RELUCTANT HEROES

best wishes

Steve Westcott

Reluctant Heroes

BOOK ONE OF THE
BLACK DRAGON TRILOGY

STEVE WESTCOTT

FrontList Books

Published by FrontList Books.
An imprint of Soft Editions Ltd,
Gullane, East Lothian, Scotland.

First published in 2003.
This revised edition published in 2007 by FrontList Books.

ISBN: 1-84350-101-5

ISBN 13: 9781843501015

Reluctant Heroes

Steve Westcott and his family live in an old farmhouse on the picturesque Isle of Man, where they have resided these past thirteen years. He fits his writing in and around his day job, when he can find the time to scribble down notes for later translation. For more information visit Steve's website at:

www.stevewestcott.com

Chapter One

The common room of The Shepherd's Cock – formerly known as The Shepherd's Crock, until someone pinched the 'r' – was in pandemonium. A mass of sweat-charged, ale-filled humanity surged and jostled around the gaming area trying to place wagers.

As the mob shrieked and yelled to get the croupier's attention, a short, squat, ugly little man shoved and battered his way through. Reaching the croupier, he shoved a pile of coins into the man's outstretched hand. "Red, number ten," he growled.

The croupier eyed the man warily for a moment, then looked down at the coins. His eyes widened at the amount of gold he held. Quickly recovering his composure, he picked up one of the coins and bit into it. A huge grin split his face and he thrust the coins into a belt-pouch before removing a pencil from behind his ear. Scribbling something on a scrap of paper he handed it over. "Red, number ten it is, my friend. And may you be lucky."

Grunting an acknowledgement, the little man disappeared from view clutching his stub as more bodies pressed forward to place their wagers.

Across the other side of the room, blissfully unaware of the tumult, Ryzak slept the sleep of the totally hammered. Blissfully unaware, that is, until a loud guttural bellow tore through his slumber with the subtlety of a finger to the eye.

"That square's mine!"

Ryzak's eyes snapped open. Honed by years of hard drinking, his survival instincts kicked in and he thrust out a leg to stop himself from sliding off the chair. The action made his forehead slip off his arms and bump onto the tankard-scarred tabletop. He rubbed at his pounding head and eased himself upright.

A shrill scream rang out. As suddenly as it had sounded it cut off, replaced by strange choking noises.

"Nice one, turd-face. Now hand over the dosh."

Ryzak groaned. This was all he needed; some smart-arse with a big mouth aggravating the throbbing in his head. By the gods, he felt rough. It must have been that last ale. For some reason it was always the last one that made him feel ill. He peered myopically around the dimly-lit, smoke-filled interior of the common room, searching for the commotion that had disturbed his sleep.

His bleary gaze fastened on his friend Jollif, the tavern-keeper, who was busy pushing his way through the mass of inebriation at the far end of the room. Despite his drunken state, Ryzak could still recognise Jollif's corpulent figure when he saw it.

"All right, Sam," he heard Jollif say. "You've won your money, now get your hands off the croupier's throat, there's a good chap."

An avenue had opened in the throng to allow Jollif through, giving Ryzak an unrestricted view. His eyes narrowed as he saw which 'Sam' Jollif was speaking to.

Sawn-off! The end result of a brief but fruitful liaison between a lonely shepherd and a sex-mad rock-trolless, Sawn-off Sam was a maniac at the best of times. When riled, he swiftly turned from a short-arsed surly half-breed into a short-arsed murderous half-breed. The man was lethal.

Sam's low, growling reply carried to where Ryzak was sitting. "Yer gonna make me?"

Ryzak groaned. He recognised the tone of Sam's voice, and hoped that Jollif also did. Otherwise this could be the point at which his friend became a dead friend.

"If I have to."

Bugger! No such luck.

Sam puffed out his barrel chest and fixed Jollif with a hard stare. "So yer think yer man enough, do yer?"

"Well," began Jollif, not appearing to notice the none-too-subtle challenge, "if you don't release the croupier he will soon be a very dead croupier. Then we won't have anyone for the gaming table and that will be the end of the gambling for a week or two, until we find another."

Sam's face puckered into a scowl as he thought it over. Suddenly he smiled, then thrust the bug-eyed croupier away, stepped forward and clapped Jollif on the back. "Yer got a point there, tavern-keep." Turning to the watching crowd, he grinned and raised his voice. "Right, me lads. The ales are on me. Seems like I 'it a lucky streak and 'ave a few crowns in me pocket."

As the crowd cheered their appreciation, Ryzak shook his head, in relief that his friend had avoided an untimely death, and dismay that the ruckus had come from the gaming area. It never ceased to amaze him how people could get so worked up over a stupid bar game. It seemed like a waste of time to Ryzak, more so since he'd lost most of his money playing the game within days of arriving in the small village of Fleshwick. He was so broke now that it was as well Jollif was the tavern-keeper, or he would have been slung out on his ear.

Another loud cheer went up. Ryzak winced and ran a grubby hand through his dishevelled mop of sandy-brown hair. He scowled at the noisy group and reached across the table for his ale. Now he was awake he might as well have another drink. He raised the tankard to his lips and took a hefty swig – and halted mid-swallow. His eyes bulged in horror as the foul-tasting liquid hit his taste-buds. His ale had gone warm! A feeling of nausea crept over him. The blood rushed from his face and a cold sweat slicked his skin. He doubled over and spewed the offending contents onto the scuffed, pockmarked floorboards, watching in sickly repugnance as the brown liquid frothed and bubbled for a moment before being absorbed by the wood. Wiping dark brown dribbles off his chin with the sleeve of his tunic, he straightened and gestured towards the bar for another drink.

By the gods, his life was a mess. Even his old friend Jollif was getting fed up with him hanging around. He had not said, as such, but Ryzak could tell. Perhaps it was time to move on. After all, he had only intended to stay for a week, reminiscing about the good old days with his pal; but that had been six months ago. It was amazing how quickly time passed you by if you let it.

The slam of a tankard on the table jolted him out of his ruminations. Looking up, his eyes met the hostile gaze of the serving girl. It looked as though Jollif was not the only one wanting to see the back of him. Ryzak attempted to give her a winning smile, but it must have come out like a drunken leer. The girl's eyes went cold and flinty. Drink-dulled reflexes prevented him from avoiding the blow. He could only sit in stunned amazement as a hand lashed out and caught him hard across the cheek with a wicked slap.

Before he had the chance to protest his innocence of whatever it was she thought he had done, she had spun on her heel and stalked away. Bewildered, Ryzak watched her go, his cheek burning from the impact. In no fit state to figure out how he had managed to upset her, he decided to drown his sorrows. As he raised the tankard to his lips his arm trembled, and he slopped some of its contents onto the table.

"I think you've had enough," scolded Jollif, easing his portly frame on to a stool beside him. "When *you* spill ale, you've definitely had enough!"

The inn-keeper removed a grubby rag from his tunic pocket and began to dab at the beads of sweat forming on his bald pate.

Ryzak's bloodshot eyes tried to focus on his friend's flabby features. "Jollif, my bes' friend," he said, smiling in recognition and clapping him affectionately on the back – slopping more ale in the process. "Bin with me through all the good times," Ryzak continued, throwing an arm over Jollif's shoulder and hugging him in a moment of drunken ebullience. "Heroes, that's what we are. Heroes. General, er, whassname, said so. Right after the Battle of Drakov, 'member? Tha's when I single-handled, hingle-san – charged the enemy all on my own. 'Turned the battle', he said. Me! Turned the battle! Those were the days."

Ryzak heaved a satisfied sigh and raised the tankard to his lips – and missed, spilling most of the contents down the front of his tunic. He stared at the wet stain in fascination for a moment, then began to dab at it with his hand.

Jollif looked on pityingly. How the mighty had fallen, even if the man was only mighty in his own mind. He well remembered the incident Ryzak referred to; the man never shut up bragging about it, which was why he always ended up drinking on his own. He told his tale to all who would listen, and to those who wouldn't, hence the ring of empty tables around him. If it were not for the gaming area, Jollif did not think he would have had a patron left.

Ryzak would never admit that he was actually trying to flee the battle at the time, of course. He was not quite that stupid. In his panic to escape, he had startled his horse and inadvertently sent it galloping the wrong way, towards the enemy. His own troops, seeing such an apparently heroic charge, had enthusiastically followed. By the time Ryzak had realised he was heading into danger it was too late, he was in the thick of it.

"That was a long time ago, Ryzak. We have to move on, make new adventures."

Ryzak abandoned his ineffectual ministrations and turned his bleary gaze on Jollif. "You're right, my frien'. I've bin thinking while I …"

The tavern door crashed open. The loud smack as it slammed against the wall, coupled with the shouts of pain from the patrons it smashed into en route, silenced the conversation in the room. Heads turned to see what the excitement was about.

Jollif rose from his stool in astonishment as a beautiful young woman hurtled into the room, her clothing in tatters, fear etched on her face. She screamed as three battle-scarred barbarians ran in after her, their unkempt black hair hanging loose over their fur-lined jackets. Swirling red patterns were tattooed on the cheeks and foreheads of their fearsome faces.

"Bugger me," murmured Jollif, recognising the tribal markings of the men. "Wolverines!"

They were the most feared of all the barbarian tribes, known the land over for their ferocious fighting skills, their reckless abandon and their passion for torturing their captives. They were right evil bastards.

The light from the oil lamps glistened on their drawn swords as they skidded to a halt just inside the door, the sinister gleam adding to the aura of menace surrounding them.

"Bugger me," Jollif whispered again, and began to back away from the table. There was only one safe place for him, and it certainly wasn't here.

Startled by the door crashing open, Ryzak swung round, nearly falling off his seat as his sense of balance deserted him. Once he had recovered, he gaped in open-mouthed admiration at the tall, dark-haired beauty who had run into the common room.

The girl's fist flew to her mouth in fear as she stumbled forward. Then, noticing Ryzak looking at her, she ran to him and threw herself at his feet. "Please, good sir," she implored, "will you help me? Those foul beasts mean to take me for their own amusement. Please save me!"

In the background, the remaining patrons beat a hasty retreat, leaving Ryzak to it. It was not their fight, after all. Why spoil a good night? Ryzak, on the other hand, ever smitten by a pretty face, grinned drunkenly down at the girl.

"Never fear, my pretty maiden. My frien' and I would be pleased to be of assistance. Wouldn't we, Jollif?" He twisted round, his gaze falling on an empty seat. "Jollif? Jollif?" he called, nervously scanning the now empty room. "Where've you gone?" The strange, sickly feeling in the pit of his stomach gripped him as he turned to face the three men. They were slowly advancing, their features distorted by smiles of cruel intent.

Ryzak gulped in apprehension and rose unsteadily to his feet.

The more heavily tattooed leader leered at him. "Give the girl to us, stranger, or you die."

Swaying from the effects of too much ale, Ryzak peered into the girl's fear-filled face, flicked a nervous glance at the three men, looked at the girl again, gave a forced smile, and began to frantically claw at his sword. For some reason it seemed to be glued into its scabbard.

The leader grinned. "It don't seem right killing a *hero* without knowing who he is," he sneered. "What's yer name?"

Ryzak looked up in terror. "Er, Ryzak," he heard himself mumble.

"Ryzak?" the barbarian repeated. He glanced at his colleagues, a hint of fear in his eyes. "Not *the* Ryzak? Hero of Drakov?"

His sword finally clear of leather, Ryzak pointed it in what he hoped was a threatening manner towards the men. "What?"

"The Ryzak? Hero of Drakov?" the leader asked again.

Taken aback by the recognition, Ryzak stood taller, puffed out his chest, and tried to appear nonchalant. "Yes. I am he."

The effect was slightly marred by the clatter of his sword falling to the floor as the effort of concentrating on the three men, holding his weapon and talking at the same time all proved too much.

The leader appeared not to notice the lapse. Casting his cohorts a nervous glance, he hastily sheathed his sword. "I'm terribly sorry to have bothered you," he said, spreading his arms wide and bowing low. "Really. You keep the girl. Plenty more where she came from. Right, lads?"

Mumbled agreement sounded from the man's companions as they slowly backed away.

"Well. We'll be off now. Sorry to have interrupted your evening." The leader turned and scrambled for the exit. In a mad dash, his men followed his example, shoving at each other in their hurry to escape.

"Oh thank you, thank you, good sir," the girl gushed as they fled. She rose to her feet and threw her arms around Ryzak's neck, kissing him soundly.

Both astonished and relieved by the men's sudden departure, Ryzak fainted.

The girl gave a startled yelp as he fell. Then, pulled over by his collapse, she landed in a crumpled heap on top of him.

* * * * *

The three Wolverines fled north along the deserted main street of Fleshwick. They did not stop running until they reached a deserted barn at the outskirts of the village. The leader skidded to a halt and cast a furtive glance behind him before sprinting the short distance to the open doorway and throwing himself through. His cohorts rapidly joined him.

Inside, all three lay on the ground, exhausted, listening for signs of pursuit. But aside from their heavy breathing, nothing could be heard. There were no loud shrieks of outrage, no heavy pounding of booted feet, no growls of anger. Nothing. Even so, five minutes had passed before the more heavily tattooed leader rose and quietly urged his men to do likewise. Once on their feet they listened for any alien noise, but all remained quiet.

Relieved that they did not appear to have been followed, the leader broke the silence with an awe-struck whisper. "Oh my, that was outrageous. Did you see the look of panic on that unkempt rascal's face?" He giggled, then clapped his hands in delight. "He was actually afraid of us."

"Of you, Rupert," one of the men gushed. "I was so scared, you nearly had me peeing my pants."

Rupert laughed and reached out to tweak the man's cheek between forefinger and thumb. "Oh, Stevie, you are a one. Fancy being scared of little old me. Come. Let us remove these loathsome wigs and wash our faces free of this filth. It is time to celebrate, my fellow thespians. We have been well paid and Troupe Dalberr has finally come of age, even though our adoring audience was blissfully unaware of his part in our act."

Accompanied by their girlish titters, Rupert ushered his companions to the back of the barn, where they had secreted some water and a change of clothing earlier that day.

Half an hour later, suitably washed and attired in clean leggings and tunic, Rupert linked arms with his two friends. "Let us away from here, my fine fellows. Now is the time for us to eat good food, drink sweet wine, and lay our weary bones upon the finest silken sheets. We have played our part to perfection, and who can gainsay us?"

As they quietly slipped away, a freshly-laundered set of lady's riding clothes swung gently on a wooden peg behind them: mute witness to their stealthy departure.

Chapter Two

Ryzak woke to sunshine streaming through the window. He winced as its brightness penetrated his eyelids with a flesh-coloured glow. The throbbing in his head intensified as the woodpecker hammering away at the inside of his skull was joined by its brothers and sisters. He worked to produce saliva in a throat that felt dry and furry, his tongue seemingly glued to the roof of his mouth, and decided he needed a drink. The least he could do was drown the little buggers.

Groaning with the effort he attempted to rise, but couldn't. His right arm appeared to be clamped to the bed. Puzzled, he tugged again, but it was no use; his arm was stuck fast. He threw his body to the left to try and free the ensnared limb.

A feminine groan sounded at the movement, alerting him to the fact that he was not alone. Astonished by the revelation, he turned his head, the woodpeckers going into overdrive at the sudden movement. Opening an eye to risk a glance, a tortured gasp escaped his lips as the light hit him.

Once the bright, dancing flecks of luminescence had stopped cavorting in front of his eyes, he managed to focus on the form lying beside him. His jaw dropped open in amazement as he viewed the figure. It was the girl from the common room, and she was naked except for the disarrayed sheet that partially covered her nubile form.

Her eyelids fluttered open. Seeing Ryzak staring at her she gave him a lazy smile and raised her head to kiss him lightly on the lips. "How is my hero this morning?" she asked.

Ryzak was stunned, the previous night's events remaining a distant, alcohol-dulled blur. "Eh?"

She gave him a coy look. "Don't be bashful. You were absolutely marvellous. I knew you were *the one* the moment I set eyes on you."

"Eh?"

"Oh, Ryzak! Don't be so modest. After saving me from those,

those fiends, you promised to help me regain my kingdom, and then," her face coloured, "you took me in your arms, carried me to your room and made mad, passionate love to me."

Ryzak was gutted. He couldn't remember a thing about his purported bedroom prowess, apart from some hazy recollection of her being on top of him. He looked at her quizzically. "I did?"

"You did. A hero and a stallion all in one man. What more could a girl ask for?" She snuggled into him, her bare breasts brushing against his upper body.

By the gods, what was a red-blooded man supposed to do in a situation like this? Ryzak immediately had his answer as arousal coursed through him, the throbbing in his head moving to another part of his anatomy.

He grinned inanely down at her and made his move. "More?" he suggested.

She placed a hand gently on his chest and pushed him away, her eyes fixing on the gold medallion that hung on a leather thong around his neck. She stared at it for a moment, the hint of a satisfied smile showing on her face, before she composed herself and looked into his eyes. "No. Not now, my love. We must leave. We have a kingdom to regain."

While Ryzak stared at her in bemusement, she reached over and lifted the medallion, turning it in her fingers to admire the cryptic script on the reverse face. "Where did you get this?" she asked, studying the strange markings intently.

"Get what?" he queried, still trying to work out what he'd managed to get himself into.

"This piece of jewellery," she answered, tilting her head to peer up at him.

"Oh, you know," he shrugged, "it was just lying around and I happened to find it."

"And where was it that you found it, 'just lying around'?" she asked sweetly.

Ryzak didn't answer. He was lost in the fathomless depths of her alluring sea-green eyes. She was gorgeous. Why could he not remember his night of passion? If only …

A raised eyebrow broke the spell, indicating that she was

waiting for a response. "Er, around some knight's neck," he reluctantly admitted.

"You stole it?" Her voice rose in indignation. She let go of the disc and backed away from him.

"No!" Ryzak cried, fixing her with an anxious look. The last thing he wanted was for her to think him some sort of petty thief. Or pervert, he thought, trying to keep from staring at her perfectly rounded breasts. Especially as she seemed to think so highly of him, in more ways than one. "He was dead, and I saw this glittering around his neck, and …" He stumbled to an embarrassed halt.

"You thought you would take it," she finished for him.

Ryzak looked at her pleadingly. "I never killed him. He was already dead when I found him, honest. He was lying on the ground; his horse must have thrown him or something, and I stopped to see if he needed any help. When I saw he was dead I decided to bury him. It was the least I could do. That's when I saw the medallion." He gave a timid smile. "It seemed such a waste to cover it with soil, seeing as he'd no need for it. And it did seem an appropriate payment for services rendered."

The girl shook her head in disapproval, tossed aside the covers and slid from the bed. She quickly crossed to the washbasin that stood in the far corner of the room. "The Great One moves in mysterious ways," she mumbled as she sluiced herself down with cold water. Frowning with irritation at the thought of the bumbling idiot she had landed herself with, she wondered where it had all gone wrong. It had all seemed so simple back at the Palace of the Sisters when she'd first broached the subject of Mishtar to Draya, her first minister, and told her of the weakening of the power that imprisoned the evil sorcerer deep in Mount Aine.

She had known of the weakening for some time. The orb, the sisterhood's sacred relic of power, had alerted her to the fact that an ancient evil was trying to break free of its chains and stalk the lands it once roamed. What it never told her was what, or who, that evil was. It had taken her years to find that one out. She hoped it did not prove to have been too long.

Neither of them could believe it when they saw the image of

Ryzak in the orb and discovered that it was he who held the missing seal to the sorcerer's prison. Now she understood why. The cretin had stolen it! Stolen it from someone who would probably have proved more beneficial to their cause than the drunken imbecile who was sprawled on the bed, drooling like a simpleton as he ogled her nakedness.

Being the matriarch of a rapidly declining sisterhood was bad enough, without having to rely on the likes of him for preservation.

"A worker should never blame her tools," she quietly scolded herself, towelling herself dry on an unsanitary-looking rag that she found on the floor next to the washbasin – Ryzak's shirt, as it turned out.

Suitably dried, she reached for her clothing, admiring the perfection of her regained youth. At least that was one benefit she'd gained from the exercise, although she had been loath to abuse the orb's powers for such a purpose. No one would guess she was over two hundred years old.

With the two most powerful sisters out in the field looking for novices to join their depleted order, she had no one else to delegate such an important mission to. It had been Draya who had convinced her of the need for her to see it through herself, and to give herself certain advantages for the difficult tasks that lay ahead. The most difficult one, it seemed, would be dealing with the imbecile wearing the seal.

Shula peered at Ryzak through lowered lashes and started to button up her shirt. The man was still staring at her, the very picture of a slack-jawed buffoon. A cold shiver ran through her body. She had a terrible foreboding about it all.

The ample charms and slender physique of the girl cast a spell of paralysis over Ryzak. He could not have moved from his voyeuristic position even if the bed had caught fire, nor would he have wanted to. He was enjoying the show. His face fell as she finished dressing and scowled in his direction. Feigning innocence, he quickly glanced away and pretended to inspect his chewed finger nails, then looked up again as she spoke.

"Come! You must make haste. We have a journey to make. I will see you in the common room in half an hour." Halfway to the door, she stopped to look back. "I assume you have a horse?"

Ryzak gave a weak smile, and hesitantly nodded his head.

Her eyes narrowed. "Your own?"

"Sort of," he replied quietly, avoiding her gaze.

She sighed in exasperation and shook her head, then opened the door to leave. "Half an hour, Ryzak. Do not keep me waiting."

Ryzak stared at the timber panels of the closed door for a moment before tumbling clumsily out of bed. "Next time," he grumbled to himself, "I'll have to stay sober enough to remember being a stud."

* * * * *

"Well?" Jollif asked with a sly wink. "What happened? Was she as good as she looks?"

Ryzak leaned against the common room counter, his aching head lightly clasped in his hands as he waited for his female companion to arrive. "What?" he mumbled, his bloodshot eyes peering at his friend. "Oh! Yes. Marvellous! Absolutely marvellous." *If I could remember anything about it,* he silently added.

"Where you off to then?"

"Er. Not quite sure on that one, I'm afraid."

"What do you mean, you're not quite sure?"

"Errr … Something to do with regaining some kingdom or other. I haven't got all the details yet."

Jollif frowned. "And just what kingdom is this, er, queen ruler of?" he enquired.

"Not quite sure on that one, either," Ryzak admitted.

The tavern-keeper's eyes narrowed. "Let me see if I've got this straight. You're off on a quest to regain a kingdom, the name of which you don't know, in the company of a girl, who may or may not be a queen, whose name you also do not know?"

Ryzak gave a thin smile. "Aye. That about sums it up."

"You must be mad, man." Jollif jabbed a stubby digit at his

temple to emphasise the point. "The drink must have messed your brain, what little you have. Or else she's cast a spell on you."

A discreet cough made them look round. The subject of their conversation was standing to one side regarding them, dressed for travel in pristine riding attire. However, being typically male, neither Ryzak nor Jollif appeared to notice the change.

"Are you ready, my love?" she asked, smiling sweetly. "We have to go now."

"Just where is it that you are taking my friend, Miss …" Jollif enquired.

"Shula," she replied, giving him an imperious look. "Ryzak has offered to help me retrieve a family heirloom, which was spirited away and hidden by my enemies in order to prevent me regaining my kingdom."

"And what is this heirloom?" Jollif asked, meeting her gaze.

She smiled enigmatically, turned her back on the tavern-keeper and strode towards the door. "Come, Ryzak," she called over her shoulder, "time to leave."

Grimacing helplessly at his friend, Ryzak slowly followed her out. "Keep my seat warm," he called, turning to give Jollif a half smile, "I'll be back."

"You'd better be!" Jollif's voice dropped to a whisper as he stared after him. "I've kind of got used to having you around." Surprised at the revelation, and slightly confused by the feeling considering how adversely Ryzak had affected his business, he realised that he meant it. Cursing himself for a sentimental old fool, he moved over to the bar to prepare for the day's trade.

* * * * *

Ryzak sat across the campfire from Shula, sulking. This was the seventh night in a row she had refused his advances. If he did not know better he would think that she had no feelings for him, other than as an unpaid escort. He could not understand it. He had been his usual witty, charming self throughout the journey but she had rebuffed him right from the start.

Women! One minute they were all over you, the next they

treated you as if you were something smelly they had just stepped in.

On the first night, when he had tried his hand, she'd firmly but politely set her stall out, sending him back to the other side of the campfire. "When we have achieved our goal, my love," she had said, smiling up at him apologetically and clasping his large hands with small, delicate fingers. "Until then, I could not possibly allow myself the pleasures of your body." Tears had welled in her pretty, sea-green eyes as she fluttered her lashes beseechingly.

It was the 'pleasures of your body' bit that swung it. Smoothing a stray lock of jet-black hair from her face, Ryzak had smiled in understanding, kissed her on the forehead and moved away.

The sleeping arrangements had remained the same ever since, despite repeated attempts by Ryzak to further his aim. He was starting to get frustrated.

The hiss and spit of green timber snapped him out of his melancholy. Glancing across the fire he saw the swaddled form of Shula and smiled. Ever the optimist, he decided she was just playing hard to get, and snuggled into his sleeping roll to settle for the night. Time would tell, and when it did, the stallion was ready and waiting for his ride.

After three more days of travelling across rolling, grassy plains, a low mountain range materialised through the heat-haze, shimmering in the distance. One tall, snow-capped peak dominated and, with a gleam of determination in her eyes, Shula steered them towards it. The land started to rise as they got closer to it, until eventually it became too steep for the horses. Finding a wooded copse where they could safely leave them, Ryzak and Shula continued the climb on foot.

The grass and shrubs quickly gave way to scree slopes and boulders and it became a struggle to make any sort of headway. The higher they climbed, the colder it became. They passed snowdrifts that remained in small, isolated pockets on the mountainside, the spring sunshine not yet warm enough to melt away these last vestiges of winter. The ascent became ever more perilous, as cold hands and feet refused to do as they were told, making it difficult to gain a secure purchase on the loose, crumbling rock.

However, despite numerous tumbles and slips by Ryzak, two days of climbing saw them arrive safely at the edge of a wide ledge. They stopped and looked around, relieved to be on level ground again. About twenty feet to their right, separated from them by a chasm, they could see that the ledge continued.

Shula pointed across the gap, her face beaming in excitement. "There! That is where we are going," she said. "We're nearing the end of our expedition."

Panting heavily, bruised and bleeding from a score of minor cuts and wounds, the result of his latest tumble down the rocky trail, Ryzak squinted across the chasm. "Where? That ledge? We've travelled all this way for a ledge?"

"Not the ledge, stupid. There! The cave," Shula snapped in exasperation, pointing towards the far end.

Stupid? Who was she calling stupid? Whatever happened to 'my love'? Ryzak scowled, then peered in the direction Shula had indicated. He could just make out the dark smudge of an opening in the rock face. Dubious about how they were going to reach it, he walked to the edge of the chasm and looked down. It was a long drop. He gulped in apprehension and turned fearful eyes at the cliff face. Glancing into the chasm again, he turned to Shula. "All right, I give up. How do we get across?"

She smiled sweetly at him, arms outstretched. "Come here, my love. Hold me. I want to feel you near me. I need your strength, your courage, your, your …"

This was more like it! Needing no second invitation, Ryzak eagerly stepped into her embrace. He knew she had wanted him, it was just a matter of being patient. It seemed a bit of a strange place for amorous liaisons, but not wanting to spoil the moment, he said nothing.

As soon as his lips met hers, bright lights exploded in his head. He felt giddy, light. Like a feather floating on air. He had never felt like that before. Breathless, he forced his lips away from hers, and fell ten feet to lie sprawling on the ledge on the other side of the chasm. He watched in amazement as Shula gently floated down to land beside him. "Who are you?" he asked, fear making his voice quaver.

"I am a girl who needs your services, my love, my hero," she replied, kneeling down and running her fingers through his hair. "Nothing has changed. I can do a few tricks, that is all."

Ryzak's panic faded as a feeling of peace and understanding pervaded his mind. Understanding of what, he was not quite sure, but he certainly felt more at ease. He gave a vacant grin.

Responding with a reassuring smile, Shula stood and helped him to his feet. Clasping one of his hands in her own she steered him towards the cave mouth. "That medallion you wear," she asked, "do you know what it is?"

Ryzak shook his head. He was still trying to come to terms with the fact that he had just floated through the air like a leaf on the wind.

"It," she informed him, "is one of the sacred seals of Mishtar."

"Oh," Ryzak murmured, none the wiser. He flicked an anxious look at the dark, threatening opening that was looming ever closer.

As they arrived at the entrance to the cave, Shula stopped and turned to face him. "In there is a sword. It is the embodiment of all evil. The seal around your neck was one of five that were set around it as a ward to prevent the creature contained within from escaping. The seal must be placed back into its mounting. The ward is weakened by its removal and Mishtar is breaking free. You must replace the seal and find out if any more are missing, then return here."

Ryzak stared at her open mouthed. "What? Me? Why? How? It's pitch black in there, I won't be able to see a thing. What about your kingdom? Are you sure you have the right man for the job?" Hysteria made his words rush out in an almost incoherent babble.

Shula's face hardened. "No woman may place the seal. It was formed by the lost magic of the wizards long ago. It would not work for me. You are the one. For whatever reason, The Great One has chosen you as the bearer. You were wearing the seal, therefore you are the one to place it. As for the kingdom you are to save, it is that of our own world, Middle Vooragh. You understand?" She gave him a determined look.

Ryzak blanched. Suddenly his heroics at Drakov seemed like child's play.

Shula scowled in irritation and swept her hands up to grasp his head. She began to murmur in a strange, singsong language. When she had finished her litany she let her hands drop. "There. That will help you to see in the darkness. Go! He is getting stronger. The longer we wait, the less time we have. I will be here when you return." Not giving him the chance to question her, she spun him round and pushed him into the opening.

Ryzak stumbled into the cave, tripped, and went sprawling to the floor, sending spirals of dust into the air. He sneezed, then spat particles of dirt from his mouth before rising to his feet. Despite what Shula had said, he could not see a thing. It was pitch black. He looked back to the opening where he could see her dark silhouette, framed by a halo of light. Although he could not distinguish her features he could feel her glare, demanding that he do as instructed.

"Bloody women," he mumbled, then turned and stepped haltingly forward, his footsteps echoing eerily around the cave.

After ten steps his confidence grew and he increased his pace. It may only have been his imagination, but he was sure his vision was improving. Perhaps his task would prove to be easier than he'd first thought. Thirty paces further on he was strolling along without a care in the world, whistling to himself and gazing around the rough rock of the cave in wonder. He had never been inside a mountain before and, although still not perfect, his sight had improved sufficiently that he could vaguely make out his surroundings.

Turning a corner, not fully concentrating on where he was going, he stepped into nothingness. Someone had stolen the ground. He yelled in surprise, then pain, as he bounced over and over, ever downwards, the hard edges of stone steps slamming into him as he tumbled. His rapid descent seemed to go on for an eternity before he came to a bone-jarring stop at the bottom.

It took him some time to realise he had stopped falling. He levered himself up and carefully rose to his feet, spitting more dirt from his mouth. Dusting himself down, he took stock of his surroundings, and was amazed to find he could see quite clearly. "Neat trick," he said aloud, peering down the long, dark corridor that led off at right angles to where he was standing.

"Do you always arrive so spectacularly?" a deep voice boomed, seeming to come from nowhere and everywhere at the same time.

Startled by the unexpected intrusion, Ryzak flattened himself against the tunnel wall. "Who's there?" he called.

A tall, black-robed, spectral figure materialised in the corridor, gliding toward him. It floated sedately across the floor and halted a few paces away, the rock-formed tunnel clearly visible through its substance.

Ryzak gulped in apprehension as he eyed the manifestation. The man's dark eyes seemed to be boring into him, evaluating him, penetrating him. Ryzak shuddered. He felt as though he was undergoing a physical examination – from the inside.

The figure's black goatee beard split as he smiled in welcome. "You are late, Ryzak. What kept you? I seem to have been waiting for ages." The apparent warmth of the smile did not reach the eyes.

Not having a clue what the man was on about, Ryzak stood immobile, a glazed expression on his face.

The figure glided closer, peering at the gold glint of the medallion at Ryzak's neck with undisguised pleasure. This time the warmth of the smile did reach his eyes. "Ah, excellent!" he beamed. "I see that you have brought the seal." He looked up and held Ryzak's gaze with eyes as hard as flint. They held no compromise. "Follow the corridor to the end. I will meet you there and tell you what you must do."

"Who are you?" Ryzak shouted, as the man's image began to fade.

"All in good time," a disembodied voice drifted back to him through the air. "Time runs short. Hurry! Once you have done as I have asked, all of your questions will be answered."

Scowling, and wondering where this 'asked' came into the equation, Ryzak began to follow the corridor. The sooner he got the seal placed the better. Things were starting to turn weird.

Ten minutes later he saw a brightening in the distance: a pale, violet glow that cast its muted radiance into the tunnel. His goal was drawing closer. Relieved, he strode forward. He had seen enough of the inside of this mountain to last him a lifetime and he wanted to breathe fresh air again.

'Stop!' a voice hammered into his head.

Unnerved by the power of the command, Ryzak slid to a halt. He looked around for the source of the voice. "What is it this time? I'm going as fast as I can."

'That is what he wants.'

Ryzak turned, scanning the corridor for the speaker. "Who wants?" he called out.

The figure of an old woman materialised in front of him, causing him to flinch. She smiled, her aged blue eyes crinkling in amusement. *'Mishtar,'* she answered, her light, feathery voice whispering around the inside of his head.

"Who?"

'Mishtar, the sorcerer. Now listen, for I do not have long. He will sense my presence and that would spoil everything. Do not do as he asks; he will try to trick you. You must place the seal in the empty clasp with the hieroglyphs facing upwards, towards the light source. Go, quickly, before he senses me and becomes suspicious.'

"But who are you?" Ryzak asked, becoming more and more unsettled by people appearing and disappearing in front of his eyes.

'A friend,' she answered mysteriously. *'Shula knows of me.'* The image of the old woman started to fade. *'Remember. Place the seal hieroglyphs up.'*

Bewildered by all these strange manifestations, Ryzak turned and began to walk towards the light, shaking his head in confusion as he tried to work out what hieroglyphs were.

The tall man with the funny goatee beard appeared in front of him again. "Are you alone?" he asked pleasantly, his dark eyes boring into Ryzak's.

Startled by his sudden appearance, Ryzak stumbled to a halt and nodded.

Mishtar gave a humourless smile. "Good. I thought I felt the presence of someone else. Someone who would not be at all helpful to our cause. Show me the seal!" he demanded.

Ryzak pulled the medallion over his head and held it towards the apparition for inspection.

The incorporeal figure drifted closer and bent down to examine the disc. Satisfied, he grunted his approval. "Free the seal from its thong," he ordered, "and take it to the light source. When you reach it you will see a sword suspended in the air. There are five raised mounts beneath. You must place the seal in one of the empty ones. This is important, so listen carefully. You must place the seal, hieroglyphs downwards, in one of those empty spaces. Hurry, it is nearly nightfall. The seal must be placed before the moon rises; I only have limited time in this form. Remember, hieroglyphs downwards. RUN!"

Like a startled rabbit, Ryzak sprinted down the tunnel, the seal clutched tightly in his fist. Running at full pelt he tried to remember which side up he should place it. By the time he reached the open area and entered the dim, violet glow, he was completely confused. And just what the hell were hieroglyphs anyway?

Still running, he aimed towards the shape of the sword and headed for the nearest pillar. He was so intent on reaching his target that he never spotted the rock on the cavern floor. As he went sprawling, the seal shot from his grasp and spun through the air. The soul of Mishtar, watching from his imprisonment within the sword, gasped in horror as the seal flew towards him. "You buffoon!" his angry voice echoed around the cavern.

Ryzak never heard it. He was too busy watching the golden disc commence its descent, heading in the general direction of one of the pillars. He looked on in astonishment as the seal changed direction in mid-air. Panicking, he lunged forward, attempting to catch the disc before it landed. But he was too late. It hit the rim of a pillar and rolled around its raised, concave lip, making half a dozen circuits before it started to descend towards the clasps at its centre. Ryzak's eyes followed every move. Still confused about which way up he should place the seal, he decided to let nature take its course.

The seal finally plopped into the recess and the delicate golden clasps closed, holding it firm, the strange markings facing upwards. A wail of anguish sounded in the chamber as a beam of violet light shot out from the pillar, intensifying the glow surrounding the sword.

Ryzak cowered as the shriek grew in volume. Then, deciding he'd had quite enough excitement for one day, he rose and made a speedy exit.

He was standing gasping for breath at the top of the stone staircase when the voice sounded in his head again. *'You remembered well, Ryzak. That seal will strengthen the hold on Mishtar. Come, join us outside.'*

Too weary to be startled, Ryzak grunted an acknowledgement and staggered the remaining distance to emerge into the night. The silvery luminescence of the full moon illuminated the two figures waiting for him as he stepped onto the ledge in front of the cave. Not so much illuminating one of the figures as shining through her. He recognised her as the old woman from the cave.

"Well, my hero. You have surpassed yourself. I never thought you would succeed," Shula's sarcastic comment greeted him. "It seems The Great One knows best after all," she added, smiling at the apparition by her side.

The manifestation returned the smile with one of her own, then turned to face Ryzak. *'One down. How many more to find?'*

"Eh?"

'How many pillars were there without seals?'

The voice in his head sounded irritated by his lack of comprehension.

"Oh," he murmured, as understanding dawned on him. "Two – I think. Tell me," he hurriedly continued, "what would have happened had the seal fallen – I mean, if I'd put it in the other way up?"

"The magic guarding Mishtar would have been irretrievably smashed," Shula answered with a half smile, "allowing him to regain human form. Probably yours. His own body turned to dust two hundred years ago."

Ryzak felt the colour drain from his face. "Oh."

'Well, Shula,' the ghostly voice said, *'it would appear that you*

and our friend still have work to do. Use the orb, it will help you.'
The voice became more distant as the transparent form began to fade. *'Find the last wizard. You already know him. He will help you unlock its secrets. I will try to aid you in your quest as much as I am able.'* A faint, *'Goodbye,'* drifted away on the breeze as the figure vanished.

"Last wizard?"

"Later, Ryzak, later. First things first! We must get back to your friend's tavern. We have plans to make." She gave him a coquettish smile and held out her arms invitingly. "Come, my hero, kiss me again."

Like a moth to a flame, Ryzak was drawn into her embrace.

Chapter Three

A vaporous shroud rippled over the uneven ground of the woodland clearing, clinging to the contours of the land as it crept across the lush grass towards the bordering trees. Hidden by a thick tangle of undergrowth at its edge, a pair of rheumy eyes peered into the mist, alert and watchful. They had spotted movement.

Carefully the elderly she-wolf edged forward, her stomach growling in hunger as she scented rabbit on the air. Although fading eyesight and the gloominess of dusk hindered her vision, there was nothing wrong with her sense of smell.

As she moved closer to the open ground, the scent grew stronger. Her stomach grumbled. She froze, not daring to move. Having not eaten for two days she was starving, and the kill was desperately needed. Moments passed and the enticing essence of rabbit remained. She relaxed and began to move forward again.

Suddenly the mist parted in front of her and the unmistakable form of supper became visible. Bunching her muscles, she made ready for the killing leap.

The rabbit looked up in startled surprise as a hunger-induced snarl echoed around the clearing. Its eyes widened in terror as it spotted the furry angel of death. Paralysed by fear, it could only sit and wait as the deadly mass of teeth and fur hurtled down.

Then something strange happened. The air around the wolf seemed to flicker and turn opaque, proceeding to wrap itself around the furry rabbit-eater. The wolf's descent came to an abrupt stop. Suspended three feet off the ground, she glared at the rabbit in amazement.

Not wanting to hang around and discuss the merits of the situation, the rabbit flicked out its hind legs in contempt and beat a hasty retreat to the safety of its burrow.

The she-wolf snapped and snarled at her elusive bonds in an attempt to break free. But her efforts proved fruitless; she was held fast. As she continued to struggle, the sound of voices came from amongst the trees across the clearing. She felt the first stirrings of panic and stopped what she was doing to prick up her ears and listen.

Her eyes widened in alarm as two figures emerged from the tangle of gnarled, twisted tree trunks and began walking towards her. A low growl issued from her throat as the two men moved closer.

"Well done, my boy. Well done! We'll make a wizard of you yet," Beulah congratulated his shorter companion. "Nice touch that, thickening the air to form a net. Much better than the fireball you were going to try; far less destructive. Now then, what have we here?"

Beulah peered at the suspended she-wolf from beneath bushy white brows. "My, we are an old girl, aren't we? Nasty looking scar over your left quarter there," he noted, walking around and studying her closely, "no wonder you were hunting rabbit. Couldn't get near the big stuff, hey? Well then, Snorkel, what are you going to do with her now?"

"Make a fur coat?"

The she-wolf snarled.

Sensing the wolf's unease, Beulah lightly patted her scarred rump as he walked back to Snorkel. "No, no, no. You're not in your mountain home now. How many times must I tell you? A wizard does not kill for pleasure or sport, only for self-preservation. Get your spell book out, it's time for another lesson."

Beulah looked on as his apprentice reached inside his cut-off grey robe. The success of the spell to entrap the wolf was as much a surprise to him as it must have been to the lupine captive. He was sure he had heard numerous mispronunciations in Snorkel's incantation, but it had still worked. He could not figure it out. The dwarf had been with him for ten years now and had never managed to successfully complete a complex spell of any sort. It had taken him three years just to get through the introduction. As Snorkel fumbled around, the wizard sighed in vexation. As well as being a bumbling idiot, the dwarf looked like one. With the sleeves of his robe chopped off to leave his long, hairy arms exposed, and the squat shape of his body, Snorkel could quite easily pass for an ape. Especially with his wiry mop of brown hair and the full beard he now sported. The only bits of Snorkel's face that Beulah could see properly were his flat nose and dark eyes. He grinned. Every downside had its bonus. Snorkel was not the prettiest sight at the best of times.

Why the dwarf had butchered his robe in the first place was another mystery. When Beulah had asked him about it, Snorkel had mumbled something about making himself look tougher. The young fool had even embroidered a death's head on the back, with the motif 'Born to Cast' scrawled above it.

Beulah crossed his arms in exasperation and tapped his foot impatiently as he waited for Snorkel to find the book. "At last," he murmured, as his apprentice pulled the familiar hide bound volume, entitled *A Beginner's Guide to Wizardry,* out of his robe and waved it in the air.

"What spell would the mighty Beulah have me use?" the dwarf shouted.

Scratching his chin thoughtfully, Beulah turned and wandered over to a fallen tree trunk and sat down, trying to decide which spell the dwarf could safely handle. The problem with Snorkel was that he was not particularly adept at, well, anything. The shout of "Oy! Wiz! You decided yet?" broke his train of thought and nearly caused him to topple from his perch.

He looked up, his bushy eyebrows pulling together in a frown of irritation at Snorkel's over-familiarity. Whatever happened to respect? He scowled, then cleared his throat before informing his apprentice of his wishes. "I want you to try a spell of healing first. Let's repair that injured leg of hers. It's a most useful spell, too, and not that difficult." Even for you, he silently added. "It's on page twenty-six."

Snorkel leafed through the book until he arrived at the stipulated page. He squinted at the small, flowing script and began to mouth the arcane phrases silently to himself.

One of the major problems he encountered when dealing with spells was pronouncing the words correctly; another being that he had no idea what most of them meant. Although he had managed to pick up a few of the meanings, full understanding was beyond him. Not that he would ever admit to the fact. He reckoned he knew enough to bluff his way through.

"Are you ready yet?"

Peering over the top of the book, Snorkel gave Beulah a grin of reassurance. Boy, the old goat sounded testy. He was probably cold and wanted to get back to Wizard's Keep. Snorkel turned back to the task in hand and closed his eyes. Once he felt composed enough to do what he must do, he opened his eyes and turned to face the she-wolf, who watched him warily from her elevated position.

Raising his arms in dramatic fashion, Snorkel uttered the first phrases of the incantation. *"Quizm quital kryon ert. Vulwit tootle grander blurt!"*

The air began to crackle with a haze of magical flux.

"Yunder chunder kronin blea. Fickle crickle bon apetit!"

At the end of the spell, Snorkel clapped his hands together, his index fingers pointing directly at the wolf. The animal's terrified expression turned to one of astonishment as a small puff of smoke spurted from the dwarf's fingertips, to be dispersed by the breeze. Her muzzle curled back in a lupine sneer.

Snorkel stood for a moment, waiting for the effects of his magic to appear. When nothing happened, he raised his hands and looked at his fingers suspiciously, keeping them at a safe distance in case he caught himself with a delayed reaction to the spell. Despite carefully scrutinising his hands and mentally going back through the incantation, he was none the wiser as to why it had not worked.

Beulah buried his head in his hands in disbelief. How on earth had the fool managed to trap the wolf in the first place if he could not even conduct a first-level healing spell? If only Snorkel would turn himself into a toad by mistake, at least he would be able to go back to Thorkel, the cretin's father, and say, 'I tried.'

It was only due to the favour that he owed Thorkel, after the latter had rescued him from an irate she-dwarf, that he had taken the idiot on as an apprentice in the first place.

During one of their many *sessions*, Thorkel had lamented his wayward son and admitted to becoming increasingly frustrated by the lad's inability to settle at anything remotely dwarfish. He was fast running out of patience with him.

He had tried placing Snorkel with the mining gang, but, after three mines collapsed and a fourth was rendered unsafe, he removed him for his own safety. Not that he was scared his son would be buried alive by a rock fall; rather that he would be buried alive by his work-mates.

Next had been the smithy. Snorkel had turned out to be the only dwarf in their long history who could take perfectly good ore, smelt it, hammer it, form it, and render it completely useless. The place ended up having more misshapen chunks of metal lying around than a used armour lot.

In a moment of drunken exuberance Beulah had offered to: 'Take the little tyke and make a man, er, Dwarf, out of him!' That was one offer he was still living to regret.

"It's okay! I've got it now," Snorkel shouted, waving the book in Beulah's direction. "Slight error in the third phrase. I must have misread it in this light. Oops!"

Beulah looked up to see Snorkel stooping to retrieve the book, which he had somehow managed to drop. He looked on in dismay as the little man quickly dusted off the cover and leafed through the pages until he found the one he was looking for.

The she-wolf was taking a nap. However, at the sound of the dwarf's voice and the crackle of magic flux in the air, her eyes flickered open.

"Quizm quital kryon ert. Vulwit tootle grander blurt!"

So far, so good, thought Beulah, adjusting his position on the log so that the rough bark did not dig in to his flesh quite so much.

"Hingle fingle shunt fertit."

Huh? That bit didn't sound right.

"Cruit tuit ma petit!"

It all seemed to happen at once. The she-wolf's eyes bulged as if they were on stalks as a blinding flash shot from Snorkel's outstretched fingertips; the power of the spell shot the little man six feet backwards to land in a tangled mass of arms and legs, and Beulah fell off his log.

The dishevelled wizard scrambled to his feet in time to witness the flash hit the suspended furball between the eyes; and watched, transfixed, as a green haze engulfed the animal. He cringed at the snarls and yelps that resounded around the clearing as whatever it was that Snorkel had unleashed started to take effect, and began to fear the worst.

The dwarf, having finished untangling his limbs, stood and smoothed down his robe, a self-satisfied smile on his face. "Yeah! Nice one," he said in self-congratulation. He strutted over to where Beulah was standing immobile, a glazed expression on his face.

"Hey, Wiz. I think I'm getting the hang of this."

"What have you done?" Beulah whispered, staring at the green mass hovering above the ground.

All had gone silent within the fog, the yelps having diminished to a few whimpers and whines before going quiet altogether.

"I did what you said," Snorkel replied, standing in front of the wizard, arms crossed, a smug smile on his face, "healed her injured leg. Neat, hey?"

"Neat? Neat?" shouted Beulah, snapping out of his paralysis. His face contorted in rage as he glared down at the little man. "Have you any idea what it is that you have done? Have you?" he roared. "Because I certainly haven't!"

"Healed its leg?" squeaked Snorkel optimistically, shrinking back in fear.

A movement behind the dwarf caught Beulah's attention. Puzzled that his mentor had halted in mid-tirade, Snorkel peeped out from under his raised forearm. Noticing that the wizard was staring at something behind him, he turned. His eyes widened in astonishment as he peered over to where the she-wolf was suspended, his gaze fixing on the hovering green mass that surrounded her. As he watched, he saw the fog begin to change. It started to shrink.

"Uh-oh!"

"Fascinating," mumbled Beulah, stepping haltingly forward.

Snorkel followed, safely tucked in behind his master for

protection and peeking round his robes, trying to see what was going on. At least if the noxious looking cloud proved to be dangerous, the testy old bugger would get it first.

As they drew closer they could hear quiet purring noises issuing from the green mass, which was now shaped like a large egg the size of a melon, and was still floating above the ground. They stopped in front of it, jumping back with a start as the egg cracked, with a sharp popping noise, and disappeared.

A surprised screech filled the air as a small green lizard, looking like an iguana with stubby knobs on its back, dropped to the ground. Righting itself it shook its head, then peered up at the two bewildered faces looking down at it and gave a happy chirp. The little knobs on its back unfurled to reveal small, perfectly formed wings, which it flapped vigorously to straighten out the creases and kinks.

"Chirrup?"

"My, my. Aren't we a sweet little thing?" crooned Beulah in astonishment. He knelt down and stretched out an index finger to tickle it under its lower jaw.

Snorkel, not quite so enamoured of the creature, remained hidden behind Beulah's robes and peered at it from a safe distance. "Wha–what is it?" he stammered.

"I don't know how you managed it," Beulah replied in amazement, still scratching the happily purring creature under the chin, "but you have metamorphosed the wolf into a baby dragonet, a sort of miniature version of a dragon. I don't understand it. It should be impossible for someone of your somewhat limited ability. Even I, with over two hundred years' experience, could not manage such a spell. The only wizards capable of such a feat died a long, long time ago. My, she is a beauty though, isn't she? Ouch!" Beulah jumped back, flattening Snorkel in the process, and jammed his nibbled finger into his mouth. He sucked at the puncture wounds where the small, needle-sharp teeth had left their mark.

Extricating himself from beneath the wizard, Snorkel scrambled clear and stared fearfully at the baby dragonet, which had spread its wings and was screeching at the top of its voice.

"You've upset it!" he screamed in terror. "It's going to kill us!" He ran off towards the log that Beulah had been sitting on.

Still sucking at his punctured finger, Beulah watched as the small creature launched itself into the air and chased after the terrified dwarf.

Reaching the log, Snorkel tucked in behind it, cowering, his arms wrapped over his head for protection. The green fury was undeterred and dived down, pecking him on the bare skin of his forearm.

Snorkel tried to bat the dragonet away with one hand whilst protecting his head with the other. "Go away!" he screamed. "Leave me alone. I'm too young to die."

'I'm hungry. Feed me!'

"Now's not the time to think of food," Snorkel cried out. "Get this brute off me!"

'It's not the wizard, you little fool. It's me, Draco. And I'm hungry. A piece of that roasted chicken that's hidden inside your robe would do just fine.'

The pecking stopped.

"What? Who said that?" Snorkel asked in puzzlement, peeping out from beneath his arm.

A pair of yellow eyes stared in at him. *'Me! Now where's that chicken? I'm starving. Is this any way to treat your daughter?'*

Snorkel shot bolt upright as if he had suddenly sat on a rather large thistle and stared. "Draco?"

'Hurrah! It speaks. Yes, me, Draco. Remember? You birthed me.'

"It was an accident, a mistake. I dropped the book and when I picked it up I must have turned to the wrong page. Well, you know how it is?" he shrugged. "All those wizardly-type words, all uit's and youit's. I can never get them right. And, and …"

'And now you have me!' Draco chirruped happily.

Beulah had walked across unnoticed and stood staring intently at the duo. "Why are you talking to yourself, Snorkel?" he asked.

Surprised by the sound of his voice, Snorkel spun round. "Er – er – I'm not. I'm talking to – to Draco."

"Aaaah." Beulah nodded sagely, placed his nibbled forefinger on his pursed lips and stared down at him thoughtfully. "And how long have we had this imaginary friend?"

'What's the wrinkly on about?' asked Draco. *'Can't he see me?'*

"He can see you, he just can't hear you."

"Hear who?" Beulah snapped.

"Draco!" Snorkel exclaimed, jabbing a stubby forefinger at the creature, which had pushed its head inside his robe to look for the secreted chicken.

"What? It speaks?"

'Of course I do.'

"Of course she does," Snorkel repeated.

"How?"

'Telepathy.'

"Telypafy?" Snorkel queried, staring at the dragonet with a puzzled frown on his face.

"Telypafy?"

"Er, that's what she said."

'Thought,' Draco corrected.

"Thought?" asked Snorkel.

'Yes. Mind-speak,' replied the dragonet, chewing blissfully on the well-cooked chicken leg that she had managed to pull off the carcass, the remains of which now protruded from the folds of Snorkel's robe.

"Mind-speak?" muttered the dwarf, confused.

"Mind-speak," murmured Beulah, "of course. Telepathy. I'd forgotten all about that. Before they became extinct, er rare," he hastily amended, "baby dragonets attached themselves to the first creature, or person, that fed them. 'Bonding' I think it's called. A sort of surrogate parent situation. It caused quite a stir the first time one of them bonded to a human. Everyone wanted one. Amazing little creatures."

Snorkel, who was completely lost by the use of words with more than two syllables, nodded his head wisely. "Oh, I see. What does that make me then?"

'Mum,' a sleep-laden voice whispered in his mind.

"Mum?"

Draco jumped up onto his shoulder and wrapped her tail lightly around his neck. *'That's right, Mum!'* she exclaimed. She curled up and immediately fell asleep.

Beulah laughed. "Well, Mummy, it appears that you have acquired a daughter. Come on. It's late and I feel the need for a stiff drink, to be drunk whilst reclining in front of a roaring fire."

As the wizard began to lead them back towards Wizard's Keep, Snorkel called after him. "What happened to the dragonets? Where'd they all go?"

"No one knows," the wizard shouted back over his shoulder, "they literally disappeared overnight, some ninety years ago. Not one of them has ever been seen from that day, until now."

A disturbance tore through the ether, causing Beulah to halt in his tracks, a fearful look on his face.

"What is it?" Snorkel asked. "You look as if you've just seen a ghost."

Beulah turned and looked down at his short companion, his face ashen. "If what I've just heard is what I think it is, I may have. Come. This night's work is not finished yet."

Chapter Four

Snorkel pumped his little legs in a frenzy, trying to keep up with Beulah. The old codger was setting a furious pace. He was negotiating the twisting, tree-lined pathways of Wizard's Wood with a skill and ease that defied belief for someone his age, and was starting to pull ahead. Snorkel dug into his reserves, put his head down and pumped faster. The last thing he wanted was to get lost – again.

It had taken him three days to get back the last time he had wandered in the woods alone. And then only because Beulah had eventually realised he was missing and decided to come looking for him. If he lost the wizard now he would never find his way back through the spell-guarded maze that protected Wizard's Keep from unwanted intruders. Although why anyone would want to visit such a cold, damp, dreary place as the Keep was beyond him, unless they were short of grey matter or clinically insane.

By sheer willpower, a lot of sweat and burning muscles, Snorkel managed to keep the tall, skinny form of the wizard in sight until they eventually arrived at the Keep.

Entering the large, iron-bound doors, Beulah made straight for his study, with the dwarf in tow – literally. Snorkel clung to the back of the wizard's robe for all he was worth as he was dragged up the twenty stone steps to the first floor, swung right, then hauled along the dim corridor before skidding left into the study.

Once inside, Beulah prised him off and ordered him to sit in one of the two chairs, telling him to keep quiet and stay out of the way. The dwarf needed no second urging. He was knackered. He only had enough energy to climb onto the tall chair, never mind interfere with whatever Beulah was about to do.

Beulah scurried to the back of the room and stood in front of a water-filled bowl. He began to chant and move his hands in intricate patterns.

Snorkel folded his arms and swung his legs to and fro as he watched and waited for the wizard to inform him what he was doing. However, true to form, no explanation was forthcoming. Becoming bored, and with the heat of the log fire working its own magic, Snorkel leaned back in the chair and started to doze, still no wiser as to what his master was up to.

The wizard passed a hand over the bowl, the passage of his power causing a faint ripple to disturb the water's surface. The image of Shula and Ryzak locked in a passionate embrace as they levitated back over the chasm faded. The stone bowl, mortared on top of its unadorned pedestal, was, once again, an ordinary water receptacle.

Beulah's bushy brows drew into a worried frown as he turned away. He rubbed at his chin with a pale, finely chiselled hand, the hand of an artist or poet, concerned and contemplating the events he had just witnessed.

"Mishtar!" he mumbled to himself, shaking his head. "After all these years."

Woken by Beulah's musings, Snorkel gave a loud yawn and stretched. "Who's this Mishtar, then?"

Beulah looked up, startled out of his meditation. His worried gaze fixed on the dwarf. "Who?"

"Mishtar!"

Beulah gave a curt nod as he walked over to the fire and sat in his favourite armchair; the black one with the worn areas on the leather arms and the white horse-hair stuffing sticking out from the seams, making it look like a balding badger. It may have been old and past its best but it was comfortable, the leather padding having been moulded to his physique by years of use.

The wizard reached across to the small table beside his chair and lifted a crystal decanter from its polished teak surface, pouring himself a stiff tot of 'Bellyrot' dwarven uiskey. He raised the glass to his mouth and took a small sip, savouring the dry, peaty flavour. He waited for the burning sensation in his gullet to work its way down to his stomach before daring to try and reply.

A look of abject pleasure lit his face as the uiskey bottomed out with the force of a flaming fireball. Nothing could best Bellyrot for stimulating the mental process as long as you restricted yourself to a couple of mouthfuls, otherwise the word 'mental' took on a whole different context. His eyes watered from the after-effects of the drink as he gazed around his cluttered study, trying to decide how much he should tell Snorkel or, rather, how much the dwarf was capable of understanding.

Pondering the matter, Beulah scanned the numerous stacks of precariously balanced books that filled the room, cobwebs linking the haphazard piles with their finely wrought mesh. Some of the book columns stood over six feet tall and were in danger of collapsing. Apart from the clear space around the two chairs and a narrow passage leading through to the door, the remainder of the floor could hardly be seen. It looked as though a gorilla had been set loose in a library and told to catalogue the books in any way it felt fit – Oh, and by the way, there's a banana hidden among them somewhere.

Heaving a sigh at the enormity of the task, he looked over at the dwarf perched on the edge of the chair opposite, watching him expectantly. Time enough, he decided. Maybe next year, if he had the inclination. There were more important considerations for him to see to first.

"Mishtar is, or rather was, an evil sorcerer who walked these lands two hundred and fifty years ago. He fed off the tormented souls of people that he captured, then tortured to death in order to increase his already substantial powers. He wanted to conquer and subjugate Middle Vooragh. Enslave all the races. He gathered an army of Orcs, Trolls, Barbarian Tribes from the Vooragh Plains and ruthless mercenary forces from Aldura City itself. A vast, marauding army."

Snorkel nodded knowingly. "Uhh. A bad wizard, huh? What happened to him?"

"The Council of Wizards got together and formed a plan of attack. They couldn't kill him, he was too powerful, so they had to lure him into a trap. While the combined armies of the Dwarves, Elves and Aldurans faced the might of his army on the Aldurain Plains, the elders of the council, the five most powerful wizards in the land, arranged to meet with Mishtar at his mountain retreat on Mount Aine, offering themselves in return for the safety of the peoples of Middle Vooragh."

"Pupff!" sneered Snorkel. "He'd have to be stupid to fall for that one."

"Or greedy," responded Beulah. "And he was very, very greedy. Anyway, he agreed to meet them, little knowing that the combined might of the Brotherhood of Wizards was channelled to the five via a telepathic link."

"Ah, telypafy! We know about that, don't we?" Snorkel winked at Draco and scratched the dragonet under the chin.

She yawned and stretching her wings. *'Yes, Mum,'* she replied.

"Will you stop calling me Mum," the dwarf retorted. "I am not your mother! I did not give birth to you. I did not suckle you and, to top it all, I am not even female!"

Draco gave him an indulgent look. *'Yes, Mum. Any more chicken left?'*

"I give up," Snorkel muttered, fishing inside his robe for the chicken. He turned back to Beulah. "Where were you up to, Wiz?" he asked.

"I was just about to tell you how they managed to trap Mishtar, if you've finished arguing with our friend here," he answered impatiently. "May I continue?"

"Yeah, sure. Feel free, Wiz."

"As I was saying …"

"Do you want a piece of chicken? It's delicious," said Snorkel, feeding a piece to Draco and chewing on a drumstick himself.

"No I do not!" Beulah shouted, slamming his glass onto the table. Some of the uiskey slopped onto the lacquered surface, causing the polish to bubble and blister. Beulah scowled.

'He looks a little upset,' Draco mind-spoke.

"Er, sorry Wiz. We'd love to hear the rest, wouldn't we Draco?"

The small lime-green dragonet peered over at the irate wizard and nodded her head solemnly. *'If we must.'*

"She said she would love to hear it," said Snorkel.

'Liar!'

A scowl formed on Beulah's face as he settled back in his chair. His eyes took on a faraway look and he continued with his tale. "The five arrived at Mount Aine carrying a sword woven by magic. 'To hold our souls', they told Mishtar. Being a sorcerer he couldn't take their souls into himself – conflicting magic, you see? So they told him that he needed a receptacle to hold their powers."

Snorkel nodded, his vacant expression confirming that he didn't have a clue what Beulah was on about.

"Anyway, Mishtar took the sword from them, not realising it was a trick, held it above his head, and spoke his evil words of command. The wizards, who were kneeling at various points around him, each wearing golden seals of containment around their necks, opened their minds to the combined might of the wizardhood. Mishtar, his own mind already open for the spell to drain the five realised, too late, what was afoot. His soul, screaming hatred and revenge, was drawn into the sword. The five wizards were turned into stone pillars by the power of the spell, the gold seals clasped at their apexes. A permanent prison, or so we thought; the violet glow of the magic imprisoning Mishtar and the sword within its power field forever. The lieutenants of Mishtar's army, sensing their master's demise, fled the field of battle at its height, just as they were about to overrun the combined armies of the defenders. Seeing their leaders flee, there followed a mass desertion in the ranks of the enemy forces. The remaining pockets of resistance were then easily overcome by the allied troops."

Beulah halted his narrative to dab at watering eyes.

"What happened to all the other wizards?" Snorkel asked.

"Dead. All of them," Beulah answered, turning his bleak gaze on the dwarf. "They knew they were going to die. It was their sacrifice for the peoples of Middle Vooragh."

"Dead? All of them? Dead?"

"All but one," Beulah replied solemnly, rising from his seat. "All except one junior wizard who had recently completed his apprenticeship. He was told to observe the proceedings and take any action that he deemed necessary, should it all go horribly wrong."

"Where is this wizard?" shouted Snorkel, launching himself out of the chair in his excitement. "Let's find him, ask for his help."

Beulah sadly shook his head. "There's no need. You are looking at him. I was that last wizard."

"Oh," said Snorkel, his excitement dissipating. Suddenly his face lit up with a grin. "Hey, Wiz! You're not the last. You've got me! That makes, er ..." He counted on his fingers. "One, two – two!"

Beulah shook his head again. "That's what worries me," he muttered to himself. Aloud he said, "Come. It appears that Mishtar is attempting to break free. We must make preparations to deal with him. We have to intercept that Sister of the New Dawn and her man to offer our help. The gods know they'll need it if they are to find the missing seals."

He strode purposefully towards the study door.

Draco fixed her gaze on Snorkel. *'Three!'*

"Eh?"

'Three. There are three of us. Or have you forgotten me?' The feigned sweetness of her tone implied that he'd better not have.

Chapter Five

The spring storm was at full force. Lightning flashed, the wind howled and the rain hammered down, beating a heavy tattoo on the shingled roof of The Shepherd's Cock – purveyors of the finest beverages – or Jollif's Piss-up Palace to the regulars. Jollif had just finished getting rid of the last drunken customer and had locked up for the night. The glasses and tankards were all washed and neatly stacked on the shelves; it was time to relax.

Ignoring such beverages as Dwarven Ale, Ale made in the Dwarven Mountains, Mountain Ale – made by dwarves, Draught Dwarf Beer and the infamous dwarven uiskey, 'Bellyrot', Jollif reached under the counter to his personal stock and pulled out a bottle of Alduran Brandy. As far as Jollif was concerned, Alduran Brandy was the nectar of the gods and not for resale. It was hard to come by and would be wasted on the heathens that frequented his hostelry. Anyway, most appeared happy with his current range.

It was not that Jollif was against stocking different drinks for his clientèle; it was just that he had found a ready – and cheap – supplier of the dwarven brews. So why reduce profits by buying more expensive ones? And it was good stuff, too. Dwarves were famous for their drinking and their potent concoctions. Hence the well known adage: 'Question – What do you call a teetotal Dwarf? Answer – Dead!' Apart from the odd case of temporary blindness, or brewer's drop-off (similar to brewer's droop, but more drastic), everyone seemed to appreciate his selection.

Jollif removed the stopper from the bottle, poured himself a beaker of brandy and carried it through to the living area. He sprawled in his favourite armchair beside the roaring fire and sipped at his drink, his thoughts miles away. Not for the first time he wondered how his old friend Ryzak was getting on.

It had been at least six weeks since the man had left and not a thing had been heard from him. Not that Jollif was unduly concerned. Ryzak was perfectly capable of taking care of himself. Somehow, no matter how poor the odds, he always seemed to come out smelling of roses. Aye, he'd soon be back, boasting to all who would listen about his adventures and heroism, and how he beat off ten, no, twenty attackers single-handed.

Sighing, Jollif gazed despondently into the dancing flames. As much as he hated to admit it, the tavern was too quiet with Ryzak gone. He missed him, drunkard that he was. Jollif smiled to himself. Not to worry, he'd soon be back.

Tossing down the remainder of his drink, Jollif eased off his boots, rested his head against the padded arm of the chair, and promptly fell asleep. Some time later – he was not sure how long, but the fire had burned down to a dull, orange glow – a loud hammering on the tavern door disturbed his slumber.

Disgruntled by the rude awakening, Jollif knuckled sleep from his eyes and lurched out of the chair, cursing himself for an idiot as he rubbed at a crick in his neck. At his age he ought to know better. Chairs were fine for the young and supple, but … "All right! All right! I'm coming," he grumbled, as the pounding increased in tempo.

He moved across to the mantle and grabbed the oil lamp. Using a glowing taper from the fire, he touched the wick, bringing it flaring into life. Holding the lamp aloft, he walked through to the common room, the meagre pool of light illuminating his way.

The hammering continued unabated as he walked to the door, rising above the howl of the wind and the incessant drumbeat of the rain. "All right! I'm here," he growled in annoyance, "so you can stop that infernal racket!"

Sliding back the cover of the peep-hole, he closed one eye and peered out. Two cloaked figures stood outside, hunched over for protection from the elements, their forms clearly outlined by the sporadic flashes of lightning.

"Who is it?" Jollif shouted.

"Ryzak," a muffled voice yelled back.

Jollif only partially heard what was said, the figure's words snatched away on the wind. "Who? Ryzak? He's not here. Off on a quest someplace. Now go away and leave me in peace!"

Muttering to himself about the cheek of some people, knocking him up in the early hours of the morning just to ask where Ryzak was, he slammed the cover back into place and turned to make his way up to his first-floor bedroom. A feather mattress would be a damned sight more comfortable than the chair.

When he was half way to the stairs the hammering started again. More insistent, more demanding.

Growing ever more annoyed, Jollif turned and stomped back to the door. He grabbed the cover and wrenched it open, using so much force that it smashed off the end-stop and went tinkling to the floor. An icy shaft of wind blasted through the hole and hit him square in the eye, enraging him still further. Blinking away the tears, he pressed his lips to the peep-hole. "I've already told you, he's not here. Now bugger off!"

The hammering stopped.

Jollif gave a satisfied smirk and headed back through the common room. That would be the last he would hear from those two.

The sound of metal squealing on metal made him stop. The hairs on the back of his neck rose. Slowly turning, he looked fearfully towards the door. Jollif hoped that he was wrong, but it sounded as though the bolt was being eased across.

His hand shook as he held the lamp higher and made his way haltingly towards the source of the sound. A quivering pool of light moved with him, gradually spreading up the door until it illuminated the bolt. Jollif's eyes nearly popped out of his head as his gaze fixed on it. The iron fastening was waggling up and down, apparently of its own volition, slowly working its way free of the retaining eye.

A shrill scream of terror escaped his lips as the bolt slid clear and the door burst open; the howl of the wind and rain gusting through the open doorway adding a harmonic counterpart to his screech. Not waiting to see who the two muffled shapes that threw themselves into the tavern were, he fled to the safety of his living quarters.

Reaching his room, he slammed the door behind him, then dragged the desk across to barricade it. Although his heart pounded and his breath came in ragged gasps, he could still hear the sound of booted feet tramping across the floor, coming closer, moving rapidly towards the door! He whimpered in fear and cowered behind the solid lump of oak.

"Jollif! Jollif! It's me, Ryzak!" called a voice he recognised. "Open the door and come out, you silly old fool!"

Jollif's astonishment at the sound of the familiar voice turned into a sigh of relief. A smile crept slowly over his face. "Ryzak? Is it really you?"

"Yes! It's really me. Now open the door. We could do with a drink."

Jollif dragged at the desk, eager to greet his friend. Once it was out of the way, he threw open the door and grabbed Ryzak in a fierce hug, slapping him heartily on the back. After a moment he stepped away and held Ryzak at arm's length, taking in every detail of his face. "Man, it's good to see you again. I thought you were dead. You look well. A little leaner maybe," he added, dropping into a fist fighter's pose and launching a playful punch at Ryzak's stomach. He laughed, then straightened and peered at Ryzak's face again. "How did you get the black eye?"

Ryzak grimaced and cast a withering glance at his shorter companion.

Shula lowered her sodden hood and folded her arms across her chest. She looked up at him, her green eyes wide with innocence, eyebrows arched in query as though daring him to answer.

Ryzak was the first to break. "I – I walked into a tree in the dark."

Jollif gave a knowing nod and quickly changed the subject. "Go through to the living room, the pair of you. Stoke up the fire; it'll soon come back to life. You look as if you need drying out. I'll go and get us some uiskey; it'll help warm us up."

Although Ryzak was his best friend, some things you didn't share. Alduran Brandy fell into that category.

Ryzak nodded his thanks and guided Shula into the living quarters.

When Jollif entered a few minutes later carrying a bottle of the dwarven spirit and three beakers they were sitting cross-legged in front of the fire, wrapped in blankets, their rain-drenched clothing piled in a corner of the room.

Jollif placed his load on the table beside his chair and filled the beakers with the uiskey. He handed one each to Ryzak and Shula before easing his large frame into the padded seat. "You can use your usual room, Ryzak," he said. "The bed's been kept ready and aired for your return."

A strange gurgling and choking sound made him turn his gaze to Shula. The poor girl seemed to be overcome by it all. Her face had turned bright red, tears ran down her cheeks and she seemed to be having trouble breathing. She was thumping at her chest and appeared to be on the verge of throwing up. Concerned, Jollif rose to go to her aid, but sat down again at her waved rebuff.

After a moment her convulsions subsided. Placing her beaker on the floor beside her, she turned watery eyes on her host. "Have you a spare room for me?" she croaked, a distinct raspy edge to her voice.

Puzzled and still a little worried about her health, Jollif nodded. He cast a surreptitious glance at Ryzak, looking for any hint of why she had requested a separate room, but there was no help coming from that quarter. Ryzak was gazing into the fire, studiously ignoring his companions. What had gone on with those two? Had true love – or lust – run its course? Pondering these unasked questions, Jollif shifted his gaze back to Shula. "Top of the stairs, turn right and it's the second door on the left."

She nodded her thanks. "If you have a spare lamp, it would also be appreciated."

"Take that one, we have no need of it," he answered, indicating the one he had left on the chest of drawers beside the door when he had flown into the room.

Shula took it and made her way to the door. She pulled it open with her free hand and turned to look back at Ryzak. "I'll see my hero in the morning?"

Without turning to acknowledge her, Ryzak mumbled a begrudging, "I suppose so."

After the door had softly closed, Jollif dug his friend in the back with his foot. "All right. Out with it. What happened out there? Is she a queen? Where's this kingdom she had to regain?"

With a resigned slump to his shoulders, Ryzak gulped down

the last of his drink before looking up at his friend. He gave a thin smile and waggled the empty beaker.

"Some things never change," muttered Jollif. He leaned forward and lifted the uiskey bottle from the floor beside him and filled the proffered vessel, topping up his own as well.

Ryzak took a large swallow of his drink and told his tale. He never elaborated on the cause of his black eye and Jollif, too shocked by the talk of spells, witches, dead sorcerers and last wizards, did not think to ask him about it.

After Ryzak had finished his account, it took Jollif a full hour to drift off to sleep. His mind was spinning with the story he had just heard. This, coupled with the fact that Ryzak had lain down in front of the fire and was snoring like a warthog with a head cold, did not make for ideal sleeping conditions.

* * * * *

Dawn broke fine and clear over the village of Fleshwick, the warmth of the sun quickly evaporating the dampness from the night's storm. The birds were working overtime, welcoming the new day with their rousing chorus, and generally making a racket.

Through the haze of the previous night's drinking, Jollif could hear the sounds of the village stirring into life. Mixed in with the general cacophony was the clanging from the neighbouring smithy. Jollif flinched at the fall of each hammer blow. Every dull, metallic clang seemed to pulse in time with his throbbing head. He groaned and cursed himself for having mixed his drinks, then turned over to try and get back to sleep. After tossing and turning for another ten minutes he gave it up as a bad idea and tumbled clumsily out of the chair.

Still in a sleep-befuddled daze, he stepped over the comatose form of Ryzak and made his way towards the washbasin, hoping that a good, cold dunking would liven him up and ease his aching temples.

Jollif felt a little more alert after his swill and, leaving Ryzak where he lay, went out to the common room to find a pick-me-up. He detested headaches, especially when it was him that had one.

When he arrived at the beer-stained, mahogany bar he leaned against it for a moment before crouching to rummage amongst the medicine bottles on the lower shelf. Discarding at least ten of them, he found the one he had been looking for: *'Dr. Morphine's Paineeze* – the instant cure for headaches, tummy ache, tooth ache, arthritis, impotence, warts, plague and toilet trotting.'

With a grunt of approval he shook the bottle and levered off the lid. Holding it under his nose, he took a cautious sniff and his eyes bulged. The yellow ick stank worse than Ryzak's socks. He felt the first stirrings of a nasal explosion. Or string of them, as it turned out.

When he had recovered from the sudden, prolonged bout of sneezing and wiped away the tears that streamed down his cheeks, he found his headache had intensified. He peered at the small, green bottle in trepidation, then steeled himself for what he must do and placed it against his lips. After a moment's hesitation, he downed the contents in one swallow.

Head up, eyes closed, arms by his sides, he stood for a full two minutes waiting for the promised cure, as the foul-tasting, viscous contents slowly worked their way down his gullet like some fat, juicy slug. His gorge rose as the amorphous mass settled, and sighed in relief as the churning stopped. Miraculously the cure appeared to be working.

Then the unexpected happened. One minute he was standing imitating a rock, the next he was running for the lavatory, gripping his clenched buttocks for all he was worth. He emerged half an hour later, feeling extremely sorry for himself and using the wall for support. The sound of a bright, breezy voice was the last thing he needed to hear.

"Good morning, Jollif. I'm pleased to see that you are up and about. Where's Ryzak? Still asleep, I suppose," it answered its own question in disgust.

Jollif slowly raised his head. His bleary gaze fell on Shula sitting at the counter. She was sipping delicately at a cup of tea. "Mornin'," he managed to croak, clutching his stomach as he slowly made his way towards her. The 'slug' was on the move again. Any minute now it was likely to make a rapid exit in the most dramatic of fashions. "Nought good about it, though. Wait till I get my hands on the quack that sold me that, that …" He groaned and doubled over as yet another stomach cramp took hold. The slug was about to make its bid for freedom.

Shula smiled to herself and placed her cup daintily on the counter, then rose from her seat. She walked across to Jollif, placed her hands either side of his bowed head and began whispering in a strange language. When she finished her litany, she pulled her hands away.

Jollif was astounded. It was as if she had drawn away all the aches and pains when she released his head from her grip. He had never felt so alive and well. A wide grin spread over his face. In an exuberant show of gratitude, he grasped hold of Shula's head and planted a wet, sloppy kiss on her lips. As he stepped back, a silly smile on his face, a right hook smashed into his jaw and sent him sprawling to the floor.

"Now you know how Ryzak acquired the black eye," Shula's amused voice said, as he lay wondering what had hit him.

Jollif looked up from his prone position and watched Shula wipe her knuckles on her robe with smug satisfaction, before walking back to the counter, where she sat down and finished her tea as if nothing had happened.

He climbed to his feet, rubbing his bruised jaw.

"Tea?" Shula enquired.

"Yes, thank you. That would be, er, very nice," Jollif replied, moving warily across to join her. As he reached out to take the proffered cup, a commotion at the door made him turn to see what was going on.

"You bumbling fool! That is the last, the very last time that I ever let you try a spell of location."

Shula and Jollif gaped as an extraordinary sight met their eyes. Two strangers had entered the room. The taller, older, white-haired man was soaking wet and had green pondweed plastered around his shoulders. His sodden black robe was clinging to his body, accentuating his painfully thin physique. He scolded his diminutive companion, wagging a finger at him in righteous indignation. The shorter of the two, a dwarf, looked suitably chagrined and scuffed his feet on the floor. An unusual green lizard was perched on his shoulder.

"It was a genuine mistake, Wiz, honest. Anyone could have made it. I thought you said a spell of locomotion. It's not my fault I didn't hear you properly," he added, giving the green lizard a withering look. The reptile ignored his glare and looked up at the ceiling, exuding an air of innocence.

The tall one stopped and stared down at the dwarf, his eyes wide. "Why on earth would I ask you to carry out a spell of loco- motion when we were standing not one hundred yards away from our destination? And when, I might add, we were standing immed- iately in front of the village duck pond!" he finished with a roar.

The dwarf shrugged helplessly. "Eager to get here?" he suggested.

"You – you – Bah! If it wasn't for your father I'd …"

"Can I help you, gentlemen?" Jollif enquired, stepping away from the bar and moving towards them.

The two men stopped their bickering and turned to face the tavern-keeper, their mouths still open, caught in mid-dispute. Casting the dwarf another withering look, the taller man brushed the pondweed off his wet robes and strode forward, gripping Jollif's hand in a firm handshake. "Good morning, my dear fellow. Allow me to introduce myself. I am Beulah!"

Jollif would have been quite impressed by the man's bearing were it not for the squelching sound his boots made as he walked, and the rather large puddle of water in the middle of the floor where he had been standing.

A choking sound from the direction of the counter made the old man glance over Jollif's shoulder. A small smile crossed his features before he turned back to Jollif.

"And this microscopic barrel of laughs is Snorkel, my assistant."

"Pleased to meet you," Snorkel rumbled, thrusting a small but muscular arm towards Jollif.

Jollif bent down to grasp Snorkel's hand and came face to face with the lizard. The small lime-green creature smiled, revealing rows of needle-sharp teeth, and waved her wings in greeting.

Yelping in surprise, Jollif jumped back. He stood trembling and pointed at the winged reptile with a wavering finger. "It's a – it's a – it's a dra – it's a drag …"

"Dragonet," breathed Shula in admiration, brushing past him. "My word, we are a beauty, aren't we?" she cooed.

'At last. Someone with sense,' mind-spoke the dragonet, moving her head around so that Shula could scratch an itch that had developed by her ear-hole.

'Ah, so you dragonets can still communicate?' Shula asked, using mind-speak.

'You can hear me?' Draco asked in surprise.

'Of course,' Shula smiled.

'Hey, Mum. She can hear me,' the dragonet enthused.

"Who can?" asked Snorkel.

'She can, of course,' Draco answered, pointing her head towards Shula. *'We're speaking now.'*

The dwarf gave Shula a hard stare.

Turning her attention back to Shula, Draco said, *'I'm called Draco, and that's my Mum.'*

Shula looked at the dwarf and inclined her head, a half smile on her face. "You have a fine daughter, Snorkel. You must be very proud. I am Shula."

Snorkel glowered at her, before turning to Draco who pointedly ignored him.

"Shula?" enquired Beulah politely. "I thought I recognised you."

Jollif shook his head and retired to the bar. He reached over the counter, grabbed a bottle of uiskey from the shelf and poured himself a stiff drink. It would appear that today was a day he was not going to forget in a hurry. He took a large gulp of the spirit and stared at the strange group. His hands were still shaking with the terror of coming face to face with a dragon. No matter what Shula had called it, he knew a dragon when he saw one. No matter how small it was.

Shula stopped scratching Draco and turned to the wizard. "Recognised me?"

"Yes, my dear. You and your colleague Ryzak? At Mount Aine?" He paused, obviously waiting for a response.

"Ummmm. Beulah, Beulah," murmured Shula, pursing her lips in concentration. She tapped her mouth lightly with her fingertips, deep in thought. "Now where have I heard that name before?"

"Surely you've heard of me, Sister of the New Dawn. The matriarch cannot have let the sisterhood slip so much that they would forget the name of the last wizard!"

"Ah, that's it!" exclaimed Shula, "the last wizard!" She looked him in the eye. "We have things to discuss, you and I. Matters of great import!"

Beulah smiled. "I do believe that we have, Sister."

"Jollif!" shouted Shula, looking over her shoulder to where he sat. "I did not cure your self-induced alcoholic poisoning for you to top yourself up with more of the demon spirit! Go and get these two gentlemen a room!" She glanced at the wizard's wet robes with a disapproving eye. "They require hot water for a bath. See to it, while I try to get some sense out of Ryzak. We meet back here in two hours."

The tavern-keeper looked on in sympathy as Shula swept by, heading towards his living quarters. He did not envy Ryzak. If the uiskey had not done for him, she soon would.

Chapter Six

"No! I will not alleviate his suffering. If the imbecile wants to poison himself that's his problem, not mine!"

"But you helped me," Jollif wheedled, "Couldn't you just ..."

"Are you deaf as well as stupid? I only cured you because you were the innocent party. He, on the other hand, was the instigator! As far as I'm concerned he's on his own."

The slam of the door made Ryzak groan in anguish. The loud reverberations sent waves of pain through his head. It felt like it was about to explode. He had been listening to their discussion through the alcoholic haze that swaddled him, in the vain hope that Jollif could persuade her to intercede in his torture. However, despite his best efforts, Shula was not to be moved.

A low moan escaped Ryzak's lips. He felt like shit. Why was the woman so anti-him? If he did not know better, he would have thought she despised him. Jollif's loud sigh of resignation drifted across the room, followed by his heavy tread as the big man came over. "Sorry, Ryzak. She wouldn't budge."

Ryzak raised his head weakly and peered into the concerned features of his friend. "I know, I heard," he managed to croak, through the burning sensation in his gullet. His throat felt as if he had swallowed a large furry animal that had shed its coat and left it in the back of his mouth while it went exploring his skull.

Ryzak fought back the nausea that gripped him and tried to smile, but winced in agony instead. Beads of sweat sprang out on his forehead. He gagged and buried his head in his hands before heaving into the bucket set on the floor between his legs.

Jollif gripped his shoulder in sympathy and crouched down beside him. "You look terrible, man. I've never seen such a shade of green. In fact, your face is the strangest colour I've ever seen in my life. Are you sure you're not dead?"

Retching again, Ryzak raised an arm to wipe dribbles of vomit from his chin. "Nah, I just feel like it," he whispered. "Can you get me a beaker of water?"

Not daring to move his head for fear of throwing up again, Ryzak felt more than saw Jollif move away. He was sure there was nothing left to bring up other than his stomach, and he was convinced half of that was floating in the mess below him.

When Jollif returned, Ryzak's fingers closed by reflex as a cold beaker was thrust into his hand. "Thanks."

He closed his eyes and cautiously raised his head, then lifted the beaker and speedily quaffed its contents. Feeling marginally better, he waggled the empty vessel in Jollif's direction. Four drinks later he was feeling nearly human. He could actually open his eyes without the room spinning out of focus and dragging him in to the middle of a mind-churning whirlpool.

"You look better," Jollif said approvingly. "At least your face has a more healthy colour about it."

Ryzak gave a weak smile. "I actually feel better. At least that rat in my head seems to have buggered off." He grinned at Jollif's mystified expression. "Never mind." He tried to stand, but felt the colour drain from his face as the room began to spin. Reaching out a steadying hand he gripped the chair to prevent himself from toppling over. Jollif stepped forward to aid him.

Noticing the movement, Ryzak waved him back. "I'm all right. Just a dizzy turn." After a moment the room stopped spinning. He breathed a sigh of relief. "When's this meeting?" he asked.

Jollif gave a wry grin. "An hour ago."

"Oh." Ryzak smiled, suddenly brightening. "So I've missed it then?"

Jollif shook his head. "Afraid not. You're not that lucky. It's been rescheduled."

Ryzak was crestfallen. "When for?"

"The minute you get out there. I've already got the tables together and locked the tavern for the day, as little Miss 'Do-whatisay' has instructed."

"Who?"

Jollif scowled. "Bloody Shula, that's who!" He shook his head in misery. "Who's going to replace my lost takings, hey? That's what I want to know." His voice grew louder as he continued. "A wagon-load of miners has just arrived in town, all fired up for a heavy session and some gambling, and she orders me to shut up shop! I tell you, I preferred it when she was the fawning little-girl-lost, not the condescending pain in the backside she is now."

Ryzak clucked in sympathy.

"I'm sorry, my friend," Jollif apologised, his voice softening, "I didn't mean to take it out on you. It's just that …"

"You hate to lose money," Ryzak finished for him. "Don't worry. I'm feeling better now. If you can get me a change of clothes I'll get washed, then we can get this meeting over and done with."

"That's the spirit." Jollif grinned and rubbed his hands together. "I'll go get them right away." Reaching the door, he turned. "Fancy some breakfast? Bacon, eggs, bre …" His voice faded at the sound of retching. "Well, maybe not," he mumbled, and yanked the door open to beat a hasty retreat.

* * * * *

An hour later Ryzak shambled into the common room. He felt much better now that he had been washed and had fresh clothes on. The red tunic and black leggings he wore smelt slightly of camphor, being stored away these past few months as they were, but at least the smell was acting as a tonic. It both masked the stench of puke and cleared his head at the same time.

He ignored the glares of annoyance that were aimed in his direction, scraped back the empty chair next to Jollif and sat down. "Have they started yet?" he whispered through the side of his mouth.

Jollif shook his head slightly, his nose twitching at the fusty smell being given off by Ryzak's clothing. "No," he whispered back. "They're too busy ignoring each other. There is a definite atmosphere in this place, and not a good one. I tell you, this day does not portend to be the highlight of my social calendar. Look at the wizard sitting at the opposite end to the dwarf there. If looks could kill, the little man would be toast by now."

Ryzak barfed.

"Oops, sorry," Jollif apologised, "I forgot."

The strident voice of feminine command rang out, Shula's crisp air of authority dragging everyone's attention to her as she rose from the chair opposite. All except Ryzak. He tried, but failed. Jollif's reference to toast had set his stomach churning. His gaze was fixed on a knot in the wood of the table. He hoped that if he stared at it for long enough the queasy feeling would pass.

"I think that we all know what this meeting is about," Shula began. "An evil from our past is attempting to break free of its chains. If it is successful, the lands of Middle Vooragh will again run with blood, death and foul deeds. In short, we are here to form a plan of attack to ensure that Mishtar remains shackled, deep in Mount Aine, where he was imprisoned by the wizards many years ago." She paused.

Ryzak managed to look up, his bleary gaze locking with Shula's hard stare. He gave her a small, winning smile, then wished he hadn't as he saw the scowl of irritation on her face. "Bloody women," he muttered to himself as she turned to the wizard. "You wouldn't think she loved me."

Jollif raised an eyebrow at the overheard remark. He was about to say something when Shula's voice intruded.

"Beulah!" she commanded, looking to her left, the timbre of her voice indicating the next was a demand not a request, "tell us what you know of Mishtar and the events leading to his containment."

"See what I mean about atmosphere?" Jollif whispered, nudging Ryzak in the ribs and nodding towards the wizard.

Ryzak looked up in time to see Beulah raise a large, bushy eyebrow in surprise at Shula's tone, before casting her an icy glare and giving a curt nod of acquiescence.

Scraping his chair back noisily, the wizard stood, placed his hands on the table and leaned forward. He let his gaze rest briefly on each of the group in turn before commencing.

"Mishtar was the most powerful wizard of his time and, unbeknownst to his colleagues, had begun to dabble in sorcery. We noticed that he was starting to spend long periods locked away in his study, or would disappear for weeks at a time, but we had no inkling of what he was up to. It was only a chance discovery that led to us finding out about his pernicious secret.

"A lowly apprentice had been out visiting some friends for the day when, on his way back to the Keep, he stumbled on a bizarre scene in the woods surrounding Misty Marsh. He was walking the paths through the trees when he became lost, ending up in a part of the wood he had never seen before."

Snorkel locked eyes with the wizard, a sly smile on his face. Beulah stumbled to a halt, his face reddening.

"Do we know the name of this apprentice?" Snorkel asked, in the pregnant pause. The feigned innocence in his voice indicated he already suspected the answer.

Beulah's face turned a deeper shade of red under the dwarf's close scrutiny. He averted his gaze. "Erm, yes. I think you do," he mumbled.

"What's all this about?" Jollif murmured to Ryzak.

"Buggered if I know," Ryzak replied, equally mystified. "But whatever it is, I don't think it's helping their relationship much."

"Would you care to enlighten us?" Snorkel urged, a hint of smugness in his voice.

"Does it really matter?" Shula asked sharply, putting a halt to the dwarf's banter. "If it has no relevance to what you are about to tell us then get to the point. Time is pressing."

"Bloody hell," mumbled Jollif. "I don't know what went on with you two out there, but she has come back a changed woman."

Ryzak cast his friend a dark look. "Nothing went on."

Jollif grinned. "Perhaps that's what the problem is, then. Something should have."

Scowling, Ryzak ignored Jollif's smirk and turned his attention back to the wizard. The man would not understand even if he explained it to him. Jollif was not as well versed in the ways of women as he was. She was just playing hard to get and, not wishing to arouse anyone's suspicions over the matter, chose to be bullish and domineering to hide the feelings she obviously held for him. He glanced across at Shula and gave her a wink. Fortunately her attention was fixed on Beulah and she did not see it.

Beulah cleared his throat before continuing. "Anyway, as I was saying before I was so rudely interrupted," he gave Snorkel a reproachful look, "the apprentice heard a voice amongst the trees.

It was chanting in some strange foreign language. Being inquisitive, he left the path to take a peek.

"Using the undergrowth for cover, he stealthily crept forward to try and discover what was behind the mysterious goings on. It did not take him long to reach the edge of the small, hidden clearing, and when he did, he wished he were anywhere else but there. Concealed by a fringe of long grass and bracken, he peered out on a spectacle that would stay with him for the rest of his life. In the middle of the clearing was Mishtar!" The wizard paused in his narrative to cast his gaze around the group, skilfully heightening the tension he was building.

His voice deepened to a low murmur. "He was standing beside a large slab of stone supported at each corner by boulders, the surface level with his waist. The hood of his black robe had fallen clear of his head and he gazed up to the heavens, chanting his weird litany."

The wizard straightened, his voice gaining power. "With arms held high, Mishtar's hands gripped a large, wickedly curved knife. The last of the sun's rays glinted menacingly off its silvered blade.

"The lad's gaze was drawn to the slab. His eyes widened in horror as he saw the unmoving form strapped to it. It was an elf. A young, very naked, female elf. Swirling red symbols had been painted on her bare flesh so that every part of her body was covered in them. The lad thought he recognised a few of the designs, but was not sure. Then he noticed the dark, sinister stains on the slab. He gasped in horror. He suddenly knew what the symbols were, and what Mishtar was about to do."

Ryzak stared at the wizard, open mouthed, captivated by the story. "Bloody hell, he's good," he murmured. He liked mystery and adventure tales, especially when there were naked women involved.

"Although there had been plenty of rumours doing the rounds at the Keep regarding Mishtar's long absences and periods of seclusion, ranging from mysterious lovers to being a covert alcoholic, no one had any idea he was up to this. Sorcery! At last his dark secret was out!

"Not stopping to think about the consequences, the apprentice gathered his somewhat limited powers to try and save the girl. He had to do something!

"About the only spell he had managed to master since joining the wizardhood was one of illusion. And then only managing to produce images of men dressed in baggy leather shorts and wearing silly hats, swatting each other about the head with wooden clubs, as they danced a jerky, hopping dance in two opposing lines. It always went down well at the village fair, but was probably not much use here.

"Then an idea came to him. Summoning inner reserves he never knew he possessed, he managed to reproduce the illusion. But this time, instead of dancers, he managed to form two lines of dark-robed wizards, materialising as a ghostly manifestation among the vegetation.

"Gathering his courage, the boy stepped out of concealment as Mishtar finished his litany and, in a voice both strong and powerful, commanded the evil sorcerer to desist from what he was doing.

"Surprise must have worked in the lad's favour. Seeing him and the two lines of advancing wizards, Mishtar's face clouded in fury and he turned and fled through the trees."

Beulah gave a small snort of amusement. "Fortunately, in his haste to evade capture, the sorcerer did not notice that the wizards were doing some strange kind of jerky dance and batting each other on the head with wooden clubs. If he had, the ploy might never have worked. However, be that as it may, it all turned out fine in the end.

"The girl revealed herself to be some sort of elven princess, next in line to the throne. She was so relieved at being saved from certain death that she rewarded her saviour in the only way she had available. It did not take long, as the lad was a complete novice in the carnal art. She wasn't!

"After that Mishtar disappeared, not to be heard of for another twenty years."

Snorkel's interest waned as the wizard went on to speak of things he'd heard before. He had quite enjoyed the bit about the *apprentice* becoming lost in the woods and the manner in which he had scared off Mishtar. He just knew the wizard had to have been the apprentice, and he could have had great fun at Beulah's expense if it were not for Shula. But one look at the sister's stern countenance had put paid to any devilment he had in mind before it could even start. One blazing look from her in her current mood would cook a rabbit, and he did not fancy being hors d'oeuvres.

As Beulah continued with the tale, Snorkel felt his eyelids growing heavier and heavier. Despite his attempts to stay awake, his head dropped lower until, with a light bump, his forehead hit the top of the table, the end of the wizard's account being accompanied by gentle snores.

"There you have it," Beulah concluded. "That is all I can tell you. We must find the last two seals before Mishtar can use his powers to influence some weak-minded fool to his cause, if he hasn't done so already. With three wards in place he can't project his image, but he can still use some of his quite substantial powers."

He surveyed the small group. "The question is, what do we do now?" His gaze fell on the sleeping form of Snorkel.

Ryzak noticed the wizard's scowl of annoyance. Jollif nudged him in the ribs. "I think our little friend's in for it," he whispered, inclining his head towards the wizard. Turning back to Beulah, Ryzak saw that the man's mouth was moving. Although he could not hear any words, the hairs on the back of his neck rose. It could only mean trouble. Beulah sat down and stared intently at the dwarf, a sly smile appearing on his face. The aroma of singed hair wafted across the table.

Jollif twitched his nose as the smell reached him. He glanced to his left and, with a startled shriek of "Fire!" jumped off his chair and ran to the counter.

Puzzled by the big man's strange behaviour, Ryzak watched Jollif's corpulent figure sprint away. He couldn't smell a thing over the stink of camphor. What was he on about, fire?

Seconds later the inn-keeper came back carrying a bucket of water, the contents sloshing over the sides due to the haste with which he was returning. Ryzak swore as Jollif angled for the throw, and dived from his chair.

Draco, who had been watching events from Snorkel's back, looked at the approaching figure, glanced down at Snorkel's smouldering beard, and beat a hasty retreat to the safety of the rafters. Oblivious to what was going on around him, Snorkel twitched and grumbled in his sleep.

Jollif skidded to a halt in front of the luckless dwarf and threw the contents of the bucket over his smouldering beard. With a scream of rage, Snorkel exploded into wakefulness. He shook his head to clear the water that streamed down his face and jumped from his chair, glaring around for the perpetrator. Jollif, who stood with the incriminating bucket still grasped in his podgy hands, became the focus of his wrath.

"You!" Snorkel roared. "You, you idiot! What did you want to do that for? You wait 'till I get my spell book out – then you're for it!"

The dwarf began to fumble frantically inside his robe.

From his prone position, Ryzak could see that Jollif had become extremely agitated by the mention of the 'spell book'. He began to back away from the dwarf and was trying to placate him. "It was your beard," Jollif spluttered. "It was on fire. I had to do something, or you would have been cooked where you sat."

Ryzak felt his stomach heave. It must have been the mention of food. Although he felt better, the thought of food still sent his stomach into spasms.

"Now you're going to get it!" Snorkel screamed.

The shrillness of the cry made Ryzak forget about his stomach. His friend was in trouble! His friend needed help! Urgent help! Where was a hero when you needed one? Not here, he concluded as he saw the dwarf pull the book from his robe and waggle it at Jollif's retreating figure. The little man had an unnerving, manic gleam in his eye. That sealed it: the big man was on his own. He was staying out of it.

"Just you wait 'till I find the right page, then I'll show you what happens when you mess with a wizard!" Snorkel yelled, leafing through the pages.

Ryzak heard the sound of deep, throaty laughter and raised his head to peer over the top of the table. He saw Beulah, tears streaming down his face, doubled over, chortling like a man gone mad. Ryzak turned back to look at the dwarf and saw the light of understanding in Snorkel's eyes.

"BOYS!" the strident voice of feminine authority rang out. "When you have quite finished!"

"It wasn't my fault," Jollif whined.

"I, er, I was looking for woodworm," said Ryzak, picking himself up off the floor.

"I was the victim!" Snorkel spat, through gritted teeth.

"Chirp, chirrup, squeak," piped Draco, gliding down to land on the dwarf's shoulder pad.

Beulah cleared his throat. "Er, sorry!" He tried to look contrite, but the mischievous smirk on his face gave lie to the words.

Shula crossed her arms and cast them all a withering glare, her right foot tapping an angry beat on the bare boards of the floor. "Thank you," she said. "Now, if you've all finished behaving like morons, we'll carry on."

She waited until they were seated and suitably attentive before turning to Beulah. "The Great One intimated that the sacred orb of the sisterhood holds secrets that we no longer have access to. Secrets that require your *wisdom* to unlock." She raised an eyebrow, indicating that recent events had not convinced her of his sanity, never mind his ability to be of any assistance to the cause.

"Ah, I see." Beulah nodded with thoughtful comprehension. "That must be because the orb once belonged to the wizards."

Shula's mouth fell open.

"You didn't know? Well, I'm sorry that I have to disillusion you, but we, the wizards that is, were the fathers behind the birth of the sisterhood, so to speak."

"Never!" shouted Shula, slamming the palms of her hands onto the table in outrage as she rose from her seat. "We have co-existed with the wizards since, since, since time began."

Beulah pursed his lips and shook his head. The others watched the interchange in silence.

Beulah's voice dropped to a soft, kindly tone. "No, I'm sorry. When I unlock the orb's full powers your matriarch will understand the import of what I have just told you. It is for her to decide what repercussions this holds for your order." His eyes held Shula's gaze with a look of compassion. "Until then, you will have to believe me. I may be many things, but a liar is not one of them." He gave her an encouraging smile. "We leave for your palace in the morning?"

Shula sullenly nodded her head and slowly sank down into her chair, a dejected slump to her shoulders.

Snorkel glowered at the wizard, wondering how he could out-magic the magic user and turn him into something ugly and horrid. He sniggered at the thought. The scrawny fool was that already; he would have to think of something else. What about something old, useless and decrepit? He covered his mouth with his hand to stifle a laugh. No. No good. Beulah was proving to be that also. The dwarf drummed his fingers on the top of the table abstractedly as he tried to think of something, anything, to enable him to get his own back.

'Mum!' Draco's mind-shout hammered into his head.

Such was the power behind the voice that the dwarf jerked back in surprise, his elbow slipping off the table. With no means of support, his chin plummeted down to meet the wooden surface with a mighty crack. Draco flapped her wings at the unexpected movement and fought to keep her balance as her perch collapsed beneath her.

Reddening under the accusing glares cast in his direction, the dwarf mumbled an apology as he righted himself, then turned to the source of his embarrassment. Singed bits of beard broke off at the movement, adding to his annoyance. It had taken him years to grow the blasted thing and now it was ruined. Damn the man!

"What'd you do that for?" Snorkel spat between gritted teeth.

'How was I to know you were sleeping?' Draco asked, her tone sweet and innocent.

"I was not sleeping!"

'Whatever,' she replied, with a toothy grin. Her yellow eyes started to whirl in excitement. *'Ask Beulah to describe the seal.'*

"Why?" the dwarf growled, folding his arms and staring at her suspiciously.

'Do you always want to play the fool, or would you like to be the hero for once? Just do as I ask!'

Surprised by her abrupt tone, Snorkel gave her one last glower of displeasure before turning his attention back to the meeting. He had better humour her or he would never get any peace. "What's this seal look like then?" he asked.

Ryzak looked up, a knowing grin plastered on his face. "It's a gold disc, about this big," he said, indicating the size with a fore-finger and thumb. "It's plain on one side and has hydro ... pyro ... er, strange symbols on the other." He looked sideways at Jollif and gave him a wink.

Beulah nodded in agreement at the description.

Snorkel flinched as Draco jumped up and down on his shoulder, flapping her wings in excitement. *'I know where one of the seals is!'*

"I know where one of the seals is," Snorkel repeated, verbatim. His features took on a stunned expression as he realised what he had just said.

"You do?" queried Beulah in astonishment.

"I do?" asked Snorkel, giving the dragonet a quizzical look.

"Well don't just sit there, out with it!"

"What?"

"Tell us where the disc is," Beulah growled, leaning menac-ingly across the table.

Panicking, Snorkel glanced at Draco, who was still dancing about on his shoulder unaware of his silent plea for help.

"Well? We're waiting."

'Reizgoth has got one! Reizgoth has got one!' Draco's voice trumpeted as she took off and began to fly around the room.

Amazed by the creature's strange behaviour, everyone forgot about Snorkel. "Reizgoth's got it," he stated.

Beulah snapped round, his attention fixing back on the dwarf. "What? But he's dead!" he exclaimed.

'No he's not,' Draco informed Snorkel, amid her frenzied aerobatics.

"No he's not."

'He's in Firestone Mountain.'

"He's in Firestone Mountain."

Beulah frowned sceptically at this latest piece of information. "How do you know?"

After a moment's pause, with no help forthcoming from the lime-green, winged lizard, Snorkel gave a nervous smile. "Old dwarf legend?"

"Bah. I lived with your people for years. No one ever mentioned anything about Reizgoth," the wizard said, folding his arms and glaring at the dwarf in disgust.

'It's true,' Draco said, having calmed down and glided in to land on Snorkel's shoulder. *'I've seen it in his cave. He's got all sorts of junk in there. As long as it's gold, he'll have it. He doesn't go far now; he's very old. That is why no one has seen him for years.'*

"It's true, Wiz. Honest. One of the seals is in his cave in Firestone Mountain."

"Who is Reizgoth?" asked Shula, her voice surprisingly quiet.

"What is more to the point, my dear," exclaimed Beulah kindly. "Reizgoth is a dragon. A full-blooded, fire-breathing, big red dragon. I thought he had died years ago."

"Big red dragon?" squeaked Jollif, his eyes like saucers. "A real, live dragon? I think I need a drink."

"I'll second that!" Snorkel agreed, suddenly brightening up at the prospect of alcohol.

"Me too," added Ryzak, half rising from his chair.

"Enough!" roared Beulah. "Time for that later. This changes matters, changes matters considerably."

Ryzak heaved a resigned sigh and sat back down. Snorkel did likewise. Just what he needed, more talking.

The ensuing discussion took over two hours. Two hours of heated debate, threats, refusals, foot stamping, finger wagging, fist clenching and, finally, agreement.

It was decided that Beulah and Shula would leave for the Palace of the Sisters the following morning, to try to unlock the orb's secrets in order that the location of the last seal could be found. They would then travel on to the seal's place of concealment, retrieve it, and travel back to meet Ryzak and Snorkel at The Shepherds Cock.

The latter duo, the most vociferous and reluctant of the group, were to journey to Firestone Mountain to ask Reizgoth for the seal.

"Ask a big red dragon for a piece of its hoard?" Ryzak had gasped, in horror-stricken disbelief. "You must be joking!"

He was assured in the most assertive fashion that 'Wiz' was not joking, and being told, "Anyway, you'll have Snorkel with you. What harm could befall you when you're travelling in the company of a wizard?" Ryzak sulkily agreed.

Jollif was to remain at the tavern to await their return, keeping his ears and eyes open for anything untoward, as it was entirely probable that Mishtar had agents who could be planning their demise. With the matter settled, the group broke up and went their separate ways; Jollif, Ryzak and Snorkel to the bar, Shula and Beulah to Jollif's living area to further debate the situation. Some things were better discussed in private.

"How did you know that Reizgoth has the seal?" Snorkel asked his lime-green companion, as he waited for his drink.

'Because I've been to his cave and seen it.'

"When? I thought I birthed you, and you certainly can't have been in the past few weeks. I would have noticed you were missing."

'Ages ago. Before you birthed me. When I used to live with my brothers and sisters.'

Confused, Snorkel decided to give up this line of questioning and down a few dwarven ales instead. He reached across the bar and grasped a brimming tankard, downing half the contents in one swig before placing it back on the counter. "Uiskey chaser?" he asked, giving Ryzak a grin.

Returning it with one of his own, Ryzak slapped Snorkel heartily on the back. "Stack 'em up, Jollif. My new friend and I are in the mood for a drink or two."

"Or three, or four," added Snorkel, rubbing his hands together in anticipation.

Beulah sat in Jollif's favourite armchair next to the fire. He was sipping a glass of expensive red wine, savouring the exquisite, full-bodied, lightly-spiced flavour.

"Do you think it wise to let those two loose at the bar? I've seen what drink does to Ryzak, and it's not pleasant," said Shula.

Beulah lowered his glass and smiled. "I know what you mean, Snorkel's the same. It won't do them any lasting harm and might even do them some good. Set them off in high spirits, so to speak. They will have easy enough travelling for the first week before they reach Elven lands. They should be sober by then." He laughed.

"Aye. I suppose the *Mighty Beulah* knows best," Shula responded, displeasure evident in her tone.

The wizard gazed at her speculatively. "Are you sure that we haven't met before?" he asked. "Some of your mannerisms seem awfully familiar."

"No! No, of course not. How could we have?" Shula spluttered hastily.

"No matter," said Beulah thoughtfully. "I must be thinking of someone else, someone I once knew."

Hours later he was still wondering why she had been so flustered and had blushed a deep crimson at the question.

* * * * *

Deep in the heart of the Plains of Fear a vociferous flight of dragonets took to the skies to find yet more food for the latest addition to their group.

The arrival of the youngster two weeks ago had caused great rejoicing and much consternation amongst the flight. After all, it is not every day that a small, fluffy, grey dragonet without any wing stubs is hatched.

Chapter Seven

The essence of Mishtar withdrew from the tavern, back to the sword that imprisoned his life-force. At least now he knew what he was up against: one old wizard and his incompetent apprentice, a witch of the sisterhood, and a drunkard.

Long years of captivity had given him plenty of time to study and test the wards. Despite what that fool Beulah had told the others, three seals were no longer enough to hold him completely chained. He still had a certain amount of freedom. It was time to play dirty; he had spent too long in this damned sword. When he was free he would make them pay. He chuckled in anticipation. Oh how they would pay!

He vaguely remembered Beulah from Wizard's Keep. He had been a tall, spotty youth, forever tripping over his own feet and apologising for his ineptitude at the most basic of spells. Unless he had miraculously improved, Mishtar had no need to fear his talents. It was a pity he had not realised it was Beulah who had surprised him in the woods all those years ago. If he had, he might not be in this predicament now. No matter, he would be free soon enough. And then he could make amends for past mistakes.

Mishtar smiled at the memory of the look on the sister's face when Beulah had told her that they, the wizards, had been the instruments behind the formation of the sisterhood. What would she say if she knew that he, Mishtar, had been the main instigator, wanting to get rid of the troublesome females who insisted that their powers were the equal of men's?

Pah! He showed them. He even gave them their precious orb to play with. Little did they know that as well as being a channel for their powers, it was also a receptacle. Every time it was used it drained a little of the user's power. Not enough that she would notice, but enough to gradually build up a sizeable well of magic for when the need arose. For when he required it.

The echoes of Mishtar's demented laughter sent vibrations through the cold, damp air of the cavern. This was getting entertaining. If he were not confined within this tomb, he would really be enjoying himself.

He wished he could be there when Beulah tried to unlock the orb's powers. The old fool would not sense the presence of the traps and snares he had set. As soon as he triggered one of them, his soul would be drawn into the orb, trapped for all eternity. Only he, Mishtar, the greatest sorcerer that ever lived, could unlock its powers. Only he could use them. Oh, yes. This was building up to be one hell of a ball. Pardon the pun.

Mishtar sighed with vexation, his thoughts drawn to the meddling sister. The only mistake he had made in his plans for freedom was not allowing for her. Then again she was only a female – no match for him. Even if she managed to influence Ryzak, he was sure that the man could be swayed to his cause to break the spell of confinement.

It was the removal of the first seal that had allowed Mishtar his opportunity to further his plans for revenge on the peoples of Middle Vooragh. Before the seal was removed he had spent over a hundred years trying to break free, without success. Then one day some religious nutter, intent on becoming a hermit in order to find his inner self, had found his way into the cavern. After spending three days kneeling in front of the sword, praying to whatever god it was he worshipped, thanking him for his guidance in finding so wondrous a temple (temple?), he had risen to his feet and walked reverently towards the stone pillars.

As soon as he spied the gold seals in their clasps all thoughts of religion had deserted him. His eyes filled with greed and he scrabbled away at a seal with his knife, until he managed to prise it free.

As it was removed, the violet glow of magic surrounding the sword flickered, plunging the cavern into darkness before it re-asserted itself, albeit slightly dimmer. Convinced that his god was about to strike him down, the once-priest fled from the cavern and back to the world of the living, taking his ill-gotten spoils with him.

Some years later, after he had manipulated the removal of further seals, Mishtar eventually tracked the man to the streets of

Aldurain. His spirit form found him standing on a podium at Speakers' Corner, dressed in rags, espousing the virtues of abstinence. Apparently, having sold the gold seal to a knight of the Court of Aldurain and being in a state of permanent inebriation for months after, he had come to realise the error of his ways and was in the process of trying to convert others to his cause. Had Speakers' Corner not been positioned between The Broken Barrel and Smeale's Wine Bar the man might well have lived a longer, less doomed lifestyle. As it was ...

Given a glimpse of freedom by the removal of the first seal, Mishtar had pushed back the boundaries until he could send his spirit into the outside world. Not very far, but far enough; sending it down the lower slopes of Mount Aine, searching for some dullard who he could influence to enter the cavern and prise the remaining discs free.

Eventually, after months of searching, he touched a mind that his restricted powers could influence. It did not take long to infiltrate the man's simple thought processes, plant the seed of untold wealth, his for the taking, and guide him to the cave mouth.

All was going exceptionally well; the man had prised one seal free and had just released a second when pandemonium broke out. Mishtar was so intent on guiding the man's thoughts and screening him from fear of the flickering violet light that he never noticed a dragonet enter the cavern.

By the time he became aware of its presence it had snatched a gold seal off the floor and hurtled out of the cavern. Mishtar's concentration had failed; the simpleton, regaining control of his pea-sized brain, panicked and fled as the light flickered, taking the other seal with him, never to be seen again. Not by Mishtar anyway.

After many days spent venting his fury, he set about locating the two stolen seals, but to no avail. They seemed to have disappeared. However, when he had calmed down enough to consider his options, he'd found that his powers were more accessible and he could now project his image to the cave entrance. He began to investigate the wards more closely, looking for an instant solution to free his containment. He found it. He discovered a small loophole in the wizards' spell. It could be undone – permanently!

The problem with having the seals removed was that they could be put back again. Even one seal back in its place would re-start the process, drawing his soul back into the sword. The threat of imprisonment would always be there if he could not destroy the magic that set it.

He discovered that if one of the seals was placed in its mount hieroglyphs down, by someone with magical powers, the spell would be smashed forever, leaving him free to take over the body of the poor fool that had broken it. It did not matter how little magic that person possessed, it would be enough.

Mishtar went searching and came across a young soldier with somewhat limited intelligence – he was not thick, just a little slow on the uptake. Mishtar could detect the small amount of latent magical ability within the man. Not much, but enough for his purposes – the man's mother having been some sort of herb woman. The soldier's name was Ryzak.

It had not taken much effort to influence him and manipulate events to Mishtar's benefit. He even managed to make the fool into a hero in the process. It had all seemed so easy when Ryzak retrieved the seal from the dead knight. Mishtar smirked at the memory of the knight's horse tripping on a perfectly level piece of ground. Such slipshod riding. One thing he had not anticipated, however, was Ryzak taking so long to reach the mountain.

Then that Sister of the New Dawn had arrived on the scene. Mishtar admired the way she had managed to recruit Ryzak; a masterful piece of deception. One that he would have been proud to be a part of, were it not set to oppose him! Matters had then taken a turn for the worse.

No matter, he now knew the location of one of the discs. That damned dragonet must have stolen it to appease Reizgoth. It was time to make his move. He had allies, and it was time to bring them into play.

Chapter Eight

A faint, ethereal light illuminated the corridor. Its translucent blue radiance reflected off the rows of white tiles that covered the floor and walls of the seemingly endless passage. The source was a mystery to Ryzak, as was how he came to be in this weird place in the first instance.

He remembered waking up, at least he thought he had awoken, to find himself in the corridor. Although slightly puzzled, the strangeness of the situation did not seem to bother him. He felt as though he'd been invited for some special purpose, and all he had to do was walk on to discover it. He eagerly strode forward, feeling uncommonly excited.

After walking for what felt like hours, the end was nowhere in sight and the tedious, white surroundings were starting to give him a headache. His initial excitement had dissipated and he was beginning to get uneasy. Ryzak stumbled to a halt and rubbed his tired eyes with a grubby thumb and forefinger, cursing to himself as he wondered when his final destination would be reached. Realising he would not get an answer standing in the corridor like a spare part, he set off on his travels again.

A small doorway appeared on his left, but he barely gave it a glance, remaining focused on his objective, whatever that might prove to be. The door would probably be locked anyway; all the others had been.

A darkening appeared in the distance. Ryzak stopped and stared, squinting against the brightness of the passage, trying to puzzle out what it meant. Then he smiled, sensing he was nearing the end of his quest. His heart beat faster, excitement vying with relief as he strode forward. But no matter how quickly he walked, the smudge remained a grey, unidentifiable *something* ahead of him. Many minutes passed and it was not getting any nearer. He fought against frustration and strode ever forwards, head down, purpose in his stride.

Looking up for what seemed like the umpteenth time he was

surprised to see that the smudge had grown bigger, closer. He grinned. He was nearly there. He started to jog. A pain appeared in his side, but he ignored it. Suddenly he was at the end and skidded to a halt. He stared around in amazement. It looked like he had stepped into someone's study.

A blazing log fire was set in the white tiled wall that formed the end of the corridor, and a small, white table and two white armchairs were arranged in front of it. A white leather-bound book lay on the table. The gold lettering on the book's cover shimmered in the fire's flickering flames, creating an air of mystery.

Intrigued, Ryzak walked across and picked it up. He began to read the inscription silently to himself, his mouth attempting to wrap itself round words that he had never heard before: *'Socialism For The Masses.'*

For The, he understood. It was the *Socialism* and *Masses* bits that baffled him. Ryzak moved around the table to the fire and began to absent-mindedly leaf through the pages, hoping that the contents would enlighten him.

"I see that you have found my treatise," a deep, baritone voice said from behind him. "Welcome to my home, Ryzak. Please, be seated."

The intrusion did not perturb Ryzak and he turned to face the speaker, his eyes fixing on the figure sitting in one of the armchairs. It was the man with the funny goatee beard; the one from the cavern. Mishtar.

"Excuse the rather spartan furnishings, my friend. My needs are few and I do so detest clutter. Please, sit down. You're making me feel uncomfortable." Mishtar's oily smile seemed like that of a predator about to coax lunch into its lair.

The look was lost on Ryzak, and he sat in the armchair Mishtar had indicated.

Deep down Ryzak realised he was here to meet with Mishtar all along. For what, he did not know, but he was sure he was about to find out. "Why am I here?" he asked. "I would have thought that I would be the last person you wanted to see."

"Quite the contrary, my friend," Mishtar replied, with a dazzling smile. He leaned forward in a conspiratorial manner, his eyes boring into Ryzak's. "We have a great deal to discuss, you and I.

A great deal. Do you like my book?" he asked, straightening and indicating the volume tucked under Ryzak's arm. "It's an ideal, I know. But one that I hope to pursue in the not too distant future. We all have a dream, Ryzak, and that is mine."

"Oh! Yes. Very interesting I'm sure. Very, er … worthwhile."

Having flicked quickly through the pages, Ryzak had not taken in anything that was written on them. He didn't have a clue what the sorcerer was on about.

His puzzlement must have been obvious. Mishtar leaned back in his chair and steepled his fingers, his dark, penetrating eyes holding Ryzak's. "My dream of equality for all men, Ryzak. We are all born the same way, therefore we should all be equal. Why let one man rule the lives of others? We all breathe the same air, walk the same earth, eat the same foodstuffs. We all defecate and fornicate. Why should the minority rule the majority?"

Ryzak was having a great deal of difficulty understanding this one. Here was a man whose soul was supposedly imprisoned in a sword, for attempting to take control of Middle Vooragh by nefarious means, championing the virtues of mass rule. Even Ryzak's limited intelligence could see that it did not add up.

"If you don't mind me asking, why the about-turn? Weren't you tric … er, trapped, because you wanted to rule Middle Vooragh like one of the tyrants you're on about?"

Mishtar growled in disgust. "That was a set up by those damned wizards. They wanted to keep control of the lands for themselves. Stifle the proletariat. They couldn't stand the thought of not being able to use their powers to dominate others, you see?"

Ryzak couldn't, but he nodded his head anyway.

"They found out that I was about to overthrow the tyrannical rulers of the land and they set me up!" Mishtar slammed the palms of his hands against the arms of his chair in indignation. His eyes lit with passion as he enthusiastically continued. "Just think. There would be no more peasants scrabbling round for cast-offs from the ruling classes, no more taxes, no more starvation. Equal rule for all! Equal shares for all! An end to unfair domination! That is the dream, Ryzak. That is the dream!" His clenched fist hammered onto the table for emphasis.

After a moment's pause, the sorcerer's expression changed to one of abject misery. "And now? Now I am trapped. Trapped for eternity. Unable to achieve my life's goal." He looked deeply into Ryzak's eyes. "Unless … Dare I say it?" He shook his head and briefly lowered his gaze from Ryzak's stupefied expression. Then, regaining his composure, he looked up and grasped Ryzak's hands tightly in undisguised fervour. "Unless … Unless I can enlist the help of someone who feels the same way as I do. Someone who is as committed to the cause as I am! I sense, Ryzak … I sense that that person is you!" Mishtar's hands trembled with passion, his grip getting stronger. "Are you he, Ryzak? Are you the man who is to set me free? Free to achieve my ultimate goal? Are you?"

The excitement and enthusiasm of Mishtar's delivery aroused a passion in Ryzak. Here was the most evil sorcerer ever to have walked Middle Vooragh, championing the cause of an end to tyrannical rule, whatever that was. It sounded too good to be true. However misguided, he found himself believing and wanting to be part of it. Although alarm bells were ringing in his head, his heart was beating to a different tune. Revolution! An end to domination by the rich and powerful. He, Ryzak, was to be important! A vital player! A smile slowly appeared on his face as he returned Mishtar's impassioned stare. He was imagining himself sitting on the people's committee, adored, a saviour of the masses.

Mishtar could see that the images he had planted were starting to germinate. He released Ryzak from his gaze and let go of his hands, a sly smile appearing on his face as he softly said, "I knew you were the one, Ryzak. I knew it!"

Now where had Ryzak heard that expression before? For the life of him he could not remember. He cast the thought to the back of his mind. In the scheme of things, it was of no consequence.

"Come, brother. Let us drink to our new alliance."

A bottle of wine and two glasses mysteriously appeared on the table. Ryzak was so taken in by *the dream* that he did not think to question where they had come from.

The sorcerer filled the glasses with generous quantities of wine and, after placing the bottle back on the table, offered one to Ryzak. He stood and raised his own glass. "A toast!" As Ryzak followed suit, Mishtar chinked their glasses together. "An end to all tyrants. To comrades in arms!"

Ryzak ardently repeated the words and raised his glass.

"Oops! Sorry about that. Never mind, it'll soon wash out."

Mishtar froze, his own drink half way to his mouth, his eyes widening in surprise.

Ryzak's hand was locked in a raised position, his glazed eyes staring vacantly at his empty fingers.

"What in hell's name are you doing here?" growled Mishtar. "And how, pray tell, did you get here?"

Snorkel shrugged. "Give up. One minute I'm lying on a sun-drenched mountainside being fanned by naked she-dwarfs who wait on my every whim, the next – Wham! I'm here, listening to you drivel on about brothers and tyrants." He shook his head forlornly. "Just my luck. Another couple of minutes and they would have been all over me like a rash."

Mishtar slammed his glass down on the table. Pieces of shattered crystal flew everywhere and red wine sprayed over the white table top. "Well you can just bugger off and return to your harem. Your presence is not required!"

"Yeah! Sure thing. Just point the way and I'll be gone," Snorkel retorted. He scanned his surroundings with disdain. "Sure beats the hell out of this place. Who was your decorator? Snow White?" He chuckled, pleased at his little joke. Snow White was one of his favourite bedtime stories. Nothing to do with the dwarfs being the heroes, of course.

"Go!" Mishtar roared.

"All right, all right. No need to get shirty. We were just leaving, weren't we?" Snorkel said, frowning with concern as he observed his immobile friend.

"Not him, cretin! Just you!" Mottled red splotches appeared on Mishtar's face as he fought for composure, the veins in his neck standing out with the effort.

Snorkel shook his head in apology. "Sorry, mate. We're a pair, him and me. Where he goes, I go. Where I go, he goes. Got it? Come on, Ryzak. Time to be off. Can't leave them lovely ladies waiting, can we?"

The dark shadow of Mishtar suddenly loomed over him and he glanced in the sorcerer's direction. The dwarf's eyes widened in fear as he saw Mishtar's body begin to expand, growing taller and more menacing. He gave a squeak of terror and recoiled in fear.

Ryzak was still standing staring at his empty hand as if he had been turned into a statue, blissfully unaware of events around him.

The figure of Mishtar continued to expand, his form filling the corridor. "You are about to learn the error of your ways, little man. You are in my domain now. I have absolute power! In this place you are at my mercy. It is time to die, you meddling pipsqueak."

The mumble of magic-sounding words reached Snorkel's ears as Mishtar stretched out his arms, ready to deliver the promised doom.

Suddenly everything slowed. Snorkel could see the haze of magical energies as if they were in slow motion. His eyes grew wide in horror as whatever spell Mishtar had summoned made it's slow but inexorable way toward him.

A click sounded in his head, as if a door latch had been opened. Instantly he knew what he had to do. His hands wove intricate patterns in the air as strange, unfamiliar words tumbled out of his mouth. As if by instinct, he clapped his hands together at the end of the incantation. Immediately a transparent bubble encapsulated Ryzak and himself.

With a thunderous roar, the magical haze hit the protective bubble and scattered, little particles of spent magic falling lifeless to the floor. Ryzak snapped out of his stupor and gaped in astonishment as he saw the little man. "What are you doing here?"

"No time to explain," yelled Snorkel, casting nervous glances at the enraged sorcerer, who was preparing himself for another attack.

Ryzak's eyes followed Snorkel's glance. "Uh-oh!"

"I can think of a more apt expression," snapped Snorkel, trying to figure out how he had managed to summon the shield that had protected them.

As Mishtar's menacing figure towered over them, the dwarf's instincts took over once more. His hands moved faster than the eye could follow as yet more strange words rushed from his mouth.

When he finished, it all went dark. Very dark. Scared, he grasped hold of Ryzak's tunic to make sure he was still there.

What had he done?

A light breeze began to tug at his hair. The breeze became a wind. The wind a gale. The gale a hurricane. The ferocious intensity of the moving air snatched them off their feet and sent them tumbling head over heels, their screams of terror joining the howl of the tempest.

Snorkel and Ryzak sat bolt upright in their sleeping furs at the same instant, their eyes snapping open. The lingering echoes of their screams shattered the silence of the night. They turned face to face, and seeing their own shock and horror mirrored on the other's face, screamed again.

An amused chuckle escaped the lips of the observer concealed in the undergrowth. Quietly laughing to himself, he decided that he had seen enough and made his way back to the camp to report his findings. Rhudrhyn would want to hear all about this.

* * * * *

Within the confines of his prison, Mishtar fumed. Ryzak had been right where he wanted him; his for the taking. It had been far easier than he thought to influence the man's weak, simple mind. It was all going according to plan. Until the runt appeared!

Where had he come from? How had he managed to enter the dreamscape? Why didn't he, Mishtar, sense the intrusion until it was too late?

These were questions that he had to address, and quickly. He could not afford to have a rogue element interfere with his plans.

Mishtar swore his hatred of all dwarfs to the gods, and began planning their eventual capture and extermination. Oh yes, when he was free they would suffer. He would make sure that the very first thing he did was torture the little buggers to death. A long, slow, lingering, painful death.

Chapter Nine

Dawn broke bright and cheery, the new day's sun beginning its leisurely ascent into clear, blue skies. Its early morning rays filtered through the leafy canopy at the edge of Border Woods, bathing Snorkel and Ryzak with green-tinged light as they broke camp in mute silence.

They had not slept much after their adventure in the dream-scape. Neither had broached the subject to the other since waking, not wanting to believe it could have happened to them, and fearful of appearing a complete jerk if it hadn't.

'Hey, I had a strange dream last night, sorcerers and magic and stuff. Guess what? You were in it too.'

'Really? You've lost it, mate. You're mental. If you think I'm travelling any further with a basket case, you've got another think coming!'

So they stashed their few belongings into their sleeping furs in silence, ready to roll them up and strap them behind their saddles.

Finishing tying his roll together, Snorkel rose to his feet and stooped to grab it and heft the dead weight onto his shoulder. He wanted to balance it before trying to move. He had learned from past experience that trying to walk and carry heavy objects at the same time can result in painful accidents.

He slowly turned to walk over to Clara, his mule. Casting a surreptitious glance at Ryzak, he moved across the uneven grass of the clearing. He could see that his companion had already tacked his horse and was looking at him expectantly. The man was leaning against his huge stallion, arms crossed, a wry smile playing about his features.

Snorkel knew why. He heaved a heavy sigh and staggered across to the foul-tempered beast that passed for his mount, glancing up at the sky for signs of Draco as he walked. She had not returned from her night's hunting and he was starting to get worried. It was unlike her to be away for so long.

The shout of, "Hurry up or it'll be dark!" distracted him from

his anxiety. Snorkel gave Ryzak a half smile and warily approached Clara, the mule from hell.

Being so small, the only steed available to suit him had been
one of Jollif's pack-mules. She was a sturdy beast, but somewhat
surly and unused to being ridden for any distance. Snorkel hated
her, or, more to the point, he was scared stiff of her. He was not a
good rider, and having to mount such a temperamental beast made
matters worse. His only previous experience of riding had been on
the back of a wooden hobbyhorse at the village fair. He had even
managed to fall off that.

Clara's lips curled back as Snorkel approached, revealing blunt,
yellowed teeth, stained from years of chewing fresh hay back in
her warm, comfortable stable. Her ears folded back and her eyes
narrowed in determination as he drew closer. Today was the day
when the dwarf would learn who was master of this little outfit.
She snorted in anticipation, causing Snorkel to falter in his stride.
Aye, today was the day he would get what he deserved.

It was not that she did not like being ridden. She used to quite
enjoy those lazy summer days, when Jollif let the village children
go for short rides on her back, her straw hat perched jauntily on
her head, her large ears poking through the purpose-made holes in
the brim. But this was different. She had to work! If shorty thought
he had mastered her he was sadly mistaken. Kids were fine, they
gave her sweets and stuff. This runt only gave her backache.

Unaware of Clara's intent, but always wary of her, Snorkel
approached the mule with trepidation. "Nice girl, Clara," he
murmured, in what he hoped was a soothing fashion, and casually
eased the roll from his shoulder. "That's a good horsy. You stand
there nice and steady while I put this small, light, er – very light,"
he hastily amended, as Clara eyed him suspiciously, "pack on your
back."

The mule snorted and flicked her ears in annoyance as the little
man tied his sleeping-roll behind the saddle but, much to Snorkel's
relief, stood perfectly still and allowed him to finish in peace. He
breathed a silent 'thank you' to Ryzak for putting the saddle on the

animal while he was waiting for him to tie his bedding together. Rolls were bad enough, but saddles were much worse.

Having finished securing his belongings, Snorkel stepped back and eyed Clara with misgiving. She had been too quiet. She had just stood there and let him get on with it without any sign of mischief. Perhaps she was getting used to him, or then again …

He rubbed at his bearded chin thoughtfully as he moved round to her side. Grasping the pommel he placed a foot in the stirrup to haul himself up.

From his now mounted position, Ryzak noticed Clara's lips curl back as the dwarf hoisted himself up to the saddle. Before he had the chance to shout a warning, the mule had turned her head and clamped her teeth into Snorkel's behind.

Ryzak cringed as the dwarf screamed in pain and was catapulted over Clara's back to land in a crumpled heap on the grass. As the mule's triumphant whinny sounded, Ryzak shook his head in disbelief. Couldn't the dwarf get anything right?

Jarred by his unexpected flying lesson, Snorkel groggily eased himself to his knees, shaking his head to clear the stars that were dancing in front of his eyes. Gradually awareness of what had happened filtered into his scrambled brain. His eyes narrowed. It was bad enough having to ride the dusty fleabag, without having to put up with her tricks every day as well. All her previous antics tumbled through his head, his anger growing with each remembered insult.

Sometimes she would move away as he was about to mount, causing him to fall flat on his face. Other times she would stand still and not move at all after he had mounted, no matter how hard he dug her in the ribs with his heels. But the worst occasion, prior to this, was when she had slipped her tether and gone running around in circles, with him running after her yelling abuse. It had taken him ages to catch her. He could still remember Ryzak's loud guffaws of amusement at the spectacle.

The damned beast had humiliated him at every opportunity. Well, that was it! That was the last straw. That was the very last time this mule would make an ass out of him.

Snorkel scrambled to his feet and stood glaring at the animal; all his anger, his humiliations, his outrage channelled in that one look. Unbidden, words of magic tumbled from his mouth as his hands began to weave intricate patterns in the air.

Ryzak's eyes widened in alarm at Snorkel's utterance of magic. Clara's eyes widened in apprehension in the realisation that maybe, just maybe, she had pushed the little man too far. Suitably replete from a successful hunt, Draco's eyes widened in astonishment as she flew into camp to witness events unfolding.

Finishing his incantation, Snorkel thrust his index fingers towards Clara. A pulse of magic flew from their tips. The mule managed one whinny of terror before disappearing in a haze of magic-charged ions.

Horror-stricken, Snorkel stared at the green fog engulfing the unfortunate beast. For some horrible reason, it seemed awfully familiar.

An eerie silence descended over the forest; not even bird-song could be heard. It was as if time stood still.

Snorkel slowly raised his hands to eye-level and peered at them warily, wondering if they were possessed. He was gob-smacked. Yet again he had done something without the faintest notion of what it was. It was getting to be rather a bad habit.

Ryzak breathed a sigh of relief as the fog started to disperse and the recognisable form of a small horse materialised. At least the twerp had not managed to blow the irascible animal away. As his view improved, he frowned in puzzlement. Something odd seemed to have happened. The mule's ears appeared to be shorter, and her legs were slightly longer. Wasn't Clara grey, not white with black splotches? Confused by the apparent transformation in the formerly stocky beast, he tethered his horse and went to take a closer look.

Snorkel was sitting on the grass, a stunned expression on his face, turning his hands in front of his eyes and staring at them in amazement. Ignoring him for the moment, Ryzak examined the impressive animal that stood before him. It was a magnificent small pony, and, by some quirk of good fortune, the dwarf's saddle was still strapped to its back, with the sleeping-roll tied behind.

"How did you manage that?" Ryzak murmured in awe. "She's a beauty."

"Chirp, chirrup, squeak?" asked Draco, as she flew down to land on Snorkel's shoulder.

The unmistakable sound of silence answered their questions.

Ryzak glanced down at the entranced dwarf and nudged him with his boot. "I said, how did you manage it?"

"Wh–wh–what?" asked Snorkel, finally showing some signs of returning to the land of the living.

"Her!" exclaimed Ryzak, nodding his head in the direction of the newly-arrived pony.

Snorkel looked where Ryzak had indicated and his mouth fell open. "Me?" he queried, "I did that?" He climbed hurriedly to his feet, staring at the piebald in astonishment. "I did that?" he murmured again.

"You did."

"I did that!" he exclaimed, growing excited. He looked up at Ryzak, his eyes shining. "I did that," he cried.

Ryzak looked down, giving the little man a hard stare. "How?"

"Ey?"

"How did you do it?"

Snorkel squirmed in discomfort and lowered his gaze. After a moment's pause he looked up, a cocky smile on his face. "Oh, you know. Wizardly type stuff. Top secret and all that." He winked and tapped the side of his nose knowingly with a stubby forefinger. "Can't let everyone know how we do magics or we'd be out of business. Come on. Let's go and say hello."

'You little liar,' came Draco's familiar mind-speak.

Snorkel turned his head and grinned at the lime-green dragonet. "Less of the little, if you don't mind."

The pony lifted her head and whickered a greeting as they approached. Snorkel, still unsure whether the new Clara would have the same temperament as the old Clara, jumped back in alarm.

"Come on. Make friends. It's time we were moving out," growled Ryzak, shoving him forward.

The push bumped Snorkel into the pony. She turned and nuzzled the startled dwarf affectionately. "She likes me!" he exclaimed in surprise, stroking the soft skin of her nose. "I think she likes me."

"Good. Now that's settled, let's be off," Ryzak snapped, turning away and stomping to his own horse.

Draco, tired now that the excitement seemed to be over, curled herself around Snorkel's neck and settled herself for sleep in the hood of his robe.

For half an hour they rode in silence, each immersed in his own thoughts; Ryzak seeming withdrawn and pensive, Snorkel with a wide smile on his face as his pony pranced happily alongside Ryzak's horse.

"Do you ever dream?" Ryzak asked suddenly.

"Um? What was that?" Snorkel questioned, shaken out of his reverie.

"Do you ever, you know, dream? Only the dream seems real? As if you were actually there?"

Snorkel looked up, an awful premonition creeping up on him as he gazed into Ryzak's troubled features.

"Why do you ask?" he queried, already beginning to fear the answer.

"Well … Oh, it doesn't matter. You'll only think I'm some sort of nut-job," Ryzak replied, and looked away.

"Try me," Snorkel responded. He definitely feared the worst.

Ryzak took a deep breath. "It's only that – It's only that I had a weird dream last night." The words were rushing out of his mouth as if he were ashamed at having to say them. "A very weird dream. And you were in it."

Snorkel's brows drew together in a worried frown. "So did I," he admitted.

Ryzak's mouth dropped open. "What?"

"I had a strange dream last night as well. And you were in it. As was our friend, Mishtar."

Ryzak heaved on the reins, making his horse pull up sharply. "Mishtar and magic and stuff?"

Snorkel reined his pony to a halt and turned serious eyes on his companion. He nodded his head solemnly.

"Then it wasn't a dream after all? It really happened?"

"Looks like it."

"How?" shouted Ryzak.

"How the hell should I know? He is a sorcerer after all," the dwarf shouted back.

"Thank you for the confidence boost, oh mighty wizard!" Ryzak retorted. "I thought you were here to help protect me. What was it Beulah said? 'What harm can befall you when you travel in the company of a wizard'? If only he knew!"

"I saved you, didn't I?" Snorkel snapped, aggrieved that Ryzak had overlooked that point.

"I suppose so," Ryzak conceded sullenly. "But what's to stop him trying again, hey? That's what I want to know."

"Me! You worry too much. He's not likely to try that again. Not when I've shown him who's boss. Come on, or we'll never get the damned seal."

Snorkel nudged his pony into a trot and quickly drew ahead. When he was safely out of earshot, he leaned over Clara's neck. "It's just as well he doesn't know I haven't a clue how I did it," he whispered.

Clara snorted in response. Draco lifted a sleep-laden eyelid and mind-spoke. *'I wouldn't want to be in your shoes if he ever finds out.'*

* * * * *

Sitting on the remains of a rotted tree trunk, Rhudrhyn waited for the two riders to appear, secure in the knowledge that twenty of his company were hidden in the surrounding trees and bushes should anything untoward happen. From what he had been told of the strangers, he need have no worries, but it did not hurt to be cautious, especially as one of them appeared to be a magic user. At the sound of approaching horses he stiffened, his eyes fixed on the opposite side of the clearing. They would soon be here.

When the two riders emerged from the gloom of the trail into the sun-dappled clearing, they did not notice the tall, slim figure with the tapered ears who stood waiting for them. They were too busy arguing.

"I tell you, we've passed this way before, not an hour ago. This will be the second time we've ridden through last night's camp in as many hours!"

"Man, you've got some imagination. There's no way even we could manage that. We're not that stupid."

"Don't call me stupid!" Ryzak stormed, glaring down at Snorkel.

"I didn't!" Snorkel snapped back, his face reddening with suppressed anger, "I only said that even we could not be that stupid. It would take the biggest idiot in Aldura to ride around in circles and not notice."

"Or two," a voice dripping with sarcasm called out.

Exchanging alarmed glances, Ryzak and Snorkel swung round to search for the speaker. They spotted a young man dressed in forest green, leaning casually on a longbow. His almond-shaped, violet eyes twinkled in amusement as he scrutinised them. Snorkel took in every detail of the figure. He noticed the pointy ears, long delicate fingers, shoulder length silver hair and the youthful complexion. "Elf!" he gasped in amazement.

"Elf?" queried Ryzak.

The elf straightened, a half smile on his face. "Well done, my dwarven friend. At least your kind remembers us. Welcome to my home. Please, be at ease. Allow me to introduce myself." He bowed low. "I am Rhudrhyn, or Rhudhi to my friends. You, how-ever, may call me 'my Lord'."

"Bu–bu–but you can't be an elf," Ryzak stammered, "you're much too tall. I mean, aren't elves supposed to be small, nervous folk who live under toadstools and such?"

Rhudrhyn laughed a rich, sing-song laugh, then suddenly stopped. His eyes glared into Ryzak's in contempt. "How quickly you forget, man!" he snapped. "It is no small wonder that my ancestors set wards within the woods to stop such as you from entering our lands."

Snorkel scowled a warning look at Ryzak. It was not wise to mess with elves, especially important ones. When one such as Rhudrhyn was facing you, calmly notching an arrow to his bow, he suddenly became very important.

"Rhudr– my Lord!" implored Snorkel. "He meant no harm. He's just a stupid human. What does he know?"

"Too much," Rhudrhyn answered, training his arrow on Ryzak.

Draco chose the moment to wake up. '*What's up, Mum?*' she asked, yawning loudly and craning her neck so that she could see what was going on.

"Nothing. Just keep quiet and stay hidden in my hood," Snorkel whispered through the side of his mouth, not wanting to attract the elf's attention.

"What did you say, dwarf?" Rhudrhyn snarled.

Snorkel gulped in apprehension. He had forgotten about their exceptional hearing. "Just telling my friend to apologise." He gave the elf a soothing smile. "He meant no harm, really." He cast Ryzak a worried look. "Say you're sorry, Ryzak, or you're dead meat!"

Ryzak's face had drained of colour and he seemed to be on the verge of throwing up. He looked pleadingly at Rhudrhyn. "I'm, I'm s–sor …" he stammered, squirming in his saddle. He glanced down, then quickly looked up again. "I think I've wet myself," he murmured in misery.

Rhudrhyn lowered his weapon. He had no choice, he was laughing so much he could not hold it up. "You can come out now," he called to his comrades, "I don't think we need fear these two."

Twenty elves rose from their places of concealment and con-verged on the two riders, longbows armed and ready for action. This only served to heighten Ryzak's discomfort. He looked even more wretched and the damp stain on his saddle began to expand.

'*Wow. Elves,*' mind-spoke Draco excitedly, '*I've never met one of them before.*' With a happy chirrup, she emerged from Snorkel's hood and launched herself into the air to investigate.

"Noooooo!" screamed Snorkel, as Draco flapped away to introduce herself.

"Noooooo!" screamed Rhudrhyn, as one of his company, fearing attack, let fly at the airborne reptile.

"Oh shit," murmured Ryzak, as the arrow took Draco in the chest, sending her cartwheeling through the air.

Snorkel let out an anguished wail, then jumped off his pony and ran to the stricken dragonet. He threw himself to the ground beside her and lifted her small body to cradle it in his arms. He whispered her name over and over again, but it was no use. The little creature showed no signs of life.

The company of elves watched in mystification, wondering what was wrong with the dwarf. It was only a flying lizard after all. Fear, coupled with wet trousers, made it impossible for Ryzak to jump down to comfort the little man. He could only sit and watch from his elevated position.

Eventually Snorkel's grief subsided. He laid the small, lifeless body on the ground and rose to his feet, shoulders slumped in dejection. As he turned to face Rhudrhyn a dramatic change came over him. His body stiffened, seeming to expand, grow taller and more menacing. His face hardened into a look of thunder and murderous intent blazed from his eyes.

It all went deathly quiet in the clearing; not a sound could be heard. Snorkel began to mouth arcane phrases as his hands wove intricate patterns in the air.

"Dringo, drucal, fraggle ..."

The dwarf never finished. A hefty whack on the back of his head from a stout branch saw to that. Unseen by the little man, two of Rhudrhyn's cohorts had crept up on him while he was otherwise engaged and, seeing him prepare to use his magic, had taken the necessary action to stop him. They dragged the unconscious figure to Clara, and expertly tossed him over her back.

"Make sure you tie his hands together," Rhudrhyn ordered, "and gag him. We don't want him trying any of his tricks. Tie him up as well," he commanded, nodding in the direction of Ryzak.

Ryzak was dragged from his horse and thrown face down on the ground. A booted foot pressed into the small of his back as ungentle hands pulled his arms behind him and tied his wrists together. Securely bound, he was kicked upright and pushed towards his horse.

Having helped him back into the saddle, the elves ran a length of rope under the horse's belly and tied Ryzak's legs together, taking care to avoid any contact with the damp, pungent areas.

"What about that?" one of the company asked, nodding towards the prone body of the dragonet.

"Leave it. Let the wolves feast on its flesh," Rhudrhyn answered indifferently. "Which of these fools killed it?" he snapped.

The elf shrugged his shoulders.

"No matter. But it's a shame. I haven't seen a dragonet for close on ninety years and it would have been nice to own one again." As the elf turned away, Rhudrhyn called after him, "Oh, and you had better make sure that our two guests are blindfolded until we reach Chlyonedse. We can't have them seeing where we are going."

The elf stopped and turned to face Rhudrhyn. "Aren't you going to kill them?"

"No. We'll take them to the queen. It has been ages since a magic user entered our woods. She may want to question him – or she may kill them both. It rather depends on what mood she is in and whether they prove to be of any interest or not."

Rhudrhyn smiled to himself. It had been a long time since they were last in the elven capital, and he knew this certain little lady who just loved to …

* * * * *

Neulee parted the bushes as the elves and their captives made their way out of the clearing. She waited until they were out of sight before emerging fully and hurrying over to the stricken dragonet.

She knelt down and placed her fingertips to its chest, feeling for a heart beat, then leaned forward so that her face was close to the dragonet's mouth. She straightened and sighed in disappointment. Not a thing could be felt. She shook her head sadly and picked up the body. Tears formed in her eyes as she ran quickly back to the bushes, the limp body of Draco cradled in her arms.

Chapter Ten

The hiss and sizzle of scorching flesh was drowned out by the protracted scream of pain, swiftly followed by silence as the patient blacked out. Relieved that she could complete her ministrations without having her eardrums shattered, Megan finished burning off the last of the warts in peace. It did not take her long to complete the task; it was always easier when the client was not interfering and getting in the way.

Although she usually asked if they wanted to be put out for this type of work, seeing who it was that entered her hut she had not offered. She wanted to make him suffer. If she had not needed the coin she would have refused him her services – being an active member of the animal welfare group she had a moral code to uphold – but coin was coin, a commodity she did not have a lot of, and she could not live off morals alone.

On the straw-filled mattress before her lay Bart the sheep-shearer, comatose and unaware of his nurse's antipathy. His leggings were down around his ankles and his battered manhood was on display for the world to see. If anyone could be bothered to look, that is. There was not a lot to view, and what there was wasn't pretty.

According to the village gossips his disgusting habits were nearly as ugly as he was, which was probably why he permanently smelled of sheep and led a rather lonely, insular existence. The latest rumour was that his most recent girlfriend had chucked him due to his insistence that she wore a sheepskin jacket and crawled around the bedroom floor bleating like a lamb.

Megan grimaced at the thought and rose from beside her makeshift cot, which also doubled as a consulting couch, pushing a stray lock of silver hair from her face as she gazed down at her handiwork. She scowled in abhorrence at the operation she had just performed.

Now she understood why the villagers called him by another name; one a lot less complementary. She had never come across a human with 'sheep pizzle' before, and there was only one way he could have been infected with that.

Her face screwed up in disgust at the thought as she held her hands out for inspection, staring at them as though they were harbingers of filth. An involuntary shudder ran through her body and she began to scrub the unclean paws vigorously on her skirts.

As she scrubbed, a mischievous smile began to appear on her face. Moving quickly to the back of the single-roomed dwelling, she rummaged around in her unguent and ointment cupboard for the items she needed.

* * * * *

Night had fallen when Bart started to regain consciousness. Gradually he became aware of a numb throbbing emanating from his nether regions. His face distorted in pain as he tried to lever himself up on the cot to look around the darkened room, the movement causing a pulling, stabbing sensation in his groin. A low moan escaped his lips.

As if on cue, an oil lamp flared into life, casting a dim, orange glow over the spartan interior of the hut. The lamp moved towards him, bobbing through the air, leaving streamers of light in the gloom. His eyes, unaccustomed to the brightness, did not see the figure of Megan until she was close to him.

"How are you feeling?" she asked, her voice flat and devoid of emotion.

Bart grunted as he rolled onto his side to make himself more comfortable. "I've felt better," he grumbled.

Megan's eyes narrowed as she placed the lamp on a small, wooden table beside the bed.

Bart yelped in surprise as she bent down and yanked the blanket off him, then in pain as he lunged forward to try and snatch it back. Failing, he shrieked, "What did you do that for?"

"Because it is time for you to go. I want my bed back." Megan replied, her voice cold.

"But I'm not well," Bart complained, a pathetic whine edging into his voice. "Can't I stay till morning?"

Megan folded her arms across her chest and glared down at him. "Out!"

"Please?" Bart wheedled, giving his best attempt at a winning smile.

"Out. Before I lose patience and curse you with the pain of a thousand fantasies."

Bart's brows pulled together in a worried frown. "A thousand what?"

With a sly smile, Megan nodded at his crotch. "A thousand fantasies, which, in your current condition, could prove to be a painful experience."

Bart looked down to where she indicated. There, illuminated by the lamp, was a huge swaddled bulge stuck between his legs, topped off with a bright red ribbon. He shrieked in horror. "What have you done? I'll never get my leggings on now. It's too big!"

Megan gave an impish grin. "Too bad. The bandage was necessary. Your, aherm, ailment was too far gone. Drastic infections require drastic treatments. Now, out! I need some sleep."

Bart looked up in panic. "But you can't send me out like this. I'll be a laughing stock if anybody sees me!"

She arched an eyebrow. "Can't I?"

Bart gulped in trepidation. He knew when he was beat. He swung his legs gingerly over the side of the cot and stood in front of the herb-woman, his legs bowed as if he had been in the saddle for two days. He could barely stand, let alone place one foot in front of the other. How on earth was he going to manage to walk home with his tackle strapped up like an overstuffed marrow?

Megan forced herself to keep a straight face as she stepped back to allow Bart to stagger past. "Your leggings are beside the door," she informed him. "You can collect them as you leave. I have taken the liberty of obtaining my payment."

She noticed the look of alarm that crossed his face. "Don't worry. I only took what was my due. No more."

She watched as he made his way over to the door to retrieve his clothing, ignoring his hostile glare as he brushed by her.

"Make sure you keep it dry," she called after him, her voice betraying a hint of amusement at his predicament, "or you will have to go through it all again. And keep the bandage on for at least a week. Your wounds need time to heal."

One hand holding his crumpled leggings, the other grasping the door latch, Bart turned and gave her one last look of enmity before yanking the door open and storming out. Not that he could move very fast; every time he haltingly stepped forward his thighs crushed the bulge between his legs and sent shooting pains through his crotch; resulting in a shambling, ungainly gait.

Megan winced as the door slammed shut. Then, giggling to herself, she hitched up her skirts and ran to the building's only window, wanting to make sure that the funny little man had gone. She rubbed a circle clear in the grime-covered glass and peered out.

She started to laugh. She could almost feel sorry for him – almost. She was amazed at how he managed to maintain his dignity as he stumbled and staggered back to his croft, past the numerous villagers who, strangely, appeared to have chosen this night to go for an evening stroll. The light from their lanterns illuminated the little man and his colourful protuberance, reflecting off his bare, pasty backside as he walked past them. To give him credit, with back straight and his gaze fixed straight ahead, Bart waddled slowly on his way as if they weren't there.

After a while, growing tired of the sport, Megan turned and moved to the back of the room to make ready for bed. A feeling of despondency crept over her as she began to unbutton her bodice. Perhaps it was time to move on. She had been here for ten years now, treating all sorts of petty ailments and problems. Pretty soon the villagers would begin to notice that she did not age as they did, and start asking questions. Or she would get slapdash in her healing and one of them would notice that the potions she used had little effect on their problems at all; that it was her use of touch that did the job. She sighed and re-buttoned her bodice. She had been through it all before in other villages, and knew when it was time to go.

Her decision made, she stopped preparing for bed and moved around the room gathering her few belongings. With any luck she could be away before the village stirred into life and someone noticed her leaving.

She was just pushing the last of her clothing into a pack when a loud hammering at the door startled her. She sprang upright in shock, her hand flying to her chest to still her racing heart, eyes staring fearfully at the door. Something felt wrong. She did not know what, but the situation did not feel right and she intended finding out who she faced before she opened the door.

The hammering sounded again, this time more urgent.

She sent her powers probing to the door and beyond, but gasped in shock as her probes were rebuffed. Whoever was out there had shields! There was only one group of people that had the use of such powers: the Sisters of the New Dawn.

She panicked, her eyes darting around for a weapon. The hut only had one door; there was no other means of escape, so she had to protect herself as best she could. She cursed herself for a fool. She should have realised it would not be long before they heard of her and sent someone to kill her. What friends she had had amongst her mother's people had warned her about the sisters and their evil ways. And now they had her right where they wanted her. Trapped!

Her gaze fell on the stout walking stick that Bart had left behind. They could not perform their evil tricks if they were out cold. As her fingers closed on the gnarled piece of wood the door blasted open, knocking her off her feet and sending her sprawling in the dust of the floor. By reflex, her powers wrapped around her to form a protective cocoon.

After a moment, amazed that no attack was forthcoming, she levered herself up on an elbow and stared at the doorway. She spat particles of dust from her mouth and gathered her powers to gain what further protection she could muster. Her eyes widened as she saw two figures, outlined by the silvery light of the moon. Although she could not make out any detail, she could tell that one of them was incapacitated, the other having to support her as they staggered into her home.

"Please help us," a whispered plea drifted across the drab room.

Despite her misgivings, Megan dropped her shields and scrambled to her feet. She could never refuse anyone in need of her services, whether they were Sisters of the New Dawn or not.

Chapter Eleven

The shadows were lengthening as the two riders guided their mounts down the last gently rolling hill to the Palace of the Sisters. Behind them the sun was dipping below the western hills, its gold and crimson afterglow forming a spectacular sunset. However, Beulah was oblivious. He was too enthralled by the magnificence of the palace to notice. It had been a long, long time since he was last here and he had forgotten how breathtaking the view was.

As he nudged his horse forward he gazed in admiration at the tall twin towers that straddled the main gates, set centrally in the front section of the low curtain wall surrounding the home of the sisters. The pale pink stone of the palace beyond and its four rounded turrets, one in each corner, glowed a richer, deeper tone as the sun bade it farewell for the day. It looked majestic, especially with the sea as a backdrop; a gently swelling, gem-spangled, shimmering carpet in the setting sun.

Beulah chuckled in fond recollection of countless climbs over the low wall, there to visit the novices' quarters to try and woo a few comely lasses. He gave a rueful smile. He had enjoyed as much success then as he had more recently – none. He snorted in amusement and urged his horse on.

In a matter of minutes he and Shula were riding through the main gates and into the cobbled yard, making their way to the stable block. The clip of the horses' hooves on the hard stone surface must have roused the stable boy from an early evening siesta. He came running from one of the low, single-storey buildings as they reined to a halt beside a hitching rail, his hair tousled, knuckling sleep from his eyes.

Weary and longing for a warm bath and something to eat, Beulah slid from his saddle. With a brief nod of thanks he left his mount in the boy's care before following Shula to the main building.

Daylight had finally disappeared as they climbed the short flight of steps leading to the entrance, the light from the oil lamps within clearly visible through the glass-panelled windows of the lower floor. As they neared the top of the steps the doors opened and a stern-faced woman of advancing years appeared, framed in the bright light that spilled out from the hallway beyond. The woman's face split in a wide smile of recognition as her gaze rested on Shula.

"Draya! Draya! It's so good to see you again," Shula enthused, running forward and wrapping her arms around the startled sister before she had the chance to say a word.

The older woman haltingly returned her embrace.

"Do not call me Matriarch," Shula whispered into Draya's ear. "Until I tell you otherwise I am Shula, a returning sister."

Draya masked a look of surprise and stepped back, letting her arms drop so that she could hold the matriarch's hands as she gazed at her thoughtfully. She suddenly smiled. "Shula!" she exclaimed warmly, "how good to see you again. We were so worried about you. Where have you been? What have you been up to? Who's he?" she asked, nodding toward Beulah, who was standing to one side, patiently observing.

The wizard bowed deeply. "Allow me to introduce myself, Matriarch. I am Beulah, the last of the wizards."

Shula raised a hand and muffled a snort of amusement at Draya's glance, as Beulah stood, head bowed, waiting for a response.

"Don't just stand there, say something," Shula mouthed at her first minister.

"Well stand straight, man!" ordered Draya, smoothing her robe as she fought for composure.

Doing as he was told, Beulah looked up, a puzzled expression on his face. "I believe that you require my assistance?" he asked, a hint of annoyance manifesting itself in his tone.

Draya visibly relaxed. "I'm terribly sorry, Beulah. But we were all a little concerned about Shula. This business with Mishtar and all that."

"Aaah! Yes," agreed the wizard. He puffed his chest out self-importantly before continuing. "Never you mind, Matriarch. I am here now and I am sure that we can resolve this minor problem of Mishtar fairly quickly. That is if all your sisters are as good as this one here." He gave his companion a patronising smile.

Shula returned it with a cool look.

"Shula is one of our brighter sisters," replied Draya, moving swiftly on and giving the matriarch a sideways glance. "Please forgive my poor manners, do come in. I'll get one of the girls to show you to the guest quarters. Mishtar can wait until the morning, when you're both fully rested and refreshed." She stepped aside and indicated that they should precede her.

Draya closed the doors behind her as she followed them in. As she drew level with the two travellers she smiled at the look of amazement on the wizard's face. He was peering around the large reception hall like an idiot.

It was not just the size of the place that affected newcomers this way; a huge square room, its floor covered in white tiles, a wide, polished timber stairway leading from its centre up to a galleried first-floor landing; nor was it the intricate murals painted on the walls, nor the high, vaulted ceiling arching high over their heads, a glass cupola at its apex. It was a combination of all of these things. It was designed to make the visitor feel small, humbled, insignificant within its confines. It certainly quietened the most vociferous of guests for a moment or two.

Draya clapped her hands twice, making Beulah flinch. As the echoes reverberated around the hallway a girl appeared from one of the side doors. She ran over and slid to a halt in front of them, her face flushed and chest heaving. She bowed reverently to the two sisters.

"Kindly show this gentleman to the guest room," Draya commanded. "He is to stay with us for a while, so please ensure that he is well looked after. He will require a hot bath and refreshments."

Draya turned to Beulah. "Leilan will take you to your room. We will meet in my quarters tomorrow morning. Leilan will show you where they are after you've finished breaking fast."

Beulah scowled in annoyance at the obvious dismissal. The scowl was still evident as he inclined his head in acknowledgement before stomping off across the tiled floor, following the retreating figure of Leilan.

"You were a little harsh, weren't you?" Shula asked, the mirth in her voice indicating that she'd found it quite amusing.

Draya returned her smile. "Not half as hard as I would suspect you've been with him on the journey here."

Shula laughed. "It was ... how shall I say? An entertaining journey. When he wasn't trying to impress me with his knowledge of magic, he was trying to discover anything he could about the matriarch. 'Fore-armed,' I think he said he wanted to be." She giggled again. "Come, let us retire to my study, where we can talk in peace and relax with a glass of that Alduran Red."

Laughing, the pair linked arms and made their way up the central staircase to Shula's room.

* * * * *

Beulah sat on the edge of his bed, a thoughtful frown on his face. He had been sitting in the same position for the past fifteen minutes, trying to work out what it was that was bothering him. Something was not quite as it appeared. They were definitely up to something, those two. Although he was sure it was nothing detrimental to their cause, he was just as sure they were not telling him something. He hated secrets, especially when he was the one they were being kept from. Try as he might, he could not fathom out what it was. Concerns about the whole venture had been troubling him since the start of their journey to the palace, mainly because Shula had been so obtuse when he had broached the subject of the matriarch. All he had managed to find out was that the older Shula he once knew was no longer in charge, not a jot of information more. That perturbed him. He found it exceedingly strange that he had not got to know that she had moved on and that this Draya, who he had just met, now controlled the sisters.

After several days of trying all angles to elicit more inform-ation he had given up, deciding that he would have to take the new head of the sisterhood as he found her. Coming to the conclusion that the change must have happened during his sojourn with the dwarfs, which was why he had never heard about it, they had completed the journey in relative silence. It was obvious that his companion was not going to be very forthcoming about matters pertaining to her order.

He sighed as memories of happier times surfaced, fondly remembering the older Shula's acid tongue. Aye, it was a shame her mouth could not have been as pleasant as her looks. A haranguing from her could strip bark from trees or cause the most thick-skinned of people to cringe in embarrassment – Beulah included.

They would be about the same age now, if she still lived. She was the girl he had tried to impress the most. She was a stunner. Long jet-black hair, that hung past her shoulders, loose and wild, just like her. And those eyes, those dazzling, sea-green eyes. The younger Shula was very much like his old flame. Perhaps it was that which was troubling him.

He gave a rueful smile and rose from the bed. The past was the past. He had more pressing matters to attend to than remembered flirtations. He had to protect the future.

Moving to kneel on the floor in front of the fire, he rested the palms of his hands lightly on his knees and closed his eyes, concentrating his powers on his inner self to free his spirit from the chains that bound it to his earthly body.

Age and lack of practice meant that nearly half an hour had passed before his spirit form finally floated free. He remembered when he could achieve the state in a matter of minutes, and it did not seem that long ago. It was amazing how quickly old age caught up with you. His spirit form gazed down at the old man in front of the fire, the two connected by a faint, golden umbilical cord of life. By the gods, he looked old. Worn out and decrepit. Was that bundle of bones wrapped up in a black robe really him?

Despondent, he remembered when the life-cord was a full, bloated, golden ribbon, strong and vibrant like the body that contained it. Now it was weak, just like its owner. There was not much longer left before the body turned to dust. And then where would the world be with no more wizards to protect it? Only that imbecile Snorkel. His thoughts turned bitter.

Countless years he had spent scouring the lands after the demise of his fellows, looking for any that showed the slightest hint of ability. Long, fruitless years. With his brothers having been too thorough in their own recruitment, selecting any human showing signs of magical ability for apprenticeship, all likely candidates had perished in the capture of Mishtar.

As a last resort he had turned his attention to the dwarven mountains. That was the only place left to look. He had discounted the elves, due to their magic being totally different to the powers wielded by the wizards. Their abilities were linked to the elemental powers of air, water and earth. Excellent if you wanted to tame badgers, grow asparagus, fly kites or drown fish, (yes, you can drown fish) but not good for much else, in his opinion.

Despite the fact that none of the little people had ever shown any signs of magical ability throughout their long history, he had discovered a spark of power. Only a small spark, but enough to work with. Had he known then what he knew now, he would never have travelled to their lands. Snorkel would have been left to suffer the mercies of his father, Thorkel, and his fellow country-men. If it wasn't for the dwarven uiskey and that damned she-dwarf he could have left him where he was.

Thinking about the little man set him to wondering what he was up to. He sent his spirit soaring towards the elven lands, and set out to locate him. The puzzle of the matriarch could wait until later; until after he made sure the squirt had not got himself into trouble. The stars streaked past in a blur as his spirit flew through the night sky. The faint glimmer of the life-cord stretched out long and thin behind him, linking him to the frail body in the guest room at the Palace of the Sisters.

Beulah sent his powers searching ahead, like antennae, feeling for Snorkel's presence. Soon he was soaring over the edge of Border Woods. He felt a tug. He had found him. His spirit veered to the left, scanning the tree line for signs of Snorkel and Ryzak.

A group of elves came into view, camped within the woods. Beulah frowned in concern, hoping that the two idiots had managed to avoid them. He remembered specifically warning them about the elves. They were a funny lot and did not take kindly to strangers entering their lands uninvited. The fey folk had turned reclusive after the escapade with Mishtar, avoiding all contact with outsiders. Especially magic users. They hated them with a passion.

The tugging became stronger, pulling him towards the camp. A sense of foreboding gripped him. Snorkel and Ryzak should have only been in the woods a short time on their way through to the Plains of Fear, not long enough for the elves to become aware of their presence. And certainly not long enough for the fools to antagonise them. What were they doing this far in, so close to elven lands?

As he dropped lower he saw the reason. They had been captured.

Ryzak was securely tied to a stake, guarded by one of the elves, while Snorkel ... What had they done to him? Beulah had never seen such a look of despair. Snorkel's eyes were blank, expressionless, peeping over the top of the gag that bound his mouth. He was also tied to a stake, and guarded by three elves. As Beulah's spirit drew closer to the dwarf he could make out the dried blood congealed in his hair, matted on the back of his head.

"Ah, Beulah. How nice of you to pay a call. Just a passing visit, or are you going to stay for a while?"

The spirit form of Mishtar manifested itself in front of Beulah. The wizard swiftly halted his descent, a feeling of panic pervading his soul as he gazed at the incorporeal form of the sorcerer.

Mishtar gave an evil smile. "Surprised to see me? Or has the cat got your tongue?"

"How ... What ..."

"Surely you did not think that three of those seals were enough to fully contain me? Me! The greatest sorcerer that ever lived. Or, should I say, still lives. Albeit somewhat confined."

"Even three seals should be enough to contain your evil soul," Beulah snapped back, recovering some of his poise.

"Oh dear! How little you know. I see that years of imprisonment have enabled me to increase my powers whilst years of idleness have limited yours. Take a good look at your friends," Mishtar sneered, glancing at the over-stretched, slender, golden ribbon of Beulah's life-cord, "it will be the last time you see them. See anything, as a matter of fact." A jet-black scimitar materialised in Mishtar's hands. He lunged at the wizard's life-cord.

Beulah was too weak and too far away from his body to

retaliate. He did the only thing he could. Just as the scimitar was about to strike the death blow, Beulah released the hold on his spirit.

The life-cord retracted faster than the speed of light, pulling the form of Beulah after it. A kaleidoscope of colours flashed past, too blurred to distinguish as they all merged into one streaming, muddled mass.

A scream of anguish still hung in the ether as the eyes of the old man kneeling in front of the fire snapped open, staring blankly ahead. Slowly, its spirit broken, Beulah's body sagged to the floor.

* * * * *

Sprawled in armchairs in front of the fire in the matriarch's study, a half empty bottle of vintage Alduran Red on the table beside them, Shula and Draya sat in companionable silence. The oil lamps had been turned low, creating a warm, comfortable atmosphere in the small, oak panelled room. Shula felt like she was worlds away from the rigours of the previous few months, and fully relaxed for the first time since she had set off on the quest for the missing seal. The combination of wine, warmth, good company and being back in familiar surroundings helped ease away her discomforts.

Tiredness began to descend on her like a cloak of darkness and her eyelids started to close. She was exhausted.

"Well?"

Draya's pointed question roused her. "Hmm?"

"Are you going to tell me what happened or not?"

Shula looked into the first minister's questioning eyes and realised she would get no sleep until she had told her what she wanted to know. She raised her glass and took a sip of her drink to compose her thoughts.

Once started, it took Shula nearly an hour to tell the tale. Draya hung on her every word, not daring to interrupt, as she would normally do, for fear of missing any of it. Although she did manage a gasp of disbelief when Shula explained how she had managed to trick Ryzak to their cause.

"So there you have it, warts and all," concluded Shula. "It

appears that there are still two seals to find. Ryzak and Snorkel are on their way to Firestone Mountain to retrieve one, the other … Who knows where that is? Hopefully our illustrious last wizard will be able to help on that one."

Draya fixed Shula with a sly look. "He is not the same Beulah who spent years trying to win your heart, is he?" she asked, eyebrows raised in enquiry. "The tall, gangly youth who, the moment he spotted you, went bright red and tongue-tied?"

Shula laughed. "I'm afraid so. By the gods, I was awful to him. The more he got embarrassed, the more I tormented him. He did blush such a nice shade of crimson! I actually quite liked him, believe it or not."

They burst into fits of giggles at the memory. As their laughter subsided, Shula's expression turned serious. "They were good times back then. Now what have we?" she asked bitterly. "A failing sisterhood, a geriatric wizard, a bumbling apprentice and an alcoholic hero. It does not bode well. Not well at all."

She sighed and lapsed into silence, staring distractedly into her wine. After a couple of minutes she came out of her trance. "Draya?"

"Yes?" Draya responded, looking up from staring into the fire.

"There are things that I have not told you yet," she said, "things that affect the sisters. Information regarding our beginnings."

Draya's features took on a worried look. "What things?"

Shula placed her glass on the table and stood up. She walked slowly to where the orb rested on its golden stand, its clear, crystalline surface reflecting the fire's dancing flames. She stared at it for a moment, deep in thought.

Draya's eyes followed her every movement. "What things, Matriarch?" she asked again.

Shula half smiled at Draya's use of her title. At least she seemed aware that what she had to say was serious. She turned to face her friend, a hand resting lightly on the top of the orb. "It would appear that our orb was made for us by the wizards."

"No! Never!" shouted Draya. She jumped out of her seat in horror and stared at her matriarch as if she had taken leave of her senses.

Shula slowly nodded her head in confirmation. "It would also appear that only a small part of its powers are available to us. Wards and shields are in place to prevent us from utilising its full potential."

Draya's face drained of colour. "What? Who told you this, this, this lie?" she spluttered, her voice rising in outrage. "Surely you don't believe it's true? Tell me it can't be true!"

With a grim smile, Shula slowly walked back to her chair and indicated for Draya to sit. "If it is true, as I suspect it is, there is nothing we can do to change it, and only we two must ever know. Not a word of it must spread to the sisters." She leaned forward, her eyes boring into Draya's. "It is to be our secret, and that of the matriarchs who follow me. You understand?"

Draya lowered her gaze and sullenly nodded her head.

Shula reached across and laid a compassionate hand on hers. As Draya looked up, Shula lightly squeezed it and gave a small smile. "I know how you are feeling," she murmured. "I, myself, felt that way when Beulah first told me. I did not want to believe it. But I have long known that we can only use a fraction of the orb's powers, and the more I thought about what he said, the more I realised it had to be true. A comment The Great One made at the entrance to Mishtar's domain suddenly made sense."

A look of astonishment crossed Draya's face. "Merrel? The Great One? She appeared to you?"

Smiling, Shula nodded her head and settled back into her chair, reclaiming her glass and taking a small sip. "It was after Ryzak had placed the seal and was on his way back. She suddenly materialised beside me and told me to look for the last wizard. That he would help us unlock the orb's secrets and that without his help we would not find the missing seals. The orb can help us find them, Draya. Or *it,* as we already know the location of one of them."

Leaning forward, she looked deeply into Draya's eyes. "That is why Beulah is here. To unlock the orb and undo the wizards' magic that shields its full powers from us. If he found out that I am really the Shula he once knew he might not fully co-operate. I was pretty awful to him in the past and I do not want to take that chance. He will find out soon enough that I, Shula, am really the matriarch."

She settled back in her chair and lifted her glass. "Anyway, enough about the orb for now. What news from the sisters?" she asked brightly, smiling warmly at her friend. "Anything of interest to report?"

"Hmm? Oh! I nearly forgot!" Draya replied, placing her hand over her mouth in realisation. "Rhissa's returned!"

"Rhissa? Here? When?"

"About two weeks ago. And she wasn't alone."

Shula leant forward, her interest aroused. "Bella?" she enquired.

Draya's face clouded. "No. Not Bella. She has not been heard of for a long time. The gods know where she is. She should have reported back by now. But there again, you know how forgetful she is. She has probably lost track of time chasing a lost cause. No. It was someone else." Her eyes shone with excitement. "A wilder! And she's here, in the palace."

"A wilder? Where was she found? What level is she?" Shula asked. This was the best piece of news she could have hoped for.

"Rhissa came across her at Jerelsport, a small fishing village up the east coast, where the girl was working as a herbalist and sometime healer. Hearing tales about a witch who lived in a shack on the outskirts of the village from the locals, she went to investigate."

"Yes, yes, yes!" interrupted Shula. "What level is she?"

"Well. As soon as they arrived here I had her tested." Draya paused and grinned.

"Go on."

"Level six!" Draya said, with undisguised glee. "Level six, and that is without any training!"

Shula collapsed back in her chair in amazement. Level six! How on earth had she managed to attain such a level without any formal training? Draya was level eight, the only sister in the sisterhood, besides Shula, to have achieved over level six in the past two hundred years.

"How?" she asked, bewildered.

Draya shrugged. "I have no idea. Neither does Rhissa. It should not be possible, but, somehow, she has achieved it."

"I don't believe it," Shula whispered, shaking her head. "Level six and we had no idea that she existed. Surely we should have been able to sense someone with that much ability."

"Obviously not," said Draya. "She does have some strong mind-shields, stronger than yours even, I dare say."

Shula arched an eyebrow and Draya quickly continued. "It would appear that she faced some severe beatings and animosity when she was younger, because she was different. She must have developed the shields to prevent her from using the power too obviously. Self-preservation."

Shula nodded her head in agreement. It made sense. With no one to help her through the difficult adolescent years when the full force of the power could have driven her insane, she would have had to develop shields or go mad.

Over the years, during the course of their search, they had come across a small number of women who had been cursed by the madness, having come into their power before the sisters had found them. There had been nothing they could do, other than leave them drooling and dribbling where they were. At least they had family and friends to look after them.

So few were being born with the power, and those that were would not come forward. Magic was a synonym for witch in the eyes of the populace. The gifted ones would sooner ignore their gift than be branded as such. Magic was a fading force in the land. Where once it would have been considered a blessing to have such a child, it was now thought of as a curse, something to be ashamed of. Whereas before they would have sent the child to the sisters at the first sign of her powers, they now locked them away and kept them out of sight. Mishtar had a lot to answer for.

"That alters our agenda for tomorrow," said Shula, "I will meet with Rhissa and ..."

"Meganrhys," Draya informed her. "Or Megan, as she likes to be called."

"Meganrhys. What an unusual name," mused Shula. "Have Rhissa and Meganrhys come to my study at first light. And now, if you will excuse me, I think I'll get some sleep. We have a long day ahead of us."

"Of course, Matriarch."

Draya rose to leave. "Remember, not a word about the *old* Shula to Beulah. If he asks any questions, just tell him that she left the sisterhood some years back and no one has seen or heard of her since," Shula called out.

"Won't that make him suspicious?" Draya asked.

"Probably. We will just have to make sure that he is kept too busy to have any spare time left to pry, won't we?"

"I'm sure we can manage that," Draya replied, a cunning smile playing about her lips. "Until tomorrow, Matriarch. Sleep well."

As the door closed, Shula moved across to the orb and gazed into its translucent, unblemished depths.

"Why would the wizards construct you for us?" she asked, half hoping for an answer. With none forthcoming, she walked to her sleeping quarters. That was one question Beulah would have to answer at the first available opportunity.

Chapter Twelve

"Don't leave me, Mummy. Please, don't leave me!"

"It is for your own good, boy!" cut in a man's harsh voice.

The voice was one he recognised; it was his father's. "But why, Daddy? Why?"

"Because we can't help you. You don't belong with us. The villagers all think you're in league with demons, that you're cursed."

The unspoken accusation was there. His father thought likewise and wanted to be rid of him.

"Please, Mummy?" Tears welled in his eyes.

His mother turned away, her own eyes puffy and red from weeping.

"Please, Mummy, please?" he begged, as the figures started to fade.

The contemptuous sound of a man's voice sounded through the emptiness as another scene unfolded before him.

"You! Yes, you! Come out here, boy, and see if you can manage to get it right this time."

He slowly shuffled to the front of the class, head held low, face bright red. He stood before the senior master, aware that twenty pairs of eyes bored into his back. He knew that the expressions on their faces ranged from sympathy, to amusement, to outright hostility.

"Turn to page thirty-seven," the tall, dark-haired man with the goatee beard ordered.

He looked up fearfully, the book having been left back on his desk.

The master's face turned red with rage at such forgetfulness. He raised a hand and struck him a heavy blow across the face. "Why do we let you country idiots in here?" he roared. "Go! Go to your room and meditate on your shortcomings. Stay there until I send for you!"

The scene shifted. He was in the courtyard at the Palace of the

Sisters. It was late afternoon and the sun was starting to dip below the western hills. He peered out from behind the hedgerow where he had hidden. There she was, walking in his direction.

He stepped boldly out from his place of concealment and strolled casually towards her.

Becoming aware of his presence, she looked up from the book she was reading. Her smile instantly disappeared and turned into a sneer of contempt.

As she drew closer he mentally recited his carefully rehearsed lines, wanting to make a good impression. But before he had the chance to say his piece, she spoke.

"Kissed any princesses lately?" she asked him, her eyebrows arched in disdain.

"Wh–what?"

"Are you deaf as well as stupid? I asked if you had kissed any princesses lately?"

"I–I don't know what you mean," he stammered.

She stopped walking and stood facing him, her deep, sea-green eyes boring into his, her book firmly clasped to her chest.

"If I was to mention small, green, slimy pond dwellers who croak a lot at night, would it give you a clue?"

He shook his head, not having the faintest idea of what she was on about.

"Never heard the one about the frog princess?" she asked primly, "only in reverse?"

He stared at her blankly.

She scowled in annoyance. "Never mind! It seems you are thick as well as ugly."

Tears of disappointment pricked at his eyes as she pushed rudely past him, his carefully prepared speech forgotten. Turning, he ran to the low outer wall to make his escape, wanting to be well away before she had the chance to call the guards.

The images of rejection and failure assailed him, one after the other without pause, battering his defenceless spirit. The one recurring picture was of Mishtar and a large black scimitar, the sorcerer's baleful eyes boring into his as he raised it for the killing stroke.

Each image and rejection took a small piece of his life-force. He knew he was dying, but could do nothing about it. Yet another failure to add to his long list. The heartbeat of the body that housed his pathetic soul was getting weaker and more erratic. It would not be long before he could finally rest.

Forlornly, he realised that the only reason he had been told to remain outside the mind-link of the full contingent of wizards as they faced Mishtar was that he was the weakest. They thought he would fail, and, if he failed, they would all fail. And allow Mishtar total control of Middle Vooragh.

'Of course they didn't,' an alien thought intruded, *'you were the best of them. They knew you had potential to rebuild the wizards. They needed you to survive. You were the best!'*

His spirit laughed a humourless laugh at the prospect of another vision of failure to come. Potential to rebuild the wizards? Pah! How he had excelled at that! One recruit. An imbecilic dwarf who could not even spell magic, never mind perform it.

'It is a start. And do not be too quick to condemn Snorkel. He has more inner talent than you have seen. Your sixth sense realised that when you apprenticed him. He is, or will be, your greatest success.' The alien thought paused to give Beulah the chance to contemplate what had just been said.

'Remember the ring your mother gave you as she hugged you and bade you farewell at the gates of Wizard's Keep? The one you wear on a chain around your neck? That was given as a token of her love for you, a reminder that a part of her will always be with you. And your father? He was not ashamed. He was proud! The whole village got fed up of him telling them all how one day you would be the greatest wizard that ever lived. You are not a failure, Beulah!'

The vision of Mishtar appeared again, an evil grin distorting his features as he raised the black scimitar. The manic gleam from his dark eyes bored into the very centre of Beulah's being.

A puzzled frown suddenly appeared on Mishtar's face as a tall young girl strode purposefully towards him. Her long, silver hair streamed out behind her as she walked. She stopped, standing in front of the sorcerer's image, arms folded, staring straight at him.

Mishtar's mouth fell open and his eyes grew wide. Giving Beulah one last glare of contempt, his image winked out.

The girl turned towards Beulah and stretched her arms out to him. She smiled warmly. *'Come to me, Beulah. Come home.'*

* * * * *

The first thing Beulah saw when his eyelids flickered open was a pair of blue, almond-shaped eyes peering down at him from a face of stunning beauty, framed by a cascade of silver hair. Seeing him wake, the eyes crinkled into a smile. "Am I dreaming?" he croaked, through a throat that felt parched and raspy.

"No, you're not dreaming," the girl replied, a musical sweetness in her voice. "Come, sit up. You need to drink. You're badly dehydrated."

Helping Beulah into a more comfortable position on the bed, she placed some pillows behind his back and fetched a beaker of water.

Comfortably supported, Beulah glanced around and was surprised to see Shula, Draya and a sister he did not recognise in the room, concern showing on their faces. "If I'd known I was to be guest of honour I would have dressed for the occasion," he remarked, before being overcome by a bout of coughing. By the gods, his throat felt as if it were on fire.

"Here, drink this," the girl ordered, passing him the beaker.

"Thank you, my dear," Beulah murmured, when he had drunk his fill. "That feels much better. May I ask the name of my guardian angel?"

"Meganrhys," she replied, lowering her lashes and blushing a deep shade of red.

Beulah covered her hands with his own. "You have my sincere thanks, Meganrhys, for nursing me through this … aherm, ailment."

As she raised her head Beulah stared intently into her eyes, suddenly understanding what she had done, and what Mishtar had tried to do. "My guardian angel," he whispered.

Flustered, she pulled her hands free and rose from the edge of the bed. Turning to Shula, she said, "I believe our wizard is cured, Matriarch. If you will excuse me, I am feeling a little tired."

"Of course, Meganrhys." Shula smiled. "Go and rest. We will speak later."

The raising of one bushy eyebrow was the only reaction from Beulah to the newfound knowledge that Shula was, in fact, the matriarch. Shula turned to the two remaining sisters. "Leave us!" she ordered. "The wizard and I need to talk – in private."

The two sisters exchanged anxious glances before rising from their seats. They bowed to the matriarch before leaving.

Shula sat in silence, her steepled forefingers idly tapping her lips as she stared at the bed-ridden wizard, who had closed his eyes and was feigning sleep. Irritated by the fact that he appeared unconcerned by her presence, sparks flashed in Shula's eyes. "Well?"

"I'm sorry, Shula, or should I say Matriarch? Did you say something?" he asked sweetly, opening one eye to look over in her direction.

"Do not play the innocent with me!" Shula stormed, rising from her chair and striding towards him. She folded her arms and glowered at the smiling wizard. "What on earth were you playing at? A man of your age should know better than to go astral-roaming. Where were you off to? What was so important that you had to risk your life and our future for?"

Beulah's face fell as he recalled Snorkel and Ryzak's predicament.

The matriarch noticed the change. She sat down on the edge of the bed and held Beulah's hands. "What is it?" she asked quietly. "What's happened?"

The wizard looked up. "They're captured."

"Who are?"

"The elves have them," he continued. "I warned them to stay clear of them. The idiots!"

Shula gasped as realisation hit home. "Snorkel, Ryzak?"

"Of course, Snorkel and Ryzak," Beulah snapped. "What other two idiots do we know? There's nothing else for it. We'll have to unlock this orb of yours, find the last seal and hope that the little cretin can somehow manage to wriggle his way free of them. Come on! There's no time to waste."

Beulah sat up. The room started to spin and he promptly fell back on the bed. "Well, maybe tomorrow," he mumbled, his eyes losing their focus. He struggled to keep them open, but within moments he was asleep.

"Yes, maybe tomorrow," Shula whispered, her words lost over the sound of gentle snores.

* * * * *

"Come!"

Shula's face lit with a smile as Meganrhys entered. "Feeling better after yesterday's exertions?" she asked.

"Yes, thank you, Matriarch."

"Come, sit down. And do call me Shula when we are in private and not on official business."

Meganrhys settled herself in the chair opposite. "Thank you, Matr– Shula."

"That's better. Tell me, how long do you think it will be before our wizard will be fully active again?"

Meganrhys smiled. "Not long," she said, and laughed her bright, breezy laugh. "He's a tough old goat; far tougher than he likes to make out. Maybe tomorrow or the day after. I will go and check on him later."

"That is more than I could have hoped for," Shula responded, pleased at the prognosis. "The sooner the better as far as I am concerned."

"Might I enquire why he is here?" Meganrhys asked.

Shula stared at her thoughtfully, trying to decide which way to play it. There was more to Meganrhys than met the eye. There was something different about her, she could sense it. For once in her life she decided to take a risk. Taking a deep breath, she briefly explained about Mishtar and the mayhem that would devastate the lands of Middle Vooragh should he regain human form. She told her of her quest to replace the first of the missing seals, of Beulah's comments regarding the sacred orb of the sisterhood, and of the implications should the remaining seals not be placed.

She spoke for an hour without pause. All the while Meganrhys listened intently. Shula did not know why she told her so much; after all, she was a virtual stranger. But it felt as if she should. She felt as if she had found a soul-mate. "So here we are," she concluded, "awaiting the recovery of the last wizard, so that we can continue with our quest to ensure that Mishtar never darkens our lands again."

"Thank you for confiding in me, Shula," Meganrhys said, with a small smile. "I did not expect so detailed an explanation, being new here. But I am pleased that you feel you can trust me."

"It is more than that, Meganrhys. I see in you a sister of great potential, far greater than any that have gone before. Excepting perhaps Merrel, The Great One, our founder. She was the most powerful sister of her time, and since. I do not have half the ability that she had and I am still the most able of the surviving sisterhood, by far."

Shula stared deeply into Meganrhys's eyes. "You are not a level six, are you?" she asked, holding her gaze.

Meganrhys looked at the desktop, her face flushed in embarrassment.

"I thought not!" Shula exclaimed triumphantly. "No sister at level six could have done what you did for Beulah. Even I, at level nine, could not manage such a feat. You have far more power and potential than I. You, my dear, are the future of our order. That is why I have confided so much in you. I need you to fully understand our situation. I get the distinct impression that you are to play a vital role in the events that lie before us." She grasped Meganrhys's hands tightly in her fervour.

Meganrhys looked up, still blushing a bright crimson. "I hope your instincts are correct, Matriarch. You should not pin such high hopes on an unknown quantity."

"I am seldom, if ever, wrong, and I do not doubt my instincts now." Shula smiled. "Come! Let us see if the cantankerous old goat is up and about. The sooner we attend to matters here, the sooner we can set about the real task in hand."

* * * * *

'How are things going?' the deep, resonant voice whispered in her mind. *'Any problems?'*

'Everything is proceeding according to plan,' she thought back. *'No one suspects.'*

'What of the other sister?'

'Bella?' she queried. *'Her flesh has fed the crows by now. She is no further concern of ours.'*

'Good. How is Beulah? Recovered from his little scare?'

'Shaken but not stirred,' her amused thought transmitted. *'He plans to attempt to unlock the orb tomorrow morning, after he has had more time to regain his strength.'*

'Excellent' Mishtar's thought replied. *'I do so wish I could see his face when his soul is drawn screaming into the orb. It will be such a shock to him when he realises that he has not bested me after all.'*

Mishtar's laughter sounded in her head. *'Keep me informed of further developments,'* he commanded.

Then he was gone, leaving her to her thoughts.

* * * * *

Beulah awoke feeling refreshed. The last two days had been frustrating. He had wanted to attempt the unlocking of the orb the first morning after his abortive astral-roam, but Meganrhys had forbidden him, telling him that he would need to regain his strength before she let him try any magic. Grumbling incessantly about his inactivity, he had spent two days alternating between pacing the room, sleeping, and reading some of the books that Shula had supplied. Concern about Snorkel and Ryzak also weighed heavily on his soul, but there was nothing he could do for them, other than pray they escaped the elves' clutches.

Although he hated to admit it, Meganrhys had been proved right. He felt better now than he had done for years. He felt as if he was twenty-one again. Well, maybe one hundred and twenty-one. But today was the day. He was up for it!

He stretched and yawned theatrically, his nose twitching in pleasure as the aroma of bacon and eggs wafted through his olfactory senses. He gave a smile of approval and threw aside the covers. On the small table next to the fire was breakfast: a plate heaped with rashers of bacon, two eggs and a loaf of freshly baked bread. The distinctive smell of coffee drifted across the room.

Grinning, he walked over and grasped the steaming mug. He took a sip, grimacing at the bitter taste, and set it back on the table. Spooning a helping of honey into the drink to sweeten it, he took another sip. That was better. He heaved a satisfied sigh, then sat down and began to devour the food.

"I see you are back to your old self again." Shula's voice said from the doorway.

"Don't you ever knock?" Beulah asked, looking up, his mouth stuffed with bacon. He had been so engrossed in feeding his stomach he had not heard her come in.

"Why?" she replied with a smile. "Scared I might see something that would shock me? I can assure you that you have nothing I haven't seen before." She lifted an eyebrow and scrutinised his grubby nightclothes as she walked over. "Although it was packaged in cleaner garments."

Beulah snorted in contempt and carried on with his meal.

"Splendid! Absolutely splendid," he remarked a short while later, dabbing his mouth with a napkin to wipe away the bacon juice. "That girl of yours, Leilan, makes a wonderful nurse. I'll have to thank her next time I see her."

"At least she is good for something," Shula replied caustically. "Unfortunately she is not one of our brightest pupils, barely a level one. She is willing enough, but the flame of aptitude is only just flickering, I'm afraid."

"Is everything ready?" Beulah asked, tossing the napkin onto the table.

"Yes. There will be a minor change of plan, however."

"Oh?" He raised a bushy eyebrow.

"Meganrhys is to link with you to make sure that your body behaves itself during your adventure."

Beulah noted the uncompromising look in her eyes as she held his gaze. "I see," he said. "You want to make sure that this old duffer does not kick the bucket before the deed is done, eh?"

"Something like that," she replied, a sly smile appearing on her face. "On the other hand, it may just be that we have come to like you and want to keep you around a bit longer."

Laughing at Beulah's snort of derision, she said, "I'll wait for you outside the door while you get dressed. Some things are best not seen on a full stomach."

Ducking smartly to avoid the cushion that Beulah threw at her, she quickly made her way to the door. "Don't take all day about it," she called from the open doorway, stepping swiftly through and closing the door behind her, as the wizard hefted a pewter plate threateningly.

Twenty minutes later, suitably attired in a freshly laundered robe, Beulah emerged from the room. His long white hair was neatly combed and he had even scraped the bristles from his face.

"That's better," Shula said, casting an approving eye over his appearance. "Follow me, the others will already be there."

Beulah caught hold of her arm and gently spun her round to face him. "Today, Matriarch, we go as equals." He crooked his arm.

Shula smiled and linked her arm through his.

Together they walked through the corridors and hallways to the matriarch's private apartments, causing the few people they encountered to stop and stare at the two most powerful magic-users in the land laughing and whispering like young lovers.

As they arrived at the door to Shula's apartments, Beulah reluctantly broke their arm-link and dipped his head in a low bow. "I thank you for your hospitality, Matriarch. I trust that my efforts on your behalf will prove ample reward."

"I am sure they will, wizard, I am sure they will," she replied.

She was about to say more when the door opened. A flustered Draya emerged.

"At last, Matriarch. We were worried something had happened. Where have you been? Everything is prepared and ready for …" she gave Beulah a withering look, "him!"

"Yes, thank you, Draya," said Shula, pushing past her into the room.

Giving Draya one of his most winning smiles Beulah followed Shula, ignoring the first minister's mordant scowl. He immediately spotted the orb on its stand and wandered over to take a look at the sisters' sacred object. He shook his head in admiration as he gazed into its unblemished depths. "Amazing," he breathed. "Such perfection." It had been made many years prior to him joining the order of the wizards. Only the hierarchy of the wizardhood knew of its origins. It was not to be common knowledge that it had been wrought by them for the sisters. Beulah only knew of this through reading the old records held at Wizard's Keep during his many years of loneliness.

Having finished his inspection he turned to look for Shula, but there was no sign of her, or Draya. He assumed they must have retired to an anteroom to discuss matters of importance. Him, most probably. He noticed Meganrhys deep in conversation with the sister he had first seen when he awoke from his abortive astral-roam, and walked over to them.

"Good morning," he said brightly. "How are we this fine day?"

Meganrhys turned to face him. "Good morning, Beulah," she replied, with a welcoming smile, "I see the rest has restored your strength."

He gave her a cheeky grin. "No small thanks to my guardian angel. I believe you are now to be my nurse, in case my old, weak heart decides to give out."

Meganrhys blushed a deep shade of red and swiftly changed the subject. "Allow me to introduce you to *my* saviour. Meet Rhissa. Without her I would still be stuck in the back of beyond, curing goatherds of gout and fishermen of colds!"

Beulah dipped his head in greeting. "Pleased to meet you, my dear. You have my eternal thanks. If you had not found Megan-rhys, I would now be a very dead last wizard."

Rhissa gave him a thin smile, her hazel eyes showing no warmth. His attempts to engage her in conversation were inter-rupted by Draya and Shula's reappearance. "Beulah!" Shula's authoritative voice rang out. "It is time. We are at your disposal."

"Until later, ladies," Beulah said with a smile, turning to join the matriarch and Draya at the orb.

"We are yours to command, wizard," Draya informed him. "What are your instructions?"

"Gather round," Beulah directed, looking across at the two sisters. "What I have to do should be a fairly simple and straight-forward operation. The …" He looked at the matriarch enquiringly.

"It is all right, Beulah. They are aware that certain restrictions have been placed in the orb. Restrictions that only a wizard of your ability can release."

"Excellent!" he remarked. Shula's expression warned him that she had not told them the whole truth.

"As I have already said, the operation to release these, aherm … restrictions, should be fairly simple and straightforward. However, one must never be too careful when dealing with matters of magic. One false …"

"We know all this, Beulah," interrupted the matriarch, not unkindly. "We do have a certain degree of experience where magic is concerned."

"Oh, yes. Sorry. Well, we have to be careful. The most simple operations sometimes turn out to be the most fraught."

A rancorous voice cut in. "I think we understand, wizard. Ouch!" Draya gave a small yelp of pain as Shula's foot connected with her shin.

Unperturbed, Beulah continued with his instructions. Satisfied that they understood his intent, he removed the orb from its stand and moved to sit in the centre of the room. Setting it on the floor in front of him, he leaned forward and placed his hands on its surface. As instructed, Meganrhys took up position behind him, ready for the mind-link. Draya and Rhissa were watching Megan-rhys's vital signs, while Shula oversaw the whole procedure, ready to help should the need arise.

Beulah concentrated his powers on his inner-self, freeing his mind from the earthly form far quicker than when he had sent his spirit searching for Snorkel. He sensed the presence of Meganrhys joining him.

'I am here, Beulah,' her voice sounded in his head.

'I know.'

'There is one thing I should tell you before we continue,' she said. *'When you send your life-force into the orb, your whole mind will be open to me. Should I choose to do so, I could destroy you.'*

'I am aware of that,' he replied. 'I am also aware that my every past thought, every past deed and every past secret will be available for you to do with as you wish, should you delve. I would never have agreed to let you link with me if I thought for one moment that you would betray me. Now, if you're ready?'

The adrenaline pumped through his body as his life-force broke free of its restraints and travelled down his arms, flowing out into the orb through his splayed fingers.

His spirit swam down through a clear, green-tinged sea. He felt alive, invigorated. He looked at his hands and was surprised to see youth and vitality in the unblemished, wrinkle-free appendages. Then, glancing down at his naked body, a smile crossed his face as he admired the suppleness of the well-muscled torso and limbs. Young again!

Giggling with pleasure, he looked back the way he had come and could just make out the fuzzy dark colours of the matriarch's room and the five light brown blobs of the faces surrounding the orb. He grinned, then turned to carry on with his swim. This was fun. By the gods, he felt so alive! Laughing with glee he turned a full somersault, revelling in his newfound youth, chortling to himself as fish-shaped parcels of magic swam and cavorted alongside him, attracted by this strange, magic-charged life-force in their midst. He had not had such a good time in years. He could stay here for ever.

'Beulah! You have work to do,' an unwanted intruder whispered in his mind. 'Ignore the lure of the magic and carry on with your mission.'

Irritated by the voice, he chose to ignore it and continued to play with his new friends; swimming with them, being pulled along by them, tickled by them, having the time of his life. He was so absorbed in their antics that he did not take much notice of where they were leading him.

'BEULAH! YOU HAVE WORK TO DO!'

The volume of the mind-speak cut through the enchanted haze causing his child-like behaviour. The fish-shaped parcels of magic, alarmed by the ripples caused by the power of the voice, scattered and dispersed.

Beulah ceased his cavorting and looked around. There was no sign of the surface where he had entered. He was all alone in a green-tinged void. Gone were the fuzzy images of Shula's room and the watching figures. He panicked, and started to thrash in an attempt to re-orient himself. If he could not find where he had come in, how could he find his way out again?

'Relax.' This time the voice was welcome. *'I am here with you. I will guide you out once you have accomplished your aim. Listen carefully. You have been in there for three hours; you have to hurry. Your heartbeat is becoming erratic. No matter how young and vital you feel within the orb, your earthly body is not! It is suffering. You have to hurry!'*

Beulah was shocked. Three hours! It only seemed like he had been here a matter of minutes. How could three hours have elapsed so quickly?

'Time runs differently in the orb. Tell me, have you seen anything out of the ordinary, something that does not seem like it belongs?'

He hadn't. Mind you, he hadn't really been looking. He'd been too busy enjoying himself. He looked around, scanning his surroundings for … what? Then he saw it! A dark blob in the dist-ance, its shape distorted as if he were looking through a heat haze.

'Yes! I see it!'

'Then that is where you must go. Please hurry. Time runs short and I do not know how long your body can survive.'

Striking out with young, supple limbs, he swam towards the distant shape, his powerful strokes moving him swiftly nearer his goal. As he drew closer it began to become more distinguishable. It was a castle.

He increased his speed, impatient to reach the target. Looking up, he gasped in amazement as he saw the castle clearly for the first time. This was too easy. He immediately knew what he had to do.

What safer place to lock the secrets of the orb than in a replica of Wizard's Keep? He shook his head in admiration at the ingenuity of the wizards. There was no way that a sister, or even four or five of them, could break through the spells that created its mirror image. They were far too powerful.

Arriving at the entrance he opened the familiar door and stepped inside, then strode purposefully across the hall to the stairway leading down to the dungeons.

At the bottom he looked around. It was all as he remembered: the four doorways leading to the small, solitary cells, set either side of the large, oak-panelled doors of the main research cell. That was the area the wizards used to carry out their experiments, the more dangerous ones. He smiled. He remembered when old Prenderghast had tried to …

'BEULAH!' the voice in his head commanded, *'GET ON WITH IT!'*

Pulled back to the present, he grunted an acknowledgement and walked around the perimeter of the central area to try the doors. They were all locked.

He stepped back to regard them, rubbing at his chin thoughtfully. Now where would the keys be? He had no idea. The doors had always been open during his time, as there was no need for them to be locked. A grin split his face. He raced back up the stairs and ran through the keep, up the main staircase and into the master's quarters, his own quarters back at the real keep. He entered the private study.

Although the room was a lot tidier than the one in the real world, the surroundings were instantly recognisable. Volumes of spells, written by past masters, filled the familiar bookshelves lining the walls. The mahogany desk sat in its usual place in the far corner, its red leather top looking in far better condition than the one he remembered.

However, there was no time to waste in idle thoughts. He ran to the desk and pulled open the drawers one by one, looking for the keys. They were empty! Not a thing was in them. He slammed the last drawer shut in disgust and slapped the top of the desk in frustration. He was so sure they would be here.

Starting to panic, he quickly scanned the bookshelves for any sign of the keys. His gaze locked on to the back of the door, which had swung closed during his search of the desk. His eyes crinkled and a smile crept over his face. There they were, hanging on a peg.

He strode across the room, snatched the keys and made his way back to the basement. Reaching the dungeon level he ran to the first door, one of the ones leading to the small cells. They would be where the minor magics were locked away.

In his haste to find the correct key, the weighty bunch dropped from his fingers to the floor. He quickly scrabbled for them and thrust one into the lock. He turned it expectantly. Nothing happened. He tried another, without success. The third key he chose fitted, and the lock opened with an audible click.

Standing with his back to the wall, he pushed the door. A rush of wind swept past his face and a purple mist shot out, swiftly disappearing up the stairs towards the main entrance. Initially startled by the sudden emergence of the magic-charged cloud, he soon gathered his wits and made his way around the remaining three minor doors, repeating the exercise.

Finally only one door remained. The door to the master cell. Overcome by apprehension, he cautiously put the last key in the lock and turned it. Instead of waiting until Beulah pushed, the door flew inwards of its own volition, the handle snatched out of his fingers. Beulah threw his arms across his face and cringed in terror, fearing the worst. When nothing happened, he hesitantly lowered his arms and opened his eyes to stare into the room beyond. It was empty.

He stepped slowly forward, ready to bolt at the first sign of danger. But it was all as he remembered. Empty. Just four stone walls, with a recess at the rear where the opening to the well was. Even the blackened scorch marks on the walls from past experiments were as he remembered.

The further he walked into the room, the more aware he became of a low humming in the air, almost too low to be audible. More of a vibration than a sound, it appeared to be emanating from the recess. Puzzled, he walked hesitantly over. The closer he got, the more insistent the humming became. His mouth went dry and fear gripped him.

Fighting the fear and forcing himself forward, he managed to reach the recess. Once there, a feeling of absolute terror rendered him immobile. He could not have run if he wanted to. His limbs refused to work. The humming had grown to a persistent roar in his head and was getting louder. He screwed his eyes shut to fight the pain. It did not work. His head seemed about to explode and he felt the warm, wet trickle of blood coming from his ears. That noise, whatever it was, was trying to kill him!

He opened his eyes, intending to search the room for something to help him, but instead they fixed on the opening to the well itself. A pulsating violet light was coming from it. His eyes widened in terror. It was getting brighter, coming closer. And the noise was getting louder.

He managed to raise his hands to cover his ears. By screwing his eyes shut, he sought to keep what remained of his sanity. Just when he thought he would be driven beyond the point of no return, the humming stopped. Silence filled the room – a silence more unnerving than the noise.

He uncovered his ears and cracked his eyes open a fraction. Just enough to witness red, scaled claws shooting out from the orifice, to drag his life-force screaming into the abyss.

Chapter Thirteen

Halting beside the partially open gates, every sense alert for danger, Neulee stood flat against the stout timber panels and peered into the courtyard beyond. Silvery moonlight bathed the cobbled yard with a ghostly glow and all was still. Satisfied the coast was clear, she quickly entered, her booted feet barely making a sound on the moss covered stones.

Keeping close to the deeper shadows of the perimeter wall, she made her stealthy way past the old stable block toward the disused barracks. From there it would be a short sprint across the intervening open ground to the prison quarters, which were annexed to the main palace.

The night was close and humid and the threat of rain hung in the air. Neulee frowned as an ominous dark cloud prepared to obscure the crescent moon. While darkness would be a welcome ally and enable her to merge more fully with her surroundings, rain would be another matter. Damp earth would make their trail easier to follow. She hoped it would not take too long to locate the dwarf and the man, if they still lived. Tales abounded of what elves did to trespassers, and they were not nice.

Voices sounded in the night.

Neulee froze. Fearful of giving herself away, she held her breath and hugged the illusory safety of the cold stone wall at her back. The voices grew louder as the speakers approached. Although she could not see them, she could tell they were getting closer. Gradually, the voices began to fade.

Neulee breathed a sigh of relief, then waited for a couple of minutes before making her move. It was as well her companion had drawn a plan of the grounds for her to memorise, otherwise she could have wandered around for hours and still not been able to find where the captives were being held. She prayed her new friend was safe and had discovered which cell the duo were being kept in. That information would aid their task enormously.

When she reached the cover of the old barracks she crept

through an opening in the back wall, barely making it before the heavens opened and rain began to fall. She swore silently to herself. A flash of lightning forked across the sky, illuminating the interior of the semi-derelict building. A clap of thunder sounded overhead.

Cautious of tripping on the rubble that littered the floor, she slowly made her way to the front of the building where, safely concealed behind the old stone wall, she poked her head around the doorway. Fortunately the door had long since fallen off, allowing her an unrestricted view across the open ground that lay between her and her objective.

Her nerves grew more ragged as she waited for her companion. "Come on!" she murmured for the umpteenth time. "Where are you?"

The sound of stone grating against stone came from somewhere behind her. She spun, her sword leaping to her hand as if by magic as she crouched down. Adrenaline pumped through her body as she waited for the expected attack.

A familiar figure materialised through the gloom.

Neulee smiled in relief and rose, sheathing her weapon. "Did you find them?"

* * * * *

"How long are they going to keep us down here?" Ryzak stormed. "We've been cooped up like rabid dogs for the past three days! Surely *her highness*," he said with a sneer, "could have seen us by now."

He glanced across at Snorkel, not really expecting a reply. The dwarf sat disconsolately at the back of the small dank cell, staring bleakly into space. Throughout their journey to Chlyonedse he had remained thus. The only time the elves would untie the gag that bound his mouth was when it was time to be fed. Even then three of them stood guard whilst one spoon-fed him, in case he tried something. His hands had not known freedom since their capture, the guards keeping them permanently bound.

Ryzak looked up at the small window opening at the top of the rear wall. It did not allow much light to enter, but what little did get in was welcome. He snorted bitterly as the bright shaft of sunlight started to fade, the sign that another day was drawing to a close.

"Damn it!" he muttered to himself, then stomped over to the door to hammer the fleshy side of a clenched fist against the timber panels. "Open up, you pointy-eared bastards!" he yelled in frustration. "You've got no right to keep us locked up in here. Tell your queen we want to see her. *NOW!*"

The corridor beyond remained silent.

Giving the door one last pounding for good measure, he turned away, worry etched into his face. He rubbed at the shadow of stubble covering his chin, then glanced up at the window opening with dull and haunted eyes. Imprisonment was getting to him.

The journey to the elves' capital had been bad enough, being blindfolded all day and strapped to his horse, but this? This was far worse. They had been cooped up in this place with only the occasional visit from their jailers for company, and they only appeared twice a day to bring food and water. Apart from those brief interludes, the days were running into each other with regular monotony. He was coming to the end of his tether; he did not know how much more he could take. He was meant for the great outdoors, not being locked up in some cold damp cell like this. He needed a drink!

Scowling in frustration, he walked over and squatted next to the dwarf, tempted, yet again, to remove the gag and untie the ropes that bound him. Tentatively, he raised his hands, but dropped them as he saw Snorkel's eyes widen in alarm.

"I don't know why you won't let me," Ryzak grumbled. "I know what the elves said about gutting me if I touched your bonds, but surely you, with your powers, would be able to get us out of here once I untied you?"

Snorkel shook his head and scrambled away from him.

Ryzak stood and began to pace the cell in frustration. Eventually, getting bored, he leaned against a wall, slid down to sit at its base, folded his arms across his raised knees and rested his head on them to try and get some sleep. Some time later the jangle of keys in the lock woke him. He came to with a start and rose to his feet, running a hand through his matted hair while he tried to focus his gaze.

The door opened and four guards entered. "You!" shouted the leader, pointing at Ryzak. "Come with us! And you!" he said, looking at Snorkel, a smile playing about his lips, "don't go anywhere. We'll be back!"

The last comment raised a few sniggers from his companions, who nudged each other and nodded towards the hapless dwarf. Two of them grabbed Ryzak by the arms and frog-marched him out of the cell. Left alone with Snorkel, the leader gave him a contemptuous look before turning and following them out. The loud bang of the door slamming shut had a sombre finality.

Snorkel glared at the locked door after the elves had left, all his anger and hatred of Draco's killers focused in his look. If he could have wiped them all out with his magic, he would have. However, he still could not figure out how to ignite the powers he obviously had. Whatever it was that caused him to summon them was deeply buried.

Some wizard he had turned out to be; he could not even protect his friends. And now he had lost the only one he held dear. Draco. When he was free he would make the elves suffer. Every last one of them! And their deaths would not be as quick and clean as Draco's. He continued to stare at the door, his eyes hard and cold.

An hour passed and there was still no sign of the jailers, or Ryzak, returning. The cell was pitch black, the evening having given way to night. Even the moon and stars, which usually cast a muted light through the high window, had disappeared, obscured by clouds. The scent of a storm filled the air and he could hear the distant rumble of thunder. Frustrated at his confinement and inability to do anything about it, Snorkel fell into a fitful sleep.

He was lying in a beautiful, rolling meadow, the vivid green of the grass heightened by the colours of the wild flowers that grew in profusion. He sighed with pleasure, and clasping his hands behind his head idly watched fluffy white clouds meander past.

134

The warmth of the sun made him feel drowsy. He decided to close his eyes for a minute or two, before heading back to his mountain home.

Sometime later he awoke to a tickling sensation on his arms and legs. He had no idea how long he had been asleep, but he could see that the sun was a good hand-span lower than it had been. Concerned that he had idled away most of the day, he decided to make a move homewards before he got in trouble with his father again.

He tried to move his arms, but they were held. Then he tried to move his legs, but they were clamped as well. In panic, he tried to wrench them free, but no matter how hard he pulled or tugged he could not move them. Struggling, he managed to raise his head a fraction and look at his ensnared limbs. In horror, he realised the grass had grown whilst he slept and wrapped itself around him, immobilising him completely.

An evil laugh sounded and a dark shadow loomed over him.

His gaze was drawn up to a frighteningly familiar face, the dark goatee beard split into a grin, revealing even, white teeth.

Mishtar glared down at him.

The sorcerer's figure expanded, growing until it completely filled Snorkel's vision, the malice he held for the dwarf radiating from his dark eyes in a wave of hatred.

Snorkel shrank back, trying to force his body into the earth for protection. But it was no use. Mishtar had him. He was staring death in the face. He screamed the first thing that came to mind. The name of his beloved friend.

"Dracooooooooooo!"

'Mum! Mum! Don't worry, I'm here! I'll save you!'

Snorkel came to with a start, the echoes of his muffled shriek reverberating around the small cell. His heart raced and his eyes darted round for signs of Mishtar. Fearfully he scuttled back until he could go no further, his body coming up against the cold, hard stone of the wall.

Awareness of where he was slowly trickled through and he gave a nervous snort. That was one hell of a nightmare. It seemed so real.

Rain was falling; he could hear the wet splatter of the large, pregnant drops as they hammered against the outer wall of the cell. Suddenly lightning flashed, the brilliance of the bolt illuminating the cell. A sinister silhouette appeared on the far wall.

Terrified, Snorkel awaited the next flash, eyes wide and fixed on the spot where the shadow had appeared. He did not have long to wait. Thirty seconds later the cell was lit by a dazzling flash of light, and there it was again. The shadow image of, of …

'*Hey, Mum. It's me, Draco!*' came the triumphant cry of the dragonet in his head.

"Ummmmmph?" queried Snorkel.

The dwarf's eyes widened as a small lime-green shape glided down from its perch on the ledge of the window to land in front of him. The dragonet began to hop up and down, her wings flapping in excitement, her eyes whirling in a frenzy of happiness.

Tears welled in his eyes as Snorkel gazed down at his long lost – dead? – friend. "Mmammo!"

'*Mum!*' the ecstatic voice of Draco pounded in his head. '*What's up with your voice?*' she added quizzically.

"Imph mm mmph. Imph mm mmph, mm aghhm!" Snorkel replied.

A puzzled expression crossed Draco's face. She jumped onto the quilted shoulder pad and cocked her head round to peer at the dwarf.

'*Ahhhh!*' she murmured, understanding. '*You're gagged!*'

"Emph!" replied Snorkel, nodding.

The dragonet moved to a better position and began to bite at the ligature that prevented the dwarf from speaking. In a matter of moments she had chewed through. Spitting bits of rope from her mouth, she hopped to the floor.

Through tears of happiness, Snorkel croaked, "Draco! I thought you were dead! What happened to you? Where have you been? How did you get here?" The words rushed out in a torrent as he tried to choke back the sobs that threatened to turn him into a blubbering wreck.

'*I very nearly was,*' she replied excitedly, '*until the nice lady found me.*'

Snorkel sniffled. "What nice lady?" he asked. Then the floodgates opened and he wept unashamedly. "Oh, Draco, I thought that I would never see you again. I thought that I'd lost you forever!"

The dragonet jumped back on to Snorkel's shoulder and nuzzled his cheek. *'I love you, Mum,'* she purred. *'You didn't think you'd get rid of me that easily did you?'*

Snorkel grinned happily and peered into her yellow eyes. "I love you too, Draco. Remind me never to complain about you calling me 'Mum' again."

'OK, Mum!' she replied cheerfully. *'Where's Ryzak?'*

"The elves have taken him to see their queen," Snorkel replied, his eyes narrowing in concern. "They've been gone for ages. He should have been back by now. I hope they haven't killed him."

'I could go and look,' Draco offered, hopping back down to the floor.

"NO! – No," Snorkel said, his voice softening. "I've only just got you back, I don't want to lose you again. I'm sure they'll bring him back soon enough. Who's this lady then?" he asked, intrigued.

'Ooooh, a very nice lady. She saved me.'

"What's her na – ooow!" Snorkel's face screwed up in agony.

'What's the matter, Mum?' Draco asked, concern in her voice.

"It's my hands. They're tied as well." He gave her a hopeful smile. "Do you think …"

'Move over!' Draco ordered. *'Let the carver see the wood.'*

Snorkel did as he was told, patiently waiting while the dragonet chewed through the bonds. As soon as his hands were free he sighed in relief, then rubbed at his wrists to try and get the circulation going, groaning as feeling started to return.

"That's better," he said, as the pain subsided. "Now then, who is this nice lady and how did you get here?"

'Her name is Neulee,' she informed him. *'She found me and made me better. Look!'* Draco pointed a long fore-claw at the puffy, raw-looking scar on her chest.

Snorkel leaned forward to inspect the damage. He could faintly make out the ragged edges in the dim light. A flash of lightning illuminated the cell, providing enough light for him to see the wound more clearly. He whistled between his teeth. "That was a close one," he murmured in amazement. "Is she a witch?"

'Noooo,' chuckled Draco, *'she can't even mind-speak. She's a good tracker though. That's how we found you, once I'd managed to show her where I wanted her to go.'*

"How did she heal you then? That shot should have killed you."

'I don't know; she can't hear me so I can't ask her. All I remember is flying to meet those nice elves and then waking up to see Neulee looking down at me, smiling. I had some pretty foul smelling stuff smeared on me though. Eeeeugh! Made my eyes water, it did.'

"There's nothing nice about elves," Snorkel growled, his eyes hardening. "If it wasn't for them we would have been at Firestone Mountain by now."

The dwarf looked up and gave a gasp of alarm as he heard the jangle of keys and the sound of footsteps approaching the cell. "You'd better get out of here, quick!" he urged. "They've come back for me. If they find you in here they'll know something is up and we'll never escape."

'I'm out of here,' Draco mind-spoke, as she launched herself into the air. *'Don't worry, Neulee and I will get you out, so don't do anything stupid. Just be your usual self. On second thoughts,'* she amended, *'keep quiet and don't say anything. It's probably safer that way!'*

Snorkel snorted in disgust. "Thanks for the show of confidence."

He stood facing the door with his arms crossed as it swung open and his captors entered. He smiled in satisfaction at the look of shock and panic on their faces when they realised he was no longer bound. "Good evening, my fine fellows. Are we off to see this queen of yours then?"

The leader of the jailers pulled out a small club and stepped forward, indicating for his men to surround the dwarf.

Snorkel raised his eyebrows and gave them a stern look. "Tut, tut, tut. There's no need for that. I'll be on my best behaviour." He smiled. "Promise!" He placed his right hand over his heart and raised his left, giving the universal sign for peace. At least he hoped it was. It always amazed him how something as simple as holding two fingers up could be so confusing. He had suffered more beatings than he could count on the fingers of both hands because of that simple mistake.

The leader glared at him. "You'd better be or she'll feed you to the wolves, magic-user or not! You two!" He ordered, turning to the elves on his right, "take an arm each. You!" he commanded the remaining elf, "follow behind. Any monkey business and club him. Got it?"

The elf nodded his understanding.

"Good." The leader turned and strode out of the cell, with Snorkel dragged along behind him.

"Oy! Slow down," the dwarf shouted, "I've only got little legs."

The two elves holding his arms gave each other a knowing smirk and, on the count of three, hoisted the little man up, leaving his legs treading air. They laughed at Snorkel's squeal of outrage and ignored his pleas to put him down and let him walk like a man.

After numerous twists and turns they arrived at a dead-end. Snorkel was still muttering about the indignity of the situation when the corridor finished at a solid wall of rock. "Ha!" he said, in undisguised delight. "Got ourselves lost, have we? Serves you right! Treating a respectable member of society like you have. It's a disgrace. Put me down and let me show you how to get out of here. I don't know, can't even find your way out of your own prison."

The leader scowled, then nodded to the elf who stood behind the dwarf.

Realising he had overstepped the mark, Snorkel hastily apologised. "Please! Please forgive me. I'm sure you know what you're doing, really. It's being tied and gagged for so long, it's affected my mind. I just don't know what I'm saying half the time." He gave the leader a hopeful smile.

The elf shook his head in disgust and turned away, placing the palm of his right hand in a recess in the rock beside him.

Snorkel watched as a panel slid back to reveal a brightly lit corridor. He squinted against the sudden glare. After the gloom of his cell the bright light was a painful experience.

Still suspended between the two guards, he was carried over the threshold and along the corridor. As he passed he glanced at the walls beside him. They were adorned with colourful tapestries depicting scenes from elven folklore. Eventually they reached another door; a solid lump of oak blocking their path. Raising his hand, the leader of the party gave three sharp raps, quickly followed by two more. A key turned in the lock and the door swung open, revealing a heavily armed elf. After a cursory inspection, his lip curling as his gaze lit on the dwarf, he nodded them through.

After a seemingly endless series of corridors, T-junctions and cross-ways, they arrived at another large, oak-panelled door guarded by two more elves. The elves carrying Snorkel stopped as their leader strode forward. A whispered conversation ensued, then one of the guards knocked on the door, opened it and went in to the room beyond.

Waiting outside the door, Snorkel fretted. He felt as if a hundred butterflies had hatched in his stomach and were trying to flutter free. By the time the guard came back, they had resorted to using pick-axes and shovels.

At the leader's curt nod, Snorkel's escort carried him forward into a vast, vaulted hall. Craning his neck, he could see the ceiling arching away high over his head, a glass dome at its apex. Lightning flashed and storm clouds scudded across the night sky, clearly visible through the rain-washed glass.

A movement from his jailers dragged his attention away from the ceiling and back to the room itself. A worried scowl crossed his face as his eyes fell on the congregation awaiting him, and he gasped in trepidation. The hall was filled with elves, dressed in a glittering variety of fine, richly coloured clothing. There seemed to be a party in progress. He could see elves talking and laughing in small groups as they sipped their drinks and nibbled delicately on little pastries that were being served by young elven girls and boys.

As soon as he and his escort passed by they stopped what they were doing and became silent, staring at him as if he were something unpleasant. Given the conditions he had recently endured, this was not too far from the truth. Even the death's head embroidered on the back of his robe was grimacing in distaste.

Snorkel was carried through the throng toward a raised dais in the middle of the room, positioned immediately below the glass canopy of the arched ceiling. As they drew closer, he became aware of a golden throne set in the centre of the dais. A stunningly beautiful elven woman, who he assumed was the queen, reclined on the red velvet material of the seat. She was enjoying the attention of a small group of admirers who spoke and laughed with her; and she ran long, delicate fingers through her waist-length silver hair as she listened politely to their jests.

As the small troop halted in front of the throne, conversation dropped to a hushed, expectant whisper. Giving the escort and its captive a quick glance, the queen waved away her fawning admirers with a flick of her long, slender arm. Bowing low, they left. All except one. Rhudrhyn!

He stayed by his queen's side, leaning casually against her throne and regarding the dwarf with a sly smile on his face.

The queen turned and gave Snorkel a withering look, her beauty marred by the cruel, hard glint in her eyes. "Release him!" she commanded, in a voice that brooked no argument.

Snorkel landed on the floor in a crumpled heap as his guards immediately did as they were ordered, much to the delight of the queen and the assembled gallery. They laughed uproariously as the little man scrambled to his feet.

With an elaborate flourish, he bowed low. "I am at your service, Your Majesty."

"Indeed you are," she replied, arching an eyebrow in disdain. "Are you a magic-user?"

Puffing out his chest importantly (he had seen Beulah do this to good effect in the past) he replied. "Indeed I am, Your Majesty. Snorkel, member of the Brotherhood of Wizards, resident of Wizard's Keep and master of magic, at your command." He placed his right hand over his heart and bowed again.

"We do not like wizards! Especially short, ugly, untidy ones," the queen sneered, eyeing his unsanitary appearance. "Dwarf, aren't you?" Snorkel stared at her in shock, before dumbly nodding his head. He suddenly realised that he was flirting with danger – danger of a terminal sort. "I can't stand them either," she muttered. "Mucky little bastards." She leaned forward threateningly, her eyes boring into his. "What were you and your friend doing in my wood?"

Snorkel blanched. He dare not tell her about their quest to see Reizgoth. The fewer people that knew about Mishtar and the seals the better. Beulah would skin him alive if he did. It was bad enough that they had been captured by the elves, especially after the wizard had warned them about straying from the path.

"Well?"

He cast a quick glance at the queen, noting the first flush of anger colouring her face. Trying to think rapidly on his feet before she decided to gut him, he replied, "Erm … We were looking for herbs for some healing spells."

Rhudrhyn strode forward and jumped off the dais, landing lightly in front of the startled dwarf. He grabbed two fistfuls of Snorkel's robe and hoisted the little man off the floor. "Wrong answer!" he snarled. "Try again. And do not attempt any of your mumbo jumbo tricks. My archers have been ordered to shoot at the first sign of mischief, no questions asked."

Snorkel managed to turn his head and make out the bowmen lining the balcony, arrows notched and ready. Swallowing nervously, he looked into the violet eyes and nodded his head.

"That's better," Rhudrhyn said, with a smile. He placed Snorkel back on the floor and casually straightened his crumpled robe, before moving back to the edge of the dais, wiping his hands on his tunic as he went. Reaching the raised section of floor, he turned and leaned against it, his hostile gaze fixed on the dwarf.

Snorkel clasped his hands in front of him and looked up at the queen. She was reclining in her throne, sipping at a glass of wine as she scrutinised him. "We were on our way to Firestone Mountain," he mumbled.

"What?" asked the queen. "Speak up, we all wish to hear."

"We were on our way to Firestone Mountain," he repeated, slightly louder.

Her face creased into a puzzled frown. "Why on earth would you want to go there?" she asked. "It's just a pile of rocks, with tribes of cannibals running all over the place."

"Cannibals?" squeaked Snorkel. No one had told him about them.

Rhudrhyn laughed at the look on the dwarf's face. "You seem a little put out," he said. "I would have thought a man of your ability would have known all about the Plains of Fear. But obviously not." He grinned.

A buzz of amused laughter spread round the room as the conversation was relayed back.

"Why were you going there, little man?" Rhudrhyn enquired.

"To see Reizgoth and ask him for a piece of his hoard," Snorkel replied morosely.

Rhudrhyn stared at the dwarf as if he were an idiot, which, technically, he probably was. He clutched at his sides as fits of laughter engulfed him. Soon the whole room was in uproar.

Snorkel shuffled his feet and looked at the floor. He could feel the heat from his face as it reddened in embarrassment.

Dabbing at watering eyes, the queen tried to ask him a question – several times, but each time gales of laughter consumed her. Eventually she composed herself. "Any particular piece? Or were you just calling on spec?" she asked.

The room filled with laughter again. The only person not sharing in the hilarity was Snorkel, who waited until the uproar abated before answering the queen's flippant question. Wanting to wipe the smiles off their faces, he informed them which piece he was after, hoping it would sober them up. It did, but not in the way he expected. As soon as he told them of his quest the room fell silent. You could have heard a gnat fart (as the well-known dwarven saying goes – they were famous for their erudite maxims).

The queen's face drained of colour and she glared at him with open contempt. "Take the little cave-rat back to the cells," she snarled to the guards at his side.

Standing up, her anger-filled voice rang out. "Everyone leave! All except the council. We have to decide what to do with the runt." Her malevolent gaze fell on Snorkel. "We have to decide whether we kill you, let the cannibals eat you, or leave you to Mishtar," she sneered. "I don't care which, as long as we elves stay out of man's troubles. If the wizards had dealt with the sorcerer properly in the first place, we wouldn't be facing this problem now. You're on your own. We're staying out of it!"

The guards dragged Snorkel back to his cell, the assembled elves glowering and muttering as he was escorted past them, as if it was his fault that Mishtar had decided to come back and haunt them. Life was so unfair sometimes; or most of the time in Snorkel's case.

Chapter Fourteen

"That's it!" exclaimed Neulee, brushing aside a bedraggled lock of sodden brown hair that had fallen across her face. She sat down on the rain-soaked grass and placed her feet either side of the window opening, then leaned forward to grasp the last remaining bar.

"Pull!" she ordered, her muscles bunching under the strain.

Draco added her weight, the rope that tied her to the bar going taut as she frantically flapped her wings. In an explosion of masonry, the rusted metal rod pulled free. Fortunately, the noise of the thunderstorm masked their endeavours.

It had taken Neulee almost an hour of chiselling with her hunting knife to weaken the mortar sufficiently for the bars to be wrenched out, the rain having made them too wet and slippery to work on easily. Now, the task complete, she sat back and breathed a sigh of relief. She should not complain too much; the weather had kept the elves inside, safely out of the way, keeping dry.

The only heart-stopping moment had been when the door of the cell had suddenly opened, and the unconscious man was thrown to the floor by his jailers. Neulee had been so engrossed in what she was doing she never heard the commotion until it was almost too late. Not daring to move until the cell door slammed shut for fear of attracting attention, she waited a good while before returning to her scraping.

"All we need now is the dwarf," she murmured, as Draco glided down to land beside her.

Neulee removed the loosely tied noose from the dragonet's shoulders and tickled her affectionately under the chin. "It's a good job you understand me, even if I can't understand you," she said, over the rumble of the happily purring creature.

Crouching, she crawled forward and poked her head through the opening. From her lofty vantage point she could make out the prone figure. He was out cold, lying where he had been thrown.

The rattle of keys sounded. Neulee backed out of the opening in the four foot thick wall and placed a forefinger to her lips.

"Get in there, runt," a harsh voice ordered. "And don't try anything stupid."

There was an indignant yelp of pain. "There's no need for …"

Thunk!

"You!" the harsh voice commanded. "Stay in the cell with those two. If the dwarf comes round, club him again. Don't kill him though. That pleasure's for the queen."

"Me? Alone? Bu–bu …"

"What's the matter? Scared? Don't worry. Chuirhyn will be just up the corridor and I'll come to relieve you in an hour or two. Just make sure you stay awake."

Neulee heard the sound of the cell door being closed. She edged herself forward on hands and knees and peered over the ledge, down into the room below. Both captives were flat out on the cell floor. The elf who had been ordered to watch over them had placed a torch in a sconce on the wall and was sitting immediately below the window, watching the two comatose forms.

As Neulee eased herself back, an idea formed. She placed a finger to her pursed lips and gestured for Draco to remain quiet then, stooping low, she ran to the old barrack building. She returned with a large stone. Placing it on the ground next to the window, she peered down into the room. The elf still sat in the same position.

Neulee silently withdrew, then bent and lifted the stone. Hefting it in her arms to test its weight, she leaned in through the window opening, holding it in outstretched hands.

"Wh–wh–where am I?" a bemused voice asked.

Neulee paused in the act of dropping her makeshift weapon on the elf's head and peered in. Damn! The man had woken. His sense of timing was impeccable.

"You're back in your cell, human," the elf answered. "Don't try anything foolish or you'll end up like your friend there. Out cold! Got it?"

The stone drooped lower and lower as Neulee's arms wilted under the strain. Beads of perspiration sprang out on her forehead as, teeth clamped together, eyes screwed shut, she fought to keep it level.

Awareness of the miracle gradually filtered through into Ryzak's head. He was alive! That was a bonus. He was sure they would kill him, especially after he had upset their queen. It was not as if it was his fault. She should not be so temperamental. He was only trying to be friendly.

It was when he had heard the collective gasp of horror from the throng and seen Rhudrhyn's eyes harden in anger that he'd realised he was in trouble. Bowing low to the queen, he had inadvertently let his eyes linger on her chest for too long. The sheer fabric of her dress, stretched tightly over her pert, rounded breasts, had fuddled his brain. Forgetting where he was, he had uttered his amazement at such a wondrous sight. But instead of being flattered by such praise she had been furious. He could not understand it.

When Rhudrhyn bounded off the dais, pulling a razor-sharp knife from its sheath, Ryzak had done the only thing he could. Fainted! In hindsight it was probably just as well, or he would be dead by now.

Feeling a little groggy, he eased himself to a sitting position, his hand rising to feel the sore spot on his head were he must have knocked it when he passed out. "Wh–wh–where am I?"

"You're back in your cell, human. Don't try anything foolish or you'll end up like your friend there. Out cold! Got it?"

Startled by the words, Ryzak glanced up. It was one of their jailers. Seeing the elf nod his head to the right, Ryzak looked across. His eyes widened in alarm as he saw Snorkel lying nearby, a pool of congealed blood staining the floor beneath his head. They've killed him, he thought in horror. He sighed in relief as he saw the gentle rise of the little man's chest. Then something caught his eye.

Turning to look above and behind the elf, Ryzak's mouth fell open in astonishment as he spied a rock, seemingly floating in the air.

The elf swivelled round to look. But before he could cry out to summon assistance, the alien object plunged down and smashed onto his head. Lifeless, his body crumpled to the floor.

"Don't just sit there, grab a hold of this!"

The sound of the voice jolted Ryzak out of his stupor. He looked up to the window opening and saw a coil of rope snake down towards him.

"Tie a loop under the dwarf's arms and I'll pull him up. MOVE!" the voice snapped. "We don't have all night."

Startled into action, Ryzak did as he was told. He needed no second urging, when it seemed as though they were finally going to get out of this place. He scrambled to Snorkel's side and gripped his arms, dragging him to the rear wall. Once he was there he passed the rope underneath the dwarf's arms and across his chest before tying it. He gave it a tug.

"Support him while I pull him up."

In a matter of moments, the dwarf's small form was lifted to the window and hauled through.

The rope struck Ryzak on the head as it came back down. He had been daydreaming about the voice. He could not be sure, but it sounded female. Nah, it couldn't be, he decided. Incarceration must be playing tricks with his mind.

"Come on, grab hold and start climbing. I won't be able to pull up your weight."

Hearing the voice again did not clarify matters. It still sounded female. Butch, but definitely female. Puzzled, he grasped the rope and started to climb. All would soon be revealed.

Reaching the opening he squeezed through. It was tight. He got half way out and became stuck. His head, arms and shoulders on the outside getting wet, his chest stuck in the wall with his legs left dangling in mid-air.

His mouth fell open as the most perfect brown eyes he had ever seen dropped into his line of vision. They peered at him from a face of stunning beauty. Framed by rain-soaked, shoulder-length brown hair, it was a face made for dreams. His dreams. He smiled, instantly smitten.

A scowl of irritation crossed the flawless features. "Come on, you dumb ox. Stop fooling around and get out here. I want to be well away by the time they discover our dead friend."

The sound of her deep, husky voice jolted him back to awareness. He gave her an apologetic smile. "I can't. I'm stuck."

His saviour groaned in frustration and sat down on the grass, placing her feet against the wall. She leaned forward and grasped his upper arms.

"Grab hold and I'll help pull you out."

Ryzak's appreciative gaze fell on the ample breasts suspended in front of his face, the rain-soaked fabric of the girl's tunic clinging to her body like a second skin. And it was obvious that she was cold.

"On the count of three."

"Eh?"

"On the count of three," she repeated, "I will pull and you wriggle."

"Oh, right. Ready."

"One, two, three!"

She tugged and Ryzak wriggled. Like a cork from a bottle, he shot out of the hole in a sudden rush to land on top of her. An inane grin lit his face as he stared down at his rescuer. He was in love.

The girl's eyes hardened under his lecherous gaze.

Oblivious to her obvious annoyance, and making no attempt to move off her, the sudden crunch between his legs came as something of a shock. His eyes nearly popped out of his head at the sharp, excruciating pain in his vitals. A feeling of nausea gripped him as strong hands pushed him into the mud.

Draco winced at Ryzak's choked cry. That sounded painful. She shook her small head in mystification. Try as she might, she would never understand the man's innate ability for self-destruction. She had only known him a short while, but it was long enough to realise that he was a liability – both to himself and to others. Not for the first time she wondered at the wisdom of the wizard including him in their plans. They might have been better leaving him at the tavern. He would be less trouble there. She glanced down to the unmoving form of Snorkel. Perhaps they would have all been better off staying at the tavern. At least it would be warm and dry, even if the tavern-keeper had taken a dislike to her.

The sound of Neulee's angry voice made her look up. Her new

friend stood over Ryzak, hands on hips, glaring down at him as he writhed in the mud nursing his injured bits in clasped hands.

"That is the last time you'll ever get on top of me, so don't get any funny ideas."

Well that should cool his ardour a bit, Draco thought, or kill it off altogether. One sight of a female form and the man seemed to lose all sense of reason, what little he had; so every little reminder that not all females were vulnerable might help cure him of his affliction. Fat chance!

She gave a questioning chirrup as Neulee joined her and bent down to examine the dwarf, placing her fingers on his neck to feel for a pulse.

"Well, he still lives," she murmured, giving Draco an encouraging smile. "But we need to be away from here, and I can't carry him." She scowled across at Ryzak, who had managed to rise to his knees. "And he's not capable." She opened the pouch at her belt and began to rummage around inside. "I think I may have something here to bring him round."

Draco wrinkled her nose in disgust as Neulee produced a small bottle and levered off the lid. The contents smelt worse than Snorkel's armpits. And that was saying something.

As soon as the bottle was wafted under the dwarf's nose it started to take effect. He twitched and a few moments later shot bolt upright, wheezing heavily as tears ran from his watering eyes.

'Mum! You're awake!' Draco jumped onto Snorkel's shoulder and began to nuzzle his neck.

Shaking his head to try and clear his nasal passages of the foul stench, Snorkel could do nothing but wheeze in response.

"Get your act together, dwarf. We need to be out of here."

"Who's she?" Snorkel croaked, wiping tears from his eyes as he looked up. "And what happened to Ryzak? He looks like he's been hit by a rock-troll."

'That's Neulee, the lady who rescued me. She's just introduced herself to Ryzak.'

"Oh!" said Snorkel, a knowing smirk on his face. He watched in admiration as the woman moved away.

Hauling Ryzak to his feet, Neulee half-dragged, half-carried him over to them, then released her hold on his arm. With no support, Ryzak slowly sank to the ground, his face ashen.

"Your horses are stabled by the main gates; mine is hobbled nearby. Follow me if you're coming," Neulee called over her shoulder as she strode away.

"Some friend," muttered Snorkel under his breath, moving over to help Ryzak to his feet.

'It could be worse,' advised Draco.

"How's that?"

'She could have taken a dislike to you.'

The dwarf snorted in amusement, then took Ryzak's weight and struggled after their rescuer.

It was some time before the dwarf and the man joined Neulee at the rear of the derelict barracks. Masking her growing anxiety, Neulee hissed at them to hurry and follow her. If she had realised it would slow their pace this much, she would not have hit the man so hard. However, old habits die hard. She shook her head and, keeping under cover of the perimeter wall, led them back towards the main gates.

She hoped it would take the elves a while to discover their captives had escaped as, although the thunderstorm had passed, rain still bucketed down and their passage left muddy footprints in the saturated ground. Footprints so obvious a blind man would have little difficulty following them.

Reaching the exit she angled past, toward the stables, hoping that the horses would not be guarded. As they approached the squat building she spotted the dull glow of an oil lamp, its muted, orange radiance visible against the dark backdrop of the night. Gesturing for Ryzak and Snorkel to stay where they were and keep quiet, Neulee ducked down low and stealthily went to take a look.

She stopped short of the doorway and raised her head to the grime-streaked glass. She could make out the recumbent form of an elf, sprawled on a hay bale. He was snoring loudly, an empty bottle of wine lying beside him. She grinned and removed her hunting knife from its sheath. Reversing the hilt, she padded inside.

"You'll have one hell of a hangover in the morning," Neulee whispered, clubbing the elf behind the ear. Moving to the door she gave a low whistle. Almost immediately Ryzak and Snorkel appeared, the former looking like some sort of mud monster as he staggered in.

"Get your horses. I'll meet you outside the gates."

Without waiting for a response, Neulee disappeared into the rain-soaked night. A shadow amongst shadows.

* * * * *

Rhudrhyn rapped sharply on the door of his queen's private chambers. As it opened he pushed past the indignant attendant and strode into the room, his face a mask of fury. The attendant scurried after him, attempting to halt his progress.

"I hope you have good reason for bursting in here un-announced," the queen said, glaring at his reflected image as she brushed the night's knots from her hair. With a flick of her eyes she dismissed the flustered aide.

Rhudrhyn bowed low. "Forgive the intrusion, Iderlrhys. I have grave news."

Her hands ceased their ministrations. "And what news might that be?" she asked, her eyes narrowing.

Rhudrhyn straightened. He held her reflected gaze. "The prisoners have escaped."

Iderlrhys angrily slammed her brush on to the dresser and spun from her chair to stand facing him. "How?" she snarled.

"It would appear they have an accomplice. The bars of the cell window have been removed and Diarhyn is dead, his skull crushed by a rock. Their horses are gone and Teevalrhyn is nursing a bludgeoned head."

"How long ago?"

"Two or three hours, I would guess. They will be half way to the Plains of Fear by now if the dwarf wasn't lying about their destination."

"They're heading that way. The cave-rat was too stupid to invent a story as bizarre as that."

After a moment's pause, a twisted grin appeared on her face. Perhaps she could still get rid of them. The last thing she wanted was for Mishtar to come seeking revenge on her and her people for not stopping them, should he ever get free.

"Have a pigeon sent to De'Athman with a message. Tell him lunch is heading his way in the form of a dwarf and two humans. Tell him I require their heads; the remaining bits he can keep for whatever. He will be well rewarded for his efforts. We shall send ten barbarians as payment when the proof is received. That will keep him and his disgusting people well fed during the winter months."

"Iderlrhys," began Rhudrhyn.

"Yes! What is it?" she snapped.

"We don't have any. The last one died last week, attacked by wolves in the fields."

"Well go and get some," she snapped. "Why is it that I have to do all the thinking around here?"

"Yes, my Queen." Rhudrhyn dipped his head in acknowledgement. "I'll attend to it right away." He turned to leave.

As he was nearing the door Iderlrhys called out to him. "Rhudi! Take two men and track them yourself. If De'Athman fails, you are to bring me their heads."

He stopped and turned, a sly smile playing about his lips. "And what is to be my reward for such an heroic act?"

"Why, Rhudi," she replied, a similar smile on her face, "a man such as you should need no reward. However, if you're a good boy and I feel the need for company, I might let you play with me for a week or two." She grinned. "It's been a long time since I enjoyed certain pleasures. Now go. Don't keep me waiting for too long or I might change my mind. Oh! And tell De'Athman we would like the pigeon back. They are in scarce supply as it is, without him and his henchmen eating them."

As the door closed she turned back to the dresser, her brows furrowed. Mishtar. Whoever would have thought he would appear back on the scene?

Chapter Fifteen

"Cannibals?" yelled Ryzak, frantically spurring his horse into a gallop, "you never said anything about cannibals!"

"It sort of slipped my mind," Snorkel yelled back, forcing his pony to heroic efforts to get her little legs pumping fast enough to keep up with the bigger mounts. "I didn't know myself until the elf queen told me!"

Snorting in fear, eyes wide with terror, the horses flew across the pockmarked landscape of the volcanic Plains of Fear as though their lives depended on it. Which, as it happened, they did. The De'Athshead were as partial to horse flesh as they were to human. To get three of each in one go would be a real bonus, even if one of the two-legs was only big enough for starters.

Risking a glance over his shoulder, Ryzak saw at least forty of the cannibals behind them. They yelled and shrieked their excitement in high-pitched warbles as they raced along. Their strong, powerful legs, bare below their fur loincloths, rapidly covered the ground.

They were bloody quick.

He felt the first stirrings of panic as he saw the front-runner jumping over craters and boulders as though they weren't there; as if the bastard had springs on his feet. Shouting encouragement, Ryzak dug his horse in the ribs to urge him to greater speed.

With Neulee leading the way, they headed down an incline between two folds of land. The echoes of the horses' hooves reverberated off the rock walls as they thundered down the old, hardened lava flow. The passage went deeper and deeper. Dark, rocky walls began to loom over them, growing higher and higher, more threatening and sinister. Arriving at a fork in the passage, Neulee reined her horse to a bone jarring halt.

"What's up?" gasped Ryzak, skidding his mount to a stop beside her.

"Which way?" Neulee screamed, struggling to control her nervously prancing mare.

"That way, I think," gasped Snorkel, pointing down the right hand passage.

Still annoyed that the little man had not mentioned anything about the cannibals, Ryzak glared down at him. "Are you sure?" he growled.

"Uh-huh," Snorkel responded, eyes wide, nodding his head.

"How come, when you've never been right about anything before?"

"Be–be–because …" the dwarf stammered, and raised a tremulous arm to point down the left fork.

Ryzak turned to look. His face drained of colour. "I believe you," he shrieked.

Kicking his stallion into motion, he barrelled after Neulee who, aware of the approaching danger, was already a good distance ahead.

The screaming cannibals waved their short jabbing spears in the air and shrieked in annoyance before giving pursuit.

The horses were tiring rapidly as Ryzak and his companions raced through the narrow, winding channel, trying to put some distance between themselves and their pursuers. They had no idea which way they were heading, nor where they would end up when they eventually reached the plain again. At the moment they did not really care – they wanted out.

Eventually the path straightened and started to rise. Daylight appeared in the distance. With no twists or turns to hinder them, they urged their flagging mounts on.

Unseen, a rope snapped taut in front of the galloping horses. In a flurry of flying hooves, frightened whinnies, screams of surprise and airborne bodies, they came to an abrupt stop. The riders hit the ground hard and lay motionless.

Eight De'Athshead emerged from concealment and quickly moved across to the prone figures. The leader bent down and pinched the muscles of Ryzak's arm. He grinned in approval.

A sudden commotion from beside the fallen dwarf made him look up. One of his men was agitated, jabbing a finger at the little man. The leader shook his head and rose to his feet. Walking over to the tribesman, he looked where the babbling man pointed and gasped in astonishment. Swiftly recovering his wits, he shouted a string of orders before running down the passage.

* * * * *

The sound of flapping wings and excited chirrups intruded on the peace of the day. Never before had so many dragonets been seen in the sky. Their screeches and screams, interspersed with occasional woofs and howls, created a veritable cacophony. The airborne creatures ducked and dived, performing countless acrobatic manoeuvres in their excitement.

Central to the aerial display was a small, lime-green dragonet. Thrown from Snorkel's shoulder when his pony tripped over the rope, Draco had recovered from her tumble to see the De'Athshead take him and her friends captive. Recognising the plains from her previous life, she went to find her brothers and sisters. Draco gazed around in wonder. She did not remember there being so many of her kind. Where had they all come from? And what was that terrible howling noise?

The urgency of her mission broke through to the forefront of her mind. She flapped her leathery wings and flew through the masses to land on an outcrop of rock and await their arrival. It took quite a while. By the time her brothers and sisters had finished their grand welcome and settled down, Draco was becoming agitated.

As she regarded the hundreds of pairs of beady, yellow eyes looking up at her, she found her gaze drawn to the *large*, yellow ones at the front of the assembled flight. Framed by a furry face and large, hairy ears, it was the strangest looking dragonet she had ever seen. And where were the wing stubs?

The young she-wolf, her pink tongue lolling out of the side of her mouth, returned Draco's quizzical look with one of her own.

Shaking her head in confusion, Draco looked away, deciding to leave that question until later. She began to project her story into the minds of her listeners. Murmurs of sympathy reached her ears when she told them about her near-death experience with the elves. A loud chorus of approving squeaks and chirrups followed when she described how Neulee had subsequently saved her.

Draco was pleased with the way it was going. She had them; they were hanging on her every word. When she reached the climax of her story, there was a deathly silence. For added melodrama, Draco paused to give them time to digest the information before screeching at the top of her mind. *'Will you help me?'* she cried, her plea timed to perfection. *'Are you with me?'*

The noise was deafening as the flight chorused their approval. *'You bet! Go for it, sister! Let's make 'em have it! We're right behind you!'*

By the dragon's teeth, it had gone better than she thought it would. At least they had agreed to help. She shook her head and gazed forlornly at the mass of dragonets that had taken to the sky again. The hard part would be getting them to calm down enough to form a plan of attack.

The wet, velvet touch of a large, soft tongue made her jump. Dipping her head to scrape slobber from her face with a foreleg, she came face to face with the excited she-wolf. With a startled squeak, Draco launched herself skywards.

* * * * *

Bright lights floated in his vision as Ryzak opened his eyes. He winced in pain and licked at dry lips, then raised a hand to gently massage his throbbing temples.

"I see there is life left after all. How are you feeling?"

Easing himself into a sitting position, Ryzak peered in the direction of the voice. "Oh. It's you. I've felt better. Wh–where are we?"

"Take a look around. I'm sure even you can work that one out." Ryzak did. They were in a small cave, about fifteen feet by ten. A rickety, timber gate barricaded the entrance and he could make out the shapes of the two men guarding it, their figures barely discernible against the twilight beyond. He groaned. Taken prisoner. Again!

A distinctive animal smell wafted into his nostrils. He sneezed, sending pains shooting through his head. Damn it. He was allergic to goats. He rubbed at his temples with the heels of his hands, then turned to face Neulee. "Where's Snorkel?" he croaked.

Neulee frowned, then walked across the small cell and crouched in front of Ryzak. "No idea," she said, gently moving his hands aside so that she could probe his head. "I've only just come round myself. It seems they've locked us up and taken the dwarf off somewhere else. Starters, perhaps?" she added, with a wry grin.

"This is no time to be joking," Ryzak retorted, immediately wishing he hadn't, as yet another sharp pain tore at the inside of his head. He collapsed to the floor, groaning in agony.

"Let me look at that," Neulee commanded, kneeling beside him.

She pulled his hands away and began to probe at his scalp. At Ryzak's sudden yelp of pain she tutted. "This looks serious."

Moving his hair to one side revealed a large discoloured lump the size of a pigeon's egg just behind his left ear.

"Sit up."

When Ryzak finally managed to work himself into a sitting position, Neulee held three fingers in front of his face. "How many fingers do you see?"

"Errrrr … errrrr … six!" he croaked, triumphantly.

She frowned. "Follow my finger," she ordered, and began to move a forefinger slowly in front of his eyes.

Ryzak's eyes didn't move. They remained fixed on a spot somewhere in front of him.

Neulee folded her arms and sat back on her heels staring at him, a thoughtful expression on her face. After a moment's reflection she opened her belt-pouch and removed several carefully wrapped bundles. Finding the one she wanted, she untied the wrapper and extracted a small, purple-coloured leaf.

"What's the verdict?" Ryzak asked anxiously.

"Cracked skull and minor concussion," she replied, thrusting the leaf into his mouth. "Chew on this while I go and find something to bandage your head: it will help relieve the pain."

She returned moments later carrying a strip of material that she had torn from her tunic and soaked in water. Ryzak was still chewing the leaf as she knelt beside him and gently bandaged his head. When she had finished, she rose and stepped back to admire her handiwork.

"Not perfect, but it will have to do," she said. "How are you feeling?"

Ryzak looked up at her. "A lot better, thanks. The pain has dulled and I can actually see properly; no bright lights!" He gave her a grateful smile.

"Good! Spit the leaf out. It's done its work."

"Eh?"

"I said spit the leaf out. You don't need it now. I'll give you another to chew on if the pain returns."

"Errrr, can't do that."

"Why?" she asked, raising an eyebrow. She folded her arms and stared down at him. "Tell me you haven't swallowed it!"

Ryzak hesitantly nodded his head. "Sorry. Didn't realise I shouldn't have."

A grin appeared on Neulee's face. "Oh dear. I think I shall move to the other side of the cave for a while, near to the gate. Get some fresh air." She tugged at the collar of her tunic, feigning discomfort, as she backed away. "Phew! Don't you think it's a bit stuffy in here?"

Ryzak watched her retreating figure anxiously. "Wh–wh–what's the matter?" he asked.

"You'll see," she giggled. "Oh, and by the way, the latrine is over there." Laughing, she pointed to a crevice at the back of the cave.

Ryzak looked over to where she indicated, just as the first spasm rippled through his gut. He jumped to his feet, the cheeks of his buttocks firmly clenched, and rushed to the crevice as fast as a man whose world is about to blow apart – in the most embarrassing manner.

* * * * *

The heat of arousal coursed through Snorkel as his nurse's bare breasts brushed the skin of his chest. He was in paradise. Having come round to find himself being ministered to by a buxom, semi-naked beauty, he had no intention of letting her know he was awake in case she stopped. He was not that stupid.

A low moan of pleasure escaped his lips. It was too much for a dwarf to take. Fighting a losing battle against self-restraint, his arms slowly rose to encircle the girl's thick waist.

At the feel of his hands against her bare flesh, his nurse's sweetly-hummed tune turned into a scream of alarm. Dropping her damp rag, her fist flew to her mouth and she scampered away safely out of arm's reach. She studied her patient with fear-filled eyes.

Realising he had frightened her, Snorkel gave a reassuring grin and levered himself up on an elbow. "Don't worry, lass. I'll not harm you," he assured. Quite the opposite, he thought, admiring her with a merry twinkle in his eye.

Her fist lowered as she returned his smile coyly, a hint of pink colouring her cheeks as she averted her gaze and scuffled a foot in the dust of the floor at his appreciative look.

Boy she's a stunner, thought Snorkel.

Except for the small loincloth that covered her pubic area, the girl was naked. Passions that he had not felt for a long time became aroused in him. His eyes feasted hungrily on her bare flesh; her large, pendulous breasts, looking like a pair of quivering jellies topped with ripe, juicy cherries; her short, chunky legs, built for stamina; the wobbling mass of her belly; the wild, sticky-out tangle of her hair; the stubble on her chin. She was the next best thing to a she-dwarf. It did not matter to him that she had 'ten-past-two' eyes; it only added to her uniqueness. He heaved a contented sigh. Now he knew how Ryzak felt. He was in love. Or lust. He was not quite sure yet.

He sat up and swung his legs over the side of the low, straw-covered slab on which he had been lying.

The girl's eyes widened in surprise and she snorted loudly. Her deep, barking laugh reverberated around the small cave. Turning on her heel, she lumbered away, the echoes of her laughter remaining long after she had disappeared.

"Wait!" Snorkel called after her retreating figure, wondering what had made her run off like that. Looking down he suddenly realised, as the object of her amusement poked into view. It would appear that she was not the only one who had been naked.

Snorkel felt the heat of embarrassment colour his face and scanned his surroundings for his robe. Apart from the slab he was sitting on, the cave was unadorned. No furnishings, no rugs, no wall-hangings, – NO ROBE! "Where are my clothes?" he called out in frustration.

"They are being repaired, Divine One," a heavily accented voice informed him from the cave entrance. "Your recent tumble damaged them."

A tall and wiry dark-skinned man entered and bowed low. He was also naked apart from a small loincloth. As he strode towards the dwarf, his matted beard split in a grin, revealing perfect white teeth. Perfect apart from the canines. They had been filed to needle-sharp points.

"Cannibals!" Snorkel yelled in terror, darting behind the slab.

The man halted his advance, a look of surprise on his face. "What is wrong, Divine One? Have I offended you?"

From his crouched position, Snorkel peered over the top of the slab. He watched in astonishment as the cannibal fell to his knees and prostrated himself on the floor, where he began rocking backwards and forwards. The palms of his hands slapped against the ground as he repeated over and over again, "I beg forgiveness, Divine One. I beg forgiveness Divine One …"

Snorkel slowly rose and stared down at the subservient, unkempt savage in front of him. "Why do you keep calling me Divine One?" he asked, nonplussed.

"Because you are," the man replied, halting his litany to kneel and stare at the dwarf.

"Oh!" responded Snorkel, none the wiser.

Seeing the little man's blank look, the savage explained. "It has been foretold by our shamans, ever since the first De'Athman, that the 'Divine One' would appear to us in our time of need. He would lead us and guide us, take us away from our miserable existence. He would be a man of great magic, a man of honour, a man of wisdom. And you are he!"

The last was said with such conviction that Snorkel dared not contradict his claim, nor did he want to. Instead, standing taller, he pulled himself up to his full four foot seven inches in height and puffed out his chest. He liked the sound of this. "Yep! That sounds like me. Tell me, er …"

"De'Athman the 23rd, Divine One."

"Tell me, De'Athman the 23rd …"

"Dee, will do," interrupted De'Athman, grinning.

"Oh! Right then. Dee it is. How did you know I was the one?"

A perplexed look crossed Dee's face. "By the sign," he replied. It was Snorkel's turn to look confused. "What sign?"

"The sign on your robe," the cannibal answered.

Noticing a hint of doubt entering the man's voice, Snorkel smiled. "Ahhhhh! And this sign means I am the one, does it?"

"Our Shaman says so," replied De'Athman, "unless you tell me it is not so." His brows knitted in a hard frown. The type of frown that said, 'you'd better be, or we're having you for supper, mate.'

The look was not lost on Snorkel. He had to stop himself taking a step back under the fierceness of the man's gaze. He gave a nervous laugh.

"No, no! I am he, as you quite rightly spotted. I was just checking. We 'Divine Ones' like to have our little jokes. Keep you on your toes." He grinned, relieved to see that Dee responded with a smile of his own. He rubbed his hands together. "Now then, where's my robe?" he asked.

"Here, Divine One."

His heart skipped a beat as he heard the voice. Her voice. Looking at the cave entrance, Snorkel saw his former nurse waddle towards him, a shy smile on her face as she brought him his repaired robe. His eyes glazed over as he drank in her beauty.

Placing the garment on the slab she gave him a bashful look. At least he thought she did. It was hard to tell when one eye seemed to be fixed on the wall beside him and the other on Dee. She gave a throaty giggle, then turned and fled.

"Aherm!" The sound of De'Athman clearing his throat dragged the dwarf's attention back to the man. Realising he was still naked, Snorkel grabbed his robe and quickly donned it. He leaned against the slab, trying to appear nonchalant under Dee's penetrating gaze.

"So, Dee. Have you any idea where my fr– my attendants are?"

"They are safe, Divine One. You will see them again tonight, at the feast we have prepared in your honour."

"Yeahhhhh, excellent!" exclaimed Snorkel, clapping his hands in delight. He loved parties. "Will, er, will …" he said, raising his eyebrows in query and nodding towards the cave mouth.

De'Athman's eyes twinkled with pride. "Yes. My daughter, Meelan, will also be there."

"Splendid," beamed Snorkel. He stepped forward to grasp Dee's arm and lead him towards the entrance. "Come. Take me to my attendants. I can't wait to tell them about this."

The little man jerked to a halt as De'Athman suddenly stopped. "Why would you want to tell them," he queried, "when they are to be the highlight of the evening?"

"In what way?"

"They are the grand finale, so to speak."

"Oh," said Snorkel, slightly disappointed they would not be joining him until later on. "So they won't be eating with us then?"

The leader of the cannibals laughed. "Eating with us? Why no, Divine One. They are to be eaten by us. They are the main course. It is a great honour for them to be chosen as such."

The dwarf was aghast. "What?"

"Is there a problem?" De'Athman enquired. "We could always have them first, if you prefer."

"Yes! No! I mean, I don't want them at all!" Snorkel shrieked. "They are my friends. I don't want to eat them. Anybody as a matter of fact." Then a brainwave hit him. "I'm a ve– er, veg– er, vegetable!" he exclaimed.

De'Athman frowned in confusion. "What's one of them?"

"I don't eat meat," Snorkel replied. "Didn't you know that?"

De'Athman shook his head and looked at the little man as if he was daft.

"Well, it's all to do with being the Divine One," Snorkel explained, his demeanour taking on a serious mien. "That's how we keep pure of body and pure of mind. Meat has all sorts … all sorts … all sorts of bad things in it, you see? Turns you mad in the end, it does. That's why we don't eat it."

De'Athman looked dejected. "So we can't cook them?"

"No!"

"Not even a little?" the leader of the De'Athshead wheedled.

"No!"

"Well that buggers that then," he said sullenly.

"Come on," said Snorkel, "it's not that bad. Take me to them. We can still have a feast. It just won't have any meat in it, that's all."

Masking his disappointment, De'Athman allowed Snorkel to lead him to the entrance.

The dwarf emerged into the light of day, squinting against the unaccustomed glare. Once his eyesight had adjusted, he gazed around in wonder at the scene of everyday activity.

Children played and laughed in the warm rays of the late afternoon sun. A few scrawny dogs yapped and chased each other around the village. Men and women carried bundles of timber to the large fire being built in the pit below the cave dwellings. You would never have guessed these people were cannibals. Apart from their pointy teeth, that is.

Fire pit?

Snorkel gasped. It was large – very large. A spit ran across its centre, supported by two large timber posts set in the ground either side of the stone hearth. A turning handle was clearly visible at one end. A cold shiver ran through him as he realised what it was for. Noticing that De'Athman had moved ahead, he quickened his pace to catch up with him. Hopefully he had done enough to convince the man that the pit would not be needed this night.

As they progressed through the village towards the dark splotches of cave-mouths, the tribespeople they passed stopped what they were doing to dip their heads in reverence. Enjoying every minute of his new-found elevated status, Snorkel grinned and waved as if he were royalty.

Soon they arrived outside a guarded cave. After a brief, muttered conversation with De'Athman the two guards moved aside and opened the timber gate for them. They waited until their leader and the dwarf had entered, then followed them in.

Ryzak and Neulee looked up in astonishment as the gate opened and Snorkel entered with the scrawny looking savage, the two guards taking protective positions beside them.

"Nothing to say?" beamed the dwarf, relieved to see his two friends unharmed.

"What? How?" mumbled Ryzak, rising to his feet.

"Out with it, dwarf," growled Neulee, also standing and taking a pace forward. "What have you been up to?"

"Nothing!" spluttered Snorkel. "Honest!"

Seeing the Divine One threatened, the guards advanced, clubs raised.

Snorkel waved them back and gave De'Athman a thin smile. "They are usually more pleased to see me than this," he assured him. "They'll be fine in a moment."

De'Athman shook his head and turned to leave. He motioned for the guards to be alert in their duties, before walking from the cave.

Moving to sit next to Ryzak, Snorkel gave Neulee a warning look and motioned for her to join them on the floor. Once settled, he attempted to make light conversation to calm the guards. The two men were scowling, as if daring Ryzak and Neulee to make a wrong move so they could put the clubs to use.

"What happened to your head?" Snorkel asked Ryzak.

"Cracked skull and concussion," he replied with a wry grin. "Fortunately, I had a good nurse."

Ignoring the compliment, Neulee fixed her gaze on Snorkel. "Well?"

"Well what?"

"Well, how come you're not in the cooking pot and why did they treat you as some sort of king?"

He gave a smug smile. "Because I am." He sniggered at the looks of astonishment on his friends' faces.

"How?" gasped Ryzak.

Snorkel grinned, enjoying his moment. "Well …" he began.

When he finished his tale, Ryzak and Neulee shook their heads in amazement.

"So let me see if I've got this right," said Ryzak. "Because you have a badly embroidered death's-head on the back of your robe they think you are some sort of god, returned from your godly abode to guide them and lead them on the path to glory?"

"Yep! That about sums it up," replied Snorkel, proudly. "Divine One, that's me," he said, puffing out his chest and tapping it with a stubby forefinger.

"So just why aren't we going to be cooked?" asked Neulee. "You still haven't explained why we are not to be the main course in this feast of theirs."

"Ahhh, yes," said Snorkel, reddening, "I was coming to that bit. A brilliant piece of fast thinking by me, if I might say so. The thought is mightier than the sword, or something like that."

"Yes, yes," snapped Neulee. "Answer the question, idiot!"

Snorkel gave her an injured look before answering. "I told them I was a vegetable," he said proudly, crossing his arms and looking at them with a self-satisfied smirk on his face.

A smile appeared on Neulee's face. She grinned and turned to Ryzak.

Puzzled by her reaction to his stroke of genius, Snorkel switched his gaze to Ryzak. The corners of the man's mouth were twitching. Just what the hell was tickling those two?

Snorkel frowned with annoyance as the smiles turned to chuckles, the chuckles to laughs. He became furious when they both fell about clutching at their sides. Jumping to his feet, he stood with hands on hips glowering at the hysterical duo. "All right, out with it. What's so damned funny?"

Ryzak looked up, tears streaming down his face. "What sort are you? A cabbage?" He keeled over, clinging to Neulee in his hysteria.

The dwarf's foot beat an angry tattoo as he waited for their laughter to subside. "When you've quite finished," he snapped, "I've just saved your miserable lives!"

"I'm sorry, Snorkel," smirked Neulee, dabbing tears from her cheeks. "It's just that, well, what you should have said was 'vegetarian'. A vegetable is what you eat. You got confused, that's all, and used the wrong word. It's just as well the savage did not know what you meant, or we'd all be in the stew by now." She fell into helpless fits of laughter again.

Now that he understood why they were laughing, Snorkel could see the funny side – sort of. The corners of his mouth began to twitch. Soon he was laughing as heartily as they.

The two guards looked on. Turning to his colleague, one of them raised his eyebrows and twirled a forefinger at his temple in the universal sign for lunatics. The other grinned and nodded his agreement. Chuckling to themselves, they moved outside to stand beside the entrance.

Chapter Sixteen

Sitting on the floor of the cave, deep in discussion, they did not hear De'Athman enter. It was only when he cleared his throat to attract their attention that they realised he was there and swiftly turned to face him. He stood a pace inside the cave, the bare skin of his scrawny body like burnished copper in the fading light of day.

"Your people are ready to receive you and your guests, Divine One," he announced, bowing low.

Ryzak cast Neulee a nervous glance. How much had the savage heard? Neulee gave an almost imperceptible shake of her head and shrugged.

Snorkel smiled up at the leader of the De'Athshead and rose to his feet. "Lead on, De'Athman the 23rd. The Divine One would like to address his people and inform them of his wishes."

The head of the tribe returned his smile, gave a curt nod of approval, then turned to leave the cave.

Ryzak sagged in relief. If the savage had heard anything, he was pretty good at pretending he hadn't. He scrambled to his feet and gripped the dwarf by the shoulder, spinning him round. "You remember what it is you have to say?" he asked, peering into his eyes for any hint of uncertainty.

"Relax," Snorkel smirked. "What do you think I am, stupid?"

Before Ryzak had a chance to answer, Neulee interrupted. "Come. It is best we do not keep him waiting. If he did overhear anything, the delay will only make him suspicious." Leading Ryzak firmly by the arm, she dragged him to the cave mouth.

De'Athman was waiting at the bottom of the short, rocky incline leading down to the basin floor, his figure a dark silhouette against the brightness of the large fire behind him. He gave a brief nod of greeting at their arrival, then turned and led them towards a raised mound set in front of the fire.

As they neared it, a bald, naked, wrinkled old man shot out in front of them, his emaciated body daubed in strange red markings.

His eyes held a fervent gleam as he danced around, chanting in some strange language and waving a bone rattle in the air. Occasionally he stopped his prancing to thrust the noisemaker at the dwarf and jabber incomprehensibly.

"Who's he?" Ryzak asked, casting Snorkel a nervous glance. He was half expecting the dwarf to be cowering from the on-slaught; however, the little man was grinning and taking it all in his stride. He appeared to actually be enjoying it.

"He is Gothurn, our shaman," answered De'Athman. "He is blessing the Divine One and his servants."

His gaze still fixed on Snorkel, Ryzak's eyes hardened. Servants?

Halting beside the mound, De'Athman gestured for the painted man to leave them, then turned to Snorkel. "Wait here, Divine One," he said, dipping his head, "I shall announce you."

As he moved away, Ryzak turned and glared at the dwarf. "Servants?"

"Shhh! You'll spoil the show," Snorkel replied. "Anyway, I had to tell them something, otherwise you'd have ended up in the pot."

The sound of De'Athman addressing the tribe cut short any retort Ryzak might have made. The man, his voice strong and powerful, spoke in excited tones. Not that Ryzak had any idea what he was saying, as he spoke in the language of the tribe. He could have been telling them dinner was fresh on the hoof, for all Ryzak knew.

De'Athman's speech ended in a high-pitched vocal flourish. He turned and gestured for them to join him.

Ryzak looked on as Snorkel strode onto the mound. The little man had a wide smile plastered over his face and his arms were raised in salute. All that was missing was a fanfare. Ryzak turned to Neulee and shook his head.

Mounting the large, flat-topped section of raised rock, Ryzak noticed a small, blackened shape on the spit over the fire. "What in hell's name is that?" he wondered aloud.

Neulee looked to where he was staring. "Looks like a pigeon to me," she answered. "Not much to feed this lot on," she added, nodding her head at the sea of expectant faces looking their way.

Turning, Ryzak saw what she meant. There were hundreds of them. Men, women and children of all ages sat on the ground before them. They looked ferocious in the fire's light. He gulped in apprehension. The dwarf had better get this right, or they would be next on the spit.

The subject of his concerns stood beside De'Athman gazing down at the mass of faces below him. A sheen of perspiration covered his face.

"He looks a little nervous," Neulee murmured.

"He's not the only one," replied Ryzak.

"My people," Snorkel began, his voice strong and firm.

Ryzak flinched in surprise as De'Athman repeated the dwarf's words in the tongue of the tribe. He frowned. Hopefully nothing would be lost in the translation.

"My people! I bring you greetings from the gods."

The eyes of the watching audience grew wide in superstitious adulation as De'Athman translated his words.

"They send you greetings through me, their humble servant."

"He's a natural," Neulee whispered. "They're hanging on his every word. Especially that girl at the front with the funny eyes."

"Aye," Ryzak muttered, not convinced the dwarf could pull it off. "Let's hope he doesn't get too carried away and start having delusions of grandeur. If he doesn't stick to the script we agreed, I'll skin him alive." He glanced at the spit behind him. "Or then again, I may just cook him."

He yelped as Neulee's elbow connected with his ribs.

"Shut up and listen, you fool. Or the dwarf will not be the only one to receive serious bodily harm."

Safely concealed by the darkness, three pairs of almond-shaped eyes watched the proceedings. Hidden from view by a rocky outcrop at the entrance to the village, the three elves listened to Snorkel's words.

"What is the dwarf up to?" Rhudrhyn muttered in disbelief, "and why haven't those savages cooked him yet?"

His astonishment grew as Snorkel informed his enthralled audience how he and his companions had travelled long and hard to be with them. They had come to inform them of the gods' wishes and to lead them, his people, to their destiny. The gods loved their children and were proud of them. However, now it was time to leave their spartan existence behind, give up their barbaric ways and travel the lands as missionaries. The world was full of heathens and non-believers. It was up to the tribe to preach to the ungodly and convert them.

"He really is rather good," murmured Rhudrhyn admiringly. "Look at the faces of those savages. They are totally in awe of him. They actually believe him."

"My people. My brothers, my sisters," Snorkel's voice boomed through the night.

Rhudrhyn shivered as if a cold breeze had just washed over him. The hairs on the back of his neck prickled and pins and needles worked their way up his body from the tips of his fingers and toes. He looked nervously across at his companions. He could tell by their apprehensive expressions that they were experiencing the same sensations.

Turning back to watch the dwarf, he gasped as his gaze rested on the little man. A haze of translucent, purple energy could be seen emanating from his outstretched hands, pulsing in time with the sound of his voice as it resounded through the still night air. The haze drifted through the tribe, touching and caressing each one of them before moving to the next.

"Magic!" snarled Rhudrhyn through gritted teeth. "I knew he was dangerous. We should have killed the little bastard when we had the chance!"

"What are we going to do?" a nervous voice asked from beside him.

"Do?" snarled Rhudrhyn. "We do what we came here to do. Kill the cave-rat and his cronies and take their heads back to the queen. String your bows!"

Snorkel's impassioned voice continued in the background as Rhudrhyn's cohorts carried out his command.

"I am here to show you the way to fulfilment, enlightenment, enrichment. From this day on we shall eat no meat. We shall live off the land. Pure in body, soul and mind. You are to be disciples.

Less than gods but more than men. This is the message of the Divine One!"

Rhudrhyn peered around the rock. His face twisted in anger as he saw the whole tribe prostrate themselves. The dwarf, his arms raised to the sky, was gazing down at his converts with a beatific expression on his face.

Rhudrhyn raised his bow. It was time to put a halt to this charade.

Snorkel gazed down in amazement. How the hell had he managed to carry this one off? Revelling in his moment of glory, he caught Meelan's eye and gave her a broad wink. He could only catch the one: the other was gazing at a spot fifty paces to his right.

His smile started to fade. The prepared speech over, he was at a loss what to do next. Hoping for a hint, he turned his head to peer anxiously at Ryzak and Neulee.

Noticing his look of alarm, Neulee mouthed, "Get them to stand up!"

"What?" Snorkel mouthed back.

"GET THEM TO STAND UP!"

Snorkel gave a relieved smile, finally understanding what she meant. Turning to address the throng, he opened his mouth to speak. Then, in panic, he swung back to face Neulee. "What then?"

Before she could answer, a low rumble filled the air. It began as a far off susurration, like pebbles falling down a mountainside, gradually growing in volume until it sounded as though the whole mountain was following.

Snorkel looked up. Icy fingers of fear clutched at his heart as the noise increased. He had an awful feeling about this. What if he had upset the real gods? What if they were so pissed they had sent winged demons down to teach the impostor a lesson? He could hear nervous mutterings amongst the tribe; they were becoming agitated. He looked around and saw fear on people's faces. Even De'Athman appeared terrified. Of the little shaman there was no sign. He appeared to have scuttled off at the first indication of trouble.

The noise level reached a crescendo, sounding as though it was coming from directly above their heads. Men, women and children clung to each other. The shaman reappeared, chanting maniacally as he danced around the fire and shook his rattle at the heavens.

Snorkel shrieked in terror and dropped to the ground as the leathery flap of wings descended from above. He curled into a ball.

Demons!

Fearing for his life, Ryzak clung to Neulee for protection.

"Well I'll be blowed," Rhudrhyn gasped in amazement, lowering his bow. "Dragonets! Hundreds of them. The dwarf's pet must have survived, after all, and brought reinforcements. Quick! Now is our chance. Let's get closer. No one will notice us with all this going on."

The she-wolf's large, yellow eyes fixed them with a deadly stare as she advanced on the elves from behind. Teeth bared, fangs dripping with saliva, she closed in.

Snorkel dared not look up to see what was going on. Although, by the screams and yells, he could imagine what the scene would look like. He just hoped his own death would be quick and painless.

The flap of wings sounded immediately over his head. He screamed. He screamed louder still when he heard a small body hitting the ground next to him.

Waving his arms to ward off attack, he kept his head safely tucked between his knees. "Go and get someone else. I'm too small to eat!"

'What are you on about, Mum?' came a voice inside his head. *'We're here to rescue you, not to eat you!'*

Bewildered, thinking he recognised the voice of Draco, Snorkel peeped out from between his legs. He spotted the lime-green dragonet standing beside him.

"Draco?"

'Of course it's me. Who else did you think it was?'

Snorkel smiled in relief and scrambled to his feet. The smile disappeared as he gazed in dismay at the devastation surrounding him. Everywhere he looked he could see tribespeople running around, swatting at the winged creatures diving down at them. "What have you done?" he murmured.

'Saved you, of course. They are my brothers and sisters,' Draco said proudly.

"Oh no," gasped Snorkel. "This has spoilt everything!"

'Well, if that's all the thanks I get, next time you can save yourself. See if I care.'

The dwarf fixed her with an anxious look. "No, no!" he shouted. "You don't understand. Listen!"

Ryzak and Neulee joined them as he was summing up. Hearing Snorkel finish, Neulee cut in. "Wait a minute. This can be turned to our advantage." She pulled them together and quickly explained what she had in mind. A wide grin spread over the dwarf's face as he listened. His people were about to see the Divine One in action. That should impress Meelan even more.

Knowing what she was to do, Draco took to the air to carry out her part of the plan. Snorkel waited for a minute before standing to address the fast-disappearing tribe. In a voice filled with power, his words boomed around the rocky basin.

"BEGONE, FOUL CREATURES OF MISHTAR! BEGONE, BEFORE YOU SUFFER THE WRATH OF THE DIVINE ONE!"

In a flurry of wings and fear-filled screeches, the dragonets disappeared. One minute they were everywhere; the next, gone.

Although still wary, the people of the De'Athshead gradually drifted back to the fire, nursing their wounds and abrasions, looking extremely sorry for themselves.

The dwarf's voice sounded again. "My people! Did I not tell you we are just below gods?"

De'Athman, blood streaming down his face from a bite on his cheek, hobbled to Snorkel's side and, with rather less enthusiasm than before, translated his words.

"You have just seen the power of the Divine One. The demons of the evil Mishtar, sent here to halt our plans, have been vanquished! You, my people, have made me proud!"

The dwarf paused to look at the dubious expressions on the faces staring at him. His gaze fell on Meelan. Although appearing terrified, she did not seem to have suffered any harm. He gave her a smile, then spoke again.

"You truly are more than men!"

Surprised by the Divine One's praise, De'Athman's eyes shone with pride as he translated the words. Then, tears of happiness streaming down his face, he turned to the dwarf and embraced him in a fierce hug.

Unprepared for such a show of enthusiasm, Snorkel found he could not breathe when his face became buried in the man's stomach. By the time De'Athman released him he was about to pass out; and not just from lack of air. The odour from the man's unwashed body would curdle milk.

As he stood recovering, the little shaman ran out of the crowd and skidded to a halt in front of him. "Moooremen?" he asked.

Somehow managing to smile, Snorkel nodded his head. "Yes," he croaked, "you are now more than men."

A wide grin spread over Gothurn's face. "Moooremen," he repeated to himself quietly. Then, shaking his rattle in delight, he turned to face the tribe. Arms spread wide, he shouted, "Mooore-men! Moooremen! Moooremen!" Repeating the refrain at the top of his voice, he ran off to dance around the fire, where he was soon joined by the rest of the tribe as the chant was taken up.

Safely concealed in the hollow they had dropped into when the dragonets disappeared, Rhudrhyn and his men trained their arrows on the dwarf and the two humans.

"On the count of three," commanded Rhudrhyn. "One, two …" A deep, threatening growl interrupted him.

The startled elves swung round. Their eyes fixed on the form of the she-wolf; a bristling mass of grey fur and bared, saliva-dripping teeth. Fifty dragonets stood behind her, emitting low grumbles of anger.

The wolf sprang. Following her lead, the dragonets launched themselves at the would-be assassins. The elves screamed in terror, dropped their bows and fled into the night, their pursuers snapping and nipping at their heels.

* * * * *

As there had been no sign of pursuit for the preceding three hours,

Rhudrhyn slowed his horse to a trot and motioned for the other riders to do the same. They needed to rest. It was time to start thinking about a camp. They all had wounds that needed attention and they were tired.

It was as well they had left their horses fully tacked for a speedy exit, or they would have suffered more. That and the elves' natural ability as runners had saved them from a severe mauling.

It took another hour of riding before a suitable place to halt was found. Sliding wearily from his mount, Rhudrhyn handed the reins to Teevalrhyn. "No fire tonight," he ordered. "That wolf may still be around and we do not want to signal our presence. You take the first watch. Stay awake and keep your eyes and ears open."

Grumbling to himself, Teevalrhyn tended to the horses, then settled himself in a small stand of bushes slightly back from the camp. From there he could safely watch the trail and also see the sleeping forms of his comrades.

"Rhudi," a warm, inviting voice whispered, "where are you?"

He looked around, trying to locate the source. "Where … Who are you?" he called, nervously scanning the unrelieved whiteness of his surroundings.

"Over here, my love," the whispery voice replied.

"Iderlrhys?"

"Of course, Rhudi. Who did you think it was? Come to me, your reward is waiting."

Rhudrhyn smiled to himself and headed in the direction he thought the voice had come from. He could not see a thing through the thick white mist that enveloped him. "Where are you?" he called.

"Over here," the voice of his queen directed. "Please hurry. My body aches for you. You have no idea how much I want you."

The voice sounded more substantial than before. He thought he could sense where Iderlrhys was. He also made out the throaty, seductive intent behind her words. Smiling in anticipation, he altered course towards the place where he thought she waited.

He jumped in alarm as a gossamer-thin veil of white silk wafted across his face. He licked nervously at dry lips and slowly made his way forward, carefully moving aside the hangings.

"There you are, my love," the queen's voice said, as he moved aside the last veil. "Come to me, run your fingers through my hair. It's been too long, Rhudi. Far too long."

Seeing his queen naked, Rhudrhyn removed his clothing and joined her on the bed at the centre of the hanging veils. Her bare back was towards him as he knelt on the soft, feather mattress behind her. He gently removed the ivory-handled brush from her long, delicate fingers and placed his hands on the alabaster skin of her shoulders. Tenderly, he pulled her round to face him.

His scream of pain and terror sounded loud and long before it was abruptly cut off.

The form of Iderlrhys stared down at the remains of Rhudrhyn lying on the gore-spattered sheets. Her face lit with an evil smile as she admired the warm heart she held in the palm of her outstretched hand.

She gave a deep, booming laugh as she gazed at the dead body, and her features slowly started to melt. The pretty face and breathtaking figure started to run into one, to disappear, revealing a darker, more masculine form beneath.

Mishtar wiped the filth from his face as he glared angrily at the corpse. "Oh yes," he snarled. "How I've been waiting to give you your reward!"

Teevalryhn awoke with a start. Someone was shaking his shoulder. He must have dozed off.

"Wh–what is it?" he asked, trying to clear his sleep-befuddled mind.

"You'd best come and look at this," a tremulous voice replied.

Teevalrhyn looked up into the pale, frightened face of Neharhyn. "What is it, Neh?" he asked, fearful of the answer.

"It's Rhudi. He's dead!"

"How?" asked Teevalrhyn, quickly scrambling to his feet.

"Just come and see," his friend urged, shaking his head. "I'd better warn you, though, it's not pretty."

Teevalrhyn followed his companion back to the unmoving form of their leader. Rhudrhyn's glazed, lifeless eyes stared up from the white, pasty flesh of his corpse.

"Looks like he died in his sleep," Teevalrhyn commented. "This will upset the queen. He was her favourite."

"This will upset her even more," stated Neharhyn. He stooped and pulled the blankets away from the body. Teevalrhyn stared down in horror at the gaping wound in Rhudrhyn's chest where the heart should have been.

* * * * *

A week after Snorkel's rousing speech, he, Ryzak and Neulee silently stole away from the De'Athshead village in the dead of night, taking their reclaimed horses with them and covering their tracks to avoid being followed.

"Do you think they will do as we've taught them?" asked Ryzak the following morning, as they rode to their prearranged meeting with Draco.

"Dunno," replied Snorkel. "They seem keen enough. But then again, they're only savages. They'll probably be back to their old ways inside a week or two."

Dropping back to join the conversation, Neulee gave the dwarf a nod. "I don't know. They appeared to be mighty impressed, specially young Meelan," she said, with a smirk and a knowing wink.

Snorkel's face flushed crimson. "I don't know what you mean," he muttered indignantly, spurring Clara ahead.

Ryzak shrugged and gave Neulee a wry grin. "Don't worry. He's always a little tetchy."

"Mmm," responded Neulee thoughtfully, gazing after the little man.

Little did the trio know how well they had taught the newly named Moremen tribe. Their name would become far more feared than that of the De'Athshead. The Divine One's mysterious dis-appearance fully convinced the savages of their gods' wishes and they set about their allotted tasks with gusto. In years to come, when pairs of them appeared in towns, espousing the virtues of purity for the body and soul, the cry would go out: "Lock the doors; pretend we're out. The bloody Moremen are here again!"

Chapter Seventeen

The higher they climbed the more tortuous their route became. More than once Snorkel wished he had wings like Draco and could fly up the mountainside. His short arms and legs could not reach the handholds and footholds that Ryzak and Neulee used and he was growing tired. "How much further?" he asked his airborne companion. "I can't take much more of this. My arms feel like they're about to drop off."

'Not much further now,' Draco replied. *'We'll be at the ledge before nightfall.'*

"Nightfall!" groaned Snorkel. "That's hours away. I'll never make it!"

"Quit moaning, dwarf!" Neulee shouted down. "If you put as much energy into climbing as you do into talking we'd be there by now."

"Humph. Women!" grumbled Snorkel under his breath.

'I heard that,' Draco informed him.

They had left their horses in a makeshift corral further down the mountain. There was enough food and water to last them three or four days, by which time they hoped to have completed their task. The trail had become too steep to risk taking the horses any further, and common sense prevailing for once, thanks to Neulee, they had decided to leave them behind.

After their rendezvous with the dragonet, the journey to Firestone Mountain had been both short and boring. The infamous mountain proved to be a higher, steeper fold in the land than the surrounding hills. Three days of looking at grey rock, sleeping on grey rock, swallowing the dust of grey rock and listening to the metallic ring of the horses' hooves striking grey rock had driven the trio into dull, melancholy moods. Their disposition only brightened when the home of the dragon's lair came into view.

"I can see it!" Ryzak shouted down.

Snorkel glanced up to see a long pair of legs disappearing over the edge of a ledge. Still a good thirty feet away, he struggled to make his arms and legs stretch to the nooks and crannies that would enable him to reach it as well. As he slowly made his way up, the handholds seemed to be further apart with each yard he climbed.

Above him his companions sprawled on the ledge to await his arrival. The climb had taken its toll and they were resting quivering limbs. Draco curled up in Neulee's lap and chirruped happily. The heat of the late afternoon sun began to work its spell. Within moments they drifted off to sleep.

"HEEEEEELP!"

The loud cry of distress roused Ryzak from his slumber. He yawned and rubbed his eyes as he sat up. He gazed around in confusion before the realisation of where he was sank in. The cry sounded again.

"HEEEEEELP!"

Draco woke with a start and bugled her alarm as she took to the air, disappearing down the mountain, waking Neulee as she went.

"It sounds like Snorkel," Ryzak said.

Neulee looked at the angle of the sun, her face creasing in worry. "He should have been here ages ago. We must have been sleeping for at least half an hour."

Ryzak crawled to the edge and poked his head over the yawning drop. He spotted the little man about fifteen feet below him, clinging to the rock face like his life depended on it. Which, unfortunately, it did.

"What's the matter?" Ryzak shouted. "We haven't got all day. Get a move on!"

"I can't," Snorkel yelled back, "I'm stuck!"

"What?"

"I can't move. The handholds are too far away. If I try to climb, I'll fall off."

Ryzak groaned. "Wait there. I'll see if I can find something to pull you up."

"If I move, the only place I'll be going is down," Snorkel grumbled, and glanced under his outstretched arms to the rocky ground below. It was the worst thing he could have done. As he stared at the vast distance between him and the base of the cliff his vision started to swim. His arms and legs began to tremble.

"Heeeeelp!" he called out in terror, screwing his eyes tight shut, concentrating on keeping his body glued to the cliff face. But no matter how hard he tried, he could not clear the image of that long drop from his mind.

'What's up, Mum?' Draco enquired, her voice full of concern.

Snorkel eased an eye open to look at the lime-green dragonet hovering nearby.

"I'm stuck," he whispered, through gritted teeth. "I can't move!"

A scraping sound from above caused him to glance up, but the rattle of small rocks bouncing down made him hug the wall even closer. His sudden movement loosened the purchase of his footholds. He screamed in terror as his feet lost their grip and he was left suspended hundreds of feet above the ground, hanging by his fingertips.

"Be quiet, I won't let you fall," came the authoritative voice of Neulee as she grabbed the back of his robe. With a swift tug she hoisted him up so that his feet could grip the rock. "Climb ahead of me," she ordered, "I'll push you from behind. When you get near the top Ryzak will pull you the rest of the way."

Eventually Snorkel managed to scramble over the lip of the ledge. He lay on the rocky outcrop, exhausted, and never moved even when Draco hopped down beside him to screech his triumph.

Helping Neulee up over the edge, Ryzak turned to stand over the dwarf. "I thought your sort were supposed to be good climbers. What *were* you doing down there?"

Snorkel levered himself up on an elbow and gave him a hard stare. His heart still raced from his near-fall and this was all he needed. A dumb human! "Just because we live in mountains doesn't mean we are good at climbing them. Where I come from we have steps! Being backward, you wouldn't know about such things!" he growled.

"Backward?" snarled Ryzak, his hands balling into fists.

"CHILDREN!" interrupted Neulee. "When you have quite finished, we have a seal to find. Now kiss and make up and let's be on our way."

Snorkel glowered and rose to his feet, then stomped off.

'Mum!' Draco's voice sounded in his head.

"What?"

'You're going the wrong way. The entrance to Reizgoth's cave is in the other direction.'

The dwarf did a swift about-turn and stomped back, ignoring the smiles of amusement as he strode past his two companions.

The pathway leading to Reizgoth's lair was both long and arduous, working its way round the mountain like a snake with belly ache; all ups and downs and sudden hairpin corners that took the path back on itself. The one constant factor was the precipitous drop waiting to catch the careless footfall. In some places the ledge was wide and level, but in others it dwindled down to a narrow ribbon, scarcely protruding from the rocky face. After both Ryzak and Neulee had suffered near-fatal mishaps with the crumbling rock of the pathway, the group proceeded with caution.

They had been walking for half an hour when they spotted the entrance to Reizgoth's cave. Relieved that their goal was in sight, they made their way down the last leg of the trail as it disappeared behind a large outcrop of rock, rising sharply before levelling out onto a small plateau immediately in front of the cave mouth. They stopped at the top of the climb and looked nervously across the open ground that stood between them and the opening.

"There are an awful lot of boulders around here," Ryzak observed, scanning the smooth rock face and trying to figure out how they could have got there.

"They're not boulders," Neulee remarked grimly, "they're bones. Look." She walked to the nearest *boulder* and picked it up, returning to Ryzak with the prize in her hand.

His face drained of colour as he looked down at the yellowed skull. "Wh–wh–what is it?"

"Looks like a sheep to me," said Snorkel, with an air of confidence. "What's the matter? Scared all of a sudden?"

"It's a goat, actually," corrected Neulee.

"Oh," said Snorkel, pretending not to notice the smile that appeared on Ryzak's face. "As long as Reizgoth sticks to eating animals I don't really care what it is."

"You needn't worry about him eating you," said Ryzak, with a grin, "after all, you can just tell him you're a cabbage. I'm sure he'll understand."

The dwarf gave him a withering look.

"Will you two stop it!" snapped Neulee. "If you carry on like this we may just as well give the whole thing up and let Mishtar get free. In some ways it may be preferable to travelling with a pair of simpletons!" Hands on hips, she glared at them.

'That goes for me too!' scolded Draco.

Looking sheepish under Neulee's hostile glare, Ryzak held out a hand and mumbled a begrudging apology.

"Accepted," rumbled the dwarf, briefly clasping it before snatching his own hand away.

'That's better,' chirruped Draco.

With lips compressed in annoyance, Neulee led them across the bone littered plateau. She signalled a halt at the cave entrance and turned to Snorkel. "Do you know the way to Reizgoth's lair?"

He shrugged. "No idea. I've never been there. Draco," he asked hopefully, "any ideas?"

Sitting on Snorkel's shoulder, Draco scratched the underside of her chin with a long, pointed fore-claw as she tried to recall the whereabouts of the large cavern where the dragon usually slept. *'I can't remember,'* she said after a moment's pause, *'I've only been there once. All I can recall is flying down a long tunnel and following the smell.'*

"What smell?" queried Snorkel.

'Bad breath, sulphur fumes, that sort of thing.'

"Oh." He turned to Neulee. "She doesn't know either. But she says she can guide us by the smell. Apparently our big red friend stinks."

"Lead on then, Draco. We are in your hands," said Neulee.

"Are you sure this is wise?" asked Ryzak. "I mean, it looks really dark in there, and …"

Neulee glared at him. "Now is not the time to be having second thoughts. If you're scared, stay behind me and I'll protect you." Her voice lowered to a whisper. "And I was just beginning to like you."

"Me? Scared?" Ryzak spluttered. Puffing out his chest, he gave a good impersonation of someone who is crapping himself but trying hard not to show it. "No, no, no, no, no. Me? Pupff! Surely not. Merely making an observation, that's all." He gave Snorkel a dazzling smile. "After you, my dwarven friend. Lead on, I'll be right behind you." So saying, he clapped the dwarf on the back and propelled him towards the dark interior of the cave.

'Don't worry, Mum. I'll guide you,' Draco whispered.

They entered the murky cave then stopped, allowing their eyes to adjust to the gloom.

'I'll fly ahead and scout the route,' said Draco. With a powerful thrust of her hind legs, she launched herself from Snorkel's shoulder and flapped her leathery wings, flying quickly down the passage.

Snorkel rubbed at his shoulder where her talons had left their imprint through the cloth, and flexed his arm to relieve the pain. She was getting far too big to do that.

'All clear, Mum,' the dragonet's thought broke through.

Flexing his arm one more time, Snorkel stepped forward. "Looks like we're off," he commented.

The three slowly made their way along the wide passage, surprised at how quickly their eyes became adjusted to the darkness. They had been walking for fifteen minutes and, although the lighting was subdued, they could still make out the rough, rocky walls of the passage stretching away in front of them.

"How come we can still see where we're going?" questioned Ryzak.

"Look above you," Neulee directed, peering up at the craggy canopy.

Doing as he was told, Ryzak could see little pinpricks of light glittered like myriad stars on a cold, clear night, seemingly embedded in the high, rocky arch of the roof.

"What are they? Diamonds?" Snorkel asked hopefully.

"I doubt it," answered Neulee. "But whatever they are, I'm pleased they are there. At least they shed some light for us."

A further ten minutes walking brought them to a junction. Draco was perched on a rock, waiting for them to arrive.

"Which way?" asked the dwarf.

'Either,' replied the dragonet. *'The two paths meet around the*

other side. There's another tunnel there. It's not lit like this one: it's very dark and I can smell that Reizgoth is somewhere down it.'

A cold shiver worked its way down Snorkel's spine. Now that they were nearing their goal, he suddenly wished he were someplace else.

"Which way, dwarf?" asked Neulee.

Giving a nervous start at the sound of her voice, it took a moment for him to compose himself. Then, leading the way, he took the left path. A short walk saw them arrive at a small opening leading into a tunnel. Snorkel peered into it. He could see the smooth, well-worn slope of the floor angling down into the dark, sinister passage for about ten paces, after which it was pitch black.

"You first," Ryzak said, a nervous tremor in his voice. He stepped back and gave the dwarf a hesitant grin. "Don't worry, we'll be right behind you."

"I'll go first," Neulee snapped, brushing him aside. "We will hold hands in case one of us slips. At least we will know where the others are."

Ryzak instantly clasped hold of one of her hands. "I can see the sense in that!" he exclaimed. "Snorkel, you grab my other hand and we'll be off."

Neulee wrenched her hand free and gave him a look of contempt. "Take my hand, Snorkel," she ordered, holding it out to the dwarf, "Ryzak will take your other one."

Draco settled on Snorkel's shoulder and cocked her head thoughtfully. *'True love never runs smooth, hey?'*

"You can say that again." Snorkel sniggered.

"What was that?" growled Ryzak.

"Oh, nothing," Snorkel replied innocently. "Draco was just saying how dark it is in there, weren't you?"

The little dragonet solemnly bobbed her head.

It was slow going after the light from the main tunnel had disappeared. They could not see a thing, so Neulee was feeling the ground ahead with a foot before taking each step forward. The floor of the passage sloped downwards and got steeper the further they went. The sulphur fumes, previously only detectable by Draco, were getting stronger.

By the time they had worked their way down the tunnel for half an hour the darkness was becoming oppressive. The temperature of the air seemed to have risen several degrees and it had become stifling. As well as the ever-present smell of dragon, a low rumbling sound was growing louder as they neared the source.

"What's that noise?" asked Snorkel, a slight quaver in his voice.

'It's only Reizgoth,' replied Draco. *'He's sleeping. That's all he does now, most of the time. He's very old. He is the last dragon, you know!'*

"Oh," grunted Snorkel, not the least bit impressed or comforted by Draco's information. "Apparently it's Reizgoth," he informed the others. "He's sleeping."

"Let's hope he stays that way," Ryzak muttered.

Another half hour saw a golden glow begin to appear in the distance. "The dragon's lair," breathed Neulee in wonder.

In her excitement she stepped forward without checking the ground first and fell over the edge of a fissure in the floor. With a shrill scream she plummeted down, dragging her companions with her. Draco, who had flown clear at the first sign of the dwarf tumbling, chirruped her concern after his falling body. Three loud splashes sounded as they plunged into a subterranean lake.

Shocked and winded, but none the worse for his fall, Snorkel thrashed his arms and legs and quickly surfaced. He blew water from his mouth and looked for signs of his companions.

Ryzak appeared nearby. "Where's Neulee?" he asked, his voice shrill with concern.

"I don't know," Snorkel replied, "I haven't seen her."

Coming to the same conclusion, they took several deep breaths to fill their lungs and dived into the murky depths to look for her.

Deep down, a vague movement caught Snorkel's eye. He gripped Ryzak's shoulder and pointed. Thrusting out, they dived deeper. The figure of Neulee came into view. She was frantically trying to free herself of her large broadsword, her efforts getting slower, more lethargic. She was drowning.

Ryzak was the first to reach her side. He began to claw at the leather belt that bound the deadly anchor to her back. She hung face down, arms limp, unmoving.

Snorkel's lungs burned, his arms ached and his vision was blurring, but he would not turn back. He tore at the belt, which Ryzak had partially lifted over Neulee's head, and, with a final tug, pulled it free. It swiftly sank out of sight.

Grabbing one of Neulee's arms each, they kicked out for the surface. When Snorkel was beginning to think he could take no more, his head bobbed clear in a shower of water. His throat burned as ragged breaths sucked air into lungs deprived for too long. His vision swam. That was the closest he had ever been to death; he could almost have reached out and touched him. He closed his eyes in relief. The bastard would have to wait a bit longer before he had the pleasure of his company.

"Snorkel!" Ryzak yelled. "We have to get her to shore."

Aided by Draco, who gripped the front of Neulee's tunic to help keep her afloat, they made it to the shore and staggered up the shingle beach, carrying the unmoving form between them. They laid her on the ground and Ryzak bent over her body. There was no sign of life. He looked at Snorkel. "What can we do?" he implored.

"We have to clear her lungs," Snorkel gasped, "to get rid of the water she's swallowed. Come on, give me a hand."

Together, they rolled Neulee on to her stomach. Snorkel pushed down on her back in an effort to expel the fluid. With a series of retches and coughs, Neulee violently spewed water, before lying limp.

Rolling her over, Ryzak placed his fingers on the side of her neck to feel for a pulse. "She lives!" he yelled in relief, his fingers having found a shallow heartbeat. "What do we do now?"

'She's going to be fine,' Draco mind-spoke to Snorkel, from her perch on a nearby rock, *'I can tell. She will come round any minute now.'*

"We still need to get large quantities of air into her lungs," Snorkel advised, the beginning of a mischievous plan hatching. "She swallowed an awful lot of water. You have to give her the kiss of life."

"What's that?" asked Ryzak, the gleam of panic reappearing in his eyes.

"You have to breathe for her," explained the dwarf. "Listen, I'll tell you what to do." Ryzak hung on every word as the dwarf explained the technicalities of the life-saving technique he must carry out. "You understand?" Snorkel asked.

Wide-eyed, Ryzak nodded, then knelt beside Neulee, a worried look on his face as he prepared himself.

Sitting on the rock beside Draco, Snorkel watched with an expectant smile on his face as Ryzak loosened Neulee's tunic. This could turn out to be the highlight of the journey so far. He smothered a snigger as Neulee's large, perfectly formed breasts popped into view.

'Does he really need to do this?' Draco's irked thought intruded. *'She's about to come round.'*

"Good," grinned the dwarf, snorting with mirth. "I can't wait to see her face when she finds Ryzak pawing at her." He cupped his hands to his mouth. "That's right," he yelled in encouragement, "hold her nose, cover her mouth with yours, then breathe deeply into it. Fill her lungs with air. Remember to rub her chest after each breath. That's vitally important. You must massage them lungs!"

Ryzak nodded his understanding and bent to the task at hand.

'Uh, oh!' murmured Draco. *'Here she comes.'*

Neulee's eyes flickered open. Having just kissed her on the lips, Ryzak had begun to rub her breasts.

"Wait for it." Snorkel chortled with glee as he spotted Neulee's eyes narrow. "Any time now she's going to give it to him."

But before Neulee had the chance to express her displeasure – and further Snorkel's enjoyment – Ryzak stopped rubbing her breasts and moved back to her face. He was so engrossed in what he was doing that he did not notice she was conscious, and clamped a thumb and forefinger over her nose before taking two deep breaths and exhaling into her mouth.

It was then that matters took a turn for the worse as far as Snorkel was concerned. Responding to Ryzak's ministrations, Neulee's arms rose to encircle his neck and she returned his kiss with enthusiasm.

"Bollocks!"

'I take it that was not supposed to happen?' Draco enquired sweetly.

Snorkel glowered at the oblivious couple. "No, it bloody well wasn't!" He rose to his feet and stomped across to stand over them, then cleared his throat to attract their attention. After three or four attempts they eventually looked up.

"When you two have quite finished rutting like animals," Snorkel growled, "there is the small matter of the seal to contend with."

He folded his arms and glared down at the amorous pair, studiously trying to ignore Neulee's exposed breasts. But it was damned hard – he had urges like the next man. Unable to avert his eyes, his face flushed crimson as she extricated herself from beneath Ryzak and stood, her voluptuous charms in full view. She gave a vampish smile and casually fastened the remains of her tunic, before brushing past him to stand beside Draco.

Snorkel's annoyance escalated to new heights as Ryzak got to his feet and gave him a sly wink. "I told you she was mad about me," he whispered.

Aggrieved by the reverse in the fortunes of his plot, Snorkel's features became stony as he walked over to join the rest of the party. If nothing else, he was consistent. Every plan he'd ever had turned out different to expectations.

"Where to now?" asked Neulee, when he reached them. A half smile played about her lips as she eyed him.

"To find some dry clothes, if you ask me," Snorkel grumbled. "I'm still soaking wet from our unexpected swim." Snorkel saw Neulee's eyes harden at his comment, and stepped back under her glare.

Fortunately Ryzak intervened. "Yes, yes. We're all wet," he said, "however, I'd feel much happier with some swords. Mine is at the bottom of that lake."

"As is mine," said Neulee.

"Right then," Ryzak continued, "it seems to me that we need to reco … recon … er, take stock of our surroundings. See what's about, if you see what I mean. Get some weapons before we face this dragon thingy."

Snorkel noticed the new air of authority in his voice. His glower deepened. It was amazing what a warm, soft body did to a man. Only ten minutes ago Ryzak was a gibbering wreck. "And some dry clothes," he muttered.

"That sounds good to me," agreed Neulee, linking her arm through Ryzak's.

'*I can do that!*' warbled Draco.

"What did she say?" asked Ryzak.

"She said that she could take a look-see," growled the dwarf.

"Good girl," enthused Neulee, giving the purring dragonet an affectionate tickle under the chin with her free hand.

"Traitor," hissed Snorkel, as Draco chirruped her delight.

It took a while for Draco to return from her scouting mission, as the cavern was huge. By the time she appeared, Snorkel was shivering. "Wh–wh–wh–what did y–you f–f–find?" he asked, his teeth chattering with cold.

'*Not much,*' Draco replied. '*No sign of Reizgoth; he must be sleeping up in one of the higher caves. All I could find where piles of gold coins, some ornaments and lots of other junk. Oh! And a pile of rotting clothing over in the far corner.*'

"C–c–clothes?" asked Snorkel, suddenly perking up. He got to his feet, his arms wrapping round himself for extra warmth, eager to be out of the wet ones he was wearing.

"Never mind the clothes," snapped Neulee. "Did she see the seal?"

"N–n–no. Sh–sh–she said there was so much junk lying about the place sh–sh–she could not see any sign of it." He gave her a pleading smile. "Sh–she found some clothes though," he reminded her.

A sudden cold shiver ran down Neulee's spine. "As much as I hate to agree with the dwarf, I think we should try and get out of these wet things before we freeze to death."

"Right you are," said Ryzak. He held his hand out and helped Neulee to her feet. "Lead on, Draco."

They emerged from behind the cover of the rocky bank and gaped in awe at the splendour of the subterranean vault. The roof arched away high over their heads and the twinkle of glow globes, similar to those in the tunnel, could be seen dotting the rocky canopy, casting their muted light. The very walls of the place seemed to radiate a surreal, golden glow. Stalactites hung down from the roof, their gleaming, calcite surfaces adding to the dreamlike panorama before them.

"Wow!" breathed Snorkel. "S–s–some place, huh?"

"What are those dark splotches in the walls?" asked Ryzak. "There's loads of them."

'They are the entrances to the dragon caves,' Draco replied. Snorkel relayed her answer to the others.

"But there's so many," gasped Ryzak. "Which one is Reizgoth in?"

'I don't know,' replied Draco, with a shrug of her small shoulders. *'And let's hope we don't find out!'*

"Come on," urged Snorkel, "let's find these clothes. My skin has gone all wrinkly."

They headed out over the rock-strewn cavern floor towards a dark corner where the light did not appear to penetrate as fully. Ryzak glanced over at the opposite end of the chamber, where a deep golden gleam reflected against the nearby wall. "I wonder what's causing that?"

"Draco says that's where Reizgoth has stashed his horde," said Snorkel. He frowned as he noticed the avaricious look that crossed Ryzak's features. "I'm sure we'll see it soon enough," he snapped, not wanting to be diverted from finding some dry clothing. "Come on, before I turn into a block of ice." So saying, he stomped off.

After giving the area of the golden glow a lingering glance, Ryzak linked arms with Neulee and followed the little man.

It did not take long to find the pile of rotting rags that Draco had spotted. They lay in a mouldering heap, hidden in a trough in the floor. Snorkel was already there when Ryzak and Neulee arrived. He was gazing disconsolately into the hollow.

"I can't see there being anything of much use in there," he groaned. "They look like they've been there for years." Not wanting to admit defeat, he jumped down and started to sift through the debris.

"We might as well wait here until the dwarf gets fed up of

poking around," said Ryzak, sitting down. As Neulee sat beside him he raised a hand to cup her chin and turned her face to him. "I'm sure we can find ways to keep warm while we wait."

Returning his smile, she leaned forward to lightly kiss his lips. "I'm sure we can," she murmured.

A sudden scream made them look up. Snorkel stood in the middle of the rags, his eyes wide in horror.

"What is it?" yelled Neulee, jumping to her feet. "What's the matter?"

"This!" exclaimed the dwarf, holding up a human skull. "It's not a dump for old clothes, it's a dump for old treasure hunters! GET ME OUT!"

'What's the matter, Mum?' Draco enquired, as she returned from exploring some of the caves.

Snorkel tossed the skull away, then placed his hands on his hips and gave the dragonet a withering look. "You … you … Bah! Why didn't you tell me that the people who owned the damned clothes were still wearing them?"

'I never thought to look,' she blithely answered. Her mind-speak rose an octave in excitement as she changed the subject. *'I've found the seal.'*

"You've what?" Snorkel asked. The news of her discovery thrust all thoughts of throttling her to the back of his mind.

'I've found the seal,' she repeated. *'It's over there in one of the lower caves, along with some other stuff. I recognised it from the description Ryzak gave us at Jollif's.'*

"She's found the seal," Snorkel yelled excitedly.

"She's what?" shouted Ryzak.

"She's found the seal, over there somewhere," Snorkel replied, waving his hand vaguely in the direction Draco had indicated. "It's in some sort of cave."

"Hurry up and get out then," grinned Ryzak. "Let's get it before that damned dragon wakes up and finds us in here. I, for one, do not fancy joining the rotting rag brigade over there. The sooner we're out of here the better."

It did not take long for Snorkel to get free of the treasure hunters' graveyard, the end of their quest being in sight adding an extra spring to his step. They followed Draco as she flew ahead, leading them towards the distant golden glow. Half way across the cavern she flew up to perch on a ledge at the entrance to a low cave.

"It's in there," Snorkel gasped, leaning against the rock face for support. He was knackered. The fall, coupled with the cold dunking and the exercise of the past few days had caught up with him. Although young for a dwarf, he was twice the age of Ryzak; but he felt a lot older.

"Can she get it?" Neulee asked.

Eager to help, Draco flapped her wings and disappeared into the cave. She returned a short time later and landed on the ledge. She shook her head.

"Apparently not," Snorkel informed them. "It's trapped under some rocks and she can't get it out."

Ryzak looked at the smooth, vertical rock face leading to the ledge above, then at the ground below, gauged the distance between the two, rubbed his chin thoughtfully and delivered his master plan.

"I've got it. We'll form a human chain. Well, human and dwarf. If I stand at the bottom, Neulee can climb up me and stand on my shoulders. Then you, Snorkel, can climb up the pair of us and pull yourself up into the cave and get the seal. Easy!"

"Easy?" squeaked Snorkel. "What happens if Reizgoth is in there?"

'He's not, Mum,' Draco informed him. *'The cave finishes after twenty or thirty yards. All that is in there is the seal and some old clothes.'*

Snorkel's interest was aroused. "Rotten clothes or good clothes?" he asked.

'They seem fine to me,' replied the dragonet. *'They're about your size, too. Small! Strange colour though,'* she added.

"Less of the small, if you don't mind! The best things come in small parcels, don't you know?"

"Good. I'm glad that's settled," said Neulee. She turned to Ryzak and gave him a coy smile. "I'm ready, my stallion."

"Stallion?" murmured Snorkel, shaking his head. Humans were

a strange lot. The only thing resembling a stallion about Ryzak was his horse. And it was a lot more attractive.

He looked on as Ryzak bent down and cupped his hands. Neulee, using them as a stirrup, clambered up his torso onto his shoulders. Ryzak grasped her ankles and forced his body upright with Neulee holding on to the rock face for support. When she was ready, Snorkel climbed up. Numerous curses and grunts of pain from the human portion of the chain later, he managed to scramble onto Neulee's shoulders. For once Ryzak had got it right. Snorkel's head and shoulders were level with the floor of the passage. He braced his arms on the rocky ledge and hauled himself up.

"Be careful, Snorkel," called Neulee, as the dwarf disappeared from view.

Snorkel paused. Neulee had called him by his name. Things must be looking up.

'Over here, Mum,' mind-called Draco from somewhere ahead. *'It's quite bright in here. One of them glow thingamabobs is in the roof.'*

Snorkel made his way down the smooth-walled passage and followed it round a bend to where it opened into a small cavern. Old, rotten straw covered the ground and a warmth radiated from the floor, seeping through the thin soles of his leather boots. Draco sat on a small mound of rocks, the glint of gold winking from the pile beneath her. But what took his breath away was not the sight of the seal, but the bright crimson clothing hung carefully on a wooden stand to one side of the cave.

"Wow!" he exclaimed in astonishment. "Some threads!"

He ran over to take a closer look and stroked the soft, supple hide of the jacket and trews in admiration, amazed at how new and fresh they felt. Crouching down to the small, pointy-toed boots that had been placed beneath the stand, he picked them up. After blowing years of accumulated dust from their polished uppers, he dropped to the floor and kicking off his old, well-worn boots tugged on the new red ones.

"Yeaaah!" he exclaimed happily, jumping to his feet and dancing a jig around the cave. "Just my size. They could have been made for me."

'Sorry to break up your party,' interrupted Draco, *'but hadn't you better be getting the seal for Ryzak?'*

Snorkel stopped his cavorting. "Oh, yes. I'd forgotten about that."

He scampered over to the rock pile and began to shift the small boulders to one side. In moments he had created enough space to thrust his hand in and pull the seal free. "There we are," he said, with a smile. "Take this to Ryzak while I try on the rest of this outfit."

With a roll of her eyes, Draco hopped over and grabbed the golden disc from him. Holding it in her front claws, she flew back the way they had come.

"I shan't be long," Snorkel called after her retreating figure.

He turned back to admire his new outfit and rubbed his hands together in anticipation. Boy, they looked cool. He couldn't wait to see Ryzak's face when he saw him dressed in those. He quickly stripped off his damp robe and walked over to the clothes stand.

"What is he doing in there?" growled Ryzak, pacing around in frustration. "He's been gone for half an hour. He should have been back by now."

"Relax," Neulee said reassuringly. "Draco is not the least bit concerned. If he was in trouble she would know about it and be creating a racket by now."

"I guess you're right," he muttered, squatting down next to her and scratching Draco behind the ear. "Now that we've got the seal, all I want to do is get out of here."

"I know what you mean," Neulee agreed. "This place is starting to give me the creeps."

Draco suddenly sat up and twisted round to stare at the entrance to the cave. Ryzak and Neulee turned to look, their mouths dropping open in surprise as Snorkel came into view. Draco covered her eyes with a leathery wing and shook her head. Standing above them, legs splayed, hands on hips, was …

"Snorkel?" queried Ryzak in disbelief.

"The very same," replied the dwarf, his beard parting in a grin.

Ryzak was dumbstruck. The dwarf was encapsulated in crimson.

The little, pointy-toed boots with the floppy turnovers; the tight-fitting trews tucked into the tops of the boots; the double-breasted, fleece-lined jacket with the padded shoulders and elbows; the little gloves that covered his hands; the long, flowing, crimson cape, and the skullcap with the little ear flaps: the little man was RED. The only relief to the monotone was the dwarf's thick, brown beard poking out of the sides of the cap and the strange glass fronted eye-covers which were held in place by a cord tied around his head.

"Very, er, very …" Ryzak struggled to find a suitable adjective to describe what he was seeing.

"Fetching?" Neulee finished for him.

"Not quite the word I was looking for," Ryzak mumbled. "Why don't you join us and let us take a closer, er, look?" he called.

"Okay!" Snorkel said, jumping off the ledge and landing lightly on the balls of his feet in front of his astonished audience.

"How'd you manage that?" asked Ryzak in amazement.

"Manage what?" queried Snorkel.

"That, that jump? You used to get dizzy climbing out of bed and now you jump off a ledge, from thirteen feet up, without batting an eyelid."

"Never mind that now," murmured Neulee. "Let's go. I need to be out in the fresh air again. Something does not feel right."

"I know what you mean," sniggered Ryzak, glancing at the dwarf.

Snorkel appeared not to hear his snide comment. "Can't we have a look at the gold first? There might even be some weapons we can use," he said.

Growing ever more worried, but feeling naked without a sword in her hand, Neulee reluctantly agreed. "As long as it is only a quick look." Her eyes darted around the cavern in nervous scrutiny. She could not put her finger on it, but something in the air had definitely changed.

Alert for signs of danger, she followed Ryzak and the crimson-clad dwarf towards the distant glow. The nearer they got, the more nervous she became. When they crested the last rise, she bumped into Ryzak's back. The man had stopped dead in his tracks.

As she peered around his bulk, her mouth dropped open in amazement. In a hollow below them was amassed what must have been the greatest treasure trove in history. Thousands upon thousands of golden artefacts littered the floor like confetti.

"Bloody hell," whispered Ryzak.

"Paradise," murmured Snorkel.

"Trouble," muttered Neulee, seeing the undisguised greed in their eyes.

Yelling their delight, the man and dwarf made their move. An overwhelming sense of danger washed over Neulee. "Wait!" she shouted.

"What is it?" asked Ryzak, stopping and casting her a quizzical look.

"Yeah, come on," pleaded Snorkel. "We'll be there and back in no time."

"Something's not right," Neulee replied, nervously chewing at her lip.

"Seems all right to me," shrugged Ryzak, glancing around. "Snorkel's right; we'll be back in a tick. Wait there if you want to. I'll see if I can find you a sword."

Before she could stop them they had scrambled down to the bottom of the slope and were running towards the treasure.

In sudden horror, Neulee realised what was different. It was quiet! The low rumbling of Reizgoth's snores had stopped! "Come back!" she shrieked. "It's Reizgoth. I think he's woken!"

The two figures skidded to a halt and stared into each other's fear-filled eyes. Screaming in terror, they quickly turned and ran back up the slippery slope.

"Going somewhere?" a deep, melodious voice enquired from behind them.

Chapter Eighteen

'Rhudrhyn has failed,' the voice informed her. 'On a brighter note, it will be the last time he will ever fail me. Fail at anything, as it happens. So it all hinges on you now, my dear. I trust I can rely on better results? Do what you must to ensure that Ryzak places the seal hieroglyphs face down. You understand? Anything! I do so hate incompetence, especially in my followers. It gets me all worked up. Upsets me for days. And you know how I get when I'm upset?'

She heard the implied threat behind the words. 'Yes, Master. You can rely on me.'

'Good' Mishtar's oily retort sounded in her head. 'You are such a pretty girl, I would hate to see anything happen to you.'

'Master?' she asked. 'Why do you not simply enter Ryzak's mind and influence him to our cause?'

'If only it were that simple,' Mishtar answered. 'Unfortunately our dwarven friend seems to have an influence in the matter. Ever since he unexpectedly appeared in the dreamscape I have not been able to get near Ryzak, and that worries me. Without the dwarf around he would have been easy. If that idiot Rhudrhyn had not failed, Ryzak would now be mine.'

She could hear the anger in his voice. 'Should I kill him?'

'No. Not yet. He intrigues me. When I'm free I shall deal with him. Leave him be for the moment. I will let you know if I change my mind. How is our wizard? Has he breathed his last mortal breath yet?'

'No. He still clings to life – just. We are nearly at that tavern in Fleshwick, where they plan to meet with Ryzak and the dwarf. They hope he can save him.'

Mishtar laughed. 'Save him? I very much doubt that. I could not save him from where his soul has gone. What chance does the dwarf have? Rest assured, it will not be long before Beulah breathes his last.'

'Yes, Master.'

'Keep me informed if there are any interesting developments. This damned shield is proving tiresome now that the third seal is in place. I cannot breach its confinement for long. I can feel myself being drawn back. You know how to reach me. Do not let me down.'

'No, Master.'

Mishtar's voice faded and she settled back in the cushions, making herself comfortable for the remaining leg of their journey. She would not fail. When her master was free, she wanted to be there with him. He would need a consort. Relishing the prospect, she looked down at the deathly-white, pasty flesh of Beulah's face, gave a humourless smile and softly caressed the waxy skin of his forehead. "Not long now," she whispered.

"How is he?" Shula asked, her head popping through the slit in the front section of the canvas cover.

The girl swiftly masked a look of alarm at the unexpected intrusion. "No change, Matriarch," she answered, turning to face her. "If the dwarf can't help, or he is not there," she shrugged her shoulders, "it's a matter of days, I fear."

Shula nodded in understanding then withdrew, closing the flaps behind her.

The girl breathed a heavy sigh. "Not long now," she repeated, smiling to herself as she closed her eyes.

Soon the rolling motion of the cart sent her into a dreamless sleep.

* * * * *

"Aherm!"

"Ouch!" Jollif rubbed the crown of his head as he rose from beneath the counter. "Can I help you, S–Shula?"

Shula smiled. "I certainly hope so, Jollif."

The tavern-keeper noticed the dark rings beneath her eyes and the tired, drawn look on her face. "Are you all right?" he asked, concerned. "Let me get you a drink. You look like you could do with one."

He turned to the shelves behind him. Maybe he could spare a

drop of his Alduran Brandy. She looked in need of it. He felt a restraining hand on his arm and turned.

Shula gave him a weak smile and released her hold. "No. No, thank you. I am fine. Just a little tired, that is all. Are Ryzak and Snorkel back yet?"

"No, they're not," Jollif replied, a worried frown crossing his ruddy features. "I must admit, I was starting to get concerned about you all. It's been two months since you left and not a sight, not a sound have I heard. I thought you'd forgotten about me," he finished.

"I am sorry, Jollif. We've been a little busy. I will explain later, I promise. But first, have you a spare room we could use, for Beulah?"

"Certainly. When he comes in I'll show him up," Jollif answered.

"That might be a little difficult." Shula grimaced. "He is not quite himself at present. In fact, we will require your assistance to get him in here. Despite his frail appearance, he is a lot heavier than he looks."

Jollif's eyes narrowed. He hastily followed her out of the tavern to the canvas-covered cart parked outside.

"He is in here," Shula said, lifting back the flaps and tying them out of the way.

Jollif stepped on to the tailgate to peer inside and gasped as he spied the apparently lifeless form of the wizard. "Is he alive?"

"Barely," a young girl he did not recognise replied. "We have done the best we can, but it is not enough. He is beyond our powers to help."

"Can we move him, Meganrhys?" Shula asked. The girl nodded.

"It will take three or four of us," pondered Jollif. He rubbed at a fleshy jowl. "Hang on, I'll be back shortly."

A couple of minutes later he returned with three villagers. With much cursing and groaning they managed to lift the unconscious wizard out of the wagon. Tightly wrapped in his blankets, they laid him on a wooden pallet and carried him inside the tavern.

The three sisters followed them. They looked on as the four men negotiated the narrow stairway leading to the first floor. At the top, Jollif directed his helpers towards one of the rooms. Inside they lifted Beulah off the pallet and on to the soft, feather mattress of the bed.

"My thanks, lads," he said, as they finished. "There's a drink for each of you downstairs. I'll be with you in a tick."

Their faces lit up. Giving each other knowing smirks and mumbling words of thanks, they quickly left the room and made their way down to the bar area. With any luck they might be able to help themselves to one or two before Jollif turned up.

Once they were out of earshot, the tavern-keeper turned to Shula. "What happened to him?" he asked, nodding at the re-cumbent form of the wizard.

"It's a long tale, Jollif," Shula sighed. "Best left until later and told over a glass of red wine. If you could fetch us some tea and food, I would be pleased to tell you all once we are refreshed."

Realising he would get no immediate answers, he gave her a contemplative look. "I'll see what I can do," he grumbled, shuffling towards the door.

Shula's voice halted him as he made to step into the hallway. He peered back over his shoulder. "Jollif. There is a wooden chest in the wagon. Be so good as to have it brought up."

Jollif scowled as he closed the door behind him. One thing was for sure, absence had not improved her manner in the slightest.

* * * * *

It was past midnight before Shula made her appearance. She looked slightly refreshed and less tired than she had done earlier. Impatient to hear what had been happening, Jollif smiled a welcome as soon as he spotted her coming down the stairs. He waved and beckoned her over. Having grown more testy as the day wore on, he felt as if a load had been lifted from his shoulders as she approached. He was never at his best where equanimity was concerned. "Red wine, was it?" he asked, as she sat down on a tall stool beside the bar.

She gave him a half smile and nodded her approval.

"Make 'at two!" a loud, gruff voice demanded.

Jollif scowled. He knew that voice. Looking up he saw Sawn-off Sam swaying towards them, and sighed. The little bastard had not been near the tavern for months, and he had to pick this night, of all nights, to turn up. And he was hammered.

Jollif's scowl of annoyance turned to a look of unease as the squat figure pulled up a stool and sat next to Shula.

"Me and the pretty lady are goin' to 'ave a drink together, aren't we?" Sam leered, wrapping a filthy arm around Shula's shoulders and giving her a gap-toothed grin.

"Er – er – S–Sam," Jollif managed to stutter. "Th–the lady and I were …" His voice tailed off under Sam's malignant gaze.

"The lady and you were what?" Sam snarled, leaning forward menacingly.

"Er, nothing." Jollif squeaked, and backed away.

"Do I have a say in this?" Shula enquired frostily, arching an eyebrow in disdain as Sam fixed his leering gaze on her.

"No!"

Jollif saw Shula's face harden and resisted the urge to smirk.

"Really?" Shula purred, a wicked smile playing about her lips. She leaned forward invitingly. "Come on then, big boy. Show me what you are made of." She gripped his squared head and pulled him towards her. Her lips parted, and her tongue flicked out playfully.

Sam started to dribble in excitement.

"Close your eyes," she invited. He did, then cried out in agony as a blinding flash shot into his head.

Turning to Jollif, Shula smiled as if nothing had happened. "A red wine would be lovely, thank you."

Jollif was stunned. Where had Sam disappeared to? One minute he was puckering up, the next he had gone. Vanished into thin air!

"Wh–where…"

"A simple spell of translocation," she answered. "He is now somewhere he cannot cause any trouble. Not for a while, anyway."

* * * * *

Sam eased himself into a sitting position and rubbed at his throbbing head. What in hell's name had happened back there? A cold shiver ran through him. He was bloody freezing. He cracked his eyes open and gazed around.

Snow? Alarmed, he lumbered to his feet. "Where the hell am I?"

His loud shout drifted across the barren, snow-covered plains towards the dim and distant mountains. It was answered by a low, threatening growl from behind him.

Sam spun, his eyes flying open in fear as he spotted the originator of the noise.

"It's a piggin' polar bear!"

Turning tail, he fled towards the far-off range, his little legs pumping away for all they were worth.

* * * * *

Recovering from the shock of Sam's vanishing act, Jollif became further disturbed as the matriarch told him her tale. When she finished, he gulped down the remainder of his drink and went to fill his glass again. Discovering the bottle empty, he placed it back on the counter, wondering whether Shula would notice if he opened another. The raising of an eyebrow told him that she would. He sighed.

"What if Ryzak and Snorkel did not escape the elves?" he asked. "Who will save the wizard then?"

"They have," Shula replied emphatically.

"How do you know?"

"The orb showed me. I used it on our way here and saw them climbing Firestone Mountain. However, once they went inside the orb's powers could not penetrate the interior, and I have not been able to see them properly since."

"So they could be dead," Jollif probed. There was something she was not telling him, of that he was certain.

Shula shook her head. "No. I have received hazy pictures; enough for me to know they are not dead, even if I cannot see what they are doing." She held his gaze. "They are alive."

Jollif nodded thoughtfully. She was not going to tell him. Time to try a different tack. "Fine. Assuming they are still alive, why would the dwarf help the wizard? I can still remember what happened the last time they were here. And, if I remember the little idiot correctly, what makes you think he is capable of saving Beulah, even if he does agree to help?"

Her features hardened. "Don't be so pessimistic!" she snapped. "Of course he will help. He is a wizard after all!"

"Apprentice," corrected Jollif.

"Apprentice wizard, then!" Shula retorted, silently cursing Jollif for voicing her own fears. She slid off her stool and stood facing him, her manner aloof. "Now, if you will excuse me, I shall retire and get some sleep. Apprentice or not, Snorkel is the best equipped out of all of us to help Beulah. I'll bid you goodnight."

Jollif watched her go, not so confident in the dwarf's abilities as Shula appeared to be. The next few days should prove eventful, one way or another. He began to clear away the empty bottle and glasses. Perhaps now was a good time to think about retiring to the country.

Jollif saw little of the sisters over the following three days. They kept themselves to themselves and only made occasional, brief excursions down to the main room of the tavern. He made sure their every need was catered for and delivered a steady supply of food and drink to them. He was only allowed into their room once after his initial visit – after nearly passing out at the sight of the gaunt, emaciated wizard they refused him entry, preferring to take their supplies from him at the door.

On the fourth morning, Jollif made his way down to the common room to begin preparing for the day's trade. He was surprised to see Shula and Meganrhys sitting quietly at the counter, solemnly sipping at cups of tea.

"What's happened?" he cried, hurrying over. "He's not dead, is he?"

Shula looked up. "No, not quite," she replied. "Although how he clings to life I shall never know."

Placing her cup on the counter, Meganrhys rose and gave the matriarch a thin smile. "I will go back to him now. It would be unfair to leave Rhissa with him any longer, especially if the worst comes to pass."

Shula covered Meganrhys's hand with one of her own and gave it an affectionate squeeze. "I understand. I'll be up shortly."

"No change then?" enquired Jollif, sitting on the departed sister's stool.

"Only for the worse, Jollif. Only for the worse," she sighed.

"How long?" he whispered.

She gave him a weary look. "Minutes? Hours? Days? Who can say? Wherever his soul has been drawn, it is beyond the reach of our powers."

"I thought your orb would be able to help, now that Beulah has released the magic."

"Whatever Beulah did inside the orb has certainly increased the powers available to us, but it is still not enough. It's as if a portion of the orb is still locked away, hidden. Perhaps we will never realise its full potential."

"I wish Ryzak and Snorkel would hurry up," Jollif muttered, reaching over the counter for a bottle of his favourite brandy. Now felt as good a time as any to have the first drink of the day.

The silence of the morning was suddenly shattered by a loud bugling noise. It filled the air, causing the windows to rattle. Taken by surprise, Jollif dropped the bottle, its loud smash making him swear involuntarily. That was his last one and his supplier did not arrive for another three days. He leaned over and stared in anguish at the large pool of spilled liquid on the floor.

"Bollocks!"

He flinched as the bugling sounded again. This time it was so loud that the bottles on the shelves rattled. Still leaning over the counter, Jollif lost his balance and toppled to the floor. He quickly scrambled to his feet, and seeing Shula run to the window hurried after her. Together they peered out.

Clouds of dust swirled outside, obscuring their view as powerful gusts of wind whipped up the dry, crumbling clay of the main street. Over the noise of the blast they could hear the screams of terrified villagers. The disturbance quietened as quickly as it had started.

"What is it?" Jollif asked nervously. "Can you see anything?"

"It is still too hazy," Shula replied. "Stay behind me while I take a look."

"You're not going outside?" he asked, aghast.

She did not answer, but strode to the tavern door and slid back the bolts. Easing it open, she stepped onto the veranda. Close behind, Jollif heard her gasp of surprise.

"Wh–wh–what is it?" he stammered, trying to peer over her shoulder. His eyes widened in terror as a huge shape started to materialise through the haze. "It's … it's …"

He never finished. His eyeballs rolled up in their sockets and he collapsed to the ground in a dead faint.

Chapter Nineteen

"Going somewhere?" Reizgoth repeated, a little more sharply. He hated it when he was ignored; it made him mad. "That's more like it," he said in approval, as the three small figures skidded to a halt twenty paces from the edge of the crater. It had been a long time since he'd had visitors and he was quite looking forward to meeting them. It got so boring living in a mountain with only rocks for company. Conversation was a trifle limited.

"Hey, you guys. What you been up to today?"

"Urgh, nothin' much. Jus' hangin' around takin' in the vibes, man."

Boring!

Emerging from behind the large treasure mound where he had been sleeping, Reizgoth made his ponderous way towards the figures. "Do turn around," he urged, "I hate talking to people's backs; it's so uncivilised, don't you think?"

He snorted in amusement as he heard a shrill, high-pitched scream. It was always like this before people got to know him and realised what a swell guy he really was. Abject terror!

He chuckled. It was good to see that he could instil such fear. Although, sometimes, he wished he did not have such an adverse affect on his visitors. Strange it should have been the male human who screamed, it was usually the females. Still chuckling to himself, he made his way forward and halted at the base of the slope. He had to squint in order to study the three figures more closely, his eyesight having deteriorated over the past fifty years or so. Yet another frailty to add to his long list. Thinking the short one looked awfully familiar, he moved closer.

Suddenly his snout twitched. He had a tickle. That was one of the irritating little problems that plagued him when he slept for long periods and dust settled in his nostrils. Trying to clear the offending particles, he shook his head and snorted. He sighed in relief as the tickle disappeared. That was better. Then, wanting to take another look at shorty, he lowered his head.

Without warning, he sneezed.

Huge globules of gritty mucus splattered everywhere. Screams of terror joined the nasal reverberations as the figures clung more tightly to each other under the viscous hail.

Reizgoth raised a foreleg and dipped his head to wipe mucus trails from the end of his snout, before offering them an embarrassed apology. What must they think of him? Contrite, he gave an endearing smile, but it only seemed to make matters worse. He sighed. They did not like him. His good humour began to evaporate. Why was it people never called to pass the time of day, always seeming to want something from him instead? Usually taken while he slept. His eyes narrowed. They appeared to be just like the rest. "Nothing to say?" he snapped.

The figures shook their heads.

"Oh dear," the dragon murmured, "it seems that I was wrong about you after all. You are only interested in my trinkets and baubles. And I thought you were different."

Reizgoth reared, spread his leathery wings and loudly trumpeted his anger, then bent his long neck so that his head was level with the interlopers. He glared at them, his smooth, silky tones changing to a deep, menacing growl. "Why is it that the only time I receive visitors is when they want to steal from me?" he hissed. "Once I was revered by all. Idolised! Thought of as something special. People visited me to discuss theology and the like, seek my wisdom in their petty disputes. Now all they do is come to steal, like thieves in the night. Well, I, Reizgoth, have had enough!" he roared. "Prepare to meet your ..."

He never finished. A searing pain shot through his chest. With a startled gasp, Reizgoth clutched his breast and toppled to the ground.

Snorkel screwed his eyes tight shut and waited for the fiery blast that would end his miserable life. This was it. The end! At least if he was about to die he was going in good company; well one of them anyway. He cringed expectantly and clung to Neulee's leg, praying for a quick death.

He was still in the same position when he heard the earth-shaking thump, but it was some time before he dared open his eyes and see what caused it. And then only because Neulee prised his arms from her leg and peeled him off her.

The dwarf peered towards where the dragon had been standing, but there was no sign of him, only clouds of dust spiralling into the air. He cast Neulee a querying look.

She shrugged, then prised Ryzak off her other leg and helped the man to his feet. Slowly she led them to the edge of the trough. Gradually the dust cleared, revealing a vast, unmoving, red form below them.

Reizgoth!

"Is he dead?" Ryzak squeaked.

Turning, Snorkel saw him standing behind Neulee. The man was quaking in terror. Snorkel smirked. Where was the stallion now? Before he had the chance to make a disparaging comment, Draco flew down from the safety of the cavern roof and chirruped a reply.

"Draco thinks so," Snorkel translated. "She says he was very old and his heart gave out under the strain."

A happy grin appeared on Ryzak's face and he moved from behind Neulee to stand beside her. "Let's take a peek then," he said, with renewed courage.

They gazed down at the huge form of the last dragon. He did not look so fearsome in death. His frame was covered in crimson scales from the end of his blunt nose to the tip of his ridged tail; except for his stomach, where the scales were a deep, golden colour.

"He looks so regal; almost kingly," breathed Neulee, a hint of sadness in her voice.

"He must be fifty feet long," whispered Ryzak in awe.

"Look at the size of them talons," grimaced Snorkel. "I'm glad I never felt them tearing into me. They would have ripped us apart before you could blink an eye."

They stood looking. It was not every day you saw a real dragon, even if it had just pegged out in front of you.

After a while, growing bored, Snorkel turned to the others. "I'm going for a closer look. Anyone coming?"

"Er, no thanks," said Ryzak. "I'll stay here with Neulee. You go if you want."

"Not even for a look at the gold?" Snorkel wheedled, rubbing his hands together at the thought of all that wealth, his for the taking.

"No."

Ryzak's arm rose to encircle Neulee's shoulders in a show of solidarity. "We could not steal from him in death. You go and gloat if you want to, but leave us out of this."

With an unconcerned shrug of his shoulders, Snorkel scampered eagerly down the slope. Bollocks to them; see if he cared! It meant all the more for him.

Ryzak watched the little man disappear over the lip, before turning to Neulee. "If he takes anything, I'll kill him," he growled.

"You and me both," she agreed.

United in their displeasure, they sat on the hard rock of the ground to await the dwarf's return.

Reaching the bottom, Snorkel's eagerness began to dissipate. The dragon was huge. Its vast bulk dwarfed him. Mind you, he *was* dwarfed by anything except a fellow dwarf. A feeling of unease gripped him. What if the dragon was only kidding? What if he suddenly raised his head and flamed him? What if …

Pushing such unnerving thoughts to the back of his mind, he silently padded past the large head towards the gold. The sight of the untold wealth before him had a calming effect. Cursing himself for a coward, he strode forward.

The dragon's body shuddered.

Snorkel halted mid-stride, his eyes widening, his face draining of colour. Was that what he thought it was?

The dragon twitched again.

Screeching in terror, Snorkel ran to hide behind a boulder.

"What's happening?" shouted Ryzak, jumping to his feet.

Peering nervously out from behind the boulder, his heart racing, Snorkel glanced at Reizgoth's prone form before looking up at Ryzak. "Beats me," he shouted. "The dragon moved. Must have been an aftershock. You know, like chickens when you cut off their heads and they still run across the yard. That sort of thing."

Ryzak raised his eyebrows doubtfully. "Get back up here," he ordered. "Leave the dead in peace. We've got what we came for. Let's be on our ... uh-oh!"

Noticing Ryzak's look of horror, Snorkel poked his head over the top of the boulder. "What's up?"

Ryzak pointed to Snorkel's right.

With a sinking feeling in his stomach, Snorkel slowly turned, then screamed. Reizgoth had raised his head from the ground and was staring at him; his huge, golden eyes holding him with their hypnotic gaze.

The dragon's mouth moved as if he were trying to say something, then, slowly, the head lowered back to the ground.

The dwarf's terror faded and a feeling of pity washed over him. The dragon was not dead, he was dying. He had never witnessed anything so sad. Reizgoth's lips moved again and the faint whisper of his voice reached Snorkel's ears. It was so hushed he could not make out the words.

For once in his life he felt compassion for a fellow living being. He stepped out from behind the boulder and, though terrified and expecting to get flamed at any moment, hesitantly walked forward.

"Help me, Galduran, help me. Please."

Shocked by the dragon's plea, Snorkel halted. Galduran? Why had he called him that? It was as if the dragon knew him. This was getting creepier by the minute. Against all his natural instincts to run, he cautiously edged closer. It was as if he were under some strange compulsion to help the beast.

"Ah, Galduran. I knew you would come back," Reizgoth murmured, as the dwarf drew level with his head. The dragon's lips curled back in a weak smile. "It is good to see you again, my friend. Albeit from a somewhat undignified position."

Licking at dry lips, Snorkel gazed down. "Wh–wh–what is it you want?"

The dragon's eyes twinkled. "Why, for you to help me, of course," he replied, "so we can be together again, like before. Rulers of the skies. It would be good to have you ride me. It's been too long, far too long, since we last journeyed together."

A lump began to form in Snorkel's throat. He felt tears form in his eyes. Why was he crying? Ten minutes ago this beast was about to rend him limb from limb, and now he was blubbering like a kid who'd just watched his pet frog get squashed. Dipping his head, he wiped the tears away with a gloved hand.

"How can I help you?" he sniffled. "I don't know the first thing about dragons."

"Use the magic," breathed Reizgoth, his eyelids closing and his voice fading. "Use the magic."

"But I don't know how," the dwarf wailed.

Watching from the safety of the upper level, Ryzak and Neulee could not hear what Reizgoth had said, they only heard Snorkel's despairing cry. Expecting the dwarf to be toast by now, it was a shock to see the little man conversing with the beast.

"What is he up to?" Ryzak murmured, spotting Snorkel move closer to Reizgoth and lay a hand on the knobbly ridges between the dragon's eyes.

"I don't know, but I am going to take a closer look," said Neulee. Moving forward, she stepped over the edge and ran down the slope towards the dwarf.

Ryzak shook his head. "Here we go again," he grumbled, then followed her down.

Snorkel closed his eyes and took deep, rapid breaths, trying to focus his energy on Reizgoth. He had no idea what he was doing, or, in fact, why he was doing it. He just knew he had to help the stricken creature. It was a feeling from deep within, a long buried emotion. He could not have refused if he wanted to.

A feeling of peace and serenity pervaded his mind as the breathing exercises had the desired effect. He could feel warmth emanating from his palms, working its way through to the rough, scaled skin. Then a familiar, audible click sounded in his head. The latch to his hidden magic came open.

But this time it was different. Whereas previously he had mumbled words he did not understand to summon unknown spells, he now understood everything. It was as if his mind were an open book of mage craft and he only had to leaf through to the right page to find the spell he needed. It was not the magic of Beulah or the wizards, either. It was an older, more eldritch kind of magic. If he'd been asked to explain the difference, he would not have been able to. It was just, well, different. He felt more complete than he had ever done in his life.

Released from its earthly constraints, his inner being soared through the dragon's body, inspecting all the vital organs and blood supplies for damage and rectifying the defects it came across. It was all so simple. Why hadn't he been able to do magic before?

Sitting on the hard, rocky ground of the trough, Ryzak and Neulee watched the little man at work. Snorkel had been at it for two hours now, two hours of standing rigidly at attention, eyes closed, palms splayed on the dragon's head. And to their complete amazement, it actually looked as if the dwarf knew what he was doing. Reizgoth's scales had taken on a more vibrant, crimson tone and the dragon appeared to be breathing more easily.

When they had first arrived at Snorkel's side, they were worried about his condition. The dwarf didn't appear to be breathing and his body was cold and rigid. He did not even acknowledge their presence with so much as an oath.

Wanting to gain the little man's attention, to make sure he was all right, Ryzak tried a variety of methods to rouse him, much to Neulee's disgust. He pinched him, waved his hands in front of his face and even kicked his shins – all with no response. When he had stepped forward with a dagger to try jabbing the dwarf, Draco had squeaked angrily and dived at Ryzak's head until he retreated. It was then that he gave up and sat down to wait. The dwarf would have to come round on his own.

Not so sure of Ryzak's surrender, Draco remained on guard and would not let him or Neulee near Snorkel, remaining alert even when it seemed they had fallen asleep.

Some time later, a loud screech of alarm made Ryzak and Neulee wake with a start. Jumping to their feet they saw Snorkel slumped over Reizgoth's head. Draco hovered above, squawking her concern.

"Don't worry, he is fine," a deep, drowsy voice informed them. "He is merely sleeping after his exertions. If you don't mind, I will join him for a while. Please make yourselves at home. Feel free to look around."

They stared at Reizgoth's huge head in surprise as the dragon closed a sleepy eyelid. Before long the deep, even snores of the dragon joined those of the dwarf.

"Did you hear what I thought I just heard?" asked Ryzak, staring at the peacefully sleeping duo in amazement.

"Uh-huh," replied Neulee, nodding.

Ryzak was stunned. He had seen the dragon keel over, apparently dead; an old, decrepit creature, way past its prime. Now he was looking at a dragon reborn; it even looked younger. There was a glossy sheen to its scaled hide and its golden belly was pure and rich in colour, not the dull yellow it had been. Even the one eye it opened when it looked at them was bright and clear. And it had made them welcome! What on earth had the dwarf done? And how?

"What should we do?" Neulee asked, unable to take her eyes off the sleeping figures.

"Huh?"

"What shall we do?" she asked again. "Are you deaf?"

"Oh sorry," he apologised, "I was just ..." His voice tailed off; he had no idea what he was just ... He suddenly smiled. "Do? Why, make ourselves at home of course, as our big red friend invited us to. Come on, let's look around for some weapons. We might even find some food. I'm starving. Come on Draco. You too!"

Ryzak grabbed hold of Neulee's hand and strode off towards the treasure pile, making for the side where Reizgoth had appeared. Draco flew above their heads, remaining close by. As they made their way around the vast mound of gold, a large dark opening came into view.

"I wonder what's in there?" Ryzak mused. "Come on, let's take a look." He led Neulee towards it.

Draco flew on ahead and perched on a rock beside the opening. As they approached she screeched loudly and shook her head.

"She doesn't want to go in," Neulee observed, halting.

"Come on," Ryzak urged. "Where's your sense of adventure? There's only one dragon and he is happily curled up with our little pal over there. Where's the harm in taking a little look around? Reizgoth did say to make ourselves at home." He gave her a winning smile.

Neulee snatched her hand from his, folded her arms and frowned in disapproval. She shook her head. "You go if you want to. I'll wait here with Draco. It does not feel right, it feels …"

"Chirp, chirrup, squeak," interrupted Draco.

"Precisely!" Neulee smiled and wandered over to the dragonet, sitting down on the rock beside her. "Not gone yet?" she enquired politely, noticing Ryzak had not moved.

He was disappointed by her reluctance, but tried not to show it. "Fine, see if I care. I won't be long. See you in a tick."

"And Ryzak, try to stay out of trouble," Neulee called after him as he turned to enter the tunnel.

Mumbling under his breath, Ryzak entered. What did she think he was, some sort of calamity magnet?

The tunnel sloped gently down, the smooth contours of the well-worn ground illuminated by the glow globes in the ceiling. It was obvious the passage was well used, as the rock of the walls was worn smooth by the passage of a large reptilian body. The deeper he travelled, the warmer the tunnel became. After ten minutes of walking he was starting to sweat. Heat from the rock of the floor was beginning to radiate through the soles of his boots.

"It's like an oven in here," he grumbled, following the pathway round a bend. As he turned the corner, the passage abruptly finished. He stood in an elevated entrance to a large, underground amphitheatre, having emerged at the top of a tiered gallery. He gazed around at the stone ledge seating surrounding the sandy basin some thirty feet below. "You could seat a hundred people in here," he murmured. "I wonder what it was used for?"

Excited by his discovery, he started to make his way down to the sandy, circular arena at the bottom. Half way there he became aware of a golden glint in the centre of the smooth sand and stopped to stare at it. Unable to see it clearly enough to make out what it was, he increased his pace, eager to find out. Reaching the last stone ledge he jumped on to the soft, yielding sand. His feet sank and his eyes widened. The bloody stuff was hot. Very hot!

Ryzak mouthed an oath and jumped back to the stone tiering. He sat down and ripped his boots off before they welded themselves to his skin, and began to massage his feet, which had already turned bright pink. Groaning in discomfort, he noticed small blisters beginning to form. Why did it always happen to him? He clambered gingerly to his feet and stared at the golden gleam in the circle of sand. He had to find out what it was.

He picked up his discarded boots and began to look around for something to help him. His eyes lit up as he spotted several pairs of wooden clogs. He hobbled over to inspect them, wincing as his burned feet touched the cool stone. Placing his boots on the edge of the tier, he bent down to inspect the clogs. At least he knew why they had thick, wooden soles; after his latest escapade it was painfully obvious.

The clogs had tough leather uppers, with laces threaded through eyelets to strap them to the wearer's legs. Sorting through to find a pair that fitted, he disgustedly threw them aside. They were all too small. The only feet they would fit would be a child's; or a dwarf's. His were much too large. He swung his feet over the edge of the stone seat to think how he could overcome the problem, knocking his boots to the hot sand below.

Muttering under his breath and wondering why the only luck he ever seemed to get was bad, he lay flat on the stone to reach down for them. A pair of larger wooden clogs lay next to his boots. He whooped in delight and retrieved them both, then tried the clogs for size. They were still a bit too small, but were larger than the other pairs. He decided to improvise.

Pulling the laces from the clogs, he put on his own boots. Then, placing his booted feet onto the wooden platforms, he tied them to his legs with the laces. He stood upright to try his new footwear and, after wobbling on the spot for a moment, managed to walk a few tottering paces. He grinned, pleased with his ingenuity, then made his way to the edge and dropped lightly down into the sand. His feet sank to just below the top of the thick, wooden soles. With a satisfied smile, he made his way to the centre of the arena.

The sweat was dripping off him by the time he reached his objective, and his tunic was plastered to his back with perspiration. The heat was stifling and he was relieved to have achieved his goal. He stooped down next to the golden object to take a closer look. He could only see a small portion of whatever it was, where it protruded above the surface of the sand. He rubbed his chin as he stared down, trying to figure out how he could dig it out without burning himself.

An idea formed. He tottered back to the seating area and grabbed one of the smaller wooden clogs. Clutching his prize he returned to the semi-buried object, stooped down and began to rake away the sand using the clog as a shovel.

"This thing's huge," he gasped. He had been scraping away for more than an hour and still not revealed the full extent of the buried mass. "I wonder what it is?"

"HOLD!" a deep, angry voice echoed round the amphitheatre. "If you value your life, desist from your endeavours!"

Ryzak dropped the clog in surprise and spun to see who had shouted. Unbalanced by turning in his ungainly footwear, he toppled sideways, screeching as the heat from the sand scorched his flesh. It felt like his skin was on fire as he hastily scrambled to his feet.

"Wh–who's there?" he called, wincing at the pain from his burns.

"Oh, Ryzak," came the disappointed sound of Neulee's voice from somewhere above. "You – you idiot!"

Ryzak looked up at the entrance where he had first come in to the subterranean amphitheatre. His gaze fixed on the glares of Neulee and Snorkel. The huge form of Reizgoth was next to them, his yellow eyes swirling in fury.

"What have I done?" he asked, holding his hands out.

"Scrape the sand back around the egg," Reizgoth ordered, "before the temperature drops and the unborn queen dies. Then you will be informed of your errors."

Ryzak's eyes widened. "Egg?"

"SCRAPE THE SAND BACK, HUMAN!" Reizgoth's voice boomed around the cavern.

With a squeak of terror as he saw the dragon spread his wings and launch himself into the air, Ryzak hastily retrieved the clog and began pushing the sand back into place.

Reizgoth landed heavily beside him, causing a small, furious sand-storm. Ryzak cowered as hot, gritty particles sandblasted his already singed flesh.

"Hurry, human," Reizgoth snarled, using his hind legs to scoop sand over the egg. "If she dies, rest assured your death will not be as quick."

Recognising a threat when it was put so bluntly, Ryzak shovelled sand with renewed vigour. Within minutes all that could be seen of the ovaloid was a small patch of golden yellow.

Ryzak was dripping with sweat, and shattered, by the time they had finished. Gasping for breath, his burns stinging, he staggered back to the comfort of the gallery to lie, exhausted, on the cool stone. Reizgoth waddled over to where he lay and settled down in the sand beside him. "It is as well she lives, human," the dragon rumbled.

Ryzak raised his head at the sound of approaching footsteps. His nervous smile of greeting was met with furious glares from Neulee and Snorkel. Even Draco glowered at him from her perch on Snorkel's shoulder.

"You can be such a fool at times, Ryzak," Neulee snapped. "What on earth did you think you were doing?"

"I didn't know it was an egg," Ryzak whined. "I only wanted to see what it was."

"Enough!" broke in Reizgoth. "No harm has been done. The egg is undamaged. Galduran has interceded on your behalf and I will take no action – this time," the dragon finished, in an ominous tone.

"Galduran?" queried Ryzak.

"He means Snorkel," Neulee whispered, inclining her head toward the crimson-draped dwarf. His arms were crossed and he was observing Ryzak with an angry scowl.

At least he's taken those stupid eye-covers off, thought Ryzak, giving the dwarf a grateful smile.

Neulee kicked Ryzak in the shins and nodded at the dragon.

Ryzak gulped in apprehension and scrambled to his feet, wincing at the pain from his burns. He faced Reizgoth. "I–I–I didn't realise it was an egg. I–I …" Ryzak stuttered to a halt.

"You just saw the gold and thought you would have it," Reizgoth finished for him.

"No!" exclaimed Ryzak. "No … well … yes. I really am sorry, Your High … er … Magnif … er …"

"Reizgoth will do, human."

"Sorry, Reizgoth," Ryzak mumbled, hanging his head in dejection.

The dragon nodded his acceptance, then turned to Neulee. "Now is the time for answers," he rumbled. "Why are you here? What were you trying to steal?" Under his baleful gaze Neulee stepped back a pace.

"Allow me to explain, Mighty Reizgoth," Snorkel offered.

Reizgoth smiled down affectionately. "Galduran, please speak," he requested. "At least I can expect the truth from you."

"He wouldn't know the truth if it hit him in the arse," muttered Ryzak under his breath, earning another kick in the shins from Neulee.

"Before I begin, I have to inform you that I am not he whom you believe me to be. I am not Galduran. I am Snorkel, a dwarf from the Dwarven Mountains."

The dragon gave an amused chuckle. "My little friend," said Reizgoth, "I know that, but it pleases me to call you after my dearly departed rider. We spent many happy years together before he passed from this plane, and I have taken no other rider since. You remind me of him. Please continue with your tale, and after I would be pleased to tell you our story."

Settling himself on the edge of the stone tiering, Snorkel related all that had befallen them. Ryzak was amazed that the dwarf did not embellish the story, even when he came to the part about inadvertently changing Clara from a mule into a fine, young pony. This was not the Snorkel he knew. Something had definitely changed him.

"Show me the seal," Reizgoth demanded, when Snorkel had finished.

Ryzak rummaged in his tunic and fished out the disc. He held out his hand, the golden disc nestling in his outstretched palm. The dragon bent down and gazed at it with a large, dinner-plate-sized eye.

"Ah, yes," he breathed, drawing his head back, "I remember. It was brought to me by one of those irritating little dragonets, many years ago. I sensed wizard's magic about it and refused the gift. I did not realise the creature had hidden it away in my lair. And this was a seal imprisoning an evil sorcerer, you say? Interesting."

"That is why we must leave," said Snorkel. "Ryzak must place the seal before Mishtar manages to break free and ravage Middle Vooragh."

"I understand," agreed Reizgoth. "But first hear my story. I have a feeling the endings of both tales are intertwined."

The dragon settled back, his eyes taking on a distant look.

"We dragons are an old race; far older than any that currently inhabit what you call Middle Vooragh. We were old when man took his first steps. We were masters of the air and all the lands, enjoying the kind of supremacy that none had previously, or since, experienced. We feared nothing; which was to be our ultimate undoing.

"One of the first races to develop were the ancestors of the dwarfs, a people called the Ogmus. They managed to evolve powers of the mind – what is now known as magic – and used their skills for healing and the general good of the land. The dragons befriended the little people, who healed sick and injured dragons, and soon became an integral part of dragon life.

"We dismissed man and the other developing races as in-significant, only taking a slight interest in them. As the years passed, man became stronger and more numerous, developing weapons of war and ravaging the lands like locusts. At first we were not troubled by this and continued raiding their herds for food. The captive beasts were far easier to catch than the wild, roaming animals. We enjoyed abundant food supplies.

"Soon man became tired of us hunting their cattle and flocks. They turned hunters themselves, trapping and killing dragons using ever more vicious and barbaric methods. They even raided our lairs, smashing the eggs and killing the yet-to-be-born infants. This troubled us greatly. Due to our longevity, young were born infrequently. Our offspring were being slaughtered faster than we could reproduce.

"The Ogmus turned from dragon healers to dragon riders. From their lofty positions they would use their abilities to strike out at the attackers to preserve the few remaining dragons.

"However, soon only myself and a handful of males were left to defend our queen. We were not enough. It would only be a matter of time before the last bastion of the dragons was overrun and we were killed, leaving no trace of our passing.

"The elders of the Ogmus spent many a year trying to find a place of refuge for us, where we could live in peace and prosper. Using the combined power of their minds, they found a path to safety, although not of this world.

"They located a place amongst the stars, abundant with wildlife and free of mankind. They told the queen of this wondrous world and it was agreed that we would depart that very same day. However, there was one problem. The queen had recently laid a golden egg, an egg containing the future queen of the dragons. It would not survive the journey. One of us had to remain to protect it. I was that last dragon, protector of our unborn queen.

"In their wisdom, the Ogmus protected the egg with spells, ensuring the queen would not enter this world until one of their kind appeared to unlock the chains that preserved the yet-to-be-born infant. I was chosen as the physical barrier to protect her. I was the youngest and strongest dragon left.

"They cast a web of concealment over the entrance to the lair, to hinder man, then opened the gateway to the other world. They passed through within moments, leaving me with my ward. Here I have remained for the last five hundred years, only occasionally leaving the confines of my mountain home to hunt for food and the odd trinket or two, waiting for he-who-is-foretold."

Reizgoth's enormous head swung towards Snorkel, his eyes sparkling with excitement. "You are the one, Galduran. I can sense the magic in you. It is not of this time; it is older. You are Ogmus!"

Ryzak expected Snorkel to splutter a denial, tell Reizgoth he was mistaken. But he was disappointed. His mouth fell open as he saw the little man, tears streaming down his face, drop to his knees and dip his head to the floor, his arms spread in supplication.

In a tone both soft and gentle, Reizgoth bade him rise. "You have no need to bow down before me, Galduran. We are equals, now and forever."

His face wet with tears, Snorkel straightened and, in a voice carrying far more presence than Ryzak had heard before, said, "I know you speak the truth. When I healed you I felt whole, complete. I knew I was where I belonged. Here, with you. The knowledge of the Ogmus is open to me."

Snorkel rose to his feet. Despite his comic appearance he seemed to have grown in stature. "I know what needs to be done. First, however, I must finish what we started in this world, and I require your assistance."

Chapter Twenty

The dust settled and a large, red, winged, reptilian shape began to materialise.

"Reizgoth," Shula murmured in awe. It could be none other.

A loud sneeze rattled the windows of the tavern behind her, the power of the minor hurricane causing her to stumble back under its foetid blast. By the gods, she had never heard of a dragon pebble-dashing its victim to death before, but she supposed there was always a first time. Wiping gritty dollops of mucus from her face, she looked at the frightening apparition with apprehension, then cringed expectantly as the dragon snorted loudly and shook its huge, scaled head.

Shula relaxed as she heard Reizgoth's sigh of relief, and was immediately bowled over as he sneezed again. This one was more forceful than the last. The rush of phlegm-charged wind lifted her from her feet and sent her crashing over the prone form of Jollif.

Windswept, bruised and damp from her latest nasal drenching, Shula scrambled to her feet and warily fixed her gaze on the dragon. She swallowed involuntarily as large, yellow eyes swung her way.

Reizgoth's lips curled back in a parody of a grin, and his head dipped lower.

Shula screamed.

So did Reizgoth.

Confused by the dragon's reaction, Shula's screech faded. The big red creature had sat on its haunches and was peering at her with solemn eyes.

"Do not be afraid. I mean you no harm," Reizgoth soothed.

"You can speak?" Shula asked in amazement.

"Of course he can," replied a small, crimson clad figure as it jumped from the dragon's back. Removing its glass-fronted eye-covers, the diminutive rider gave her a cheery grin.

Shula's eyes widened in surprise. "Snorkel?" she gasped, recognising the bearded face peering out from beneath the strange red hat. "Is it really you?"

"None other," Snorkel grinned. "Allow me to introduce my friend Reizgoth. Reizgoth, meet Shula, Matriarch of the Sisters of the New Dawn."

The dragon dipped his head in greeting. "It is an honour, Matriarch," his deep, mellow voice boomed.

"Likewise," Shula responded. "And, I might add, your timely delivery of Snorkel may just have averted a catastrophe." She glanced at her stained, bespattered robe and gave a wry grin. "Although you might also have caused one," she murmured.

The redness of the dragon's face appeared to deepen under her accusing look.

"Why? What's the matter?" queried Snorkel.

"Beulah," Shula replied. "He is at death's door. Something happened while he was unlocking the secrets of the orb and his soul has been trapped inside. We can't get him back. We brought him here in the hope that you can save him."

"If he can be saved, I will save him," Snorkel replied confidently.

Shula looked deeply into his eyes, taken aback by the hard, assured gaze that was levelled in her direction. Whatever had befallen the dwarf on his travels had certainly changed him. She was no longer facing a dim, retarded little cretin, but a person with – intelligence?

"Is something the matter?" Snorkel asked.

"N–n–no. I am just worried about Beulah, that's all," Shula stammered, realising she had been staring at him for too long.

"Remind me who this Beulah is," Reizgoth requested.

"He is, or was, my master," answered Snorkel, turning to face the dragon. "I must help him, or try at least."

Reizgoth lowered his head to dwarf level. "Is there anything I can do to help?" he offered.

Snorkel gave a chuckle and rubbed the soft skin of the dragon's snout affectionately. "No, my friend. You go and hunt. I will call you when I am finished. You need to build your strength for our journey."

Letting his gaze linger on the little man for a moment, Reizgoth nodded, then raised his head. "Take care, Galduran. I could not bear losing you so soon after being reunited. Think of the yet-to-be-born queen. We shall await your call."

Reizgoth bugled a farewell and stretched his wing membranes, then launched himself into the air, the dust created by his departure making Snorkel and Shula duck and cover their eyes. By the time they could see clearly again, the dragon had become a small speck on the distant horizon.

"What happened to him?" Snorkel asked, spotting Jollif's prone figure.

Shula chuckled and gave a shrug. "You know Jollif and dragons."

A smile of understanding split Snorkel's face. Walking over to the still form of the tavern-keeper, he stooped down and placed his fingertips either side of the man's head. In a matter of seconds Jollif's eyes blinked open to stare into the dwarf's dirt-encrusted features. "Wa–wa–was that a dragon?" he whispered.

"Sure was," answered Snorkel. "A big red one!"

Jollif's eyes glazed over and he passed out again.

"I think we'd best leave him where he is," Snorkel laughed. "Now. Where's Beulah?"

"Follow me," Shula instructed. She stepped over Jollif and led Snorkel into the tavern and up the stairs to the first floor.

The small village of Fleshwick gradually stirred to life. Doors slowly opened as nervous inhabitants poked their heads out, wanting to make sure the big red beast had gone before they dared venture outside. Soon the whole population was in the main street, discussing the frightening apparition in tense, huddled groups with friends and neighbours.

By the time the tale was relayed around the surrounding country-side it had been substantially embellished, each storyteller adding their own little bit: Reizgoth was at least two hundred feet long, had curved horns of burnished gold, breathed huge flames, had eaten half the villagers of Fleshwick and was ridden by the Devil himself. It became a tale oft repeated to recalcitrant children, late at night, by parents who had had enough for the day.

"If you don't behave and go straight to sleep, the Devil will fly down and roast you in your beds. And don't expect to come running to us when he's eaten you."

Shula halted outside the door leading to the rooms they were using and turned to Snorkel. "Where are Ryzak and the girl?" she asked.

"Following on with the horses," Snorkel replied. "Reizgoth is still weak since I cured him. He could not carry us all. Anyway, I had become rather fond of Clara and did not want to leave her behind."

"Clara?"

"My pony," Snorkel replied. His eyes narrowed as he gave her a thoughtful look. "How did you know about Neulee?"

"The orb," she answered, then turned to lift the latch. "Beulah is in here," she said, opening the door and ushering the dwarf inside.

As he entered, Snorkel flicked his gaze round the small, nondescript living area for signs of the wizard. He could not see him. However, his gaze did linger briefly on each of the two robed sisters sitting in chairs beside the fire. They looked up, regarding him with astonishment.

"Where is he?" Snorkel asked, turning to Shula.

"Through here," she answered, leading the way across the room to a small door to their right.

Snorkel gasped in alarm when he saw the swaddled form of the wizard. He hurried to the side of the bed and leaned over, placing his hands on Beulah's temples. "How long has he been like this?" he asked, his voice tinged with anxiety.

"A couple of weeks now," Shula replied. "We have tried everything in our power to reach him, but we can't. Wherever his soul has gone, it is beyond our reach."

"Where's the orb?" Snorkel demanded.

"In here," a voice answered from the doorway.

The dwarf looked at the girl who stood there. "Well bring it here," he ordered. "Time is of the essence. If I am to save the wizard I need to be about it straight away."

"Matriarch?" the sister queried. The look on her face hinted at her doubts as to whether the funny little man in the red suit was capable of any such thing.

"Do as he asks, Megan," Shula replied softly, giving her a reassuring smile. "I am sure Snorkel knows what is best."

Snorkel removed his flying hat, gloves and cape and laid them on the floor beside the bed, then rose and leaned over the wizard. Placing his hands on Beulah's head, he closed his eyes and allowed his inner being to merge with him. When he opened them again Megan was standing beside him, the crystal sphere clasped in her hands.

The dwarf gave a curt nod of approval. "Excellent. Place it here, on Beulah's stomach."

Meganrhys did as she was bid and stepped back. Snorkel pulled the blankets aside and lifted Beulah's arms, arranging them so his hands cupped the top of the sphere. He grew more worried when he saw the man's skeletal limbs. The wizard had been like a stick insect before, but was even thinner now. There was no weight in his arms and the skin had the appearance and texture of ancient parchment, the veins narrow and clearly defined. How Beulah still lived he would never know.

Satisfied that the wizard's hands would not slip off the top of the orb, Snorkel turned to face the sisters. "Leave me now," he commanded. "It is best I am alone."

"But what happens if it all goes wrong?" Meganrhys asked. "Then we will have two of you beyond our reach."

He fixed her with a steely gaze. "That will not happen," he stated. Turning to Shula, he said, "I know where Beulah's soul is imprisoned. I can get there, and get back again. Whether I can bring him back with me remains to be seen. I need to be alone to prepare myself. You understand?"

Shula held his gaze for a moment then nodded. "Come. Let us leave Snorkel to his task," she said quietly, placing a hand on Meganrhys's arm.

As the door closed softly behind them, Snorkel gave a humourless smile at the hushed conversation that reached his ears.

"I thought you said the dwarf was a cretin?"

"He is, or was. But at this moment he is our only hope. Come, let us see if Jollif has regained consciousness, and get him to brew us a pot of that herbal tea. There is nothing for us to do here but wait."

"Yes, Matriarch. What happened to your robe?"

A heavy sigh, then: "It's a long story, Megan."

The outer door closed. Snorkel frowned as he knelt on the floor next to the bed and closed his eyes. He'd better get this right, or being thought of as a cretin would be the least of his worries.

Entering the wizard's being, he re-checked all the vital organs and arteries; invigorating them; making them whole; rejuvenating them. The last thing he needed was for the body to fail while he was in the abyss with the man's soul. There would be no return for either of them if that happened.

Satisfied that Beulah was stable, his inner being flowed down the wizard's arm, through the fingers and into the orb. He did not have time to spend admiring the fish-shaped parcels of magic that swam to greet him; he was totally focused on what he had to do.

His arms and legs struck out strong and determined towards the distant, vague copy of Wizard's Keep. In no time at all he was entering the open doorway of the main hall and heading to the stairway leading to the basement. Leaping down the steps two at a time, he soon reached the bottom, and became aware of a low hum as he made his way to the large, central cell.

Warily he slowed his pace and entered the room. The humming got louder. He winced. A pulsating, violet light appeared at the head of the well in the rear wall. With his hands cupped over his ears, he slowly moved closer.

The brain-numbing throb intensified.

Snorkel felt the wet trickle of blood between his fingers and panicked. There must be some way of blocking out the sound, but he could not think straight.

"HEEEEEELLLP MEEEEEEEE!" The words were out of his mouth before he realised that he'd shrieked them. If he could, he would have laughed at his stupidity, but the pain was too great.

A feathery voice whispered in his head. He did not catch the words.

"WHHHHAAAAAAT!"

'Use the magic, Galduran. Use the magic.'

Reizgoth?

Breaking free of its paralysis, his mind focused on the magic of the Ogmus, forcing out the noise. Immediately, there was silence. He felt as though he had gone deaf. He groaned and sank to his knees as his strength deserted him. Weakly raising his head, he looked at the well. Although the noise had stopped, the violet glow was still there. He grimaced, rose to his feet, and approached it – then stopped.

He was in no condition to free Beulah. He could only just walk, never mind fight whatever it was that held the wizard. He mouthed another spell and felt strength and vitality fill his spirit. He smiled and glanced down at his nakedness. "This will never do."

In an instant he was clad in crimson armour from head to toe. "Now for some weapons." Moments later he was grasping two gleaming, steel scimitars.

He had no idea how to use them, but feeling confident with them in his hands, he strode towards the well. He stopped beside it, alert for any sign of danger. The suddenness of the red, scaled claw shooting out of the orifice took him completely by surprise. A shrill scream of terror escaped his lips as he was dragged in.

Colours blurred into one, the speed at which he was moving almost making him pass out. He could not have struck at the scaled claw even if he wanted to, being rendered powerless by the rapidity of his progress. At the bottom of the descent the claw released him, sending him sprawling on a hard, cobbled surface. The scimitars struck sparks as they clattered from nerveless fingers.

Dazed, but not unconscious, Snorkel struggled to his feet and looked frantically around for his weapons, but could not see them. The large, domed cell in which he had landed was devoid of any-thing resembling his swords. There was not even a sign of where he had entered. The dull, ochre stone of the room was unbroken.

"Looking for theethe?" a smug-sounding voice enquired.

Snorkel turned to face the speaker, his eyes widening in astonishment. "Dad?"

"Thtill a failure, hey, boy?" his father said disappointedly. "It would appear that even Beulah could not help you. Well, you'll be no great loth."

Springing forward, the scimitars twirling in glittering arcs, his father lunged at him.

"No, Dad. No!" wailed Snorkel, diving out of the way as a razor sharp blade whizzed past his head.

"You can dodge all you like, boy," his father snarled, "but I'll finith you thoon enough. Make it eathy on yourthelf, thtand thtill. I'll make it quick."

Snorkel circled as his father closed in, keeping out of reach of the keen, curved blades.

"Thtop running, boy. Fathe it like a man. You can't ethcape."

Ignoring the mumbled threats, Snorkel concentrated on staying alive, his mind racing. Something was not quite as it appeared. For the life of him he could not think what it was. His father suddenly lunged with a lightening quick manoeuvre, far faster than he had any right to move. In his haste to avoid the twin blades, Snorkel tripped. Sparks flew from the cobbles as he rolled clear of a descending blade. Spinning on his back, he kicked the feet from under his attacker, sending him crashing to the ground. A scimitar flew free. Snorkel scrambled over and grasped the hilt of the spilled blade, then sprang to his feet with it firmly clenched in his hand. He turned to face his adversary.

"I thee you've got thome fight in you, boy. That'th better. Don't want to make it too eathy now, do we?" his father growled, rising to his feet.

They circled, each looking for an opening. Snorkel suddenly stopped, a stunned expression on his face. Standing straight, he threw his blade to one side, then magicked the armour away. Naked, he stood before the being that professed to be his father.

"I'll not fight you," Snorkel informed his startled adversary, folding his arms across his barrel-like chest.

"But you mutht!" exclaimed the nonplussed image of his father.

"Why?" Snorkel asked.

"Becauthe ... becauthe you have to!"

Snorkel shook his head. "No I don't."

"You have to!" his father ordered, his voice becoming a deep, menacing growl.

Snorkel sat down on the ground, then lay on his side, his head propped on the palm of his hand. "No I don't."

The features of his father wavered, as if Snorkel were looking at a reflected image in a pool of water that had been disturbed by ripples. The gnarled face distorted and became bloated, the scaled red skin of a demon erupting through the flesh. The figure grew until it towered above him. All resemblance to his father disappeared, replaced by a seven foot lizard with glowing, red eyes.

"Fight me then," the demon growled, advancing on the dwarf.

Instead of looking terrified, Snorkel smiled a welcome. "Come. Sit with me," he invited. "There's no need for us to fight; it's too energetic. Fancy a drink?" He waved a hand and a table appeared beside him, laden with pastries and beakers of fruit juice.

The demon halted his advance and shook his head in confusion, staring at the dwarf as if he had taken leave of his senses. "But you mutht fight me," he repeated, a whine entering his voice.

Snorkel picked a pastry off the table and took a bite. "You really should try one of these," he said, "they're delicious. Why not join me and tell me how you got to be here?"

"Fight me!" the demon pleaded.

"No."

"Why not?"

"Because adults shouldn't fight. That's kids stuff: they don't know any better. We, on the other hand, do." Snorkel smiled, hoping this demon was as thick as his new-found knowledge suggested most demons were. The signs were excellent on that score at the moment. "What's your name?"

"Er, Chrysothenalazm. But you can call me Chryth," the demon replied shyly.

"Right then, Chryth," Snorkel said, with a relieved smile, "want a drink?"

"That would be nithe," Chrysothenalazm answered, squatting on the floor next to the table and helping himself to a beaker of juice. "And the name is Chryth, not Chryth."

Masking his puzzlement, Snorkel tried to work this one out. "Ahhh, *Chrys*," he said, as understanding hit him. Even with the knowledge of the Ogmus he sometimes had to rely on his own mental process, which could be damned inconvenient.

"That'th what I thaid," Chrys said reproachfully, reaching across the table to pluck a pastry from one of the bowls.

"Yeah, sorry about that one. The fall must have jangled my hearing." Snorkel grinned.

Aware he was still naked, the dwarf clicked his fingers and was immediately clothed in a long, white, flowing robe. He picked up a drink and took a mouthful before turning back to the demon. "Been here long?" he asked.

"Ageth," the demon grumbled.

Snorkel tutted sympathetically. "That must be hard. Locked away from all your friends with no one to speak to."

"It'th not tho bad," Chrysothenalazm said, shovelling another pastry into his maw. "Mmmm, theethe are nithe. Mind if I have another?"

"Not at all. Help yourself," replied Snorkel magnanimously. "Plenty more where they came from. Don't you get bored down here on your own?"

"No. I have a friend," said Chrysothenalazm, leaning forward conspiratorially. The demon glanced nervously around, his voice dropping to a whisper. "I've not had him long, and if the bad man found out I wath being nithe to my friend he would not be happy, not happy at all."

"What bad man?" Snorkel asked. "I would have thought such as you would not be scared of anyone."

Chrysothenalazm shook his head sadly. "Thith ith a very bad man, a thtrong magic-uther. He tricked me and locked me down here. He told me to torment anybody who entered. Not to kill them, jutht to play with them a little, or he would never let me free."

"But you were going to kill me," Snorkel pointed out.

The demon gave a small smile and looked embarrassed. "Naaaah, I wath only playing. I wouldn't really have killed you. Jutht roughed you up a little."

"That's reassuring," mumbled the dwarf. "Where's this friend of yours, then?" he asked, "I'd like to meet him."

"He'th not very well," Chrysothenalazm said sadly, his eyes downcast.

"Oh?" Snorkel tried to hide his panic. "What's the matter with him?" he asked.

"I don't know," replied the demon, looking up and shrugging. "He jutht lieth there now, not moving."

"Take me to him," Snorkel urged, "I might be able to help him."

"Really?" said the demon. His eyes lit up briefly, before a wary look took over. "Why would you want to help me?"

"If you can't help a friend in need, who can you help?"

Chrysothenalazm pondered this for a moment, then stood up. "You thure you won't tell the bad man?" he asked, nervously fidgeting with a bread roll until all that remained was a pile of crumbs on the floor.

"Promise!" replied Snorkel, rising to his feet. "Cross my heart and hope to … er, lead on, Chrys."

"He'th not far away," rumbled the demon.

Snorkel followed the reptile to the opposite side of the cell and gasped as he disappeared through the ochre blocks of the wall. Quickening his pace, he pushed through as well, shivering at the crawling sensation that ran through his body. He emerged in a different cell, similar to the one he had just left, only this one had an occupant. The spirit form of Beulah lay in the centre of the cobbled floor, apparently lifeless. His eyes were open but not seeing, and his pale, naked, scrawny body was covered with a mass of bruises and cuts.

Snorkel ran over and knelt by the wizard's side. He glanced up at the sound of the demon's voice.

"He'th not been much fun lately," Chrysothenalazm grumbled. "Ever thince he tried to kith me and I whacked him one, he'th just lain there."

If this is the way he treats his friends, who would want to be an enemy? thought Snorkel as he felt for signs of life. He was reassured by a flicker of recognition in Beulah's eyes.

"Why would he try to kiss you?" Snorkel asked, amazed at the idea of anyone wanting to pucker up to a big, smelly red lizard.

The demon shrugged his shoulders. "Something I thaid?" he replied innocently.

Shaking his head Snorkel rose to his feet. "I'm afraid your friend is dying," he said. A tinge of sadness entered his voice as he put on his most sorrowful expression.

Chrys looked crestfallen. Then he suddenly smiled. "It doethn't matter now," he said, "I've jutht realithed. I've got you."

Perhaps this was not working out quite as he intended. Snorkel gave the demon a hard look. "Er, no. It doesn't quite work like that. When you have friends, you help them when they are in trouble. You don't just dump them when another pops along. That's not being a true friend."

"Oh," said the demon, despondently.

"Anyway," Snorkel continued, "the bad man would not be pleased if you let him die, would he?"

A gleam of panic appeared in the demon's eye. "What can I do?" he implored. "The bad man would do nathty thingth to me if he found out."

Snorkel tapped his chin with a stubby digit, deep in thought. After a few moments he looked up. "I have an idea," he said, "but I need your help. Carry Beu– the man through to the cell we have just come from and lay him on the floor."

Nodding with enthusiasm, Chrysothenalazm walked over and picked up the limp form of the wizard. Chuckling to himself, he carried Beulah into the adjoining cell.

"Two friendth now, how lucky can one demon get?"

Snorkel snorted in bemusement and followed Chrys through the wall. He watched as the lizard carefully laid Beulah down, then moved forward and knelt behind the wizard, lifting his head and laying it on his lap.

"This is the tricky part," Snorkel said, looking up at the demon. "I need you to kneel down by his feet, close your eyes, and focus your mind on your friend. Don't open them until I tell you to, otherwise it will spoil the magic and your friend will die."

Chrysothenalazm did as he was told, then fixed his glowing eyes on the dwarf. "You would not trick me, would you?" he asked.

"Would a true friend trick another?" Snorkel responded, assuming a hurt expression.

"Thuppothe not," lisped the demon.

"Right then," said Snorkel. "Close your eyes and we'll begin. Remember. Don't open them until I tell you to."

Snorkel closed his own eyes first, wanting to reassure Chrys, then waited a moment before cracking one open to check whether the demon had done as he was told. Seeing that he had, he gave a satisfied smile and closed his eye, readying himself for their journey. He placed his hands either side of Beulah's head and silently intoned the incantation that would transport them back to the real world.

A light breeze ruffled Snorkel's hair, gradually growing until it became a wind. It was a feeling he recognised from his escape from Mishtar's dreamscape. The wind became a gale, snatching him from his feet. Together he and the wizard were blown along by the tempest, tumbling through a pitch-black void.

Feeling the press of boards under his knees, Snorkel opened his eyes, relieved to find himself in the room at Jollif's tavern. He scrambled to his feet, wincing as his joints clicked from being bent for too long, and moved to check on the unconscious form of Beulah. His probing fingertips found a strong pulse. He looked down at the sleeping figure of his ex-master and gawked in astonishment.

Gone were the wrinkles from Beulah's face. Gone were the large, bushy, white eyebrows. Gone was the long, straggly mop of white hair. He was staring down at the face of a young man in the prime of his life.

"Bugger me," Snorkel murmured. "I must have cured more than his dickey heart when I checked him over."

* * * * *

Deep in the heart of the orb, the demon knelt on the hard, cobbled surface of the floor, his eyes still closed. He had been in the same position for hours and his new friend had still not told him to open them. His knees were starting to ache. "Can I open my eyeth now?" he asked.

When no answer was forthcoming he started to get nervous. Should he take a look and risk spoiling the magic, or should he wait a little longer? Deciding the strange little man had had time enough to cure the human, he opened his eyes.

Staring at the bare floor, it took a while before he realised he had been tricked. Then, jumping to his feet, he roared his anger to the stones. "You ... you ... you little bastard!" he shrieked. "You wait until I get fwee. Then I will week my wevenge! Bugger!"

His tirade halted mid-yell. What had the little man done? He had quite liked his lisp and now he had a ...

"You're dead-meat, you bloody wunt! You hear me? Dead-meat!"

So saying he burst into tears. How could anyone take him seriously with a speech impediment like this?

Chapter Twenty One

Snorkel walked through to the living area and stopped dead in his tracks. "Ryzak, Neulee? How did you get here so quickly?"

'Mum!' The ecstatic mind-speak of Draco blasted into his head, as she launched herself from the mantle. *'You're alive!'* Chirruping happily, she landed on the dwarf's shoulder and nuzzled his neck.

"Hello, little one," Snorkel chuckled, giving her an affectionate tickle under her chin. "Pleased to see me?"

'You bet, Mum,' she replied. *'They thought you were dying.'*

Shula, Ryzak, Neulee and Jollif leapt from their seats and surrounded him, all firing questions, demanding explanations.

"Whoa," shouted Snorkel, raising his hands to ward off the verbal onslaught. "Let me breathe. Beulah's fine. He just needs some rest."

Reluctantly, they quietened.

"That's better," smiled the dwarf. "Now then. First things first." He rubbed his hands together in anticipation and fixed his gaze on Jollif. "Any chance of a drink?"

Seeing his hopeful expression, Jollif snorted in amusement. "Some things never change," he grinned. "There's something over here that might do the trick. Real dwarven ale. Go and sit down and I'll bring you a tankard."

Snorkel sank into the soft, down-filled cushions of the low couch with a contented sigh, and gave a brief smile to the two sisters sitting opposite. Not giving him a chance to relax, his friends immediately sat round him and started with their questions again.

"Well, what happened?" asked Shula eagerly. "And why does Beulah look so young?"

The dwarf gave a thin smile and shrugged. "Not quite sure," he replied. "I guess I must have fixed more than his heart before I went into the orb. I only wanted to make sure he didn't peg it while I was trying to rescue his spirit. Let's hope I improved his temper as well as his looks, hey?" he added, with a wink.

"What happened in there?" Ryzak asked, echoing Shula's question. "And why did it take you so long?"

Snorkel turned to peer at Ryzak, who was sitting on the other side of him. He raised an eyebrow as he saw Neulee sitting on his knee, an arm draped lovingly round his shoulders. "How did you get here so quickly?" Snorkel countered. "You had only just started back when Reizgoth and myself flew off."

"Quickly?" snorted Ryzak. "It's taken us nearly two weeks. You've been inside the orb for at least seven days."

"What? Seven days? No wonder I'm starving."

"Time runs differently in the orb," Shula advised. "Beulah told us about that, after the first time we had to rescue him." Her eyebrows rose in mock sufferance.

Jollif arrived with a brimming tankard in his hand. "Here's your drink. You look like you could do with it."

Snorkel smiled and took the proffered vessel. "Damn right I could, it's thirsty work rescuing wizards from demons."

"Demons?" his friends chorused.

"Well, one actually," Snorkel admitted. He took a huge gulp of his drink, then wiped froth from his lips with the back of his hand before continuing.

"So there you have it," he concluded, giving Shula a tight-lipped smile. "Until the demon is dead or removed from the orb, you won't have full access to its power. Although one thing I did discover …"

"Was that Mishtar has created a reservoir to store magic," a voice finished for him from the direction of the bedroom. Everyone turned to look at the doorway.

Shula's face lit with a happy smile. "Beulah!" she cried, running into his outstretched arms.

"Blimey, things have certainly changed since he was last here," muttered Jollif.

"More than one, actually," said Ryzak, with a grin. He turned to look at Neulee and clasped her hand. "Neulee and I are to be wed."

Reddening as Jollif and Snorkel enthusiastically offered their congratulations, and commiserations, Neulee squirmed in discomfort at their vociferous attention. The more so when the dwarf puckered up to plant a wet, sloppy kiss on her lips. Beulah's approach rescued her.

"I see you are all still alive then?" the wizard remarked, gripping Snorkel's shoulder in thanks and offering him a grateful smile.

Snorkel looked up and grinned an acknowledgement, then gave Shula a broad wink. She was clinging to the wizard's arm as if expecting him to disappear at any moment.

"Just about," muttered Ryzak. "Despite his," he nodded toward the dwarf, "best attempts to get us all killed. Between elves, cannibals and big red dragons, I never thought we would live through it."

Jollif blanched. The mere mention of dragons was enough to send him into paroxysms.

"We're here, aren't we?" snapped Snorkel, his eyes flashing. "And," he pointed out, "if it were not for our little adventure, you would not now be getting wed."

Ryzak pulled a face and shrugged, then glanced at Neulee. "I suppose so," he conceded. "And we did get one of the seals."

"Excellent," beamed the wizard. "That means there is only one more to find."

"You mean you haven't found it?" said Ryzak.

Beulah glared down at him. "Unfortunately I was a little tied up." Turning to Shula, he looked into her eyes and smiled. "However, I am sure the matriarch can use the orb to help us, now I've managed to free most of the locked magic."

Shula blushed and lowered her lashes.

"What does it feel like to be young again?" Jollif asked suddenly.

The wizard's brow creased in confusion as he fixed the tavern-keeper with a puzzled look. "Being what again?" he asked.

"You know, being young? No more wrinkles and all that?"

"My dear man, I haven't the faintest idea what you are talking about."

Snorkel squirmed in his seat as Jollif walked over to the table and picked up a hand mirror, then passed it to Beulah.

Raising it to his face, the wizard's eyebrows rose in disbelief as he gazed at the wrinkle-free features reflected back. Framed by a thick mass of long, brown hair, it was the face of a young man.

"My word. How?" he whispered, his stunned gaze switching to the dwarf.

How was he going to get out of this one? Deciding on his best plan of attack, Snorkel met the wizard's querying look with a vacant grin.

"Never mind, you can tell me later," Beulah muttered, shaking his head. "I am sure it will make for interesting listening."

* * * * *

Later in the day, Beulah and Snorkel sat in Jollif's private room tucking into a welcome meal of meat and vegetables. Washed down with some fine, Alduran Brandy, it was a meal fit for kings. Or so it felt to their growling stomachs.

They hadn't spoken much since the gathering had broken up: Ryzak and Neulee to go to a bedroom to further their relationship; Jollif to tend the bar; Draco for a nap; Shula and the two sisters to see if they could trace the last seal with the orb. Each was absorbed in their own thoughts. Or, in Snorkel's case, his stomach.

After dabbing gravy from his chin with a cloth, Beulah leaned back in his chair and heaved a satisfied sigh. He chuckled in amusement as Snorkel heaped more meat and vegetables onto his plate. "It beats me where you put it all," he said. "For such a small person, you sure eat a lot."

"Keeping body and soul together," mumbled the dwarf, globules of food spraying out as he replied with his mouth full. "Being informed that I wasted a week in that damned orb, with only weak broth being forced down my throat for sustenance, set my stomach to protesting. I'm making up for lost time."

As if to make his point, Snorkel mopped gravy from his plate with a chunk of bread and rammed the saturated piece into his mouth. Dribbles of brown liquid ran into his beard.

Beulah chuckled. It was a shame the dwarf's table manners had not improved as much as his powers. He grasped his beaker and raised it to his mouth, taking a small, appreciative sip of brandy. By the gods, it was good stuff. He must ask Jollif where he had got it. His thoughts turned serious.

Swirling the drink absent-mindedly in the beaker, he gazed into space as he wondered, not for the first time, how on earth the dwarf had managed to save him. Where had the power come from? As far as he could discern, Snorkel was still no wizard, yet he had entered the orb, defeated a demon and managed to rescue him. Things did not add up. Although he could sense an aura around the little man, it was not the aura of earth magic, or any type of magic he knew. He was confused. Just what was he? Having listened intently as the dwarf regaled them with tales of their adventure and how they befriended Reizgoth, he was still none the wiser. But of one thing he was sure: Snorkel had not told him everything.

Beulah placed his beaker on the table and leaned forward. He cleared his throat. "What are you?" he asked.

The serious manner in which the question was delivered made Snorkel halt mid-chew. He briefly locked eyes with Beulah, then gave a tight-lipped smile and nodded. "I am a descendant of the Ogmus," he replied. "One of the first races of mankind, or dwarven-kind to be exact."

Beulah's brows rose in surprise at Snorkel's words. "I was aware of the legend of the Ogmus. But I always thought that is what it was, a legend," he murmured. "If you had not told me the dragon's tale I would not have put any credence to it. It always sounded, still sounds, far fetched."

"As hard as it may be to believe, it is no legend. I know."

Studying his former apprentice's solemn expression, Beulah saw the full extent of the transformation. Although he had not quite come to terms with the apparel the dwarf currently wore, though it was marginally better than his previous attire, he could see that all aspects of his former, somewhat asinine persona had gone. He indicated for the dwarf to continue.

"When it was time to leave this world for another, Reizgoth was left to protect the unborn queen from physical harm. The Ogmus protected the egg with spells to ensure she would not hatch until the time was right. They also concealed the entrance to the lair to ensure it would be years, hundreds of years, before man could again discover its whereabouts. When they were sure they had done all they could to protect the future queen, they departed.

"However, they also left one of their own behind to continue the line of the Ogmus. Salvorkel was his name."

Beulah gaped in astonishment at the familiar appellation.

Snorkel smiled. "I can see in your eyes that you understand. However, I will continue with the tale."

"Salvorkel wandered the land looking for the dwarfs, distant cousins of the Ogmus but with no magical ability, intent on joining the small mountain tribe to transfer his seed down their line. The spark of magic would be passed down to each generation until it was time to be germinated. That time is now. You were the catalyst for that germination and I am the result of Salvorkel's lineage. I am the last Ogmus on Middle Vooragh and, unfortunately, I must leave tomorrow to fulfil my destiny. My Queen and our New World await."

Beulah nodded his understanding and reached across the table to grip Snorkel's forearm. "Thank you for sharing your knowledge with me. I now know what has changed about you, my friend. I could sense something was different, but until your explanation I had no idea what." He grinned and released his hold. "I am proud to have been a part of your destiny, even though I knew nothing about it and thought you were a damned pain in the rear-end when I first took you on. You have my best wishes and deepest thanks for all your help and friendship. Even though I have not always shown it."

The door of the room suddenly flew open and slammed against the wall. Shula rushed in, her face creased with worry. The two magic users spun to face the gatecrasher and rose from their seats.

"What is it?" Beulah asked, hurrying to her side.

"We've found the seal," she cried, sagging into his arms.

Lifting his hands to grasp her shoulders, Beulah gently prised her away and smiled into her upturned face. "Why the frown, then?"

"It's the orb," she gasped, a hint of fear showing in her eyes. "It's completely open to us. There are no blocks preventing me using its powers!"

"That's fantastic," said Beulah, hugging her.

"No it's not," said Snorkel ominously, moving to join them.

"What do you mean?" asked Beulah.

"It means the demon is loose," the dwarf replied. "The last block was where Mishtar was storing the magic. The demon set to guard it. If the magic is free, so is the demon."

Beulah's mouth dropped open. By the gods, he was a fool sometimes. He should have realised. "Where's the last seal?" he asked Shula softly.

"In the lands of the barbarians."

"We had better get Ryzak and Neulee, then," said the wizard, his lips compressed. "It would appear their tasks are not yet finished. Not a word about the demon though; it would only upset them."

"Are you sure that is wise?" asked Shula.

Beulah looked at Snorkel.

"I agree," he concurred. "We'll keep it on a 'need to know' basis. At the moment, they don't need to know."

* * * * *

A loud, insistent knocking on the door roused Ryzak. He groaned at the rude awakening. "Who is it?" he yelled.

A door-muffled voice answered. "It's me, Jollif. I need to speak to you."

Ryzak scowled and gently lifted Neulee's arm off his chest, then gazing fondly down he smiled. She was beautiful, and she was his. Pleased that his luck seemed to have taken a change for the better, he eased himself out of the bed and staggered, naked, to the door. He half opened it and poked his head around the jamb. "What is it?" he asked, stifling a yawn with the back of his hand.

"Sorry, Ryzak," Jollif apologised, his gaze drawn past Ryzak's shoulder to the sleeping figure in the bed, "but we need you and Neulee downstairs straight away. They've found out where the last seal is."

Noticing the direction of his friend's crafty look, Ryzak moved to block his view, and had the pleasure of witnessing Jollif redden in embarrassment. "So?"

"Er, s–so your presence is required," Jollif stammered, looking at the floor.

"Oh," grunted Ryzak. "I suppose that means we're off on our travels again, does it?"

The tavern-keeper looked up and gave a lop-sided grin.

Ryzak sighed. "Tell them we'll be down shortly."

Closing the door he walked over to the bed and sat on the edge. He brushed a stray lock of hair from Neulee's face before leaning down to kiss her lightly on the forehead. At the feel of his lips, her eyelids flickered open. With a seductive smile, her arms snaked out from the covers and wrapped around his neck, drawing him into a passionate embrace. Aroused by her throaty chuckle, the urgency of Jollif's request was forgotten as Ryzak responded.

An hour later there was another knock on the door. Their passions spent, Ryzak and Neulee lay on top of the bed, their naked bodies covered with beads of perspiration.

"Who is it?" called Ryzak.

"It's me, Jollif," came the reply. "They're still waiting for you. Beulah's threatened to shrivel your manhood if you're not down in ten minutes."

Ryzak frowned. "We're coming," he shouted. Neulee sniggered. "What's the matter with you?" he asked, wondering what she found so amusing.

"I'd say we came about twenty minutes ago, my stallion," she replied.

* * * * *

"It's about time," Beulah remonstrated, as Ryzak and Neulee entered Jollif's living room half an hour later. "We have important matters to attend to and the longer you keep us waiting the less time we have left!"

Trying not to smirk, Ryzak apologised. He still could not get used to seeing Beulah looking so young and healthy. "We were tired after our ..." The glower of disapproval from Shula wiped the smirk off Ryzak's face. "Er, sorry," he mumbled, and led Neulee to a spare chair beside the table.

His back to the hearth, Beulah glared as Ryzak took his seat, and scowled as Neulee sat on his lap and draped an arm round his shoulders. "What's up?" asked Ryzak, not in the least perturbed by the wizard's dark look.

Beulah sighed in exasperation at the man's effrontery. "We know roughly where the last seal is."

"Great," responded Ryzak, giving Neulee an affectionate squeeze.

Beulah's scowl deepened at the sound of her girlish giggle. "When you two have quite finished," he scolded, "we have serious matters to discuss."

Ryzak gave Neulee a cheery wink and turned to the wizard. "Carry on, we're right with you. So where is this seal then?"

"In the barbarian lands," Shula's voice answered.

Ryzak's smile faded.

"It is somewhere in the northwest," Shula continued. "We could not get an exact location, but we know it is close to the borders."

Ryzak had a terrible foreboding about where all this was leading. And he did not like the sound of it one bit.

Beulah interjected. "We have decided that you and Neulee must go into the plains to seek the seal whilst …"

"Why us?" interrupted Ryzak, a note of panic in his voice. "Why not Snorkel, or you? Or Shula, for that matter?"

"Because you and your partner have a natural advantage over any of us here. With Neulee having come from the plains, you can succeed where we would fail," Beulah replied, his eyes hard and voice cold.

There was no compromise in the wizard's features. The decision had been made, with or without Ryzak's consent. Turning troubled eyes to Neulee, he was comforted by her half smile. Reassured, but still not happy, he turned to face the wizard. "What are you lot going to be doing while we go trekking around the countryside?"

"We," snapped Beulah, "will be placing the seal that is currently in your possession into its rightful place. Jollif has managed to persuade some of the villagers to help us build a walkway over the chasm that separates the cave ledge from the remainder of the trail. By the time you meet up with us at Mount Aine, there should only be the last seal to place. Then, my boy, you can go and do what the devil you like!"

The roar of Beulah's voice as he finished made Ryzak recoil in shock. Why was it that he always managed to upset the man? It was a perfectly reasonable question. He couldn't understand it. That seemed to be the story of his life – permanently misunderstood.

"Perhaps I should have improved his temper while I was at it," Snorkel said, with a snort of amusement.

Looking to where the dwarf sat on a low stool next to Shula, Beulah glared at him, then broke into a smile. He chuckled and shook his head. "You are right, my friend. Please accept my apologies, Ryzak. I should not be so grumpy. With everything that has happened lately, my temper is not what it should be."

"He accepts," broke in Neulee, sensing that Ryzak was preparing to deliver an angry rebuke. "Don't you?" she asked sweetly.

Ryzak's glower faded and he sullenly agreed. "You coming with us again?" he asked, turning to fix the dwarf with a hopeful look.

Snorkel shook his head. "Not this time. I have other matters to attend to. Reizgoth awaits me."

"Oh," grunted Ryzak in disappointment. He quite liked the little man and would miss having him around, despite his annoying habits. Breathing being one of them. On the bright side, it meant he had more time on his own with Neulee.

"However, I will walk with you some of the way before I call Reizgoth. I doubt whether the villagers could stand another visit from him; he's already been elevated into some kind of monster. If he came here again I dread to think what they would make of him."

"Pass me the seal, Ryzak," commanded Beulah, "I will take care of it from here."

Ryzak rummaged in his tunic pocket and pulled the gold disc out, handing it to Neulee to pass on to the wizard.

Taking it from him, Neulee twirled it in her hand to take a closer look. As she turned it over and gazed at the strange markings on the reverse, her face drained of colour.

"What's the matter?" Ryzak asked, disturbed by her fearful expression.

"I–it's the seal," she gasped.

"What about it?"

"I think I know where the missing one is," she whispered. "I've seen one exactly the same. It was a few years ago now, but I could never forget it. I was always fascinated by the strange markings."

"Well, out with it girl," rumbled Beulah. "Who has it?"

"My father," murmured Neulee, her eyes downcast.

The expression was lost on Ryzak. "Wow, that's great!" he enthused. "That makes our trip one hell of a lot easier."

"Not exactly," murmured Neulee.

His excitement dissipated at her disconsolate tone and he gave her a querying look. "Why's that?" he asked.

"My father and I do not get on too well. At least, not after the last time we met."

"Why? What happened?" quizzed Ryzak.

"I sort of stabbed him a bit," Neulee answered miserably.

"Sort of stabbed him a bit?" repeated Ryzak in astonishment. He knew she had a temper, he had been on the receiving end of it often enough, but to stab her father? "How much, exactly, is 'a bit'?"

"I didn't kill him!" she shouted defensively.

"Easy, easy," soothed Ryzak, raising a hand to stroke her face. "I didn't say you had." He smiled lovingly at her. "And even if you had, it would not make any difference to the way I feel about you. So tell me, how badly was he injured?"

"He needed the herb woman to heal the wounds on his buttocks, and he could not sit down for two weeks," she replied quietly.

"You stabbed him in the arse!" exclaimed Ryzak, with a loud guffaw. "Excellent! What did he do to deserve that?"

"He promised me to the chieftain of a neighbouring tribe, without asking me!" she exclaimed, her voice rising in indignation. "An old man with more wrinkles than muscle and not a tooth in his head, who smelled like an incontinent pig that had rolled in its own muck! And all because the old bastard had promised my father prime hunting land in return for my hand. Land that used to be ours before my father lost it to him, gambling on a race in the inter-tribal games!"

Her eyes hardened. "Anyway. I refused to marry him. My father was furious. He locked me up until the day of the wedding and then dragged me out so that our shaman could marry us. He had to carry me, screaming and kicking. But no matter how hard I kicked, scratched or bit him I could not break free. I went limp to fool him into thinking I was submissive. Then, when we were nearing the marriage stone, I pulled his hunting knife free of his belt and stabbed him in the backside. I can still remember his cry of pain, and the look of horror on the old goat's face as he realised his future bride was about to run off. As soon as my father's arms lost their grip I ran, and I've never been back since."

From her perch on Snorkel's shoulder, Draco chirruped her congratulations at Neulee's escape, causing the dwarf to flinch as the high-pitched warbles hammered into his eardrums with the subtlety of a banshee.

"Didn't he come after you?" Ryzak asked.

"Oh, he tried. He sent some of his warriors, but they all knew me, so they let me get away after they had given me some food and weapons." She gave Ryzak a rueful smile. "So there you have it. I don't really expect I will be welcomed back with open arms."

"Nonsense, my dear," Beulah disagreed, his voice bright with optimism. "He's your father! He'll be over it by now, don't you worry. Look at it this way; he'll not only be regaining a daughter, he'll be acquiring a son!"

Neulee's worried frown expressed what she thought of that.

* * * * *

The sound of footsteps disturbed her, making her move away from the door. Smoothing her robe, she walked quickly and silently down the corridor.

"Evenin', miss," a man's gruff voice greeted her, as she turned the corner leading to the common room.

"Good evening, Samuel," she replied with a smile, recognising him as one of the men who had helped Jollif transport the unconscious wizard upstairs on their arrival.

With a secretive smile, she continued on her way. It had been a good evening all right. She had heard enough to inform her master what was going on, so that he could make his plans in plenty of time for Ryzak's arrival.

* * * * *

The watery, autumnal sun slowly worked its way over the horizon, bathing the vast swathe of grasslands with its weak rays. Despite its brightness, it did not offer much in the way of heat to ward off the chill of the morning. Wrapped in heavy sheepskin jackets, the three riders slowly made their way towards the border with the barbarian plains.

They had left the village very early that morning, Snorkel wanting to be far away before the villagers rose. Ever since his spectacular arrival, the dwarf had been the subject of whispered threats and hate mail (usually in the form of a rock hurled in his direction, thrown from some dark corner while he took his daily walk) and he wanted to ensure their departure was not witnessed. It was bad enough knowing he would probably never see his friends again, without having to worry about rock-throwing villagers chasing them out of town as well.

One of them, Jobe, the local tramp, had even taken to pacing the veranda outside Jollif's tavern with a sandwich board over his shoulders stating 'The end is nigh' in big red letters on one side and 'Spare a copper for a cripple' in bigger red letters on the other. He hobbled along in a pathetic manner, dragging his left leg behind him. As soon as he acquired enough coin for a drink, he would heave the sandwich board to one side, spring through the tavern door and quaff a few dwarven ales. When his money was spent, he would scuttle back outside to scrounge enough coin for some more, still dragging his leg behind him. Sometimes it was his right leg, depending on how many ales he had drunk and how clear his memory was.

Snorkel sighed. Leaving Beulah and Shula had been the hardest part. He had been with the wizard for a long time and, in spite of the man's cantankerous nature, loved him like a father. It was quite a wrench knowing he would not see him again. They had bid him farewell the evening before, planning to leave the day after Snorkel, and wanting to get a good rest. Snorkel chuckled to himself. They seemed to be having a lot of early nights the past few days.

Jollif had arranged for the carpenters and materials to build the bridge across the chasm and would join the wizard and sisters at Mishtar's mountain prison. By the time Ryzak and Neulee arrived there, it should all be over bar the shouting. Not that he would be around to worry about it. Still, he hoped it all went according to plan and that Ryzak did not manage to screw things up. At least the man had Neulee to look after him.

They were a good five miles out of the village when he decided to call a halt; far enough for Reizgoth to collect him without being spotted. Reining in their horses, the three riders dismounted. Snorkel stood, eyes lowered, scuffling the ground with a pointy-toed red boot, not knowing what to say now that the time for going their separate ways had arrived. Even Draco seemed crestfallen as she perched on his shoulder. Her normally bright yellow eyes looked dull and sad.

"You'll look after her?" Snorkel burst out, thrusting Clara's reins at Ryzak.

"Like my own," promised Ryzak, taking them from him. He offered the little man his other hand and gave a despondent smile. "Take care, my friend. I'll miss you."

Snorkel chuckled. "Yeah, like a hole in the head." He clasped Ryzak's hand in a firm grip, before turning to Neulee.

Neulee stepped forward and stooped down to embrace the dwarf in a fierce hug. "Goodbye, Snorkel," she whispered. "You take care of yourself." Straightening, she gave Draco an affectionate tickle under the chin. "And you, my little friend."

The wet glimmer of tears was in his eyes as Snorkel watched his friends remount and ride away. He stared after them until they were out of sight before summoning Reizgoth. By the gods, he would miss them.

'Here he comes, Mum,' Draco mind-spoke, intruding on his melancholy.

"I know, my friend. I know," Snorkel replied quietly.

Chapter Twenty Two

The clip-clop of their horses' hooves echoed around the sprawl of tumbledown buildings as Ryzak and Neulee slowly rode through what remained of Dracov; their eerie reverberations augmenting the pall of desolation that hung over the once thriving border town.

Ryzak sighed as his hooded gaze scanned the derelict buildings lining the road. Very little remained of the Dracov he once knew. What few buildings still stood were mere shells of their former selves: roofless skeletons, precariously balanced stone walls waiting to topple into the dry, dusty street. The place had changed dramatically from the one he remembered.

Before the war, Dracov had been full of hustle and bustle as traders from the barbarian tribes bargained for the best deals with their counterparts from Middle Vooragh. Situated near a narrowing of the River Voor, one of the few places where a bridge could span its banks, it was an ideal place for a prosperous community to develop. From a small farming village, Dracov rapidly grew into a sprawling market town, all thoughts of farming being swiftly forgotten as easier money poured into the once sleepy hamlet.

Then, during the war, commerce died a death. The town was full to capacity with soldiers and ladies of little moral fibre. Trade took on a totally different meaning to the inhabitants. By the gods, they were good days. That was Ryzak's most abiding memory of the place. He'd never managed to keep his money for long while garrisoned in Dracov, but he'd sure had a fine time. However, that was before the fighting headed his way and spoiled his soldiering days forever.

And now? And now it was a pile of rubble, home to four-legged scavengers and vermin; something else that had died with the war.

A door slammed shut, startling him. He glanced across the street and saw a pack of wild dogs eyeing the riders warily from the safety of a pile of rubble.

"Away with yer," he shouted, and laughed as the dogs scattered and quickly disappeared from sight. The smile soon faded and his sombre mood returned, his thoughts turning to Snorkel.

It had been two days since they had left him and it seemed strange not having the little man around. Although he'd wished Snorkel well and promised to see him soon, he knew that was the last time he would ever set eyes on him. As much as he hated to admit it, he missed the little runt – strange outfits and all. He glanced across at Neulee. She was unhappy as well, although for different reasons. The meeting with her father was not one she was looking forward to.

As they neared the outskirts of the town, he could see the trail continuing through the countryside ahead, making its way between gently rolling, grassy hillocks towards the bridge over the River Voor. Once on the other side they would be in the lands of the barbarians, or plains tribes, as Neulee preferred to call them. He winced. The only heated exchange between them had been the previous day, when he had inadvertently referred to the tribes as barbarians. He had apologised profusely on realising his mistake, but it hadn't helped. Her eyes had hardened and seconds later he was picking himself off the ground, nursing a bruised chin. She still wasn't speaking to him properly, despite his numerous apologies.

Half an hour later they arrived at the fast-flowing river. Ryzak groaned as he saw the rickety condition of the bridge. Now that Dracov was deserted, there was no need to maintain the crossing point, and it showed. "Will it take our weight?" he asked in dismay.

"Only one way to find out," snapped Neulee, giving him an icy glare as she jumped from her horse.

Ryzak looked away and sighed. It would appear her mood had not improved.

After tying Clara to the back of her saddle with a lead rope, Neulee stepped onto the bridge to test it. Although its timbers creaked and groaned at the unaccustomed weight, she managed to make it safely to the other side. She turned and beckoned Ryzak over. "Just take your time," she called. "It appears safe enough."

"That's easy for you to say," muttered Ryzak, not so sure.

He stepped apprehensively on to the planks and slowly inched his way forward, coaxing his wary horse onto the bridge after him.

Growing more confident in the structure as he reached the mid-point, he increased his pace, eager to be back on firm ground.

Unmindful of the condition of the rotted decking, he never saw the fractured plank – until his foot shot through it. With a scream of terror he plunged down, before coming to a bone-jarring stop. It was as well he had his horse's reins wrapped around his wrist, or he would have plummeted into the torrent below.

His horse whinnied in fright and dug its forelegs into the wooden slats as it started to slide forward. Ryzak clung to the reins for dear life, the leather cutting into his hands as he hung in mid-air. Suspended over the rapidly flowing water, his mind raced as he tried to think of a way out of his predicament. He suddenly lurched lower. The horse was struggling to hold his weight.

With adroitness born from fear, he swung his legs up, hooking his heels on the planking above him. Using them as a lever, he hauled on the reins and pulled his body up before the horse could lose its footing.

Ryzak sat beside the gaping hole and stared at the swirling torrent below, his body quivering in shock. He felt the hot breath of his horse on his neck and looked up with a nervous smile as it rubbed its velvety nose on his cheek.

An ominous groaning sounded from the bridge.

Startled into action, Ryzak quickly rose and moved forward, stepping over the hole. He wanted to feel solid ground beneath his feet again. Giving Neulee a wave and a sheepish grin, he proceeded cautiously.

"I don't think I want to try that again," he said, when he arrived by her side.

"You never do things the easy way, do you?" Neulee scowled.

"Too boring," Ryzak said. "I need some excitement every now and again. Keeps the old heart fit and active."

Neulee's stern demeanour dissolved and a wry smile appeared on her face. She laughed and threw her arms around his neck, lightly kissing his lips. "Come on, you fool. Let's be on our way. One thing's for sure, it's never dull when you're around."

Two nights later Ryzak and Neulee finished the last of their travel rations. If they did not find Neulee's tribe on the morrow they would have to hunt for their food. Since the only thing he was good at catching was a cold, Ryzak did not relish the prospect.

Leaving Neulee stacking the fire with wood to ensure it did not go out during the night, he went to make sure the horses were safely hobbled. It was bad enough having their food run out, without the horses running off as well. Or being stolen. Neulee had warned him of the plains people's penchant for things not belonging to them.

Returning, Ryzak spread the sleeping furs on the ground near the fire, then climbed in and waited for Neulee to join him. Moments later he felt her warm, fully clothed body snuggle in next to him.

"When do you think we will find them?" he asked.

"They will find us before we find them," she replied. "Don't worry, we'll meet with them soon enough."

"Any time now, as a matter of fact," a voice sounded in the darkness. "It's nice to see you again, Neulee."

Ryzak and Neulee shot upright in their furs to see a tall, thin figure hobble into view around the side of the fire.

"Father?" gasped Neulee, peering at the dark form silhouetted by the fire's light.

"You still recognise me then?" Her father snorted as he squatted down beside the fire. The light from the flames illuminated the zigzag tribal markings etched onto his cheeks.

Ryzak gulped in apprehension. The man looked like a devil as his eyes bored into him.

"I see you've brought us a puppy to play with," Neulee's father growled.

"He is not here for your sport," snapped Neulee, jumping free of the furs' confinement and glowering at him. "He is to be my husband. We have come here for your blessing!"

The chieftain barked a humourless laugh. "Husband? My blessing? What makes you think I will let you have either, after what happened the last time we were together? I still walk with a limp and I know the tribe snigger about it behind my back."

Neulee lowered her gaze. "I am truly sorry, Father," she whispered. Then, looking up, she defiantly locked eyes with him. "But I could not marry that … that pig!"

The old man sighed, the gleam of confrontation fading from his eyes. "You're too much like your mother," he murmured, "may the gods take care of her soul. I could never do anything with her either."

Ryzak decided that discretion remained the better part of valour and remained seated, silently observing.

Neulee stepped forward and knelt on the ground beside her father, then threw her arms around his neck, hugging him fiercely.

Hesitantly the old man's arms came up and he returned her embrace. "I thought I had lost you," he whispered. "You were all I had left after your mother died. Will you forgive me?"

"Forgive you?" Neulee said. "What is there to forgive?"

He pulled away and stared into her eyes. "For not being the father you wished me to be," he said quietly.

Tears rolled down Neulee's cheeks. She buried her head in his shoulder and sobbed. Her father's hand rose to stroke her head and he murmured soothing words.

Relieved that their meeting appeared to be going better than he had anticipated, Ryzak stood up. All they needed now was permission to marry and to ask for the disc as a wedding present, and they could be on their way back home. He cleared his throat. "I bid you good evening, sir. Allow me to introduce myself. I am Ryzak."

Neulee's father looked up, his eyes narrowing. "Not the Dracov Ryzak?" he queried.

Ryzak bowed low, pleased that his fame had spread this far. "The very same."

"The Ryzak who led that damned charge, and turned the course of the battle? And, in the process, the war?" Neulee's father said, his voice low and threatening.

Ryzak grew nervous at his tone. "Er, yes. Is there a problem?"

"You want to marry him?" asked Neulee's father, gripping her shoulders and ignoring Ryzak's question. "The man who caused the death of hundreds of tribesmen?"

"Yes, Father," she replied, a steely resolve in her voice. "That was a long time ago. He was a warrior, doing what he was ordered to do. You, of all people, should appreciate that."

"There is a difference between appreciation and forgiveness," her father retorted. "Thanks to that man we lost half the fighting men of the tribes, and control of the bridge. There are those amongst us who would gladly rip out his heart with their bare hands for what he did."

"He was a soldier, Father," Neulee argued, her voice rising, "doing what a soldier does best – killing people!" Her voice dropped to a whisper. "And I love him."

The chieftain's lips compressed into a thin line as he glared at Ryzak. "Come here, boy," he commanded.

With a gulp of apprehension, Ryzak reluctantly moved to stand next to them.

"Do you love my daughter?" the old man demanded.

His voice deserting him in his hour of need, Ryzak nodded solemnly.

Neulee's father sighed, his expression softening. "It was a brave thing you did that day, son," he said, staring up at him. "As one warrior to another, and for the love of my daughter," he lowered his eyes and smiled at Neulee, "I, Azrak, grant you permission to marry my daughter."

Ryzak gave a whoop of joy. Embarrassed by his lapse, he cut it short.

"But," her father continued, his eyes hard, "as I have already said, there are those amongst us who would not forgive or forget. You must not reveal your identity to the tribe or it will mean your death, and my daughter's. You will be known as Rye during your stay with us."

The old man eased Neulee away and stood up. He grasped Ryzak's hand in a warrior's grip, wrist to wrist. "Welcome to my family, Rye. Come. An escort waits beyond the light of the fire. We will be at the camp in an hour or two."

Inwardly relieved it had all gone so smoothly, Ryzak tried not to let his delight show. He did not want to antagonise his future father-in-law so early in their relationship. He packed the sleeping furs away and went to prepare their horses for the journey. Leading the three mounts, he scuffed dirt over the fire to extinguish it before joining his betrothed.

As they left the camp, Ryzak became aware of other warriors joining them, appearing out of the dark as if by magic until at least twenty ringed them. "How long have you known we were here?" he asked, nervously eyeing the newcomers.

"Ever since you crossed, or should I say fell through, the bridge," the old man replied with a chuckle.

"Oh," mumbled Ryzak. Just his luck. Witnesses to his misadventure.

It took just over an hour to reach the small tents of the barbarians' makeshift camp. Apart from the odd word from Neulee's father, the journey was made in silence. By the time they reached their destination Ryzak was cold, tired and becoming extremely bored. He was relieved their trek was at an end. Six more heavily armed warriors joined them as the group made their way to the centre of the camp, startling Ryzak as they materialised from their positions of concealment.

Neulee's father turned to him. "Give me your weapons," he demanded. "You are a stranger amongst us. Until you are wed to Neulee and have been accepted by the tribe you must remain weaponless."

Ryzak glanced at his promised bride for guidance. At the slight nod of her head he unbuckled his sword belt and removed his knives, handing them over.

"You will sleep over there with the horses," the old man said, with a grin. "Have a good night. We'll see you in the morning."

Putting his arm around his daughter's shoulder, the old man drew her away. Looking back, Neulee gave Ryzak a bright smile and a wink, mouthing the words, 'I love you,' as she walked.

Not happy with the sleeping arrangements, but stuck with them, Ryzak grimaced and followed the warriors to the pitching rail to strip his horse for the night. As he wormed his way into his sleeping furs, he became aware of two men standing over him. "Not sleeping then, boys?" he asked with a smile.

The men glanced down in contempt, not deigning to answer.

"Guess not," Ryzak muttered, and rolled over to make himself more comfortable.

The following morning broke cold and clear. A frost had formed during the night and the grass glistened with a silvery sheen as the rays of the newly-risen sun bathed the land. Ryzak yawned and stretched his arms to ease the kinks and aches in his back where the rocky ground had been digging in to him.

He shook his head to clear the haze from his mind and propped himself on an elbow to look around. His guards had disappeared and everywhere he looked there was activity. The tents were mostly dismantled and being packed away for the journey, and the smell of breakfast was in the air.

With an appreciative smile he climbed out of his furs and made his way to the cooking fire. "Any room for a small one?" he asked as he arrived, rubbing his hands together to ward off the chill.

The men around the fire turned to look at him, their eyes narrowed in hostility.

"I'll take that as a no then, shall I?" gulped Ryzak, taking a step back.

One of the men ladled a helping of a thick, gooey, porridge-like substance into a clay bowl and thrust it towards Ryzak. He took it with a smile of thanks and studied its contents with distaste. The congealed mass looked like something a dog had thrown up.

"I see you're making friends, Rye," Neulee's amused voice sounded from behind him.

Ryzak turned and gave her a welcoming grin. "Just being my normal, charming self," he responded.

Neulee stepped closer and wrapped her arms around his neck, kissing him lightly on the cheek. "Ryzak," she whispered, nibbling his earlobe and causing ribald comments from the watching men, "we need to talk." She pulled away from him. "Come, my father wishes to speak with you in his tent," she said, in a louder voice.

The watching tribesmen gave knowing smirks and continued with their breakfast.

Neulee closed the hide flaps as soon as she and Ryzak were inside the chieftain's shelter and flew into his arms, kissing him passionately.

"Where's your father?" Ryzak asked when he had the chance to draw breath. "I thought he wanted to see me?"

"He's out with some of the men," she answered. "If I hadn't said he wanted to see you we would have had at least two of them listening to what we said." Her face turned serious. "He no longer has the seal."

"What!" exclaimed Ryzak in disbelief.

"Shhhhh!" urged Neulee, raising a finger to her pursed lips, her eyes flashing in irritation. "We don't want to attract unwanted attention."

"Sorry," Ryzak whispered. "But where is the seal if your father hasn't got it?"

"Pig-Breath has it," she answered. "When I ran off he demanded recompense from my father. All he had to offer was the gold disc. If he had not given it to him it would have meant war between our tribes."

Ryzak gave a sigh of frustration. He might have known something would crop up; it was all going too well. "So how do we get it?" he asked.

Neulee smiled. "We don't. You do!"

"Huh?" queried Ryzak.

"It works in our favour, don't you see?" said Neulee, her eyes shining with excitement.

"No, I don't," said Ryzak, an awful feeling of impending disaster creeping up on him. "Please enlighten me."

"When you get it back," she said enthusiastically, "my father has promised it to me as a wedding present, and," she added with a grin, "it will prove your worth to the tribe, so that none can stand in our way."

"That simple, huh?" Ryzak said, gloomily.

"Yes." Neulee giggled.

The tent flap was suddenly pulled aside and the balding pate of Neulee's father came into view as he ducked through the opening. His face betrayed no emotion at seeing his daughter and Ryzak alone in his tent. "It is time to leave," he snapped. "Go and get ready." Ryzak cast Neulee a worried glance as he left the tent.

The main village of the Prairie Dogs, as he had discovered Neulee's tribe were called, was four hours' ride from the night

259

camp. They came upon it quite suddenly, in a clearing where two small streams met; a flattened oasis amongst the endless, grassy plains. Ryzak could have passed within half a mile of the place and not known it was there, it was so well concealed.

As they approached the tented village men, women and children dropped what they were doing and ran to greet their arrival. Dogs yapped around the horses, chickens flew everywhere, goats mixed with the tribesfolk and an escaped piglet ran amok, doing its best to get trampled under the horses' hooves. It was chaos. It seemed to take an age before they managed to negotiate the hubbub and arrive at the tethering area.

"Is it always like this?" asked Ryzak, removing the saddle from his horse under the watchful gaze of his escort.

"Mostly," replied Neulee, her face lit by a radiant smile. "Wonderful, isn't it?"

She never heard his reply. She was whisked away by friends she had not seen in years, leaving a bemused Ryzak standing forlorn, his saddle clutched in his hands.

"Never mind, boy," said Azrak, slapping him heartily on the back. "Come. I'll show you where you'll stay while you are with us."

Having lost sight of his beloved in the crowd, Ryzak followed Azrak to a quieter area of the village, next to the pig-pens. His face fell as he spotted the one, lone, tattered excuse for a tent, erected next to the steaming quagmire of the pigs' home. As he was led towards it, Ryzak's intuition looked to be well founded.

"This will do you." Azrak sneered, pulling aside the moth-eaten flap.

Peering in, Ryzak wrinkled his nose in disgust at the foul stench. It smelled as though the pigs were using it for a latrine.

Azrak gave an amused chuckle. "What's the matter, boy? Not good enough for you?"

Ryzak bit back a retort and smiled instead. "As you say," he replied through gritted teeth, "it will do for now."

"That's the spirit, boy. Make yourself at home. Feel free to look round the camp, but don't get into any trouble. Can't have you getting injured before your wedding day, can we?" Azrak grinned, his unsmiling eyes boring into Ryzak's.

Ryzak watched the old man saunter away, his expression doleful. So that was the way of it, was it? He mouthed an oath and shoved his saddle and roll into the tent, then stooped to enter. As well as being the smelliest tent around, it was probably the smallest. He could only just fit in. Deciding he would have to grin and bear it, he pulled the flap closed behind him. If Azrak's hospitality was the warmest he was to receive, he would sooner spend the day in the tent, no matter how badly it stank. He rolled out his sleeping fur and climbed inside, falling asleep almost immediately.

He was awakened by a warrior shaking his shoulder. Ryzak jumped up with a start, stifling a shriek of fear as he gazed into a pair of cold eyes.

"Azrak demands your presence," the man informed him in a gruff voice. Satisfied that Ryzak understood, he waited outside.

Emerging moments later, Ryzak followed the man to the middle of the village. His mouth fell open in surprise as he saw the masses surrounding a raised hummock at its centre. The whole tribe appeared to have gathered. There were thousands of them. Becoming ever more nervous, Ryzak spotted Azrak and Neulee as they mounted the mound. Neulee looked disconsolate. Seeing Ryzak approach she gave him a grim smile, which did little to reassure him.

Becoming aware of his presence, the throng drifted apart to form an avenue leading to the hummock. Ryzak's face burned bright red as he walked down the aisle, aware of the thousands of pairs of eyes looking in his direction. As he neared Neulee and her father, Azrak beckoned to him.

"My people," the chieftain's voice rang out, quieting the dissenting murmurs. "Here is the man who would wed Neulee, my daughter." He paused to let them view the stranger in their midst. "As you can see, he is not of the tribe. He is not even of the plains!" he roared, an outflung arm pointing at Ryzak.

An indignant ripple ran through the crowd. Ryzak glanced at Neulee in apprehension.

Azrak's hands waved them quiet, then he continued. "But, my people, he has promised to prove himself worthy of us. Worthy enough to marry my daughter. Worthy enough to wear the tribal markings of a warrior!"

Another murmur went through the crowd. This time it was one of amused derision.

"He has offered to take back that which was taken from us, using the ways of the hand. Unarmed and unaided, he will enter the camp of the Wolverines and reclaim the gold disc of Umph!"

Ryzak's expression showed open horror as he realised what he had to do. He looked at Neulee, a plea for help on his face, but her eyes only held sadness as she stared dismally back at him.

Ryzak, in a rare moment of perception, suddenly knew why she looked so miserable. Azrak expected him to fail! Not only would he have got rid of *'Ryzak of Dracov',* he would have regained his daughter to barter for the return of the disc! He had had it all planned from the moment they entered his lands. What a bastard! So much for paternal affection. His features set, he stared out over the heads of the crowd, ignoring their grinning faces, open amusement and finger pointing.

"Has our hero anything to say?" Azrak leered, a mocking smile twisting his features.

Ryzak turned to face him and gave a cheery grin. "Why thank you, Father. I have."

Azrak's face clouded in anger.

Pleased that his barb had struck home, Ryzak turned to face his audience. It had worked for Snorkel; why not him? He raised his arms and gave the barbarians his most winning smile. His voice loud and strong, he proceeded. "People of the Prairie Dog," he shouted.

The crowd quieted, waiting to hear what the outsider had to say.

"I would like to thank the great chieftain, Azrak, for the opportunity of proving myself. It is an honour for me to be considered for such an important task. In my country we have heard many tales of the bravery and strength of the people of the plains, and it is a privilege for me to be standing before you."

Ryzak paused, taking pleasure in the look of astonishment registering on most of the faces looking his way. He gave a small smile of satisfaction as he glimpsed Azrak's scowl.

Glancing to his right, he shot Neulee a confident wink, but missed her frown of concern and warning look as he turned back to face the masses.

"This night I go to retrieve the disc of Umph for you, my chosen people. I will not return until my task is complete and I have proved myself worthy. On this you have my promise."

Finishing with a flamboyant bow, Ryzak straightened. Head held high, he waited for the cheers and shouts of encouragement. However, only silence met his boast.

Puzzled, he lowered his gaze and was surprised to see the crowd drifting away, shaking their heads and laughing to themselves. Pretty soon all that was left was a small boy and his dog. Even the dog appeared to have a smile on its face.

Ryzak dejectedly surveyed the scene of his intended triumph, his misery further compounded when the young lad laughed and stuck out his tongue before running off, the scruffy little dog yapping happily at his heels.

"One thing you have just learned, boy," Azrak snarled in contempt, "is that we never brag about what we are going to do; we just do it. The boasting and celebrations are left until after we succeed."

Ryzak looked at the grinning, supercilious old man angrily, wanting to do nothing more than punch him in the mouth. Yet again he had been made to look a fool, tricked and taken for an idiot. And yet again he had fallen for it. Did he have the word 'PRAT' stamped on his head or something?

"Leave us, Father," Neulee commanded. "Let us have a few moments together before he goes on this fool's errand."

"Anything you say, daughter," the old man sneered. "But don't be too long. *Rye* has to prepare himself for tonight."

At the sound of the old man's cackles, Ryzak's eyes hardened. He watched in impotent rage as Azrak limped triumphantly away.

"Oh, Ryzak," cried Neulee, running into his arms.

Ryzak returned her embrace and gently stroked the back of her head. "I take it I have been set up?" he asked.

Neulee raised her head and looked into his pale-blue eyes. "The old bastard never intended for us to be married. He only wanted me back so that he could trade me with Pig-Breath. He's probably warned the Wolverines that you are to make an attempt to take the disc of Umph. Then he gets rid of me, gains back the disc and the land in the process, and also gets rid of you – permanently!"

"I might have known," Ryzak whispered, "I thought things were going too well. I had my suspicions when I saw the look on your face, but thought I could sway the people to my cause. At least get some allies."

"Come, outsider," a warrior's curt command interrupted them. "It is time to make ready."

Strong hands grabbed hold of Ryzak's arms and pulled him roughly away. His last view of Neulee was of the misery on her face as he was dragged to his horse, stripped to his underclothes and thrown over its back. Powerless to offer comfort she ran, weeping, to one of the tents.

'Bastard barbarians,' he thought, as his hands were grabbed and bound with rope.

Chapter Twenty Three

The thick soles of Snorkel's clogs left worm-like trails in the hot sand. Unaccustomed to the cumbersome footwear, he was having a devil of a job moving one foot in front of the other. They made walking a very slow process.

"You do vine, Norkel," a deep, throaty voice said from behind him.

Turning, Snorkel flailed for balance and wobbled for a moment before recovering his poise to give Meelan a little wave. By the gods she was gorgeous. Seeing her sitting there, stumpy legs dangling over the edge of the lowest stone tier with Draco curled up in her lap set his pulse racing. He was so glad that Reizgoth had agreed to the little detour on the way back to Firestone Mountain. It was a wrench to leave his friends behind, but if he had to leave Meelan as well? He shuddered to think of a lifetime with no female company; or without Meelan's, to be more precise.

The object of his desire returned his wave and blew him a kiss.

Pretending to catch it, Snorkel almost fell. Grinning, he gave a small shrug, then turned to continue his trek to the egg.

Yes, it was the happiest day of his life when Meelan agreed to come with him to the home of the Divine One. He chuckled. So, he lied. Who was going to tell? It had made his tale more plausible when he'd *spirited* to their village in the dead of night, unnoticed by the tribe's guards, and appeared at her bedside to ask her to accompany him. She seemed only too pleased to come, especially when the 'chariot of the gods' flew down. He could still see the look of abject terror on her face when Reizgoth landed beside them. He had almost lost her then. Almost. If it were not for the dragon swooping down the precipitous drop above the village and grabbing her plummeting form, only feet from a hard, rocky landing, the whole world would have lost her. Snorkel shook his head. Boy, that was a close call.

Reaching the egg he placed his palms on the thick, golden shell and pressed an ear to its surface to listen for any signs of life, all thoughts of past escapades pushed firmly to the back of his mind. He had a job to do.

"Is she all right?" Reizgoth's concerned voice enquired from beside him.

"Give me a chance," muttered Snorkel, "I've only just got here!"

The big red dragon sat in the sand and watched as the little man carried on with his inspection. Reizgoth had been a permanent fixture at its side since their arrival at the mountain, only moving when the dwarf had insisted he fly out and find some fresh meat for the queen's hatching. And then only because Draco kept buzzing his head and annoying him until he agreed to go.

Curiosity getting the better of him, Reizgoth dipped his head lower and peered over Snorkel's shoulder.

The dwarf pursed his lips and looked at his scaled companion. "Everything appears to be fine," he said.

The dragon's eyes swirled with excitement. "When can we birth her?" he asked.

Snorkel chuckled and playfully batted the dragon's snout. "No time like the present." He frowned. "Now then, where's the food for when she hatches?"

"Up there," Reizgoth answered, indicating the entrance at the top of the gallery.

"Good! Be ready to bring it here as soon as she pops out. We can't have her going hungry. Not when she's been stuck in there for the last few hundred years or so. Be off with you and leave me in peace. The fewer distractions I have the better."

Reizgoth dipped his head in sullen acknowledgement, then rose and waddled over to where Meelan sat.

As soon as he was satisfied he was alone, Snorkel again caressed the smooth, golden carapace of the queen's confinement. He murmured and crooned to the yet-to-be-born queen, finding the inner harmony he needed to begin his task. When he was ready he placed his palms on the egg's surface and allowed his powers to flow down his arms, through his outstretched fingers and into the ovaloid, inspecting the contents for any sign of damage.

His brows rose in surprise at the apparent size of the young queen. She was huge! He rapidly checked her vital signs and sighed in relief as he found them to be functioning correctly. Next was the tricky bit. He had to find and undo the spells that had been used to preserve her, keeping her in hibernation until it was time for the hatching.

They did not prove too difficult to find. He came across their tangled web almost straight away, covering the shell like varicose veins on a spindly leg. He suffered a moment of anxiety as he saw the complexity of them: how would he be able to unravel that mess?

Seeking inner calm, he focused his mind, searching his acquired lore for the answer to his problem. As he explored his reservoir of knowledge the spells underwent a dramatic change. In his minds eye, each became a different colour. Suddenly he could easily make out the different spells, where they started and where they finished. Like an old woman unravelling a tapestry pattern that had gone wrong, he began to pull the separate threads free. The more he unravelled, the more the queen moved within the egg. She was becoming active.

After an hour sweat was running off Snorkel in buckets. His concentration and the heat from the sand were taking their toll. "Only two more to go," he mumbled to himself, unravelling yet another spell and blinking a bead of sweat from his eyes.

As he removed the penultimate spell a tremor ran through the egg. The baby queen was agitated and beginning to hammer at the inside with her head, trying to force her way out. Snorkel knew he must hurry. She would not be able to break free until the final spell was removed, and the last thing he needed was for her to get stressed and damage herself. With a triumphant yell, he managed it. Panting from his mental exertion, a look of exultation on his face, he viewed the rocking egg with pride. His bright crimson tunic had dulled with perspiration and was stuck to his body like a second skin. But what the hell? He had done it!

The egg began to rock more vigorously and hairline cracks started appearing in its golden surface. His smile faded. Not wanting to be in the vicinity when the hungry queen emerged and mistook him for breakfast, Snorkel waded back through the sand towards his companions as fast as the heavy, wooden footwear would allow.

"Get the goat carcass, quick," he shouted to Reizgoth, as he staggered to the stone seating. "She'll break out any second now."

The dragon hopped up the stone tiers and clamped his jaws round the goat's body, then spread his wings and glided down to land on the sand. After depositing the goat, he quickly waddled over to join his companions.

The watching audience were wide-eyed as the egg's rocking grew more frenetic, the hairline cracks widening. A hole appeared in its side and the unmistakable scaled head of a dragon pushed through. Gasps of awe greeted the sight. The queen was the colour of pure gold.

"Bloody hell," said Snorkel. "She's colossal."

Meelan let loose a terrified scream and clung more tightly to Snorkel's arm as a loud screeching filled the air of the amphitheatre. Hugging her close, Snorkel's eyes widened as he watched the queen. She was tearing at the tough, leathery shell with her jaws in an attempt to force her way out.

His amazement turned to alarm as her efforts appeared to be in vain. "She's stuck," he yelled. He prised Meelan off and made to jump into the arena.

"NO!" boomed Reizgoth, placing a restraining foreleg in his path. "Stay here. She will eventually break free. If you go near her before she has eaten she will turn on you."

As if to prove his point, the queen forced her way out with a final roar of rage. Standing in the sand, seemingly not sure of her surroundings, she screeched at the top of her voice.

Meelan squealed and ducked for cover, and Draco retreated to the upper tiers.

The queen scented fresh blood. Her snout began to twitch as she sniffed the air. Her head swivelled round and her eyes fixed on the carcass beside her. With another loud roar she sprang on the body and began to tear it to pieces, hungrily thrusting chunks of meat into her mouth.

Snorkel barfed. The last time he had witnessed anything so bloody was when his mother had caught his father casting a lecherous eye at another she-dwarf. He never did that again. Not to his – or his mother's – knowledge anyway.

Noticing the dwarf's discomfort, Reizgoth chuckled. "That is not how we usually eat. You must remember that she is very hungry and very young. I assure you, her manners will improve."

Snorkel gave a wry grimace and retreated to the second tier where Meelan was trying to burrow into the stone for protection. He put his arms around her and pulled her to him, smiling in amusement when she buried her head in his chest and refused to look up. Having overcome his nausea, Snorkel watched as the queen finished her meal. Soon there was nothing left to indicate the goat had ever been there, except a dark, red splotch on the sand.

The golden dragon wiped her mouth with the back of a foreleg, then stared at her observers inquisitively.

"It is safe to approach her now," Reizgoth informed the dwarf.

"Are you sure?" whispered Snorkel, nervously eyeing the young queen.

Reizgoth chuckled. "I am sure. She will not require another feed for at least two hours. Come, we had better introduce ourselves or she will think us rude."

"Better than thinking us dinner," Snorkel muttered, trying to prise Meelan off him. Eventually succeeding, he looked into her troubled eyes and gave a reassuring smile. "You coming with us?" he asked.

Meelan shook her head and burrowed into his body again. Snorkel laughed and eased her away. Smoothing her hair with his hand, he leaned forward and kissed her lightly on the forehead. "Maybe later then."

Rising, he moved down the stone tiering and followed Reizgoth out onto the sand. It was time to meet his queen.

Chapter Twenty Four

For the last two hours the Wolverines had danced, hopped and shrieked around Ryzak and he was starting to get dizzy. If they were going to kill him, he wished they would hurry up about it; their high-pitched caterwauling was driving him insane.

It had not taken them long to capture him; roughly two minutes after Azrak had dragged him off his horse and thrown him to the ground, kicking him in the ribs as a parting gift. By the time Ryzak had staggered to his feet there were at least thirty grinning savages surrounding him. They'd herded him back to their nearby camp, then tied him where he now lay, spread-eagled, his arms and legs secured to timber stakes.

Becoming aware of a presence looming over him, Ryzak opened his eyes and scowled up at a leering barbarian. The man pulled a grotesque face and threatened him with his hunting knife before dancing off to join the rest of his comrades. Ryzak grimaced. Neulee's tribe appeared positively civilised compared to these animals.

A blood-curdling shriek made the dancers stop their freakish cavorting. Ryzak raised his head and saw a small, wrinkled, semi-naked old man walk through the throng toward him.

The old man stopped beside Ryzak and looked down with a toothless grin, then gave another loud shriek. After making an obscene gesture, much to the amusement of the watching men, he pulled down his leggings and grabbed hold of his shrivelled penis. Urged on by raucous shouts of encouragement, he directed a spray of urine over Ryzak's face.

Ryzak closed his eyes and clamped his lips together as the foul-smelling liquid splashed over him. He waited for the old man to finish before opening them again. "You must be Pig-Breath," he snapped, recognising the gold disc tied around the man's neck.

Pig-Breath's face turned thunderous. He snarled with rage and stamped a booted foot down on Ryzak's head. Blood spurted from his smashed nose as Pig-Breath continued to rain kick after kick about his head and body. Mercifully, he blacked out.

It was dark when he finally came to. His captors, appearing to have had enough entertainment for one night, had buggered off. He tried to open his eyes, but the dried blood congealed over the left one would not allow it to open. He groaned. His head ached, his nose ached, his chest ached; there was not a part of his body that did not give him pain. Using his good eye to look around, fresh pains throbbed through his head. He winced, but managed to see that there was no sign of activity.

"The bastards must have gone to sleep," he murmured, through split lips.

He tested his bonds, but they were too secure for him to be able to pull free. He snorted in wry amusement. What the hell was he going to do if he broke free anyway? He did not have a clue where he was and, in his current condition, would not get very far before they caught him again.

His one eye widened in alarm as a hand clamped over his mouth.

"Shhhhhh!" a voice whispered into his ear. Relief washed over him as a face he recognised swam into focus. Neulee! Despite his pain, he managed a small smile of welcome.

Neulee looked down at him. Taking her hunting knife from its sheath, she worked her way around Ryzak's bonds, sawing through the ropes that tied him. When she had finished, she gently eased him into a sitting position.

"Your timing couldn't have been better," he mumbled.

"Sorry it could not have been sooner," she murmured.

Her eyes hardened as she viewed the full extent of his battering. "Wait here," she commanded. "Lie down and pretend that you are still tied, in case any of the Wolverines decide to take a look. I will not be long."

"Where are you going?" Ryzak asked, panic making his voice shriller than he intended.

"I think you know the answer to that," she replied, her features distorted by cold, hard fury.

She gave him a tight-lipped smile and leaned forward to kiss his forehead. Then, angling towards the tents, she disappeared into the night.

With a feeling of grim satisfaction Ryzak lay back, knowing exactly where she was heading.

Neulee made her way through the haphazard sprawl of tents towards the one she knew Pig-Breath would be sleeping in. She had only been to it once, many years ago, when her father had taken her there. But she would never forget it. At the time she did not know she had been taken for inspection, for approval as payment against her father's gambling debts. If she had realised the wrinkled, smelly old goat was to be her intended husband, she would have run off long before.

She scowled as the moon emerged from behind a screen of clouds, illuminating the tented village with a pale, silvery light. While helping her see where she was going, it also improved the chances of her being discovered. Quickly moving into the darker shadows, she made her way through the camp, only venturing across the better illuminated areas when she had no other choice.

It did not take her long to find Pig-Breath's hide-covered tent; it was the largest in the village. That and the fact that it was the only one to have a wolverine head emblazoned on the hide, its baleful eyes painted red, made it the obvious choice. She gave a humourless smile of satisfaction and crouched low to quietly run across the small strip of open ground. Placing an ear next to the flap, she listened for any sign of movement from within. Except for the rattling snores of the old man, she could sense nothing.

Reversing her knife, she held onto the blade and eased her way between the flaps. It took a moment for her eyes to adjust to the dark interior. When they did, she spotted the mound of Pig-Breath's sleeping form on the floor. The blade felt like a writhing eel in her hand as sweat slicked her grip. She licked at dry lips, silently cursing herself for a coward, then stole across the floor. Reaching Pig-Breath's side, she raised the knife, ready to bring it hammering down on the side of his head.

As her arm thundered down, the old man's hand flew up and held her in a vice-like grip. His wizened features crinkled in amusement. "Is this any way to greet your intended husband?" he cackled.

"No," she snarled, wincing in pain. "But this is!" Not being acquainted with Neulee's pugilistic skills, he was unprepared for the left hook that caught him on the chin, knocking him cold.

"I must be getting slow in my old age," Neulee muttered to herself, rubbing her wrist where the old man's grip had left its mark.

She retrieved her knife from the floor and put it back in its sheath before lifting the unconscious man and throwing him over her shoulder. She grunted at his unexpected weight. He was far heavier than his short, skinny frame suggested. Her load suitably settled, she staggered to the front of the tent and poked her head through the opening to check that the coast was clear. Satisfied that all was quiet, she stealthily made her way back to Ryzak.

Her paramour was drifting in and out of consciousness when she returned with her burden. The beating had taken its toll. At the sound of the old man's body hitting the ground Ryzak's eyes opened. He smiled when he realised it was Neulee, then climbed slowly to his feet.

Neulee dragged the unconscious man to the centre of the four stakes and used the ropes to bind him as Ryzak had been bound. Once he was tied, she ripped a strip of cloth from her tunic and formed a gag to secure Pig-Breath's mouth. The last thing they needed was for him to rouse the whole camp with his screams before they could get away. After securing the gag she grasped the medallion and tore it free. "Time to leave," she whispered.

"Wait. There is something I have to do first."

"Hurry up!" urged Neulee. "We have to get away.

Ryzak stood over the captive and dropped his underclothes, then began to urinate over Pig-Breath's face. The old man came to with a start, his eyes glaring hatred as he realised what was happening. He thrashed his head to try and avoid the steady stream, but to no avail.

"Consider that a gift returned," growled Ryzak, pulling up his underclothes. Then, glowering in contempt at the source of his beating, he raised his foot and brought it stamping down on the old man's nose, grinning in satisfaction at the loud crack and spray of sticky wetness.

"Now I'm ready," he whispered.

Daybreak found the fugitives many miles from the Wolverines' camp. When they had arrived where she had secreted the horses, Neulee had quickly tended to the worst of Ryzak's injuries, strapping his ribs and seeing to his swollen eye, before helping him dress in the clothing she had brought along. Then, insisting he sit astride his mount while she led them clear of the village on foot, they made good their escape. Although he felt foolish at being treated like a child, Ryzak did not put up much of a fight. The trek to the horses had used what little strength he had left.

After an hour of hard riding, Ryzak called for a brief halt. He was done in. It was all he could do to remain in the saddle. Neulee reined her horse to a stop and turned to look back at her companion, in time to see him slump in the saddle and topple to the ground. She leapt from her mount and ran to his side. By the time she reached him he had levered himself up on an elbow and was staring groggily around.

She knelt beside him and helped him into a sitting position. "How are you feeling?" she asked.

"Like shit," he murmured, with a thin smile.

Neulee frowned, then rose and walked to her horse, taking a flask of water and some smoked meat from the saddlebag. "Here, chew on this while I find something to help you," she said, handing him the meat.

Ryzak took the proffered strip. He chewed on the tough, dried jerky and watched as she removed a small, carefully wrapped packet from the pouch on her belt and poured the contents into the flask. "What is it?" he asked as she shook it.

"Ground poppy seeds," she replied, handing him the container. "It should mask the pain. But don't drink too much at once. Only take sips when you need it."

"Why?"

"No reason." She smiled. "It can sometimes have some rather interesting side-effects if not used sparingly, that's all."

Ryzak paused as he raised the flask to his lips. He remembered the *interesting* side-effects from the last time he had sampled one of her cures, and was in no condition to withstand another bout of toilet trotting.

Neulee smiled. "It is not harmful," she reassured him. "Quite the opposite, in fact. Drink some. It will make you feel better."

Although not entirely convinced, Ryzak raised the flask to his lips and took a small sip. Wiping his mouth on his sleeve, he stoppered the container. "Where are we headed?" he asked. "This does not look like the way we came."

"East," Neulee stated, rising to her feet. "Towards the border with the dwarven lands."

Still feeling shaky, Ryzak gripped her arm for support as he rose. "Why east?" he asked dubiously. "I thought Dracov was the only crossing point."

"It is to most, but I know of a crossing that is closer to Mount Aine. From there we can cut south, then east again to meet with Beulah and the others. Dracov will be the first place my father and Pig-Breath will look once they discover you are gone. With any luck it will be a while before they realise we have gone in the other direction."

Ryzak hoped it would prove as easy as it sounded. Somehow he doubted it. Nothing in his life ever ran that smoothly. He gave a small smile. "I am in your hands, fair lady. Lead on." He turned and tried to walk to his horse – and collapsed.

Neulee laughed and hauled him to his feet. "It's like looking after a child." She giggled, then guided him to his mount and helped him into the saddle.

The effects of the medicine kicked in half an hour later. Neulee was right; he felt much better. A little light-headed, maybe, but much better. As they rode, he gazed around in wonder. Why had he never noticed how vibrant the colours were before? The greens seemed so *green*, the blue of the sky so *blue*. He could feel the light breeze tickle his exposed flesh with its probing breaths. He giggled. He was enjoying this trip.

Looking ahead, he saw that Neulee was some way in front. No problem. If he stretched out his arms he could fly to her in no time. He stood in the stirrups, laughed uproariously, and began to wave his arms maniacally.

At the sound of demented laughter, Neulee hauled on the reins and brought her horse to a halt. As she turned, she saw Ryzak climb onto his saddle and precariously balance as his horse slowly ambled along. Her eyes widened in amazement as he flapped his arms, gave a mighty yell and jumped into the air, falling flat on his face on the ground. She galloped to his side and vaulted from her horse to kneel beside him, surprised to see him laughing and gurgling as he rolled onto his back, an inane grin on his face.

As she looked down, his bright, shining eyes met hers. "Did you see me?" he asked excitedly. "I flew like a bird." Then he passed out.

Neulee rolled her eyes and shook her head. Perhaps she had put too much of the powder in the drink.

* * * * *

"Do you think we could have a proper camp tonight?" Ryzak asked, as they followed the trail towards a narrow opening between two large outcrops of rock. "I could do with something warm to eat. This cold air is getting to me."

Neulee glanced over her shoulder and smiled. It was good to see Ryzak almost back to his old self again. The swellings on his body had reduced and, although he still looked as though he had been trampled by a herd of wild horses, he seemed a lot stronger; although his attempt at flying had not helped matters. It was as well she'd managed to dilute the mind-bending drink before he could take another sip; the gods only knew what he would have got up to if she hadn't.

The last two days had seen them make good headway. They had only taken brief stops to rest tired horses and snatch some sleep, so she knew what he meant by having a proper camp. She could do with a hot meal herself. Now that they had entered the foothills, the air was getting colder with every foot they climbed. They had not spotted any sign of pursuit, so it should be safe to have a fire.

"I don't see why not," Neulee replied. "I doubt whether they would follow us this far. They are very superstitious about the foothills. I know of somewhere further up the trail where we can safely call a halt."

"How come you know so much about this place if your people fear it?" asked Ryzak.

Neulee shrugged. "When I ran away I found myself running in this direction. I was more scared of being caught by my father and Pig-Breath than I was of superstitions, so I carried on until I found a place to cross over into Aldura. I never saw anything here to be scared of, just wind whistling through rocks."

The trail narrowed as they guided their horses through the cleft, their knees almost touching the rock either side as they progressed. Half way through, a rattle of stones cascaded down on their heads. Looking up in surprise, Neulee thought she saw a head duck from view above her. She gave a cry of alarm and kicked her horse into a gallop, racing through the narrow defile.

"Bollocks," swore Ryzak, spurring his horse and hurtling after her.

Rocks hailed down as they sped along. By good fortune neither of them was hit with enough force to knock them from their horses. It seemed like an age before the twisting, turning trail started to widen and the rain from above lessened. With a cry of relief, Neulee charged her horse around the final twist in the trail, then hauled on the reins to drag it to a skidding halt.

Ryzak nearly clattered in to her, barely managing to steer his horse to the side in time. His mount reared, its forelegs pawing the air as it snorted its disapproval. Bringing the nervously prancing stallion under control, Ryzak ended up facing Neulee. "What's the matter with you?" he gasped. "Why the sudden stop?"

Without a word, Neulee met his wild gaze and nodded to a point behind him.

Ryzak turned to look.

Ringing the trail ahead were at least twenty tribesmen. They formed a semi-circle across the defile. Each had a strung bow, arrows notched and trained on them.

"Wolverines!" spat Neulee, fixing her gaze on the wrinkled, bruised, broken-nosed face of Pig-Breath as he staggered out from the massed ranks.

Yells and shouts sounded from the trail behind them. More of the bastards. They were trapped!

Her eyes wide with fear, Neulee cast Ryzak a sorrowful look. It would appear they were not to escape and be together after all. She was taken aback to see him grinning. It was a little manic, but it was definitely a grin. Had he been at that damned drink again? "I don't see anything to be happy about," she snapped.

Turning his horse to stand alongside hers, he leaned over and kissed her gently on the cheek. "Care for a race?" he asked mischievously.

Looking at the advancing Pig-Breath, a smile appeared on her face. "What's the wager?"

"Do we need one?" he countered, flicking a glance at the Wolverines.

Neulee shook her head.

With loud shouts of encouragement, they dug their horses in the ribs and galloped at full pelt towards the startled ring of tribesmen. Pig-Breath, now only a matter of yards away, gave a shrill squeal of terror and started to run back to his men as the horses closed on him. Taken by surprise, the bowmen held fire in case they skewered him by mistake.

With heads bent over their horses' necks, the two riders bowled the old man over as they charged past, aiming for the apex of the semi-circle. It was too late for the tribesmen to do anything and they broke ranks before the approaching riders.

Ryzak and Neulee whooped and yelled as they galloped through and careered up the trail. There could be no more rest until they rendezvoused with Beulah.

Chapter Twenty Five

It took a moment for the realisation of why he was there to filter through. The sight of the sword, suspended in its violet beam of magic, had taken his breath away. All thoughts of placing the seal on an empty pillar had been pushed to the back of his mind in its hypnotic presence. Beulah was overawed.

Many times over the years he had been tempted to pay his respects to his departed brothers, but had never quite mustered the courage. Visiting the site of the wizardhood's demise was not high on his list of things to do. His own weakness prevented him, he supposed.

Gazing at the five stone pillars, he was overcome by a deep sadness. Although Shula had told him what to expect, seeing the final resting place of his past masters he was filled with a sense of sombre reverence. So many deaths just to ensnare one man. Was it worth it? He heaved a rueful sigh. Of course it was. There would have been many more deaths if the wizards had not given themselves for the cause. He felt the sting of tears in his eyes and wiped them away with the back of his hand.

Keeping his protective shield in place, warding him from any mischief Mishtar might have prepared, he hesitantly made his way to the pillars. He stopped before the sword to gaze up at it. Shaking his head in sorrow, he spotted an empty pillar and moved across to place the seal.

He removed the gold disc from a pocket in his robe and turned it over in his fingers to view the hieroglyphs. He gave a wry grin. So much emphasis had been given to the strange markings, yet there was nothing mysterious about them. For those with the eyes to see, they merely spelled the name of the master who had given his life. He fingered the disc thoughtfully. Methaniel. Not one he knew well, but one of his tutors nonetheless.

He felt the power from the pillar tug at the seal and smiled. "Goodbye, my friend," he whispered, placing it in the indent, hieroglyphs up. "May you continue your rest in peace."

As the small, delicate clasps closed over the disc, Beulah thought he heard a groan. When he looked round he could see nothing. It must have been his imagination. Turning, his thoughts sombre, he made his slow way back to the upper levels of the cave. Ryzak and Neulee should be there by now.

His companions were sitting around the fire when Beulah emerged on the upper level. It was cold in the cave. His breath vaporised in the air, leaving misty trails as he walked. Winter was close and it would not be long before the mountain trail became blocked with snowdrifts. Hopefully that would not be a concern for them.

Seeing him approach, Shula rose and ran to hug him in relief. "How did it go? Did you place the seal?"

Beulah gave a grim smile. "Aye, it is done." His eyes misted. "Although it was …"

"I understand," Shula murmured, placing a finger over his lips, forestalling the rest of what he was about to say.

He could see the empathy in her eyes, and loved her all the more for it. "Are they here yet?" he asked.

Shula shook her head.

Beulah's eyes narrowed in concern. "Where are they? Those blasted builders took so damned long to build the bridge, I thought they would have been here days before it was completed."

"I'm sure they will be here soon," Shula placated, with a rueful smile. "If only I had brought the orb we would have been able to track them."

Beulah lifted her head with his fingertips and kissed her gently on the lips. "No matter," he murmured. "At least we know they are on their way. My powers discovered that much." He wrapped an arm around her shoulders and guided her to the fire. "Stay here with the others and keep warm," he said. "I shan't be long. I will go to the entrance and see if I can trace them."

He strode to the cave mouth, returning a short while later with snowflakes melting on his head and shoulders. "They are close," he said to the expectant faces. "I can sense them."

The sound of cursing from the cave entrance made him turn.

"Will one of you idiots come and help me?"

Beulah's eyebrows rose in surprise. "I didn't think they were that close," he mumbled, recognising Neulee's voice.

He ran back to the opening and saw Neulee staggering towards him with the unconscious form of Ryzak slumped against her. She looked like she was done in. Grasping Ryzak's arm, he wrapped it over his own shoulder and helped Neulee carry him further into the cave.

"Wh–what happened? panted Jollif, gasping for breath as he arrived with the others. His eyes widened in alarm as he observed the form of his friend. "By the gods, his skin is all blue," he said.

"Not now, Jollif," snapped Beulah. "Help us carry him to the fire."

Suitably chastened, Jollif stepped forward and took Ryzak from Neulee, who, relieved of her burden, collapsed to the floor. Shula sprang to her side. She knelt beside her and placed her fingers on Neulee's neck to feel for a pulse. "She lives, though barely," she muttered in relief. Looking up she called to the two sisters. "Meganrhys, Rhissa. Help me carry her to the fire."

Stripped of their damp clothing and wrapped in warm blankets, the two frozen figures were made as comfortable as circumstances permitted. They looked like swaddled corpses as they lay beside the fire, stiff and unmoving.

Concerned by their condition, Shula moved to Meganrhys's side and placed a hand on her shoulder. "Can you help them, Megan?" she asked.

Meeting the matriarch's enquiring gaze, Meganrhys shook her head and sighed, her lips compressed into a narrow ribbon. "I don't know," she answered. "They are badly frozen. And by the look of Ryzak, he has suffered a severe beating as well. Some of those bruises are at least a week old."

"But can you help them?" Shula repeated softly.

Meganrhys gave a thin smile. "I think so. It all depends on whether the cold has taken too much of a hold of them or not."

Shula gave her shoulder a gentle squeeze. "Do your best," she urged.

Meganrhys nodded. She turned and knelt on the floor beside

Ryzak, then closed her eyes and placed her hands either side of his head.

Stepping into Beulah's waiting arms, Shula snuggled into his side as she watched the girl perform. She smiled as the wizard kissed the top of her head, moving her arm to encircle his waist.

"Do you think she can help?" an anxious voice asked. Jollif stood beside her, wringing his hands. His eyes held a worried look as he watched Meganrhys at work.

"If anyone can, Megan can," she replied, encouragingly. "Why don't you go and sit with Rhissa? There is nothing you can do here. We will let you know if there is any change."

Pondering her advice for a moment, Jollif gave a nod of understanding and moved away.

It seemed like an age before a noticeable, healthy glow started to assert itself on Ryzak's features; the purple and yellow bruising started to fade and the swelling around his eyes receded; his breathing deepened and he appeared to be resting peacefully. At Beulah's gasp, Shula looked up and could not help laughing at the expression of open-mouthed astonishment on the wizard's face.

"If I had not seen it with my own eyes, I would never have believed it," he murmured. "She's brought him back from death's door."

"I told you she was something special," Shula whispered. "A rare jewel, in a sea of glass baubles."

Meganrhys's eyes flickered open. She released her grip on Ryzak's head and rose wearily to her feet, walking across to where Neulee lay.

Easing herself from Beulah's embrace, Shula intercepted her. She gripped the girl's shoulders and stared into her tired eyes. "Are you sure you're up to it?" she asked.

Meganrhys smiled weakly and nodded her head at the sleeping form of Ryzak. "If Neulee is in as bad a state as he was it will be a struggle, but I'll manage it. How he managed to survive his injuries and the cold I'll never know. He must be stronger than he looks."

Shula nodded and moved aside, allowing Meganrhys access to Neulee.

It only seemed a matter of moments before the young sister

rose to her feet, her work done. Neulee's chest rose and fell evenly and she had a healthy glow to her face. Meganrhys staggered and nearly fell. In an instant Shula and Beulah were at her side, steadying her with supporting hands.

"Are you all right?" Shula asked.

Nodding, Meganrhys raised a fine, delicate hand and mopped her perspiring brow. Despite the chill air, she was sweating profusely. Shula wrapped a motherly arm around her shoulders and gave her a comforting hug.

"You did well," she said. "None of us could have done what you just did." Noticing the dark shadows beneath her eyes, she ordered her to go and rest.

Meganrhys squeezed the matriarch's hand in appreciation and shook her head. "I have to check Ryzak first, to make sure he's stable. I wouldn't like him to pass away through neglect on my part."

Seeing the matriarch's eyes narrow and the makings of a rebuke on her lips, Meganrhys smiled. "It will not take long," she assured. "And I would hate for all my efforts to have been in vain."

Later that evening, when all but Shula and Beulah were sleeping, the wizard gently lifted the matriarch's chin off his chest with the tips of his fingers. He looked deeply into her eyes. "That Meganrhys is some girl," he murmured.

"A rare and wonderful find," smiled Shula, kissing the wizard lightly on the cheek.

"Any idea where she comes from?" Beulah asked. "Her name has an elven ring to it, but she is not an elf. Although she may be a hybrid," he mused.

"Too deep for me." Shula smiled and snuggled back in to him. "She claims she is an orphan, but I have my doubts. I'm sure she will tell me the truth of it in due course. At the moment I am just relieved to have her." She yawned. "Get some rest, my love. It will be a long day tomorrow."

"Goodnight," Beulah responded abstractedly. His mind was filled with thoughts of the latest recruit to the sisterhood. How on earth did she manage to wield such power?

* * * * *

When Beulah awoke he was surprised to see Meganrhys up and about, tending to the sleeping forms of Ryzak and Neulee. He had expected her to be the last one to rise after her exertions the previous night.

Easing the matriarch's arm from his chest, he slipped out of the sleeping furs and rose, quietly walking round the fire to join the sister. "Are they all right?" he asked quietly.

Meganrhys jumped at the sound of his voice. "Yes. Yes, they are doing fine," she replied, recovering her composure and smiling.

Returning her smile, the wizard nodded. "Good. The sooner Ryzak wakes, the sooner we can complete what we started out to do and be out of this place."

He bent to the fire and began to prod it to life with a length of wood, before throwing fresh fuel on. At least the off-cuts from the bridge had come in useful. He gave a grunt of satisfaction as flames started to consume the fresh timber, then fumbled in his robe and removed a small pouch of herbal tea. He looked up as Rhissa joined him. "Nothing like a good cup of tea to start the day, hey?"

The girl gave him a frosty look before crouching and holding her hands out to the flames, blanking him completely.

Beulah scowled. He was about to deliver a smart rejoinder when Shula appeared at his side.

"Up bright and early, I see," she said, stooping to give him an affectionate hug and a kiss on the cheek.

"Good morning, Matriarch," intoned Rhissa, casting a disapproving look at their closeness.

"Rhissa," nodded the matriarch coolly. She turned her attention back to Beulah. "How are our two invalids this morning?"

"Why not ask them yourself?"

Shula looked round and was astonished to see Ryzak limping towards them, his arm draped around Neulee.

"That's some nurse you've got there," Ryzak said approvingly. He looked sideways and gave Meganrhys a wink.

"I see he's back to normal," remarked Shula wryly.

"I take it you were successful?" enquired the wizard, as Ryzak joined them.

"Just about," grumbled Ryzak. "You would not believe what we've been through to get the damn thing."

"I am sure we will hear all about it before too long," said Beulah. He looked at Shula and raised his eyebrows, his face taking on a pained expression.

"Yeah, well, I just hope it's appreciated, that's all," pouted Ryzak, squatting down to prod at the fire with a stick.

Realising that he was still a little tetchy, Beulah patted him on the back. "It is, my boy. Don't you worry. It is." He gave him a warm smile, hoping to diffuse the man's irritability.

Neulee crouched beside Ryzak and threaded her arm around his waist. Ryzak wrapped his round her shoulders and kissed the top of her head. "When do you want me to start?" he asked, turning to the wizard.

"What?"

"The seal," prompted Ryzak. "When do you want me to place it?"

"You?" Beulah shook his head. "No, no, no, my boy. You've been through enough. I'll take the responsibility from here. I'll leave straight after I've had a cup of that tea." He held out his hand. "Give it here."

Ryzak shot to his feet and glared at the wizard. "Now wait a second," he snapped. "Don't you think I've earned the right to finish what I started? I will be the one to place the seal!" He folded his arms and gave the wizard an uncompromising stare.

"As much as I hate to pull rank, my boy, it is to be me that places the seal. Now pass it over!" Beulah commanded, thrusting out a hand.

"No!"

"Now!" snarled the wizard, his eyes flashing angrily.

"Make me!" growled Ryzak.

"Boys, boys, boys," Shula interrupted, stepping between them. "Does it really matter who places the seal?"

"Yes!" they answered in unison.

Shula shook her head and sighed. Turning to the wizard she said, "I know you feel it should be you to finish what the wizards started all those years ago, but Ryzak does have a point. We never would have got this far if it weren't for him and Neulee."

Beulah scowled and paused to consider her words. He supposed she did have a point. What could possibly go wrong now? Looking into Ryzak's doltish features, he had his answer. Everything!

Realising he would not get any peace if he did not accede to Shula's request, he gave Ryzak one last glare. "If that is the way of it, Ryzak it is," he fumed.

Ignoring the smile that appeared on the man's face, he stomped away.

* * * * *

Beulah sulked as he watched Ryzak prepare to descend into the cavern. By rights it should have been him placing the last seal. He was a wizard after all. However, Shula was correct; they would never have got this far without Ryzak. If it were not for him helping her at the very beginning, he would never have known about the weakening of Mishtar's prison until it was too late. And he had to admit the man seemed to have matured since they'd first met. He watched as Neulee stepped forward to embrace Ryzak, and gave a small snort. She appeared to be the reason why.

He looked sideways at Shula. It was strange what love could do to a man. Normally he would not have conceded defeat to Ryzak quite so easily, if at all. But love was a funny thing. It completely buggered your sense of reason.

As Neulee moved away, Jollif moved in to wish his friend luck. Ryzak turned and gave Beulah and the matriarch a brief nod before descending.

"If you are not back in half an hour, I will come down looking for you. And remember …"

"I know," Ryzak interrupted, "those funny squiggles face up."

"He'll be fine," Shula whispered into Beulah's ear. "Ease up on him a little."

"Just making sure," Beulah said through the side of his mouth, the reference to *funny squiggles* not reassuring him much. He gave Ryzak a smile of encouragement. "We'll have the tea ready for when you get back."

The look on Ryzak's face showed what he thought about drinking tea.

"Talking about tea …" Beulah linked his arm through Shula's and headed back to the cave entrance.

When they reached the fire the wizard was surprised to see the area deserted. "Anybody seen Meganrhys or Rhissa?" he asked, frowning.

"Not since breakfast," replied Shula. "Why?"

"I think I saw them by the cave entrance a little while ago," said Jollif. "Is there a problem?"

The wizard gave a small shrug. "No. I was just wondering where they were, that's all. They must have gone out for some fresh air."

* * * * *

Reaching the bottom of the steps, Ryzak walked quickly along the subterranean corridor. Now there was only one seal to place he was unconcerned about the possibility of ghostly manifestations. After all, Beulah had placed the other seal without mishap, why not him? Whistling tunelessly to himself, he made his way towards the cavern at the corridor's end.

Before long the familiar violet glow began to materialise in the gloom ahead. He quickened his pace, eager to finish the job he had started so many months before. As he rounded the last bend he halted in his tracks. The violet radiance within the vault had deepened. It was much more tangible than when he was last here. Everything seemed to shimmer with a reddish-blue tinge, as if he were looking through tinted glass.

He opened his hand to inspect the seal and turned it to make sure it was ready for placement. Satisfied it was the right way up, he walked haltingly forward, making his way to the one remaining pillar without a golden glint at its summit.

As he got closer his hands started to feel clammy and damp stains formed under his armpits. If the truth be known, he was crapping himself now that he was alone in the chamber; scared that Mishtar would appear after all. He did not fancy the idea of being possessed and began to wish he had given in to Beulah and let him place the seal. It was only false bravado, and opening his mouth before checking with his brain first, that had landed him with the job. He really would have to learn to curb his verbal excesses.

He gritted his teeth, pushing all thoughts of evil sorcerers to the back of his mind, and concentrated on placing one foot in front of the other. When he was within a few feet of the pillar a dizzy sensation gripped him. He stumbled to a halt and, raising his hand to his forehead, dropped the seal.

It was a moment before the dizziness faded and he felt able to move on. Perhaps he was not as fully recovered as he thought. He stooped to retrieve the spilled disc, and after turning it in his palm until the familiar writing was facing him, he started towards the pillar again.

A loud shriek of rage sounded behind him. Ryzak spun, almost dropping the seal again in his surprise. His mouth fell open in astonishment as he spotted Rhissa, her back to him, arms raised as she faced the entrance. He could tell she was furious.

Side-stepping so he could see around her, he was even more surprised to see Meganrhys stride into the subterranean vault. As he looked on a pale-blue flash shot from Rhissa's outstretched hands, straight at Meganrhys.

Magic!

With a squeak of terror he covered the last few feet to the pillar and ducked behind it for protection. The last thing he needed was to be hit by a stray spell. It was war out there!

Peering out from his position of relative safety he saw Meganrhys circling Rhissa, her eyes wary. They reminded him of fist-fighters searching for an opening. As he watched, Rhissa recited words of command and hurled another spell. Knocked back by the blast, Meganrhys parried it with one of her own, then retaliated with a silver barb that flew at her adversary like an arrow. Rhissa's magic shattered it.

Shrieks and yells filled the air as they fired spell after spell at each other, detonations and bright flashes filling the chamber. Ryzak ducked behind the pillar as the sisters went at it, avoiding the odd, stray spell-bolts that hurtled in his direction.

Unable to take his eyes off the combatants, he became aware of them starting to tire. The flashes of magic were getting more sporadic and the girls were stumbling with fatigue.

Suddenly Meganrhys tripped and fell sprawling to the ground. Ryzak groaned. He was enthralled by the fight and she was his favourite. If Jollif were with him they would have had a nice little wager going.

In a flash Rhissa was over her prone adversary, an evil smile on her face. She raised her arms and prepared to deliver Megan's doom.

Ryzak grunted in surprise as the smile on Rhissa's face froze, replaced by a look of shock. Very slowly she toppled sideways and fell motionless to the floor. A movement at the entrance caught his eye. Looking across he saw the frighteningly familiar figure of Beulah, a glower of rage on his face.

Seeing Ryzak staring at him, the look on the wizard's face turned thunderous. "Hurry up and place the seal, you fool! Unless you want me to do it for you!" he roared.

Startled into action, Ryzak turned and stumbled to the empty pillar. Giving the disc one final check to make sure it was the correct way up, he moved his hand to position it over the clasp. As he readied himself to drop it into place, he felt the pull of magic trying to tear it from his grasp.

"Hold!"

"Huh?" grunted Ryzak, glancing over his shoulder.

"Hold!" Meganrhys screamed again. Supported by Beulah, she hobbled towards him, her face a mask of fear. "Rhissa has placed a glamour on the seal to make you place it the wrong way up. She was in league with Mishtar. Do not place the seal!"

Ryzak pulled his hand back and looked at the gold object. It certainly seemed to be the right way up; he could see the hieroglyphs as plain as the scowl on Beulah's face. Turning the seal in his hand, he viewed the other side. It was unmarked.

Ignore her, a voice whispered in his mind. What does she think you are, stupid? Of course it's the correct way up. Put it in and get it over with! What does she know?

Ryzak's hand moved to hover over the clasps.

"What are you doing?" Beulah's loud cry boomed from behind him. "Drop the seal, you nincompoop."

Drop the seal? That sounded like a good idea. No sooner was the thought in his head than his hand released its hold and the gold disc dropped free. An anguished cry of, "Nooooo!" sounded in the background as he watched the seal fall the short distance onto the pillar.

Astonished, Ryzak gave an "Ooo!" of surprise as the disc rebounded off the air above the pillar and fell to the floor. He stooped to pick it up and turned it over in his hand, gazing at it in bewilderment.

"What happened?" Meganrhys asked, arriving beside him.

"I don't know," mumbled Ryzak, staring at the disc as if it were possessed. "It just sort of bounced into the air and landed on the floor."

"I can explain that," said Beulah, with a smug smile. "When I replaced the other seal I put certain safeguards over the last pillar, to ensure that the seal could not be put in the wrong way and undo all our good work. I knew Mishtar had allies and I wanted to make sure they did not upset our plans. I cast a spell over the pillar so that it would only allow the disc to be placed hieroglyphs up. If it were to be placed the other way, it would refuse to accept it."

"But the disc was hyro– writing up," said Ryzak. "I saw them myself."

"Try again then," urged Beulah, "and see what happens." Ryzak did, with the same result.

"Now try it the other way," Beulah said with a smirk.

Ryzak looked at the disc. He remembered what Shula had said after he placed the first seal. There was no way some freak of a sorcerer was taking over his body. He shook his head and handed it to Beulah. The wizard rolled his eyes. He turned the disc so that the plain side was up, then moved forward to drop it into position.

Fearing the worst, Ryzak cowered and covered his eyes with a raised forearm as the seal dropped, shrieking in terror as the light dimmed before reasserting itself. When nothing else happened, he lowered his arm.

Beulah arched an eyebrow and gave him a knowing smile.

Suddenly feeling braver, Ryzak stepped forward and peered at the pillar. The gold disc glinted up at him, hieroglyphs in plain view.

"See? Nothing to it," the wizard said smugly. "Come. It is time we returned to the others. They will be worried about us."

"Nothing to it," murmured Ryzak disbelievingly. He was convinced the wizard had put it in the wrong way. Maybe Meganrhys was right and he had been bewitched by Rhissa. The strange, dizzy feeling that had affected him suddenly made sense. Especially as he'd dropped the disc and had to pick it up again. He gave a nervous start as a hand gripped his arm. Looking round, he met Beulah's amused gaze.

"Come, my boy," the wizard urged. "There is nothing else for us to do here. Let's be on our way."

Ryzak allowed himself to be steered towards the corridor. As they passed the unmoving body of Rhissa, he glanced down. "What about her?" he asked, nodding at the corpse.

"Leave her be," Beulah replied, his eyes hardening. "She has done nothing to warrant our help."

"How did you know it was her and not me that had betrayed you?" Meganrhys asked.

Beulah's face crinkled into a smile. "I didn't," he answered. "It was the spell over the pillar that proved the truth of the matter. If you had not tried to warn Ryzak, the end result would have given you away."

"B–b–but you killed Rhissa," she said, shock showing on her face. "What if it had been her that had been telling the truth?"

"Fortunately that possibility did not occur," he said brightly. "Let's go. I feel the need for a drink, and not that awful herbal tea. The sooner we get back to Jollif's, the sooner we can enjoy a real drink."

With Ryzak and Meganrhys in tow, he strode along the corridor with nary a backward glance.

* * * * *

Firmly shackled within the sword, Mishtar's spirit howled and raged. All his plans, all his plotting, all for nothing!

Chapter Twenty Six

Standing behind his serving counter, Jollif was in his element. He was serving tankards of ale as fast as he was able. Trade was the best he had ever known and The Shepherd's Cock was full to overflowing. The couple of weeks it had been closed during his escapades on Mount Aine must have weighed heavy on the surrounding populace, and they appeared to be making up for lost time. He had been back for three days and it had been the same every day since their return. He was getting worried that he would not have enough ale left for the weekend. Although he had sent a runner to his suppliers urgently requesting a delivery, he doubted whether it would arrive before his current stock ran out.

Handing a brimming tankard to yet another satisfied customer, he looked across to where his companions sat. The red flush on Ryzak's face suggested that things were definitely getting back to normal.

A shout intruded on his thoughts.

"Oy, lardy! You serving or what?"

Instead of becoming annoyed by the disparaging call, Jollif merely grinned at the surly man across the bar. It would take more than a little name-calling to upset him today. He was home!

"For you, sir? What would you like? Dwarven ale, ale brewed in …"

"So what you gonna do now?" Ryzak asked Beulah, the slurring of his words showing that he had had more than his fair share of Jollif's hospitality.

"Back to Wizard's Keep, I suppose. There are things I need to sort out and plans I – we – need to make," Beulah corrected, smiling happily at Shula.

"You two a couple then?" queried Ryzak, noticing the loving look.

"It would appear that way," replied Beulah. "We have decided to pool our resources, so to speak, and create one academy for the gifted at the Palace of the Sisters, now that I really am the last wizard."

"Oh," said Ryzak, frowning in confusion as he tried to figure out what he meant. Coming to the wrong conclusion, he grinned and patted Neulee's stomach. "Me and her have already pooled ours."

"Congratulations!" beamed Shula. "When is the baby due?"

"Baby?" gasped Ryzak, completely horror-struck by the idea. "We're not having a baby! We're jus' practisin'. Much more fun." He giggled. He was so taken by the amusing notion that he did not notice the knowing look from Meganrhys and the answering smile from Neulee.

Ryzak's eyes lost their focus, his thoughts miles away. "I wonder how Snorkel is?" he said to no one in particular.

"I am sure he is fine. He is one of life's survivors," Beulah answered. "Now, if you will excuse us, I think it is time to get some sleep. We have an early start in the morning."

The wizard rose and helped Shula to her feet. Before leaving he looked into Ryzak's bloodshot eyes. "I would like to say it's been nice knowing you, however …" He chuckled at his little jest. "I wish you both all the best, anyway." Laughing, he linked his arm through Shula's and headed for the staircase. Meganrhys also made her excuses and rose, following them up the stairs.

Ryzak's face fell as he watched them go. There was only himself and Neulee now. Ever quick on the uptake, a smile slowly appeared as the realisation hit him. There was only him and Neulee! Together at last!

He turned to her with a happy grin. "Jus' you and me now, babe. Fancy another drink?"

Neulee met his bleary gaze with a coy look. "No thank you. It is not wise to drink in my condition."

"Ey?" He could not believe she had refused an ale; she could usually out-drink him.

"Well," began Neulee. "Remember what Shula …"

Meganrhys heard Ryzak's joyous shout and call for ales from the head of the stairs. She smiled to herself, wishing the baby a better childhood than she had enjoyed. At least it would not have to deal with the same prejudices she had suffered as the daughter of an elf and a human. Her own mother had sent her out to foster parents when she was still very young. Even being a princess of the elves was no protection against intolerance of mixed-race consummation.

Meganrhys sighed. Her dear, estranged mother was probably queen by now. Her grandmother had been extremely old when she last saw her, and that was over a hundred years ago. So she was probably dead.

She stopped outside the door of the room Beulah shared with Shula. She could not blame her father; he did not even know he had a daughter and, from what she could discover, he was both young and innocent when her mother had taken him. But now she had found him she was not going to leave him. Maybe she would tell him one day, when the time was right.

"Goodnight, father," she whispered, before padding down the hallway to her own room.

* * * * *

Snorkel mentally recited the spells once again, hoping his knowledge was correct and that time had not played tricks with the implanted memories. It would not do to open a gateway to a world where they could not survive.

"Are you ready yet?" a voice queried.

"Give me a chance," Snorkel replied, irritation showing in his voice. "You can't be too careful where magic is concerned. One wrong turn and wham! Back to square one. I'm nearly through."

"Leave him be, Kraelin," Reizgoth scolded the young queen. "He will let us know when he is finished."

"There. That's it!" Snorkel exclaimed, a few minutes later. "Ready when you are, Your Majesty." He bowed low. Regarding her glowing bulk, Snorkel was amazed how fast she had developed. Although only three weeks old, she was already half as big as Reizgoth. Her skin was a deep, golden colour and she had the prettiest eyes he had ever seen. On a dragon, anyway.

"It's about time," Kraelin said haughtily. "My people are waiting."

Snorkel humpffed. It was a shame her temperament was not as pleasant as her looks.

Reizgoth lowered his head and whispered in Snorkel's ear. "Forgive her, she is young. Her manners will improve."

"Like her eating habits?" Snorkel asked, raising an eyebrow.

"Some things take longer than others," Reizgoth replied, a long suffering expression on his face.

"Will you two come on," Kraelin's voice cut in impatiently. "And what are you whispering about?"

"Galduran and I were just deciding when would be the best time to undertake our journey, Kraelin," Reizgoth answered.

"Liar," whispered Snorkel. The dragon gave him an icy glare.

"Now sounds good to me," Kraelin retorted.

"We'd better do as she says or we will get no peace," Reizgoth murmured, rolling his eyes.

Snorkel turned to Meelan. "Are you sure you still want to come with us?" he asked.

Meelan's face lit up with excitement. She squealed in delight and flew into his arms, crushing him with the force of her powerful embrace.

Snorkel grunted as the air rushed out of his body. Arms like hers could crush rocks. At the queen's snort of displeasure, Snorkel eased Meelan away, letting his hands slide down her arms to grasp hers.

"I'll take that as a yes, shall I?"

"You try stop me, Norkel, I be ver' 'noyed."

Snorkel shook his head. He was the luckiest dwarf alive. He wished his father could see him now; he would be so proud. He grinned and kissed Meelan on the end of her flat nose. She must be keen, he thought, she's even had a shave for the occasion.

Kraelin's snort of impatience intruded.

Giving Meelan a wink, Snorkel turned and began to prepare himself to open the gateway. He closed his eyes, mentally reciting the spell before speaking it aloud. A sudden feeling of something being wrong disturbed his concentration.

He opened his eyes. "Anyone seen Draco?" he asked.

"No," said Kraelin. "Do get on with it, she is of no importance."

Snorkel's eyes hardened at the queen's comment.

"Not since this morning when you began checking the spells, for the third time," rumbled Reizgoth, giving Kraelin a warning look.

Snorkel frowned and turned to face the upper entrance. It was unlike the dragonet to go missing, especially at a time like this. "Draco!" he called.

'What's up, Mum?' her voice sounded in his head.

He sighed in relief. "Where are you? We are just about to open the gateway."

'We're nearly there,' Draco replied.

"We?" queried Snorkel.

The distant drone of happy squeaks and chirrups, intermingled with the odd woof and howl, started to impinge on his awareness, growing louder as the source of the noise got closer. Suddenly the air was filled with the sound of hundreds of ecstatic dragonets as they erupted through the entrance and flew into the underground amphitheatre, somersaulting and cavorting in their happiness. In their midst a large, grey she-wolf bounded down the steps to join in the fun. She jumped off the stone tiering, her happy howls turning to yelps of pain as her feet touched the hot sand.

'We're here, Mum,' said Draco, landing on Snorkel's shoulder and rubbing her head affectionately up and down his cheek.

Snorkel chuckled with pleasure and scratched her under the chin.

"Really!" snorted Kraelin. "If he thinks we are taking this rabble to meet our public, he has another think coming."

"Either they come or we all stay," growled Snorkel, folding his arms and holding the young queen's gaze.

Flicking anxious glances between them, Reizgoth addressed his queen. "Let them come," he urged, in his most persuasive manner. "I am sure it is a big enough world for all of us. Look on the positive side; it means more subjects to worship you. They will be forever in your debt once they are through. Trust me, it is for the best."

The squeaks and chirrups quietened as the dragonets waited for the queen to decide their fate. Even the she-wolf stifled her yelps and hopped quietly from foot to foot instead.

Kraelin turned to look at the pensive horde.

"If they must," she sniffed, exuding an air of indifference.

The noise of the resultant jubilation nearly deafened Snorkel. "Tell them to shut up," he yelled to Draco, "or I will not be able to concentrate and we won't be going anywhere!"

Within seconds the message had been relayed and quiet descended on the amphitheatre.

"That's better," said Snorkel approvingly.

Closing his eyes, the little man started the incantation that would open the gateway. As he recited the words of power a hazy, pale mist began to form before him. It started as a small ball, but grew until it was thirty feet in diameter.

Within the sphere, the mist swirled, gradually moving faster and faster until it seemed to migrate to the edge, forming a circle. A tunnel stretched out before him.

"It's ready," shouted Snorkel, beads of perspiration forming on his face. "Hurry. I can't keep it open for long!"

Eager to be in her new world, Kraelin waddled quickly past him and into the tunnel beyond, Reizgoth following closely behind. The she-wolf, wanting to escape the burning sand, bounded through after them.

Teeth clamped together and sweat pouring down his face, Snorkel fought to keep the gateway open. He opened his eyes and watched the steady flow of dragonets fly through. After the last one had entered, he grabbed Meelan's arm and hurtled after them before the portal closed. As soon as he entered, the magic began to fade and the entrance started to shrink.

Safely concealed from prying eyes, a tall, lizard-like figure sprang out from its hiding place and sprinted for the fast-closing gateway, just managing to throw itself through before it snapped shut.

Chuckling to himself, Chrysothenalazm followed the horde through to the new world. "You can't escape me," he chortled. "Wherever you wun, wherever you hide, Chrysothenalazm will be waiting for you."

Chapter Twenty Seven

Pig-Breath snarled an oath as he stumbled on the uneven ground, and slapped away the hand that was offered to steady him. Yet again he cursed the splint strapped to his leg and the two responsible for his injuries. As soon as he found out what they had been up to in this cave he would seek them out. Then they would learn what it meant to mess with the Wolverines.

Accompanied by two of his warriors, he limped forward and made his ungainly way down the corridor. Before long he became aware of a lightening in the distance. A deep, violet glow illuminated the tunnel ahead. Suddenly wary, he commanded his men to take the lead, then followed at a discreet distance. As chieftain, he had to think of the future of the tribe. Where would they be if anything happened to him? All went smoothly until they rounded the last corner and his escort halted abruptly.

Hearing their gasps of amazement but unable to see around them, Pig-Breath pushed his way through. His eyes widened as he saw the sword suspended in the air. Then they lit upon the pillars. He thought he saw something glinting. Curiosity overcame his fear and he motioned for his men to follow him as he went to take a closer look.

Hesitantly they followed their chieftain across the floor of the vaulted grotto, casting nervous glances at the body of a young girl as they passed it.

Sensing their discomfort, Pig-Breath turned and gestured impatiently for them to keep up with him. They were Wolverines, feared and hated throughout the lands, not mice. What was wrong with them? Scared of a dead body?

When they arrived at the first pillar, Pig-Breath peered at its apex and a slow smile crept over his face. An avaricious gleam entered his eye. Gold!

He removed his knife from its sheath and worked at the clasps, giving a squeal of delight as the disc popped free. He thrust out a hand to grab it as it sprang clear. Three loud shrieks rang out as the cavern was plunged into darkness, then sounded again as the glow returned.

Pig-Breath and his men looked into each other's fear-filled faces and ran from the chamber, the seal still clasped in the chieftain's grubby fingers.

A deep, throaty chuckle filled the chamber as the men fled, its sinister overtones further fuelling their terror. From the confines of his prison, Mishtar snorted in amusement as the old man fell, yet again, in his haste to get away.

He tested the remaining wards and was pleased to note that he could breach their confinement. Quickly sending the power of his mind after the limping barbarian before he moved too far away, he soon caught up with him. The old man had not even reached the stairway. He probed at the man's puny intellect and sneered as he found it to be as simple as he expected. To make things easier, this one did not have the power of a wizard, or dwarf, to protect him. He worked on the man's fear, and filled him with thoughts of peace and harmony.

Mishtar's pleasure increased as Pig-Breath shambled to a halt, his eyes glazing over as he slowly turned to face back the way he had come. Mishtar planted images of wealth, his for the taking, if only he would come back to the sword and prise the other discs free. Slowly the old man's face creased into a rapacious grin. Placing one foot in front of the other, he limped back to the cavern.

Mishtar's good humour evaporated as the man drew closer. He began to have second thoughts. He'd seen gargoyles with acute toothache that were better looking than the mangy savage who was to be his living host when he got free. So much for making a grand entrance back into the world of man. He would find himself hard pushed to impress a blind courtesan who hadn't been near a punter in years, inhabiting a body like that one.

He examined him more closely, looking for any redeeming qualities that would make the possession more bearable until he was in a position to do something about it. No such luck. In addition to going by the name of Pig-Breath, the man was pig-ugly. Mishtar sighed. It could only happen to him. If it were not for that damned wizard and dwarf ... He halted his train of thought. That was another story. He had to concentrate on the here and now before it all went pear-shaped – again!

He coaxed the man closer, urging him to pry the remaining gold discs from the stone pillars surrounding the sword and shatter the haze of violet magic that held the weapon floating in the air.

Mishtar's spirit eyes hardened as they glanced around the small underground grotto; his home for the past two centuries. How he hated the place. He felt as though he knew every nook and cranny, every craggy outcropping of his jail by name. By the gods, how he longed to breathe fresh air again, feel the caress of wind on bare flesh, get even with the bastards who'd caged him like some wild animal.

He smiled suddenly, his mood lifting as the old man reached one of the pillars below him. It was almost time. Revenge!

That was what had kept him going all these long, lonely years. The chance to crush the people of Aldura beneath his heel; to make them suffer; to enslave them; to rule them; to grind the buggers down and make them his, to do with as he pleased. By the gods, he would pay them back for what they had done to him. Reprisal would become his middle name.

Freedom to carry out his plans was so close he could taste it, and it tasted good. It had the flavour of fine wine; sweet honey; exquisite candies; maple syrup; expensive perfume on a young boy's neck ...

Bloody hell! The prospect of emancipation after so long must be getting to him. He thought he had got over his little, ahhh ... problem. Annoyed by his mental slip, he fixed his attention on Pig-Breath as the man slid his long-bladed hunting knife from its sheath.

Mishtar kept the man's pea-sized intellect fully shielded as the savage eased his knife under one of the remaining discs and levered it free. The last thing he needed was for him to become terrified by the flickering violet light and run. It could be years, centuries even, before he could coerce another simple-minded fool to undertake the task.

Slowly and carefully Mishtar steered Pig-Breath around the remaining pillars, blanketing the man's mind against fear as he eased the discs free until, eventually, he reached the final one. Mishtar fought to curb his excitement, and readied his powers for the transfer.

Pig-Breath's eyes were dull and haunted as he exerted pressure on the blade, the muscles in his arm rippling with power. Suddenly his hand shot forward.

With a triumphant cry, Mishtar made to hurl his spirit into the man's body, but came to an abrupt halt. It was as if he had hit a stone wall. His spirit refused to leave the sword.

Bugger! False alarm. The knife had slipped on the smooth stone. Pig-Breath stumbled into the pillar as it flew from his grasp and landed on the floor.

Mishtar glanced down and saw that the seal was still in position, winking mischievously up at him under the violet light of the magic; taunting him. He glared at it with renewed hatred. He saw the old man steady himself and stoop to pick up the spilled blade. With only one disc of containment to hold him, Mishtar could feel his powers heightened, and he wanted out. This time there'd better be no mistake. He watched as Pig-Breath positioned the knife under the seal and gave it a savage twist and a wrench.

The golden disc flew free.

Mishtar's spirit form flew from the sword as it plummeted to the floor, and hurtled in to the figure of the old man, fighting the pull of the weapon that had held him for so long.

Alarmed by the alien presence within, the man's eyes flew wide in terror. His ancient body jerked and thrashed like a puppet whose strings were being maniacally pulled. Fighting Pig-Breath's inner being for dominance, Mishtar felt a wave of panic grip him. What was happening? This should have been so easy. Why the resistance? And why did the sword appear to be dragging him back?

Suddenly the conflict ceased. The old man's body went rigid. Managing not to laugh, Mishtar's spirit flowed to the man's control centres with the ease of water through sand. Nothing could stop him now!

Except for one catastrophic development: a development so

unexpected that it caught the sorcerer completely by surprise. Pig-Breath had suffered a terminal heart attack. The strain of the hike to get to the cavern, the mishaps he had suffered on the way and the fight to repel an incorporeal intruder had taken its toll. His decrepit body had had enough. It was packing it in.

Fear gripped Mishtar in a crushing embrace as the old man's heart stopped pumping and his body collapsed to the floor. Not thinking straight, and not knowing the first thing about resurrecting the dead or dying, he did the only thing he could. He gave in to the pull of the sword and fled to the safety of familiar surroundings.

If he thought his problems were over, however, he was sadly mistaken.

No sooner had he flowed back into the weapon than clasps woven of magic wrapped around him, manacling him in the pure, unblemished silver-steel blade.

Held in the crucifixion position; head in the pommel; arms in the hilt; legs and body in the blade, it was a moment before he realised what had happened. It was the exact same moment that the stone pillars split and cracked apart. The exact same moment that the roof of the cavern came crashing down, burying the sword beneath mountains of rubble. The exact same moment that he realised he had been completely and utterly shafted.

He had been tricked. Those damned wizards had had a backup plan in case he ever got free, and he'd fallen for it. He managed one last shriek of outrage before the magic gagged him forever, his anger-filled voice hammering through the tons of fallen rock.

"You interfering, lice-infested, worm-ridden, black robed, dead bastaaarrrrrds!"

The End

Printed in the United Kingdom
by Lightning Source UK Ltd.
126249UK00001B/46/A